STORMSPELL

'I am *not* like your father!' he countered,
with some heat. 'I don't think like your
father, I don't act like your father, and
God knows, I don't *feel* like your father!'
He took her by the shoulders then, when
she persisted in avoiding his gaze, his
thumb bruising her throat, forcing her to
lift her chin. 'Be sensible, Ruth,' he
snapped, 'and don't invite difficulties.
Believe me, I can be nothing but trouble
to you.'

STORMSPELL

BY

ANNE MATHER

WORLDWIDE ROMANCE

LONDON•SYDNEY•TORONTO

First published 1982
Australian copyright 1982
Philippine copyright 1982

© Anne Mather 1982

ISBN 0 263 73779 9

Photoset by Rowland Photosetting Ltd
Bury St Edmunds, Suffolk
Printed and bound in Great Britain by
Collins, Glasgow.

CHAPTER ONE

It was a rain-washed morning, yet as calm as the night that preceded it had been violent. It was a dull morning, a muted morning, when even the song of the birds had a tentative sound. The earth was recovering from the savagery of the storm, a watery sun thrusting out fingers of promise—as if to pledge atonement for the barbarity of darkness.

Ruth was awake at dawn. The uncanny silence after the howling of the wind, that had whistled beneath the corrugated roof of the bungalow, was as unnatural in its way as the tempest had been, and she lay for several minutes listening to the blessed peace.

Then, pushing back the single sheet which was all that covered her, she padded barefoot to the window, unfastening the shutters and pushing them wide.

Everywhere, the consequences of the storm were evident. Trees had been torn up at the roots, and those that had survived were still crushed and cowed by the torrential downpour that had danced like silver pennies along the verandah. Lightning had left arrowed lesions in the trunks of trees still standing, stripping the bark and laying them bare.

The verandah was littered with debris—leaves and twigs, seaweed from the beach, nuts and shells, and tiny pebbles that had rattled against the shutters, like hailstones. Ruth couldn't remember ever having seen hailstones, but her father had made the comparison.

Now, however, the warmth of the day was beginning to send spirals of steam rising from the damp wood, to mingle with the low-lying mist that swirled around the roots of the trees. It gave the garden below the bungalow a faintly mysterious appearance, shrouding the earth in eddying folds of opacity.

Aware of the coolness of the air against her warm skin, Ruth turned back into the room with undisguised eagerness. She would dress and go down to the beach. Who knew what one might find on the beach after such a storm, and she had time before breakfast to make a preliminary exploration.

Stripping off the cotton nightshirt which was all that covered her, she sluiced her face and hands in cold water poured from a tall jug on the nearby stand. Then, after giving her hair the most perfunctory of brushes, she pulled on the shorts and tee-shirt that were her usual mode of dress. A leather thong secured her hair at her nape, and without even looking at her reflection in the fly-spotted mirror of her dressing table, she left the room.

She paused long enough to check that her father was still sleeping, opening his door, and examining his increasingly pain-racked features with anxious eyes. The strain of his illness was rapidly depriving him of all flesh, and the bones of his skull had a skeletal appearance. Ruth's lower lip was caught painfully between her teeth as she closed his door again, and much of the excitement went out of the morning. How much longer could the medicine Doctor Francis had supplied succeed in holding the pain at bay? How much longer before that drug-induced inertia gave way to tortured consciousness?

Shaking her head, she continued along the hall that divided the bungalow into two separate halves, with the kitchen, dining room and bathroom on one side, and the living room and bedrooms on the other. There was no point in agonising over something she could do nothing about. Doctor Francis had told her—her father's condition was terminal. It was only a matter of time before the strain on his heart became unbearable. It was hard, and it was unfair, but somehow she had to accept it. Her father had accepted it. It was not fair to him that she should allow her own anxieties to impinge on what little time they had left together.

Nevertheless, as she stepped out on to the verandah, her heart plunged a little at the thought of how lonely she would be. For as long as she could remember there had been just the two of them, and while she was not afraid of being alone, she dreaded the isolation. Indigo was such a small island. Its population was not more than thirty. And aside from themselves, there was only one other white man on the island: the priest, Father Andreas. She could not see herself having the same conversations with Father Andreas that she enjoyed with her father, and the priest himself would miss their sometimes rancorous games of chess.

She sighed. She was wasting time. Her father would not approve of such maudlin sentimentality. She had a job of work to do—to go down to the beach and make sure no serious damage had been

done, so that she could give her father a first-hand
report at breakfast.

Celeste's hens were pecking in the twig-strewn
ruins of the vegetable garden, and Ruth clapped her
hands in mock aggression, driving them out. The
feathery bodies scattered noisily into the yard at the
back of the bungalow, and a smile lifted Ruth's lips
as she picked her way over the dunes towards the
beach. Poor creatures, they probably thought the
storm had returned, she thought in some amusement, bending to pick up a narrow twig. She doubted
Celeste would find many unbroken eggs today.

The rain had ceased by the time she reached the
ridge of crab grass above the beach, and the sun's
rays picked out the evidence of devastation. What
had been an unbroken stretch of almost-white coral
sand was now strewn with all the debris of the island,
and that of the sea as well. Torn branches, stricken
saplings, seaweed, rocks and shells—the whole place
had an air of desolation, the shredded blossoms of an
oleander like scattered petals at a funeral. Somehow
the sea had dredged up its bounty, and as Ruth
stepped carefully along the beach, she found rusted
strips of metal, and shards of broken pottery, as if
torn from some long-sunken vessel, ravaged on the
jagged ramparts of the reef. Some Spanish galleon
perhaps, she mused, examining a shining object,
which she discovered to be a coin. Swashbuckling
pirates and pieces of eight, she thought, remembering the stories her father had told her of the fleets of
vessels bearing Spanish gold from the Americas, that
had floundered in these waters in the seventeenth
century. Who knew what treasure still lay buried

beneath the blue-green waters of the Caribbean? Only now and then did the ocean allow a glimpse of the riches still stored beneath the waves.

With a shrug of her slim shoulders, Ruth pocketed the coin and continued her beachcombing. With the sun increasing in warmth, and the air fresh and clean after the storm, she felt a growing feeling of exhilaration, and the anxieties she had experienced earlier were forced into perspective. People lived for years in her father's condition. Doctors were making continual progress in their search for a cure. And with such sophisticated medication, surely life could be sustained indefinitely.

The cries of the seabirds accompanied her, herring gulls scavenging among the debris. Sand crabs scutled sideways out of her path, and fat waders paddled expectantly at the water's edge. There was a whole world of life on the island, she thought with sudden anticipation. How could anyone be lonely with so many companions?

Beyond the curve of the beach, where a rocky headland laced the surging waters of the lagoon with foam, she paused to shade her eyes against the glare. A clump of mangrove trees grew almost to the water's edge, their twisted trunks gnarled and dark against the brightness. As she watched, she seemed to see something move against the roots of one of the trees, and as her eyes adjusted to the shadow, she was almost convinced it was some huge sea-creature, washed up upon their shores.

Curiosity set her legs moving forward, although doubt, and Celeste's superstition, made her wary. Could it be a shark, or a barracuda, tossed into the lagoon by the force of the storm, or was it just the bole of a tree, torn up and moving with the tide? She automatically crossed herself as she drew nearer to the object, then chided herself severely for the blasphemy. Her fears were based on a belief in the old religion, and Celeste's stories of possession and destruction stirred a kind of panic inside her.

It was a man!

As she reached the stretching shadows of the trees, she saw him distinctly in the sun-dappled light. He was lying on his face, with one hand outstretched, as if grasping for the shore, and the other trapped beneath him, hidden from her sight. He was naked to the waist, wearing a pair of the denim trousers that were so popular among the young people of St Vincent, and which her father found so objectionable, and his bare feet were lapped by the waters of the lagoon.

Ruth stood still for several seconds, just staring, and then apprehension sent her running across the damp sand to drop to her knees beside him. Her fingers probed his neck, trembling at the intimacy, finding the pulse behind his ear before her shoulders sagged in relief. He was alive. He was unconscious but his pulse was not unsteady. How on earth had he got here?

With timid fingers she rolled him on to his back, sitting back on her heels in sudden trepidation when he made a protesting sound. But he didn't open his eyes, and she licked her lips in consternation as she gazed down at him.

He was a white man, that much was obvious, even though his skin was darkly tanned, as if he had spent some time out of doors. His hair was blond, silvery pale against his brown skin, and thick and smooth-straight. His lashes were long and gold-tipped, fanning against narrow cheekbones and a strong nose, and a mouth that was thin-lipped yet sensitive. Ruth knew an almost overwhelming impulse to touch that pale hair, so unlike her own long rope of black silk, but she restrained herself and allowed her eyes to move lower.

Immediately, her breath escaped her on a gasp. There was blood on his chest, some of it dried and encrusted, and coated with sand. Her hands went automatically to her lips, and she pressed her finger-tips to them as she glanced around helplessly for something to cleanse the wound.

There was nothing suitable, and out of desperation she tore a strip from the hem of her tee-shirt and dipped it into the water. It would have to do. It was clean at least, and it might serve as a bandage. Then she would have to leave him while she went for assistance.

She moved the arm he still held clasped to his chest, and as she did so she blanched as she saw the source of the oozing blood. In one way she was relieved. It was not his chest that was injured, but his arm. However, the ill-advised movement had exposed the ugly gash that gaped wetly from just below his elbow to his wrist, and more blood smeared her fingers as she returned the limb to its resting place.

Dear God, she thought faintly. How much blood had he lost? Did he require a transfusion? Then she remembered the steadiness of his pulse. It was not critical, but it could become so, if she didn't get help soon.

After a moment's hesitation she bound the improvised bandage tightly round his upper arm. At least that would stop the bleeding, she thought, although prolonged absence of blood from the arm could be dangerous. Her father had taught her elementary first aid. Without the free flow of blood, gangrene could set in, and the man, whoever he was, would not thank her for depriving him of an arm.

Satisfied that she had done all she could, she endeavoured to pull the man farther up the beach. But it was hopeless. Even with her hands firmly beneath his arms, she could not move him, and she sweated in the aftermath of so much wasted effort.

He stirred as she squatted panting beside him, and to her amazement his eyes opened. She had not speculated on what colour his eyes might be. If she had been asked, she would most likely have guessed blue. But they were not. They were brown, with curious yellow flecks in them, like amber, and when they alighted on her, they narrowed in obvious lack of recognition.

Ruth scrambled on to her knees, bending beside him anxiously. 'Hello,' she said, realising the greeting must sound foolish, but unable to think of an alternative. 'How—how do you feel?'

The man continued to stare at her, but he didn't say anything, and she stumbled into further speech.

'You're injured,' she said. 'You've got a gash on your arm. I've stopped the bleeding, but I have to go for help. If you'll just lie here, I shan't be long—'

Her words broke off abruptly as his hand reached out with unexpected strength and gripped her arm. 'Where am I?' he demanded, in a curiously harsh voice. 'And who the hell are you?'

No one. least of all her father. had ever used such words to Ruth before, and her indignation kindled as his fingers bit deeply into her soft flesh. She would not have believed him capable of asserting such energy, and her own miscalculation added to her sense of outrage.

'You—you're on Indigo.' she answered him, somewhat stiffly. 'And I'm Ruth Jason. My father and I live here.'

'Indigo!' he echoed blankly. 'What and where is Indigo? And where's the yacht?'

Ruth stopped trying to prise his fingers from her arm and stared at him. 'You were sailing!' she exclaimed. 'Then you must have capsized.'

He blinked. his brows drawing together in a puzzled frown. 'Capsized,' he repeated, considering her words. Then: 'Yes—yes, I'm beginning to remember. There was a storm . . .'

Ruth succeeded in freeing herself, and drew her arm away. rubbing it painfully. 'Who on earth allowed you to go sailing yesterday?' she protested. 'There were plenty of warnings of bad weather. They were broadcast regularly—'

'No one *allowed* me to go sailing,' he retorted, in those same harsh, but now slightly mocking, tones. 'I chose to take the risk, and obviously I've paid the penalty. Is the yacht a complete write-off?'

'The yacht?' Ruth shook her head, scrambling to her feet. 'I can't see any yacht. But if there is one, it's probably been washed up on the Serpent's Teeth.'

The man endeavoured to prop himself up on his uninjured arm, and looked up at her half impatiently. 'Oh, there was a yacht, believe me,' he assured her dryly. 'I didn't swim here from Barbados.'

'Barbados.' Ruth was astounded. 'But that's almost a hundred miles away!'

'Is it?' The man shrugged, and then winced as if his arm pained him. 'So where am I?' He touched the gaping wound with probing fingers. 'Some other island, I guess. I've never heard of it.'

'You wouldn't,' said Ruth, shifting her weight uneasily from one foot to the other. 'It's only a small island. Daddy and I and Father Andreas are the only Europeans here.' She paused. 'But now I must go and get some assistance. I've put a tourniquet on your arm, but as you can see, it needs urgent treatment. If you'll just rest here—'

'No—wait!'

Much to her dismay, he hauled himself into a sitting position and thrust long fingers through the slick wetness of his hair. The effort of sitting up drained what little colour still remained in his cheeks, but when she would have protested, he held up his hand as if bidding her to give him a few moments to recover.

Then he looked up at her once more. 'I'll come with you,' he said, cutting off her immediate objections. 'If you'll just be patient . . .'

'But your arm will start bleeding again,' she pointed out frustratedly. 'You're not fit to make the journey to the house without help.'

'I'll decide whether I'm fit or not,' he told her shortly, abnegating her attempts to restrain him. 'I'm not an invalid. I've merely gashed my arm, that's all.

The sooner I get up off my back, and get to a tele-phone, the better.'

'There are no telephones on Indigo,' declared Ruth stiffly, and his mouth assumed a resigned slant.

'No?'

'No.'

'So how do you make contact with the outside world? You do make contact with the outside world, don't you? Where is it? Trinidad? Martinique?'

'It's St Vincent, actually,' replied Ruth, naming one of the smaller islands west of Barbados, and he grimaced. 'And most of our contacts are by sea.' She paused. 'We have a two-way radio to use in an emer-gency.'

The man quirked an eyebrow. 'But you wouldn't call this an emergency?'

'I didn't say so.' Ruth was confused by his mocking humour. 'But—if you insist on coming with me—'

'I know.' He took a deep breath. 'If you could just help me up . . .'

Ruth bent so that he could put his uninjured arm about her shoulders, then straightened slowly as he struggled to his feet. He was much heavier than she had expected, and she staggered a little under his weight. But more disturbingly, it was the first time she had been so close to any man other than her father, and his hard body weighing down on hers was both distracting and unfamiliar. His body was much different from her father's; for one thing, it was firm and muscular, whereas his was soft and flaccid, and the long thigh pressing against her hip was disrup-tively masculine. It gave her a curious sensation in the pit of her stomach, one that was not entirely unpleasant. and she glanced sideways at him. as if seeking a similar response. But the man beside her was only intent on gaining his balance. and he apologised for his weakness as sweat beaded on his forehead.

'I'm sorry.' he muttered. holding his injured arm to his chest. 'I feel so bloody dizzy. I must have lost more blood than I thought.'

Ruth caught her lower lip between her teeth. 'Won't you stay here and let me get asistance?' she pleaded. but he shook his head.

'I'll make it.' he determined. through gritted teeth. and she had no alternative but to acquiesce.

It was an arduous walk to the bungalow. True to his word. he made it. but she knew he was in pain every step of the way. How could he be otherwise. with his flesh gaping almost to the bone. and the weariness of exhaustion upon him? She could hear his laboured breathing. feel the warmth of his breath against her temple. for even in that slumped state he was taller than she was. and smell the sweat on his body as he strove to sustain what little strength he had left.

Celeste must have seen their approach. because as they neared the bungalow she came hurrying out to meet them. round and black and bustling. her ample girth wobbling beneath the loose flowered smock she wore. her face creasing into a dozen different expressions as she endeavoured to identify their unexpected visitor.

'What been going on. Missy?' she exclaimed. examining the man beside her with a shrewd inquisitive gaze. 'What you been doing. spending so long at the beach? Don't you know your daddy's awake and been asking for you this last half hour?'

Ruth sighed. 'You can see what's been going on, Celeste.' she protested impatiently, aware of the older woman's sudden interest. 'I found—*him*—' this. as she realised she didn't even know his name, '—washed up on the shore. His arm's quite badly injured. Can you help us indoors?'

'I wish you wouldn't talk about me as if I wasn't here.' objected the man huskily. 'I may be tired, but I'm not unconscious—yet.' He acknowledged Celeste's curious stare. 'I presume you have seen a white man before?'

Celeste's cheeks dimpled. 'Oh, yes'm, sir. I seen a lot of white men. But they ain't all as pretty as you are.'

'Celeste!' Ruth made a sound of disbelief. 'Celeste. will you mind your own business. and help me? Look if you could position yourself here—we could get up the steps—'

'I can get up the steps myself,' the man insisted, releasing his hold on her to reach for the handrail. He succeeded in making the transfer. but he swayed as he clung to the wooden banister, and Ruth exchanged an impatient look with the black woman as she went to help him again.

'It's this way.' she said, propelling him along the hall towards her bedroom, and pushing open the door with her foot. she edged him to the bed. She sagged, too. as he slumped down on to the mattress, and weakness made her grasp at the door frame for support. It had been a strain for both of them, and she could feel the moisture trickling down her own back.

'Thanks,' he said, bracing himself against the iron bedpost, and as he looked around the room, she wished she had made her bed before leaving. But he had to rest, and this was the only place, and regaining her breath, she began to pull the covers straight beneath him.

Celeste hovered in the doorway, and Ruth turned to her impatiently. The black woman seemed fascinated by their visitor, and Ruth didn't appreciate having to issue her instructions which ought not to have been needed.

'Will you tell Daddy what's happened?' she suggested, her eyes flashing messages that Celeste either couldn't or wouldn't understand. 'Ask him if he'll come here, will you? And then make some tea—hot and strong, with plenty of sugar.'

'Yes'm.' Unwillingly, Celeste complied, sauntering off down the hall with evident reluctance. It was not every day they had visitors and she would obviously have much preferred to stay and hear where he had come from.

'She's intrigued,' the man declared, resting back against the pillows Ruth had newly shaken. There was a faintly humorous twist to his mouth as he spoke, but the evidence of the pain he was still suffering was there in the darkness of his eyes. 'I'm sorry to be such a nuisance to you. I'll get out of your way as fast as I can. But, for now—if I could just rest—'

'Your arm needs stitching,' said Ruth, when he would have closed his eyes. 'That tourniquet has to come off. My father will know what to do.'

The man's lids lifted heavily. 'Is your father a doctor?'

'No.' Ruth hesitated. 'He—he was a university professor. But he knows about such things. He's attended to the village people. And when Celeste's cousin was bitten by a barracuda—'

'That's enough.' The man licked his lips weakly. 'Could I have some water, do you suppose? I'm very thirsty.'

'Of course.'

With reluctance, she went to the door, but as she reached it her father appeared in the aperture, his lined face drawn into a puzzled frown.

'Celeste told me—she said—'

'That's right, Daddy.' Ruth gestured towards the bed behind her. 'This man's yacht capsized in the storm. I found him on the beach.'

Professor Jason entered the room with his slow, somewhat breathless gait. Even the smallest exercise tired him these days, and it was all he could do to get about the bungalow, or sit on the verandah with his pipe and his books. Age, and illness, had emaciated his always spare frame, and he stooped slightly, as if his body was curving in on itself.

Ruth placed a chair for her father beside the bed, near enough for him to examine the injured man's arm without effort, and then waited hesitantly for his verdict. Like Celeste, she found, she was curiously loath to leave him, and she felt a certain amount of responsibility for his being there.

'I'm sorry for the intrusion, sir.' He was speaking now, addressing her father, giving the older man time to regain his breath. 'But it was one hell of a storm, and I vaguely recall the keel scraping over some rocks before we turned over.'

Professor Jason frowned, reaching for his arm and examining the wound. 'You were alone?' he asked, voicing the question Ruth had been considering, and the man nodded.

'I guess no one else was crazy enough to come with me,' he remarked, glancing mockingly at Ruth, and she felt again that curious stirring in the pit of her stomach.

'Tell me, Mr—er—' Her father waited expectantly, and the man complied.

'Howard,' he said, after a moment. 'Dominic Howard,' and her father inclined his head.

'Tell me, Mr Howard,' he continued, 'have you had any anti-tetanus shots in the last six months?'

The younger man frowned. 'Not that I can recall, sir. Is it important?'

'It may be,' replied Professor Jason levelly. 'This is a deep wound. It can be dangerous. I think some kind of anti-toxin is necessary. I can stitch up the wound, but I think a doctor's diagnosis is warranted.'

'That's okay.' Dominic Howard shifted on the bed. 'I'll have a doctor take a look at it as soon as I get back to Bridgetown—'

'You can't leave today!'

Ruth's impulsive interjection was followed by an intense feeling of embarrassment, as both men's eyes turned in her direction, but to her relief her father seconded her declaration.

'I agree,' he said, getting up from the chair. 'I'd advise you to rest for the remainder of the day, Mr Howard. Tomorrow . . . well, tomorrow is another day.'

The younger man took a deep breath and swung

his legs to the floor, pulling himself into an upright position. 'Really,' he said, obviously fighting against the dizziness that had once again gripped him. 'I'm all right. Just stitch me up, and I'll be on my way. Can I get a flight from—St Vincent to Bridgetown?'

Ruth looked imploringly at her father, and after a moment's hesitation he said: 'I can't force you to stay here, Mr Howard, but I do ask you to consider seriously before ignoring my advice. You're in a state of complete exhaustion. You could permanently damage your health by over-exerting yourself. You're welcome to stay here. You're welcome to our hospitality. Have the goodness to accept my counsel and wait—at least until tomorrow.'

Dominic's shoulders hunched, his uninjured arm hanging loosely between his spread knees. Then, with a weary look of acceptance, he half turned and slumped back against the pillows. 'All right,' he said heavily, and Ruth didn't know if it was her father's advice or his own weakness which had convinced him. 'Till tomorrow,' he muttered, closing his eyes, and they all breathed a sigh of relief. 'And now, could I have that glass of water?'

CHAPTER TWO

It was lunchtime before Ruth spoke to him again.

Professor Jason had her fetch him a dish of clean water and some towels, and the chest containing his medical equipment. Then he asked her to leave while he examined his patient. Even Celeste, carrying in the tray of tea Ruth had ordered, was banished from the room, and the door firmly closed behind her.

'Who is he?' she asked of Ruth, when the girl joined her in the kitchen for breakfast. 'He some man, that one. So strong and brown. Me, I don't care for white men, but him—he something else!'

Ruth smiled. 'His name is Dominic Howard,' she confided steadily. 'That's all I know about him. That, and the fact that he set off from Bridgetown.'

'Bridgetown? Bridgetown, Barbados?' Celeste's dark eyes widened. 'How he get so far?'

'He had a yacht,' explained Ruth patiently, helping herself to a glass of orange juice. 'It capsized. It was lucky he wasn't drowned.'

Celeste nodded. 'He not drown—not that one.' Her lips curved expressively. 'He lucky man—I know.'

'How do you know?' Ruth made a face at her. 'You don't know any more about him than I do.'

Celeste sniffed, and tapped her nose with a knowledgeable finger. 'Celeste knows,' she insisted, and Ruth shook her head as she reached for a roll.

'Anyway,' she went on, 'Daddy's persuaded him to stay until tomorrow. He wanted to leave today, but he's really not strong enough. He leaned on me all the way up from the beach.'

'I know. I see.' Celeste's eyes twinkled insinuatingly. 'You not sorry he staying, no? You think him some big man, too, don't you?'

'Celeste!' Ruth was affronted. 'Don't be so silly!'

'What so silly?' Celeste shrugged. 'You seventeen now. It time you learn about men.'

'With Mr Howard?' Ruth almost laughed. 'Celeste, he's old!'

'He not old.' Celeste was impatient. 'He twenty-five, twenty-eight, maybe. Twenty-eight not old. Thirty not old!'

'It's old to me,' replied Ruth firmly, concentrating on spreading butter on her roll, but those disturbing feelings had started inside her once more. Celeste was crazy, she told herself severely. And she was man-mad! Daddy said so. Hadn't she got three children already, and none of them within the bonds of wedlock? She was no connoisseur of the opposite sex, and if Professor Jason could hear what she was saying, she would be sternly reprimanded for spreading such gossip to his daughter.

Nevertheless, as Ruth munched her way through three rolls and a slice of melon, topping it up with two cups of the strong black coffee Celeste provided, she couldn't help remembering the supple smoothness of the man's skin against her arm, and the pain-filled intensity of those curiously feline eyes as they looked down at her. She had never met a man quite like him before, and if Celeste was to be believed, neither had she, which was unusual. Celeste always maintained she had had experience with all kinds of men, and even if half what she said was true, she knew what she was talking about.

Ruth sighed, running an exploratory finger round the rim of her cup. For the first time she wished she had listened with more interest to the stories Celeste had told her. But mostly her highly-dramatised narratives of what this man or that man had said to her had left Ruth cold, and certainly in no way convinced that she herself might entertain such feelings. She had found the whole business of the relationship between a man and a woman rather silly, and truth to tell, a little boring, and the idea of letting any man touch her in the ways Celeste had described had always aroused sheer disbelief. It simply didn't seem credible that one day she might permit some member of the opposite sex such liberties, and she half suspected Celeste was teasing her when she spoke of such things. She sometimes wished she had a mother, or that her father was not such an unworldly man. Apart from a rather embarrassed soliloquy on the facts of life, when Ruth had felt he was talking more to himself than to her, he had told her nothing of love, or marriage, and she had not been sufficiently curious to find out for herself. She supposed there were ways of finding out, books one could buy; but swimming and snorkelling, fishing and hunting for seashells, had always seemed infinitely more exciting, and it was only now that she was realising her ignorance.

Dominic Howard was a disturbing man—she acknowledged that. And he was to blame for this sudden introspection. Even with the overnight roughness of his beard upon his chin, and his eyes heavy with exhaustion, he emanated a totally incomprehensible sexuality, and she was not immune to it. He was not a handsome man—at least, not handsome in the way the models were handsome in the mail-order catalogues her father had delivered from time to time. His features were too irregular—his eyes were too deeply set, his cheekbones were too high, his nose was too prominent, his mouth was too thin—and yet the whole combined to make a face she found quite fascinating, and her knees shook as she contemplated this conclusion. Here she was at seventeen—almost eighteen—years of age, and for the first time she was actually considering what it might be like to be married. Heavens, at seventeen Celeste had already had a baby, although she believed her father when he said that this was much too young. Nevertheless, it meant that she was old enough to have a baby, too, and her tongue circled her lips in trembling anticipation.

Then she shook her head, irritated by her own naïveté. Imagine contemplating what it might be like to have a baby when she didn't even know what a man looked like! She had never seen a man without clothes, and even her own nakedness aroused a kind of guilty excitement, as if by looking at herself she was committing some terrible sin. Usually she undressed and dressed without giving herself a second

glance. and she had given no thought to the burgeon-
ing maturity of her body.

'You going to sit there with that cup of coffee all
morning?'

Celeste's faintly malicious tones aroused her from
her reverie, and she glanced up almost absently.
'Why, I—no. No, of course not. I was just—thinking, that's all.'

'About that Mr Howard?' insinuated Celeste
mockingly, and Ruth felt the hot colour sweeping up
her cheeks. 'I seen that mooning face before,' the
black woman went on knowingly. 'You just realising
what manner of man he is, ain't you? You thinking
what it be like to have a man like that making love to
you.'

'No!' Ruth sprang to her feet, hot and embarrassed. 'You have a one-track mind, Celeste. I was
thinking about what we might have for dinner, that's
all. Can't I even think without you putting some
sordid purpose to it?'

'Ain't nothing sordid about making love!' retorted
Celeste shortly. 'You just don't know what you're
missing, that's all. If'n you did—'

'That will do, Celeste.' Ruth clenched her fists at
her sides. 'I don't want to talk about it any more.
And I'd be grateful if you'd refrain from making
those kind of comments in the future.'

With this unequivocal statement Ruth left her,
marching out of the kitchen with her head held high.
But once she was outside, out of sight of the black
woman's resentful glare, her shoulders sagged, and
she thrust her trembling hands into the pockets of
her shorts. Was Celeste right? Was that what she had

really been thinking? And if so, what kind of girl did that make her?

Her father came out on to the verandah, as she was leaning over the rail, securing the ravaged stem of the vine that had been torn from its bedding by the storm. She glanced round at the sound of his measured footsteps, and exclaimed at the evidence of fatigue in his face.

'Sit down,' she insisted, dragging a cane chair forward, and helping him into it. 'You look worn out, Daddy. Let me get you a drink—some coffee perhaps. Or would you prefer something stronger?'

'I don't want anything.' Professor Jason lay back in the chair and let his head relax against the cushion. 'I'll be all right in a couple of minutes. I just need a few moments to rest.'

Ruth studied his pale face with unconcealed concern. Every time she saw him he seemed to look frailer, and her heart beat fast at the realisation. How unfair life was! Why, when they were so happy together, did something like this have to happen?

After a few minutes the look of exhaustion eased, and a faint smile lifted the corners of his lips. 'You're a good girl, Ruth,' he said, taking an unsteady breath. 'What would I do without you?'

Ruth returned his smile tremulously, crouching down beside his chair and stroking his sleeve with tender fingers. 'You won't have to try,' she assured him firmly. Then, adopting a deliberately casual tone: 'Did you manage to dress Mr Howard's arm?'

'It's done,' her father replied, nodding. 'It was quite a wound. Thank heavens for disinfectants.'

'Will it be all right?' Ruth watched him anxiously. 'It won't go bad, will it? I mean, it's not infected or anything?'

Her father moved his shoulders wearily. 'I don't think so. I've given him an anti-tetanus injection, and the wound seems clean enough. He's lost a lot of blood, but he's a strong man. His body will soon recover that.'

Ruth bent her head. 'Did he—did he tell you any more about himself? Did he say where he was from?'

'Well, he's English, of course.' Professor Jason frowned. 'I don't think he belongs in the Islands. He was probably on holiday.' He paused. 'As a matter of fact, he has asked me to contact the telegraph office on St Vincent. He wants a telegram sent to his friends in Bridgetown, informing them that he's safe and well, and requesting that they transfer funds to the bank in Kingstown. He insists that I don't reveal his exact whereabouts, and he intends to use the money to buy some clothes and pay for his air ticket back to Barbados.'

'But what about the yacht?' exclaimed Ruth in surprise, and her father nodded.

'He intends to employ a salvage company, I believe. Right now, he has other things on his mind. He doesn't seem to care that the charter company may sue him for damages.'

Ruth shook her head. 'Won't there be insurance?'

'Possibly. But the fact that he apparently set off alone, in the face of a storm warning—' Professor Jason sighed. 'Insurance companies take all these things into account, you know.'

Ruth made a helpless gesture. 'Perhaps he borrowed the yacht from a friend.'

Her father looked doubtful. 'I hardly think so. Yachts are expensive, and while I get the impression that Mr Howard is unaccustomed to taking anyone's advice but his own, I don't think any friend would have permitted him to leave Barbados.'

Ruth straightened and walked a little impatiently over to the verandah rail. 'It sounds as though you don't like him, Daddy,' she ventured tentatively, turning her face up to the sun.

'I don't.' Professor Jason was blunt. 'The man's too sure of himself, too—arrogant for my liking.'

Ruth turned, resting her slim hips against the wooden spar. 'Celeste thinks he's quite a man.'

'She would.' Her father was unmoved. 'Celeste's interest is skin deep. A man's character means nothing to her.'

'She thinks he's very attractive.' Ruth paused. 'Do you think he's attractive, Daddy?'

Professor Jason's expression hardened. 'Oh, he's a good-looking man, I'll grant her that,' he admitted offhandedly. 'And I've no doubt he knows it.' He frowned. 'What did Celeste say to you? I expect she finds your attitude hard to understand.'

'My—attitude?' Ruth was puzzled.

'Of course.' Her father relaxed. 'If I've succeeded in anything in my life, I hope it's been in teaching you that an intelligent woman is worth a dozen empty-headed morons. It's natural that Celeste should try to influence you, particularly as you're growing older. But I hope you have more sense than to listen to her.'

'Yes.' Ruth managed to answer him, but inside she was torn by the knowledge of her own duplicity.

'In any case,' said Professor Jason, pressing his hands down on the arms of his chair and getting to his feet once more, 'this is a pointless discussion. You're much too young to be interested in a man like Mr Howard. Celeste should have more sense than to discuss him with you. I must have a few words with her when I have the time. But now I'd better go and attend to his wishes.'

Ruth smoothed her moist palms down over her hips. 'Will—will you use the radio?'

'No.' Her father shook his head. 'I'll send Celeste for Joseph. He can go over in the launch. There are one or two things I need in Kingstown, and I prefer to send my instructions in writing.'

Ruth took a step forward. 'Would you like me to go with him?' For some reason it seemed imperative that she should get off the island for a while, but her father shook his head.

'I need you here,' he replied. 'I shall need your assistance when I examine Mr Howard's arm again after lunch. Joseph is quite competent. I can leave the matter comfortably to him.'

Ruth nodded. 'Yes, Daddy.'

'And now I suggest you go and get on with your studying, as usual. Did you read that chapter of Ovid as I asked you?'

'Some of it,' answered Ruth reluctantly, feeling in no mood for Latin translation, but her father seemed unaware of her lack of enthusiasm.

'Good,' he said. 'So you won't require my assistance for the rest of the morning. We'll discuss it at lunch. After I've attended to Mr Howard's affairs.'

After her father had left her, Ruth obediently made her way to the tiny room adjoining the dining room which Professor Jason had adopted as his study. Small, and cluttered with books, it was not the most agreeable place to spend a sunny morning, but normally Ruth forgot her surroundings in the delight of learning. Her father had taught her since she was a small girl, and although she had never taken any formal examinations, her education was in advance of most girls of her own age. Languages came easily to her, and she was as proficient in French and Spanish as she was in English.

Her present studies in Greek and Latin had proved less enjoyable, but usually she succeeded in absorbing her. This morning, however, the words of the *Metamorphoses* just danced meaninglessly before her eyes, and her eyes constantly turned towards the window, as her thoughts ran in an entirely different direction. Who was Dominic Howard? Where did he come from? Why had he taken the yacht out in the teeth of the storm? And what reason did he have for keeping his whereabouts a secret?

By lunchtime, her head was aching and only one line more of the chapter had been translated. She hoped her father would not suspect the reasons for her lack of concentration, and she was uneasy when she entered the dining room to find him talking with Celeste.

'Ah, there you are, Ruth,' her father said, somewhat absently, moving away from the black woman and taking a seat at the table. 'We'll have our meal now, Celeste, and then you can prepare a tray for our guest.'

'Yes, sir.'

Celeste cast a knowing look at Ruth's white face, and left the room through the swing doors that led into the kitchen. It was obvious what she was thinking, and Ruth seated herself hurriedly, hoping to avoid a personal discussion.

'Joseph's gone,' her father informed her, shaking out his napkin. 'And I've set some of the boys to cleaning up the beach. Naturally, the devastation the storm caused can't be rectified in a matter of hours, but we can make a concerted effort to restore order.'

'Yes.' Ruth nodded, spreading her own napkin over her bare knees.

'Fortunately, no one appears to have been injured in the storm.' Professor Jason went on steadily. 'Apart from our unexpected guest, of course.' His keen grey eyes came to rest on Ruth's pale cheeks. 'Though I must say, now I come to notice it, you look a little drawn yourself. Didn't you sleep?'

Ruth fidgeted with the cutlery. 'Yes, I slept,' she assured him, avoiding his eyes. 'I've got a bit of a headache, that's all.' She glanced up. 'I'm afraid I haven't made a very good effort with the Ovid.'

Her father frowned. 'You're not worrying about this man, are you? I've told you, he's going to be perfectly all right.'

'Of course not.' Ruth hunched her shoulders, pushing her hands into the pockets of her shorts, and then drawing her brows together as her fingers encountered something hard and round. It was the coin he had found earlier, and she pulled it out eagerly.

'I found this on the beach this morning,' she said, pushing it across the table towards her father, successfully diverting his interest. 'Is it Spanish? The lettering is almost obscured, but you might be able to identify the engraving.'

'How interesting!' To her relief, Professor Jason drew his reading glasses out of his breast pocket and placed them on his nose. 'An old coin. I haven't seen one quite like this before.'

'Do you think it's valuable?'

Ruth was anxious to sustain his curiosity in her mind, and her father tipped the coin towards the light, turning it this way and that to ascertain its origin. It successfully distracted his attention from herself, and by the time Celeste appeared with their food, he was talking quite happily about the Spanish conquest of South America.

However, Celeste had other ideas.

'You want I should take a tray in to Mr Howard?' she suggested, setting down a bowl of fish chowder. 'Seems like he might be hungry, too.'

Professor Jason frowned, the problem of their visitor once more in the forefront of his thoughts. 'Yes,' he decided after a moment. 'Yes, that might be a good idea, Celeste.' He paused, and then went on evenly: 'Just don't make a nuisance of yourself, will you? I don't want you hanging about his room. Deliver the food and leave him to eat it. I'll retrieve the tray when I go to examine his dressing.'

Celeste's dark eyes flashed angrily at the implied insult, and she glared at Ruth as if blaming the girl for her father's warning. Ruth's helpless movement

of her shoulders, disclaiming any responsibility fo
the admonition, went unacknowledged, and th
door closed with unnecessary emphasis behin
Celeste's billowing skirts.

'Dear me!' Professor Jason broke a crust from th
long roll Celeste had baked that morning. 'I thin
I've offended her.' He sighed. 'Oh, well, it's for he
own good. I don't want Howard imagining my ser
vants are—well, importunate.'

Ruth ladled stew on to plates. 'Celeste is–
friendly, that's all.' She defended the black woma
reluctantly, but her father was not appeased.

'She's too friendly,' he declared, taking the plat
Ruth offered him. 'And I don't want her influenc
rubbing off on you.'

'Oh, Daddy . . .'

Ruth concentrated on the chowder, but its appe
tising flavour was like sawdust in her mouth. He
appetite was practically non-existent, and she starte
when her father suddenly covered one of her hand
with his.

'Listen to me, Ruth,' he urged gently. 'I know yo
still think and feel like a child, but you're growing up
In a little while you'll be a young woman.' He waite
until she looked up at him, and then went on: 'An
while Mr Howard's here, I think you ought to pay
little more attention to your appearance.'

'My appearance?' Ruth's eyes widened.

'Yes.' Then, seeing the confusion in her face, Pro
fessor Jason hastened on: 'Oh, don't misunderstan
me, my dear. I don't want you to behave any diffe
ently from the way you have always done. It's ju
that—well, those shorts you're wearing, for ex

ample. They're a little skimpy, don't you think?'

'They're too small,' Ruth conceded, her embarrassment at this discussion increasing as she contemplated what Dominic Howard's reactions might have been, and her father seized on the admission.

'That's what I mean,' he exclaimed, squeezing her fingers. 'I think a nice frock—or perhaps a skirt and blouse—would look infinitely more suitable, don't you?' He smiled. 'I suggest you get changed immediately after lunch.'

'But, Daddy—'

'Now don't be tiresome, Ruth,' Professor Jason interrupted her wearily. 'Just do as I ask, and don't argue. As soon as you're ready, let me know.'

'You're not eating any more?'

Ruth looked up at him anxiously as he pushed back his chair and got to his feet, and Professor Jason shook his head.

'I'll sit on the verandah for a while,' he said, finding it an obvious effort to open the door, and Ruth watched him leave with a helpless sense of guilt.

Her own appetite had disappeared completely, and when Celeste returned to clear the table, she looked with disapproval at the scarcely-touched plates.

'Is something wrong?' she demanded, clattering them on to a tray. 'You don't like my clam chowder any more?'

'The chowder was delicious,' Ruth assured her unhappily. 'We just weren't—hungry, that's all.'

'Well, I hope Mr Howard isn't so fussy,' retorted Celeste, impaling her with a malevolent stare.

'Seems to me like he's old enough to think for himself.'

'Oh. Celeste . . .'

Ruth had no wish to get embroiled in an argument with the black woman, and with an awkward pat on the woman's shoulder, she made good her escape.

It was only as she started along the hall to get changed that she remembered Dominic Howard was occupying her room. Her father had obviously overlooked that fact, too, and she turned reluctantly back towards the verandah, realising he would have to sanction her remaining as she was.

But when she emerged into the dappled shade of the verandah, she found her father was asleep. His efforts that morning had evidently exhausted him, and she was half relieved that nature had taken its natural course. Rest was what he needed, and unwilling to disturb him, she turned back into the house.

In the hall, she hesitated. She could hear Celeste clattering about in the kitchen, expunging her frustration in her own way, and she knew if she joined her she would be drawn into the conflict. She could return to her studies, of course, but the prospect of translating Latin cases did not appeal to her, and besides, the little room was stuffy in the afternoons.

She could sit in the living room, of course, or go and help the boys from the village who were clearing the beach. She could even offer her services to Tomas, who tended the vegetable garden for them and was presently at work restoring the ravages of the storm, but none of these alternatives appealed to her. Like it or not, she was irresistibly drawn to the door of her bedroom, and she placed her ear against the panels, listening for any sound from within.

Perhaps he was asleep, she thought, drawing back, thwarted by the silence. Perhaps she could slip inside, collect some clothes, and get out without his being aware of it. Her father need never know. She could always tell him the clothes were newly washed, and she had merely collected them from Celeste.

Her own duplicity alarmed her. What was happening to her? What was she thinking of? She had never deceived her father before, never wanted to. So why was she considering it now?

But an inner voice chided at her hesitation. Where was the harm? it argued. What possible deception was there in entering her own bedroom? She was not a child, she was a young woman. Celeste said so. And Celeste knew more about such things.

Taking a deep breath, she gripped the handle of the door and turned. It opened easily, and she took a tentative step forward, peering rather myopically into the shadowy room. Someone had half closed the shutters again, and what light there was was slatted in bars of gold across the bed.

Dominic was lying on the bed, where she had last seen him, but now his left arm was swathed in bandages from wrist to elbow, and instead of the wet jeans he was wearing a pair of her father's silk pyjama trousers. His eyes were closed, she saw, and her own feelings were mixed as she glided across the room to the dressing table. In spite of the cajoling voice inside her, she told herself she was glad he was asleep, and she opened the dressing table drawer with stealthy fingers.

She didn't need long to decide what to wear. She had few clothes. spending most of her days in shorts or swimsuits. and the floral skirt and cotton blouse she chose were well washed and faded. Until now, she had not considered clothes of much importance. and she wished her father had not made her so self-conscious.

'How much longer are you going to be?'

Ruth started guiltily at the sound of Dominic Howard's voice. Gathering the skirt and blouse to her. she closed the drawer with her knee and turned to face the man on the bed. His eyes were wide open now. and she gazed at him uncertainly, not knowing exactly how to reply.

'What are you doing?' he enquired, propping himself up on one elbow. 'Why the secrecy?'

'Secrecy—'

'Yes. secrecy. I saw the way you came in here, and I intended to let you get away with it. But you took so long. I got impatient. What's that you've got there?'

Ruth's face flamed. 'They're mine,' she declared reluctantly. 'My clothes. Daddy said—well, I was going to get changed, but you were in here, and I didn't want to disturb you.'

Dominic relaxed against the pillows, indolent, like a panther, exuding that disturbing influence she had sensed before. He troubled her, this man with the lean. brown body and strangely feline eyes. He aroused feelings she neither recognised nor understood, and although she guessed that this was what Celeste had tried to explain to her, she was half afraid of the turmoil of her emotions.

'So,' he said now. 'I'm sorry, I didn't mean to be rude. Not when I owe you—and your father—so much.'

'It was nothing.' Ruth gave a deprecatory shrug of her shoulders. 'I—we would do the same for anyone.' She paused. 'How do you feel? Is your arm any easier?'

'It's much improved,' he assured her firmly. 'Your father gave me something to ease the pain. He's quite professional, your old man, isn't he? But I guess you know that.'

Ruth bent her head. 'He—I—yes.' She pressed her lips together, lifting the corners of her mouth in an apology for a smile. 'Well, I'm pleased to hear that you feel better. You could have drowned out there.'

'I know it.' His eyes narrowed. 'I do appreciate it, you know.'

Ruth shifted her weight from one foot to the other, knowing she should leave yet reluctant to do so. 'I—Daddy's sent Joseph to St Vincent. He should have despatched your message by now.'

'Good.'

Dominic Howard drew his eyes from her to stare broodingly towards the window, and she wondered what thoughts were going through his mind. Who were his friends in Bridgetown? Male, or female? Was he married? Her thoughts shied away from such a conclusion, yet it was a definite possibility. But if he had a wife, would he have insisted on concealing his whereabouts?

As if becoming aware of her troubled concentration, Dominic turned his head to look at her again. and she coloured in embarrassment. 'How old are you. Ruth?' he asked softly, and she gathered her clothes defensively to her as she answered him.

'Seventeen,' he murmured, his mouth twisting a trifle wryly. 'Oh, to be seventeen again!'

'I'm almost eighteen, actually,' she added hurriedly, and when his brows arched interrogatively. she went on: 'In seven months, to be exact.'

'Eighteen.' His smile was mocking. 'Do you know I'm just about old enough to be your father?'

'You're not like my father,' she protested hotly. 'He—he's much older.'

'Oh, I agree. Much older. Too old to have a daughter as young as you, I'd have thought.'

Ruth held up her head. 'He and Mummy were married almost twenty years before they had me.'

'I can believe it.' Dominic frowned suddenly. 'Where is—Mummy?'

'She's dead.' Ruth was philosophical. 'I never knew her. She died when I was born.'

'What a tragedy!' Dominic Howard was sympathetic. 'Your father must have felt he was to blame.'

Ruth's eyes widened. 'Daddy? Oh, no, Daddy wasn't to blame. It was the system. He said it had lost credibility.'

'The system?' Dominic was puzzled.

'Yes.' Ruth sighed. 'With all the advances in modern surgery, it was still not possible to prevent a woman dying in childbirth.'

Dominic shook his head. 'Your mother may have been too old. Had you thought of that?'

Ruth considered. 'She was forty-four. That's not really old, is it?'

'It is for having a baby,' he replied dryly. 'Particularly if it's the first.'

Ruth shrugged. 'Oh, well, perhaps you're right. I don't suppose Daddy thought of that. I expect he was too upset.' She moved her shoulders inconsequently. 'Anyway, that was why he decided to leave England. He said he had lost faith in a society that put more money into guns and armaments than into medical research.'

Dominic levered himself into an upright position, and sat cross-legged, staring at her. 'Tell me, how long have you lived on the island?'

Ruth bit her lip. 'A long time. At least twelve years.'

He said a word she didn't recognise, but she thought it wasn't very polite. 'You mean you've lived here since you were four or five years old?' he demanded.

Ruth nodded.

'Good lord!' He seemed astounded. 'But your education—'

'Didn't Daddy tell you? He used to be a university professor. He taught me himself.'

Dominic gazed at her as if he couldn't comprehend what she was saying. Then he made a blank gesture. 'I don't believe it.'

'Why not?' Ruth was perplexed. 'It's quite simple really. Daddy has this private income, you see. Something to do with some money my grandmother left Mummy. It's enough, living here, growing our own vegetables, spending little—'

'But you've got no friends,' he overrode her roughly. 'No companions of your own age! You told

me. You said there was only you and your father and
some old priest on the island!'

'I said we were the only Europeans,' Ruth corrected swiftly. 'There are several families in the
village—'

'And what about your family?' Dominic interrupted again. 'What about this—grandmother? Your
mother's mother. Where is she? Dead, I suppose.'

'Of course.' Ruth couldn't quite understand why
he seemed to be getting so angry. 'There's only
Daddy and me.' She paused. 'He's all the family I
need.'

'I don't believe it.' said Dominic again, plucking
impatiently at the sheet beneath him. 'I just don't
believe it. You really don't know any other life, do
you?'

Ruth shifted a little uncomfortably now. 'I know
all I need to know,' she declared a little stiffly. 'I'm
not ignorant. I've had a good education—better than
some girls in England. Daddy says.'

'I don't doubt it.' retorted Dominic, the harsh
tones of his voice deepening into violence. 'But the
kind of education you're talking about is a poor
substitute for the school of life!'

Ruth felt the warm colour creeping up her cheeks
once more. Watching him, witnessing the change of
expression in his dark face, made her feel uneasy and
anxious. What had she said? What had she done to
arouse such strong feelings? She was certainly ignorant in the ways of men, as Celeste had said, and she
wished she knew how to dispel the sudden anger that
had come between them. She had enjoyed talking to
him. It had been a new and exciting experience. Now

she had spoiled it all, and she didn't know how to make amends.

'I—I'd better tell my father you're awake,' she said, seizing on her only avenue of escape, and he turned his face up to hers once more.

There was a curious expression in his eyes, a puzzled, probing expression, that sought the tentative uncertainty of hers, and searched their depths with disturbing intensity. To avoid that intense appraisal, her eyes dropped, down, over the grim planes of his face to the muscular expanse of his chest, that was lightly covered with sunbronzed hair. The hair was spread evenly over the upper part of his torso, and then arrowed down to disappear beneath the corded waistband of her father's pyjama trousers. She wondered if the lower part of his body was hairy, too, and then turned scarlet in mortification at the direction of her thoughts.

'How often do you leave here?'

She heard the question as if from a great distance, and she forced herself to concentrate on what he was saying.

'Leave?' she echoed unevenly. 'I—I don't know what—'

'How often do you visit the other islands?' asked Dominic patiently. 'St Vincent, for example?'

Ruth blinked. 'Twice—maybe three times a year,' she said, not understanding his reasons for asking, and he made a sound of disbelief.

'You're wasting your youth, do you know that?' he demanded, shaking his head. 'Ruth, you're missing out on life!'

'I don't think my daughter would agree with you.

Mr Howard.' Professor Jason's voice from the open doorway was cold with disapproval. 'Ruth—kindly go and change your clothes, as I asked you. And don't bother to come back. I will attend to Mr Howard's dressing myself.'

CHAPTER THREE

Supper was a subdued meal. Sitting opposite her father, Ruth was aware that he had still not forgiven her for disobeying his instructions and chattering to Dominic Howard, and she wondered how, in the space of a day, one man could cause so much conflict.

Since leaving the bedroom, Professor Jason had not said more than half a dozen words to her, and although she had tried several times to start a conversation, he had answered only in monosyllables.

For her part, Ruth found his antagonism almost as hard to understand as Dominic's anger. What had she done to either of them to arouse such strong feelings? And where was the harm in talking to a man who by his own admission was old enough to be her father?

Deciding she had to bring up the subject that was the cause of their disagreement, she took a deep breath. 'Do you think Mr Howard will be well enough to leave here tomorrow?' she asked, deliberately treading into deep waters, and she had the satisfaction of seeing that her words caused some reaction.

'I'm sure he will,' her father responded, his clenched fist on the table beside his plate evidence of his feelings. 'I see no reason why he should not leave in the morning.'

'I see.' Ruth looked down at her plate, aware of a sense of disappointment out of all proportion to the information he had imparted. 'His arm isn't infected, then? I'm glad to hear it.'

'You're glad he's leaving?' enquired her father, making his first overture since the scene in the bedroom, and Ruth nodded.

'Of course,' she said, ignoring the small voice inside her which told her she was lying again. 'Why shouldn't I be? I hardly know the man.'

Professor Jason's shoulders slumped. 'Thank God!'

Ruth's brows drew together. 'What do you mean?'

Her father shook his head. 'I don't know. I don't know what I mean, exactly. I don't know what I was thinking. Except that ever since I heard Howard telling you that you were wasting your life, staying here with me, I've been—afraid.'

'Afraid?' Ruth's own problems dissolved beneath her concern for her father. 'Daddy, what on earth have you to be afraid of?'

'You,' said Professor Jason simply. 'Your leaving me. I was afraid Howard might have unsettled you—made you dissatisfied—'

'Oh, Daddy!' Ruth pushed back her chair and went to him, kneeling down beside him and resting her head on his knee. 'Daddy, don't be so silly. You know I'd never leave you. Never!'

'Oh, my dear . . .' His gnarled fingers stroked the silken curtain of hair that loosened from its leather thong fell in night-dark splendour down her back. 'I'm such a coward. I don't think I could bear it if you were not with me.'

Ruth sighed, cradling his hand against her cheek, looking up at him with eyes that glistened with unshed tears. 'I thought you were angry with me,' she said. 'I thought you were annoyed because I had disobeyed you. But my clothes were in there, you see, and—'

'We'll say no more about it,' Professor Jason silenced her firmly. 'I can't deny—seeing you there, with that man, I was a little—displeased. But I know you were not to blame. He was asking you questions. I heard him. As I told you—he's aggressive, arrogant! I shall be glad when he has gone.'

Ruth nodded, lowering her lids so that he should not see the sudden pain in her eyes. It was so foolish, so stupid to feel sorry that the stranger was leaving their lives as abruptly as he had entered them. He was nothing to her. There was a saying—ships that pass in the night. He had been on such a ship, and for a brief spell their paths had crossed.

Ruth slept in the living room. Although her father made the suggestion that he should sleep on the couch, his relief was evident when she insisted that he must have the bed. It was his bed, after all, and she was perfectly capable of curling up on the couch. She was smaller, for one thing, and younger, and there was no question in her mind that Professor Jason needed his rest.

In consequence, Ruth slept shallowly, and she was awakened instantly when she heard someone cry out. For a few seconds she lay there, her heart pounding a little unsteadily as she contemplated the possibility of her having imagined it, but when it was repeated, she got hurriedly off the couch and going to the door, she switched on the light.

Her father's room was at the end of the hall, and she sped along the tiled floor on anxious feet. The efforts of the day must have been too much for him, she thought apprehensively, and almost cried out herself when the door of her room opened and Dominic Howard appeared, swaying, in the aperture.

He blinked perplexedly when he saw Ruth, almost as if he didn't recognise her, she thought curiously, and then she wrapped her arms about herself protectively as she realised she was only wearing the skimpy cotton nightshirt that barely covered her thighs.

'A drink,' he said, licking his lips as if they were dry. 'I want a drink. Where the hell's the telephone around here?'

'The telephone?' Ruth was torn between the knowledge of her father's needs and Dominic's strangely confusing demands. 'There are no telephones on Indigo, Mr Howard. Go back to bed and I'll fetch you a glass of water, after I've attended to my father.'

'Your father?' He looked down at her blankly. 'Who are you? Where am I? What the hell do you think you're doing to me?'

'Mr Howard—'

Ruth put out her hand to indicate the room behind him, hoping to divert him back into the bedroom until she had had time to see to her father, but somehow her fingers brushed his arm, and the burning heat of him made her snatch her hand back in horror.

With another helpless look towards her father's

room, she hesitated only a moment before taking his arm again, and urging him back into the bedroom.

'Get into bed, Mr Howard,' she appealed, making little progress. 'You've got a temperature. Now you don't want to get pneumonia, do you?'

'I want a drink,' he persisted, pushing against her tugging hands. 'Let me go! I want a drink, I tell you.'

'I'll get you a drink,' Ruth promised, gazing helplessly up at him. 'Oh, please—won't you get back into bed? I can't leave you like this. You're burning up!'

Dominic's tawny eyes encountered hers, searching her pleading face with sudden emotion. 'I'll get back into bed, if you'll come with me,' he said, ceasing the struggle, and Ruth was suddenly faced with an entirely new situation. His abrupt transformation from hostile adversary to willing advocate was disturbing, and she was overwhelmingly aware of the lateness of the hour and the unexpected intimacy between them. She supposed he was not himself or he would never have made such a suggestion, but that didn't alter the fact that the suggestion had been made, and he expected an answer.

'Get—get into bed, Mr Howard,' she said at length, drawing away from him, but now his fingers fastened about her wrist, firm and resistant, compelling her towards him.

She couldn't believe this was happening. She couldn't believe that he was holding her astonished gaze in an hypnotic trance, or that his free hand was sliding about her waist. It was the first time any man, other than her father, had laid hands upon her body, and the terrifying thing was, she felt incapable of preventing him.

'Who are you?' he murmured huskily, the tawny eyes glazing as he endeavoured to remember where he was, and his hoarse demand brought Ruth to her senses. As he bent his head, seeking a more physical contact, she twisted in his arms and succeeded in breaking his hold.

'Get into bed, Mr Howard,' she begged, somewhat breathlessly, from the doorway, and closed the door firmly behind her.

In the hall, she took several gulping breaths of air before feeling ready to face her father. On no account must he suspect what had happened, and her heart palpitated at the realisation of how vulnerable he was. But when she opened his door, she found Professor Jason was fast asleep, and with sudden hindsight she realised it had been Dominic Howard who had called out.

That left her in a difficult position. What should she do? Should she wake her father up and tell him that Dominic was ill? She was loath to do so. He had looked so fragile that evening, and the last thing he needed was a broken night's sleep. And yet how could she go back into Dominic's bedroom knowing her own vulnerability? She had to do something— that much was obvious. But what? *What?*

There was only one solution. With a feeling of reluctance she padded back along the hall, going out through the kitchen into the yard at the back of the house. She paid no attention to the fact that her feet were bare. She had gone barefoot as often as not since she was old enough to remember, and as she crossed the cobbled area to Celeste's cabin her only concern was that she might not find the woman alone.

Celeste's protesting voice answered her third knock, and presently she pulled open the door, huge and voluminous, in her cambric nightgown.

'What time you call this?' she complained, pushing stubby fingers through her tight curls and leaving them standing on end. Then, seeing Ruth's anxious face in the moonlight, she exclaimed: 'Is it your daddy? Oh, honey, Celeste didn't mean no harm.'

'It's not Daddy,' Ruth admitted uncomfortably, hearing the mattress on Celeste's bed creak, as if someone had turned over on it. Celeste always had a man in tow, and since her children lived with her mother in Kingstown, she felt free to invite whom she liked into her bed. Recently, Ruth had suspected it was Joseph who was occupying that special place, but as Joseph already had a wife and six children, she had decided she must be mistaken. Now, however, she was not so certain, and Celeste's eyes narrowed as she realised it was not the emergency she had thought.

'Not your daddy?' she repeated, pursing her lips. 'What then? What you want waking me up at this time of night? I'se a working woman. I needs my sleep.'

'We all need our sleep, Celeste,' said Ruth, rubbing her bare arms as the coolness of the night air chilled her flesh. 'But I'm worried about—about Mr Howard. I think he's got a temperature.'

Celeste gasped. 'You come here, bothering me about that man!' she exclaimed indignantly, making to close the door, but Ruth would not let her.

'Please, Celeste,' she appealed, 'listen to me. He really is ill. And I don't know what to do. I don't

want to wake Daddy. unless I have to. I thought—
well. I though you might help me.'

'How you find out Mr Howard sick?' Celeste
asked suspiciously. 'You sleeping in his bed?'

'Of course not!' Ruth was horrified. 'He cried out.
that's all. And—and I thought it was Daddy.'

Celeste sniffed. 'You been attending him like
that?' she grunted, and Ruth touched her night-shirt
and the silken curtain of her hair with discomfited
fingers. 'What you expect me to do anyway? I ain't
no doctor.'

'He's thirsty.' said Ruth, glancing back towards
the house. 'He said so. Perhaps, if we gave him a
drink, and some aspirin—'

'Huh!' Celeste was sceptical. 'Why can't you do
that yourself? You a big girl now. You don't need me
to hold your hand.'

'I do. That is—' Ruther broke off in embarrassment. 'Please, Celeste, won't you come? I do need
your help.'

Celeste looked doubtful. but she was hesitating.
and Ruth pressed her advantage. 'You're so much
more experienced in these things than I am,' she
pleaded. 'I know he would appreciate it.'

Celeste sniffed. 'Well—' she murmured consideringly. 'all right.'

'Oh. thank you.'

Ruth's shoulders sagged with relief, and Celeste
turned back into the cabin. 'I'll get my robe.' she
said. scratching her head as she went. and Ruth
breathed more easily as she walked back to the
house.

By the time Celeste appeared. wrapped about in a

scarlet woollen dressing gown that had once belonged to Ruth's father. Ruth had added shorts to supplement her provocative attire. She had no idea how Dominic might react faced with two women, but she hoped there was safety in numbers.

'He still sleeping in your room?' Celeste asked, bustling along the hall, and Ruth, trailing in her wake, nodded.

'I'm sleeping in the living room,' she added, her pulses racing as they neared Dominic's door. 'Daddy offered me his bed, but I refused. I'm quite comfortable on the couch.'

'Hmm!' Celeste snorted, reaching for the handle and flinging open the door. Then both women stopped, aghast. In the light shed from the hall they could see Dominic was no longer occupying the bed. He was stretched out on the floor, and judging by the way he was lying, he must have collapsed.

'Oh, gosh!'

Ruth turned anxious eyes in Celeste's direction, but the black woman was already moving forward, bending over the unconscious man. 'He have a fever,' she exclaimed, laying her hand against his forehead. 'Why you not tell me this before, Missy? Mr Howard, he poorly sick!'

Ruth expelled her breath unsteadily. 'I did tell you, Celeste,' she protested, pushing her hands into the pockets of her shorts and pulling them out again. 'Oh, lord, what are we going to do?'

Celeste straightened. 'It that cut in his arm,' she declared, her black face brooding as she considered her diagnosis. 'Sometime it happen this way. Feller feels okay, think it not going to trouble him. Then them little germs, they come along and throw you to the sharks.'

'All right, Celeste, I understand that,' said Ruth, trying to be patient. 'But what can we do?'

'I could have told you this was going to happen,' went on Celeste, as if Ruth hadn't spoken. 'I seen it all before. You remember that time little Bobby was bitten by his pet mongoose? Your daddy thought his leg was going to be all right, and what happened? Day after, it swell up like a balloon—'

'Celeste, please!' Ruth took hold of the other woman's arm and shook it. 'I know about secondary infection. And I'm not interested in what happened to little Bobby! I want to know what we ought to do now. Shouldn't we get him back on to the bed?'

Celeste looked as though she might take umbrage from the irritation in Ruth's voice, but the desperation in the younger girl's face won her compassion. 'Help me lift him,' she directed, taking charge of Dominic's shoulders, and with a struggle they managed to lever him back on to the mattress.

Ruth was panting with exertion by the time Celeste was satisfied, and she stood looking down at their patient with troubled eyes. The hectic flush which had coloured his face earlier had now drained away, and his pallor was frightening. His skin had an unhealthy grey sheen, and when Celeste put her thumb against his eyelid the pupil rolled sightlessly upward.

'What can we do?' Ruth appealed again. 'Oh, Celeste, he's not going to die, is he?'

Celeste looked at her curiously. 'You care?' she probed sardonically, and Ruth gave her an indignant stare.

'Of course I care,' she declared, aware of Celeste's interpretation of her flaming cheeks. 'I'd care about anybody in the same circumstances. I care about human life, Celeste. Don't you?'

'Perhaps not so passionately,' retorted the black woman dryly, making her own assessment. 'But if you feel so strongly about it, I guess you better wake your daddy. We need a doctor here, and ain't no way you and me's going to conjure one.'

The rest of the night passed in a blur of anxious speculation, of restlessness and impatience, and helpless impotence. Once her father was awakened, he took charge of the situation, and in no time at all Ruth found herself banished to his bed, there to remain until she was summoned.

'But I can help,' she protested, only to come up against an implacable opposition.

'Try to get some sleep,' her father told her firmly, and she had no choice but to do as he asked. Arguing would have proved time-wasting and futile, she knew that, and besides, her father could ill afford to waste his energies.

In consequence, she spent the night pacing the floor of Professor Jason's bedroom, not knowing what was going on, unable to do anything but wait in fretful impatience for the morning. She knew Celeste and her father would do everything they could, but that didn't help her, and frustration drew dark circles around her eyes as the hours passed. Had they sent for Doctor Francis? Would he come in time? Had Dominic regained consciousness? Had they succeeded in lowering his temperature? Her mind buzzed with questions, and despite her weariness she could not relax.

Nevertheless, towards morning exhaustion drove her to lie down on the bed. She would just rest for a while, she thought drowsily, and knew nothing more until the fingers of sunlight, creeping through the shutters, probed her heavy eyelids.

She rose hurriedly, and opening the bedroom door, peered down the hall. All was quiet. Her bedroom door was closed, and there was no sign of either her father or Celeste.

Feeling rather like the sole survivor of some awful disaster, she stole along the hall to the kitchen, then expelled her breath in some relief when she saw Celeste busy at the stove. The black woman was dressed now, her buxom form exaggerated by a dress with gaudy red and white flowers all over it, and Ruth felt guiltily aware that she had contributed nothing to the previous night's activities.

'Hi,' she said, supporting herself in the doorway. 'Where's Daddy?'

Celeste turned with a start, snorting impatiently when she saw Ruth's uneasy expression. 'So there you are at last,' she declared, placing her hands squarely on her hips. 'Some nurse you are, abandoning your patient!'

'How is he?' Ruth asked eagerly. 'Did Daddy send for Doctor Francis? I was so worried, but nobody came to tell me what was going on.'

'Mmm.' Celeste looked sceptical. 'You were worried all right. You were fast asleep when I looked in on you a couple of hours ago.'

'I know.' Ruth sighed. 'I stayed awake for ages, but then I must have closed my eyes. I don't remember anything else.' She moved her shoulders helplessly. 'So what happened? Where is—Mr Howard? Is he better?'

'Me, I don't get tired, I suppose,' Celeste grumbled, not answering her. 'I stay awake all night, but no one asks how I am.'

'Oh, Celeste!' Ruth came into the kitchen, spreading her arms apologetically. 'I'm sorry. I did want to help, but Daddy said—'

'I know what your daddy said,' declared Celeste, nodding vigorously. 'He say you too young, he say you not old enough to know about such things. You want I should disobey your daddy and tell you things he don't want you to know?'

Ruth kept her temper with difficulty. 'Celeste, please, tell me what's happened. Did Daddy send for Doctor Francis? If you don't tell me soon, I'll scream!'

'Don't do that.' Celeste glanced apprehensively towards the door. 'Why you so interested, anyway?'

'Celeste!'

'All right, all right.' The black woman hunched her shoulders resignedly and turned back to the stove. 'Mr Howard, he pretty sick man. His arm, it infected. Doctor say it could be matter of life and death.'

Ruth blanched. 'Doctor Francis has been here?'

'He here,' said Celeste nonchalantly, nodding towards the door of the dining room. 'What you think I doing? I making breakfast for your daddy and the doctor.'

'But Mr Howard!' exclaimed Ruth, resting her trembling hands on the table. 'Celeste, what do you mean? A matter of life and death?'

Celeste hesitated a moment. and then, as if feeling compassion for the girl's obvious distress. she added offhandedly: 'I didn't say it was a matter of life and death. I said doctor say it *could* be.'

Ruth felt suddenly weak. 'Celeste, what are you talking about?'

The black woman shrugged. 'If'n we hadn't called Doctor Francis like we did, your Mr Howard might have died.'

Ruth sank down slackly into a chair. 'But he's not going to?'

'No.' Celeste broke eggs into a basin and began beating them up. 'Leastways. it ain't so likely.'

Ruth licked her dry lips. 'You said he was a sick man.'

'He is. Pretty sick.' Celeste agreed. pouring the eggs into a pan. 'That fever. it draining all the strength out of him.'

Ruth stared at her. 'You mean he's still got the fever?'

'Yes'm.' Celeste could be obtuse when she chose. 'You want breakfast. too? Go see your daddy. I'll fetch it in.'

'I don't want any breakfast.' said Ruth impatiently. turning to stare over her shoulder for a moment. before looking back at Celeste. 'Are they going to take him to hospital?'

'Not to my knowing.' replied Celeste indifferently. 'You want some coffee?'

'I've told you. I don't want anything.' said Ruth shortly. and Celeste arched her eyebrows.

'You mighty worried about that man. ain't you,

honey?' she observed tormentingly. 'I wonder what your daddy think about that.'

'It's none of your business,' retorted Ruth irritably, and then sighed. 'Celeste, don't taunt me. I told you last night how I felt.'

'So you did, so you did.' Celeste's lips tightened. 'Only, seems to me you letting this man's trouble get to you.'

'I found him, didn't I?'

'So what that make you?'

'Nothing. I'm worried about him, that's all.'

'He your responsibility, is that it?'

'No.' Ruth's pale cheeks suffused with colour. 'I just want to know what's happening. Where is he? Is he still unconscious?'

Celeste considered her words, and then expanded. 'Seems like he's sleeping right now. Doctor given him some injection to cool his blood. Ain't nothing they can do but wait. Leastways, that's what I heard.'

Ruth expelled her breath unsteadily. 'And his arm?'

'All swollen, it was. Oozing that there pus, your daddy called it. Looked pretty ugly.'

Celeste seemed to be enjoying relating this part of her story, and Ruth wondered how she could handle food without feeling sick. Ruth felt sick, physically sick, and she looked up rather apprehensively when the door opened to admit her father.

'I thought I heard voices,' Professor Jason remarked heavily, weariness etched in every line of his face. 'Celeste, aren't those eggs almost ready? Doctor Francis doesn't have all day.'

'And I don't have more'n one pair of hands,'

mumbled the black woman resentfully. 'They're ready. Go sit yourself down, and I'll fetch them to you.'

Professor Jason permitted his daughter a slight smile. 'Are you coming to join us, my dear?' he asked, gesturing behind him, and aware of Celeste standing impatiently with the tray in her hands, waiting for her reply, Ruth nodded and got to her feet. If she wanted information, why not from the horse's mouth? she thought wryly, ignoring the black woman's knowing stare, although the prospect of watching the two men devour the dish of eggs brought bile to the back of her throat.

Doctor Francis was a man in his early fifties. A Scotsman, he had settled in Kingstown after the last war, and his family had grown up in the islands. He and Ruth's father were good friends, their professional relationship spilling over into a more personal one. At least once a month the medical practitioner came over to the island to play chess with Professor Jason, and even his professional visits lately had become social occasions. Ruth knew he was worried about her father, knew that he saw little hope for the older man, and knew, too, that he worried about her and what she would do after her father was dead.

'Hello there, lassie,' he greeted her now, his accent still as unmistakable as it had ever been. 'I hear you're responsible for finding our piece of human flotsam on the beach. I think your father wishes you hadn't taken the trouble.'

Ruth looked at her father, and he quickly demurred. 'I didn't say that, John,' he protested, waving his daughter into a chair. 'I merely said the man's been nothing but trouble ever since he arrived.'

'How is he. Doctor Francis?' asked Ruth eagerly, seating herself at the table. 'Is he going to get better? He's not in any danger, is he?'

Doctor Francis pushed his horn-rimmed spectacles up his nose and surveyed her expectant face with humorous eyes. 'You sound very anxious, Ruth,' he remarked teasingly. 'Has this young man taken your fancy?'

'Don't talk nonsense. John.' Professor Jason's lips thinned. and Celeste, serving the eggs, cast the girl a mocking look. 'Naturally, Ruth is interested. Aren't we all? There's nothing very unusual about that.'

Doctor Francis pulled a wry face. 'If you say so, Curtis. if you say so.' He turned his attention back to Ruth, who was looking quite mortified now, and smiled encouragingly. 'Mr Howard will survive,' he assured her gently. 'I'd stake my life on it. But he owes his thanks to you for alerting your father as you did.'

Ruth flushed. 'Oh, really—'

'No, I mean it.' Doctor Francis was serious. 'Had he lain unconscious until morning, I doubt I could have saved him. The arm had become infected. If the poison had spread throughout his bloodstream . . .'

'You mean you had to open his arm again?' Ruth's lips quivered.

'It was unavoidable,' said her father shortly. 'Thank you, Celeste. You may leave us. I'll call if we need any more coffee.'

'We had to relieve the pressure,' explained Doctor Francis patiently, as Celeste unwillingly left the room. 'The cavity had to be evacuated and sterilised. There was no other way we could reduce the fever.'

'And now?'

'Now he's sleeping. The fever has greatly subsided, but as you can imagine, some poison did succeed in escaping into his bloodstream. Until his system is free of the infection, he'll continue to run a low temperature. But it's under control.'

Ruth nodded, watching dry-mouthed as Doctor Francis stopped speaking to fill his mouth with scrambled eggs. She wondered how he could eat after making such a statement, and her own stomach revolted at the fleshy food. But relief at hearing that Dominic was not going to lose either his arm, or his life, steadied her reeling senses.

'A storm in a tea-cup,' declared Professor Jason, buttering a slice of toast. 'Get your breakfast, child. You've got work to do later.'

Ruth shook her head. 'I'm not hungry,' she said, folding her hands in her lap, but her father's disapproving gaze was compelling.

'Of course you're hungry,' he insisted, holding the toast rack towards her. 'Come along, eat up. One invalid on my hands is quite enough!'

'Leave her alone, Curtis, there's a good fellow.'

Doctor Francis's request was delivered in deceptively mild tones, but they both knew it was only slightly above a command, and Professor Jason's nostrils flared.

'You handle your patients, John,' he advised brusquely. 'Leave me to handle my daughter, if you don't mind.'

Doctor Francis laid down his knife and fork.

'Can't you see the girl's upset? The last time I saw a face like that was in the operating theatre, just before one of my students keeled over. Believe me, I know what I'm talking about.'

'Sentimental drivel!' exclaimed Professor Jason harshly. 'Ruth's not upset. Why should she be? Howard is a stranger to her.'

Doctor Francis looked at Ruth, and she returned his stare unhappily. She knew he expected her to say something in her own defence, but she couldn't. Not after the conversation she and her father had had the night before.

'Perhaps—perhaps I will have a slice of toast,' she murmured basely, and avoided Doctor Francis's eyes as she stuffed the dry bread into her mouth.

CHAPTER FOUR

Ruth had only a glimpse of Dominic that day. She was passing the bedroom later that morning when Doctor Francis came out, and he deliberately delayed in closing the door so that she might look into the room.

Dominic's eyes were closed, his face pale where it rested on the pillows. Celeste had complained that she had had to change the sheets twice during the night, and the whiteness of the covering contrasted sharply with the darkness of his skin rising above it. The unhealthy glaze of the fever was much less pronounced now, but his hair was damp with sweat, heavy strands straying across his forehead. Ruth knew a quite overwhelming impulse to go in there and bathe his temples with a cool cloth, and smooth away those untidy strands of hair. But of course, that was not possible. Her father had forbidden her to enter the bedroom, and he himself had emptied the drawers of her clothes, removing the necessity for her to have any contact with their visitor. He was quite fanatical when it came to her association with the man, and she could only assume that it was his own dislike of him that motivated his actions.

Now Doctor Francis closed the door and looked down at her sympathetically. 'He's going to be all right. I promise you,' he told her gently, and Ruth made a helpless gesture.

'I don't know why I was so worried,' she commented, running a nervous hand round the back of her neck. 'Like Daddy said, he's a stranger—a drifter, probably. Why should I care about him?'

Doctor Francis's mouth softened. 'Don't you know?'

Ruth coloured. 'What do you mean?'

Doctor Francis shook his head. 'What are you, Ruth? Sixteen? Seventeen? Old enough to understand that one doesn't always need reasons for caring.' He put his hand on her shoulder, squeezing gently. 'You're growing up, Ruth. And I guess you've never encountered a man quite like Mr Howard before.'

Ruth drew back. 'What are you saying?'

'Oh, Ruth!' He gazed at her impatiently. 'I wish— oh, I wish—' He broke off abruptly, and turned away, saying as he did so: 'Didn't I hear your father telling you to finish some translation? I think you'd better go and get on with it.'

He would have walked away then, but she caught his arm, releasing it at once when he turned to face her. 'Please,' she ventured, not quite knowing whether she was doing the right thing, 'won't you tell me what it is you wish? I mean, I got the feeling—is it something to do with me?'

'Yes.' The doctor inclined his head.

'Then—what?'

'You really want to know?'

Ruth nodded.

'Well . . .' He hesitated. 'I wish Curtis didn't keep

you imprisoned in this place. I wish he'd let you out into the real world. You're going to find it very hard after—well, after he's not here any more.'

'Oh, I see.' Ruth didn't want to hear this. 'I— please, don't worry about me—'

'But I do,' retorted Francis forcefully, aroused by her acceptance of the situation. 'Your father's keeping you in a cocoon here, Ruth. You haven't got room to breathe. It's not unreasonable that you should be interested in Howard. Don't let anyone tell you it is. He's an attractive man, it's perfectly natural that you should be curious about him.' He shook his head. 'Don't get me wrong. I'm not saying you should get involved with him. In fact, I'd argue strongly against it. He's too old for one thing, and he's probably known more women than—well! I doubt you're to his taste, anyway. But you must accept that you're an attractive girl, and men are unlikely to be indifferent to it.'

'Me? Attractive?'

Ruth stared at him disbelievingly, and Doctor Francis made a helpless gesture. 'Of course you're attractive,' he muttered huskily. 'That hair, those eyes—Ruth, you're going to be a beauty. And the sooner your father accepts that, the better.'

'But I—'

'I know what I'm talking about, my dear. And I know it's not easy for you to understand with the upbringing you've had, but you've got to learn not to be afraid of your emotions.'

Ruth looked up at him bravely. 'I—I do know about love—'

'Love?' Francis grunted frustratedly. 'I'm not talking about love, Ruth, I'm talking about sex! Good old-fashioned sex! That's why you're so tied up in knots over Howard. You haven't learned yet what it's like to want something you can't have.'

Ruth moved her head helplessly from side to side. 'I don't understand—'

'I know it.' Doctor Francis pushed back his thinning hair with baffled fingers. 'If you had a mother, she'd explain it to you. As it is—'

He looked as if he would have liked to say more, but he couldn't. With an upraised movement of his hand he left her, striding down the hall as if impatient with her and himself, and Ruth was left with the uneasy feeling that once again she was to blame.

On impulse, she went into the bathroom and closed the door, sliding home the bolt before examining her reflection in the mirror above the washbasin. For the first time she studied her image without shame, and felt the quickening beat of her heart as she searched the features Doctor Francis had said had the promise of beauty.

Could he be right? Had he been telling the truth, or just reassuring her? She found it hard to see beauty in the vaguely slanted depths of her eyes, eyes that were disappointingly blue and susceptible to bright sunlight. She had always wished for brown eyes, strong brown eyes, like Celeste's, that were apparently immune to the glare of the sun.

Her nose was unremarkable too, she decided, running a probing finger down its length, and her mouth was definitely too wide. She pushed her lips forward, as she had seen the models doing in the mail order catalogues, and grimaced at the result. She was no *femme fatale*, she assured herself firmly, remembering the term from her French grammar. Whatever Doctor Francis had seen in her must have been coloured by his affection for her, and she turned away disconsolately.

As she did so her hair, unconfined for once, swung against her cheek, and she put up a tentative hand to stroke its silky length. Her hair must be her best feature, she decided, looping it behind her ears. It had been loose last night when Dominic had touched her, when he had pulled her close against his hard body, and said those outrageous things to her. Her face burned with the memory, but it was not an entirely unpleasant sensation. He had made her feel excited and grown-up, and she wondered what he might have done if she had not made good her escape. Her lips parted in recollection of the disturbing curve of his. He had been going to kiss her—she had known that. And now she half regretted the panic which had denied her that experience. She was curious to know how a man kissed a woman. Not the circumspect peck that Doctor Francis had given her, but a meeting of the lips, as she had only read in Colette and Flaubert. She sighed. Doctor Francis was right. She did not understand the needs of her own body, and she left the bathroom quickly, before she was tempted to explore further.

Doctor Francis departed that afternoon, after assuring himself that his patient was on the mend. Ruth accompanied him down to the harbour, where the motor launch was waiting to take him back to Kingstown, and as they reached the small quay he gripped her hand very tightly.

'Take care,' he said, bending to bestow a warm kiss on her forehead. 'And remember what I told you. Get your father to let you come to Kingstown and stay with Mary and me. You could do with a few days' holiday, couldn't you? And some new clothes, from the look of these.'

Ruth looked down at the shabby tee-shirt and cotton skirt in inconsequent appraisal. 'I never wear skirts normally,' she confessed. 'But Daddy said—'

'I can guess what Daddy said,' retorted Doctor Francis dryly, and Ruth looked a little unhappy as she remembered the terse way the two men had bade goodbye to one another. 'But believe me, it's time you stretched the apron strings. Promise me you'll mention my invitation to your father.'

'I will,' Ruth nodded. But she didn't hold out much hope for its expedition. The Francises had invited her to St Vincent before, but her father had always maintained she was too young to leave the island without an escort. And as he never stayed away from Indigo, she hadn't either.

She bought some fish for supper, before going back to the bungalow. One could buy all kinds of seafood from the stalls on the quay, the men of the island relying on their catch to supplement their income. There was a small workers' co-operative, organised by Father Andreas, and the fruit and vegetables that grew so plentifully beneath the hot Caribbean sun were harvested and transported to St Vincent, and sold in the market there; but the island was small and in consequence the income was small also. Still, the West Indians managed to survive, and

Ruth had always envied them their evident joy of living.

She was sauntering up from the harbour when she encountered the elderly priest himself, coming down the path that led to the chapel. Some years ago, with the villagers' help, he had succeeded in erecting a wooden building that served as both a house of worship and a dwelling place, and as Father Andreas's needs were small, he was well content. His contacts with Ruth and her father were mostly infrequent, Professor Jason's strong views on the weaknesses of religion and the power of the church vying with the priest's vows of allegiance. But he was always happy to see Ruth and now he smiled his welcome.

'I hear you have a visitor,' he continued, after their initial greetings were over, in the faintly guttural accent that still lingered, in spite of the fact that he had left Salonika many years ago. 'An Englishman, by all accounts. And you were his benefactor.'

'Oh . . .' Ruth waved her arm deprecatingly, 'all I did was find him on the beach. His yacht was wrecked in the storm, and he was lucky to survive.'

'Indeed he was.' Father Andreas scratched his bald pate. 'The Lord moves in mysterious ways, as they say.'

Ruth smiled, her own beliefs less implacable than her father's. 'You must come and visit him, Father,' she invited. 'Doctor Francis says he'll probably have to stay here for several days.'

'Ah, yes, Doctor Francis,' the priest nodded. 'A good man, a god-fearing man. A man one can trust implicitly.'

Ruth knew this was a sideways knock at her father.

but she didn't respond to his remarks. Instead, she indicated the newspaper parcel in her hand, and said: 'I must go. I don't want the fish to go off. Daddy wouldn't thank me if I spoiled his supper.'

'That I can believe,' retorted Father Andreas dryly. 'God go with you, my child,' and with the sign of the cross he stepped aside to allow her to continue her journey.

But as Ruth passed him she turned hesitantly: 'Father Andreas?'

'Yes?' The priest stopped, too, and looked back at her.

Ruth coloured. 'I wanted to ask you something, Father.'

'Yes?' Father Andreas was patient.

'Yes.' Ruth explored her upper lip with her tongue. 'I wondered—that is—would you say I lived an unnatural life, Father? I mean,' she hastened on, as his button-bright eyes opened ever wider in surprise, 'would you say I was cocooned? That I was missing out on—well, on life?'

Father Andreas frowned then. 'Who has been saying such things to you? This young man? This Englishman? I thought he was in a state of collapse when you found him.'

'Does it matter who said it?' Ruth exclaimed. 'Is it true?'

The priest tugged at his chin with a thoughtful hand. 'I suppose one might say your situation here was not usual,' he admitted at last. 'Most girls of your age are in school or in work. But that has always been so.'

'But am I so different from them?' Ruth appealed.

'Just because my friends are black, not white, does that matter?'

'No!' Father Andreas conceded that point energetically. 'In fact, it might be said that your life is everything a young girl's should be. You're intelligent, you don't discriminate between races, you care for your father; this is as it used to be. Perhaps,' he hesitated, 'perhaps your life is fuller than that of other girls. It is, after all, only a rehearsal for the next world. Myself, I think what some people call life is simply the devil's alternative.'

Ruth nodded, not altogether satisfied with his answer. She should have known. A priest was hardly likely to sanction any other course. And in any case, she didn't really know what it was she was supposed to be missing. Perhaps if she had told Father Andreas that Doctor Francis had made the comparison, he would have had more sympathy for her case, but he might not have believed her, and that would have been worse.

'Does that answer your question?'

Father Andreas was looking at her anxiously now, and Ruth forced a smile. 'Thank you, Father,' she said, avoiding a direct response, and with a nod the priest went on his way, his cassock flapping in the breeze that blew up from the ocean.

The next morning Dominic was much improved. Celeste told Ruth as she served her breakfast, giving the news with a certain air of smugness, as if she, and she alone, had the right to such privileged information. She was in Professor Jason's confidence, and the only nurse he had, and she took great pleasure in telling Ruth how she had assisted in changing the dressing on Dominic's arm, and that she had exchanged a few words with him when she had taken in his breakfast earlier.

'He feeling more himself,' she declared, setting a rack of toast on the table. 'He even get up to go to the bathroom. Doctor Francis going to be real pleased with him.'

Ruth looked down at her plate, propping her head on one hand. 'You've been a great help,' she conceded flatly. 'I'm sure Daddy much appreciates it.'

'I think so.' Celeste was complacent. 'I think he trust me to know what's what. He ain't even seen Mr Howard for himself yet today, so I knows he don't worry none.'

Ruth looked up at this. 'What do you mean? He hasn't seen Mr Howard for himself? Where is Daddy?'

'He ain't up yet,' retorted Celeste, pouring her coffee. 'You sure you don't want no eggs?'

Ruth pushed back her chair. The night before she had insisted her father returned to his bed, and once again she had slept on the couch. But it was unusual for him not to be up, particularly in the circumstances, and her mouth was dry as she left a startled Celeste and hurried along the hall to his room.

To her relief, her father's eyes were open, but the strain of the last two days had left its mark upon him. He looked drawn and grey, and when he would have struggled up in the bed, she urged him down again.

'You look tired,' she said, and it was an understatement. 'I think you should stay where you are this morning. Celeste and I can manage.'

Professor Jason shook his head. 'Celeste,' he said, obviously finding it an effort to articulate, 'Celeste can mange. Just make sure she gives Howard his tablets. Francis will be over later today to check on his progress. I may stay in bed until he arrives.'

Ruth sighed. 'All right. Would you like some breakfast? I can easily fetch you something.'

'Perhaps some coffee,' conceded her father weakly. 'Nothing to eat. And would you pass my tablets from the table beside you?'

Ruth handed him the bottle, and watched as he shook two out on to his palm. Then she poured him a glass of water from the jug he kept covered on the table beside the bed, and raised his shoulders slightly while he swallowed them.

'Thank you, my dear,' he said, offering her a faint smile as he fell back on the pillows. 'And now I think I'll rest. If I'm asleep when you bring the coffee, just leave it beside the bed.'

Celeste looked disturbed when Ruth related the conversation to her. 'Your daddy, he overwork himself yesterday,' she declared. 'He stay in bed all day. You and me, we'll look after Mr Howard, hmm?'

Ruth looked uncertain. 'Daddy said—'

'I don't want to know what your daddy said,' retorted Celeste shortly. 'What he don't know about won't hurt him. Now you finish your breakfast, and then go and fetch me Mr Howard's tray. I got plenty to do, 'stead of running round after some fool man!'

Ruth opened her mouth to protest, then closed it again. Why not? she thought, dismissing the stirrings of her conscience. She couldn't expect Celeste to do everything, and her father shouldn't expect it either. Besides, he need never know.

None the less, it was with a sense of duplicity that she delivered her father's tray to his room, knowing that when she left there she intended going into Dominic's bedroom. However, her father was asleep, as she had expected, and it was easier to be defiant when she wasn't observed.

It was a little unnerving opening Dominic's bedroom door. Somehow she never quite knew what she might find on the other side, and her breath eased out more evenly when she found him propped against the pillows. The plate of eggs Celeste had provided lay scarcely touched beside him, but some orange juice and coffee had been drunk, and some toast had also disappeared from the tray.

'Hi,' he greeted her in some surprise as she came into the room. 'I wondered where you'd got to. Don't you care about your patient now he's on the mend?'

Ruth's cheeks were pink as she surveyed his teasing face, so much less haggard now than on the previous day. Two days' growth of beard had left a stubbly bristle on his chin, but in spite of this dishevelment, he was still a distractingly attractive man. After her own introspection, she was doubly aware of him in a way she had not been before, and the memory of their last encounter coloured her reactions towards him.

'How—how are you?' she ventured, approaching the bed with caution. 'You've been very sick. We've all been very worried about you.'

'Have you?' His lips twisted. 'And I thought you'd abandoned me.'

'Oh, no.' Ruth linked her fingers together. 'It was just—what with Doctor Francis being here, and—and Daddy——'

'You decided to keep out of the way. Having done your bit, you wanted no part of the blood-letting!'

'It wasn't like that.' Ruth moved her shoulders unhappily. 'Anyway, I'm glad you're feeling better.'

'Oh, yes, much better.' He inclined his head, running probing fingers over the bandages that covered the lower part of his arm. 'Thanks to you. I hear that you saved my life.'

Ruth caught her breath. 'I—hardly—'

'That's not what I heard. That doctor—Francis—he said that if you hadn't alerted your father—'

Ruth shook her head. 'You'd probably have come round and summoned help.'

'I don't think so.' He ran an exploratory hand over his bare chest, and she averted her eyes from the curiously disturbing gesture. 'I don't remember much at all of what happened that night.' He frowned. 'How did you know I was out of bed?'

'Didn't Daddy tell you?' Ruth reached for the tray and endeavoured to appear busy, gathering the plates together, and checking the contents of the coffee pot. 'You—you called out. You must have been delirious.'

'And you heard me?' he asked, leaning forward, so that the sheet that was covering him slipped lower to display an absence of any pyjama trousers. His long fingers curved gently round her arm, just above her wrist. 'Thanks.'

Ruth could hardly breathe. She couldn't swallow, and her lungs felt constricted. His face was so close to hers. she could have touched it by turning her head, and the scent of his warm flesh was disruptive.

'I—it was nothing.' she articulated chokily, but he didn't let her go. and short of making a silly scene she was obliged to humour him.

'I don't agree.' he averred, smoothing his thumb against the inner veins of her wrist, and she found the action aroused almost as much emotion as his words of two nights before. 'I think I owe you a lot. Much more than I can ever repay.'

Ruth's knees shook. 'Re—really, it's not necessary for you to—to feel this way,' she stammered. alarmed at the sensation of weakness he was evoking. She wanted desperately to turn her head and look at him. and she guessed if she did so, he wouldn't draw away. But she was too afraid. It was obvious he didn't remember what had happened two nights ago. and she was too timid to promote the same kind of intimacy.

The situation was rapidly becoming untenable. and with a shrug of his broad shoulders he released her to lounge back against the pillows once again. The action drew the sheet back into place, and the lean suppleness of his hips was again concealed from her. Ruth released the breath she had been holding and gathered up the tray, praying her trembling hands would not betray her. The cutlery rattled a little as she hurried towards the door, but it didn't disgrace her, and she was almost through the aperture when he spoke to her again.

'Do you think I could borrow a razor?' he enquired, rubbing a hand over the stubble on his chin. 'I'd like to make myself look more human, but as you know, I didn't bring any luggage."

'Oh, I—I'm sure my father has a razor you could borrow,' she murmured, glancing apprehensively along the hall, as if afraid Professor Jason might overhear her. 'I—I'll get Celeste to bring it to you,' she added, reaching for the handle of the door, but once again he arrested her.

'I'd rather you brought it,' he said, his voice soft, and curiously gentle. 'Not that I have anything against Celeste, you understand me? She's been of great assistance, I know.' He grinned ruefully, running significant hands down the outline of his legs. 'Believe me, I know.' He shrugged. 'I just find you better to look at,' he explained, and Ruth nodded her head vigorously as she hastily closed the door.

In the hall, she composed herself before walking its length to the kitchen. She had never known anyone who could disconcert her so easily, and his provoking words left her feeling both shaken and excited. It was not exactly what he said, she realised, but the way that he said it, and her heart still pounded from the recollection of his thumb upon her wrist. She didn't understand why so simple an action should arouse so urgent a response, but it did inspire the speculation of how it might feel to have Dominic caress the more intimate parts of her anatomy—like her shoulders perhaps, or her waist, or maybe—and she blushed at the thought—her breasts.

She thought Celeste looked at her rather searchingly when she went into the kitchen with the tray. She guessed the other woman had noticed the heated colour in her cheeks, which she had been unable to disguise, unaware of that fact that there were other indications of her agitation. Her eyes were sparkling, but she didn't know that, and her lips were parted in eager anticipation. Celeste's wide mouth curved a little knowingly as she took in this evidence of her young charge's excitement, and she rested her hands on her broad hips as she commented:

'You been talking with Mr Howard? What he been saying to you? Why you looking like the cat that been at the cream?'

Ruth put down the tray on the table and thrust her trembling hands behind her back. 'I don't know what you mean,' she protested, trapping them in the folds of her skirt. 'I just collected the tray, like you asked me. What's wrong with that?'

Celeste moved her shoulders indolently. 'Seems like you been a little longer than it take to collect a tray,' she declared dryly. 'Come on, you can tell Celeste. She won't go blabbing to your daddy.'

'There's nothing to tell,' Ruth retorted firmly. 'He —I—he wants a razor. Do you think Daddy would mind if I lent him his?'

Celeste grimaced. 'Who knows? You going to ask him?'

Ruth shook her head. 'He's sleeping—Daddy, I mean. I suppose I could just—lend Mr Howard the razor, couldn't I? Daddy need never know.'

'And I suppose your daddy's going to think he just chewed that there hair off his face, is he?' Celeste suggested caustically, bringing a furrow to Ruth's brow.

'I never thought of that,' she confessed, tugging at a strand of night-dark silk, and Celeste sighed.

'Tell you what,' she said. 'I guess you could borrow a razor I got lying there in the cabin.' She made a resigned gesture. 'I don't know where it come from, I only know it there, doing nothing.'

'Oh, thank you, Celeste!' Ruth could have hugged her. Then she hesitated. 'Will—will you get it and give it to him?'

'Why can't you do that?'

'I—I've got some work to do for Daddy,' Ruth explained evasively, avoiding Celeste's eyes. 'You don't mind, surely?'

Celeste shrugged. 'Seems to me there's more to this than meets the eye, but I'll do it. I'll give him the razor. Shave him, too, if'n he wants it.' She allowed her words to sink in, then added deliberately: 'Ain't a lot I'd refuse to do for Mr Howard, no, sir. And I've done most everything else, 'cept'n getting into bed with him.'

Her words had the desired effect, but Ruth couldn't help the bloom of colour that covered her body from head to toe. 'What—what you choose to do is your own affair, Celeste,' she declared, deliberately slowing her steps as they would have hastened her towards the door. 'I'll be in the study, if Daddy wants me. See you later.'

CHAPTER FIVE

Professor Jason insisted on getting up for supper, and Ruth faced him across the dining table with some misgivings. She was beginning to realise there was more to deceiving someone than simply doing something without their cognisance. She had to beware in so many other ways, not least in confining her knowledge of their visitor to things Celeste could have told her.

Doctor Francis had paid a fleeting visit that afternoon, but although Ruth was disappointed, he refused to stay and eat with them. 'I promised Mary I'd take her out to dinner this evening,' he said, touching her cheek with a regretful finger, 'and besides, I doubt your father would welcome my company.'

'Don't be silly.' Ruth spoke ruefully. 'You know what Daddy's like. He'll have forgotten all about your differences by now, and I know he enjoys your conversation.'

'Well, maybe,' Doctor Francis acknowledged, nodding his head. 'But I really can't stay this evening. I've spent so much time working lately, and Mary deserves a break.'

'Couldn't you bring her to supper one evening?' Ruth offered impulsively, even though her father had never made such a suggestion, but the doctor only smiled.

'Have you given any thought to what I said yesterday?' he countered, reminding her of his invitation, and she sighed.

'There really hasn't been time,' she demurred, moving her shoulders. 'Perhaps when—when Mr Howard leaves . . .'

'Perhaps,' agreed the Scotsman, not pressing her, and went to examine his patients before she could say more.

Professor Jason helped himself to a little soup now, from the tureen Celeste had placed on the table, and regarded his daughter thoughtfully.

'Did Francis tell you our patient should be ready to leave in a day or two?' he asked, causing Ruth's fingers to tighten around her spoon. 'I for one shall be quite relieved. He's disrupted our lives far too much.'

Ruth applied herself to breaking a roll, and then, realising he expected a response, she said: 'Celeste told me his arm was no longer inflamed. But Doctor Francis said he was very weak.'

'Oh, he is.' Professor Jason's lips thinned. 'And I'm not suggesting he should leave here before he's capable of doing so. Nevertheless,' he spooned soup into his mouth, 'he's a disturbing influence on the household, and obviously he creates more work for Celeste.'

Ruth bent her head. 'I could help her—'

'No.' Her father was adamant. 'Celeste can manage. I have no intention of encouraging you to associate with that man. Whatever Francis says, you're far too young to be involved. You're not a nurse, and it's not at all suitable that you should enter his bed-room.'

Ruth glanced up. 'Celeste does,' she ventured, but her lids lowered at her father's scathing stare.

'Celeste's is an entirely different situation,' he retorted. 'She's older, for one thing, and in spite of your age and—er—innocence, I'm sure you're not unaware of her—well, for want of a better word—experience.'

'No.' Ruth sighed.

'So,' her father drew a deep breath, 'having settled that matter, there's something I want you to do for Mr Howard.'

'There is?' Ruth looked up, her heart beating a little faster.

'Yes.' Her father pushed his plate aside. 'I was talking to him earlier this evening, and he's quite concerned about this money he has had transferred to the bank in Kingstown. Obviously, as he didn't collect it as he expected, there may be some query.' He paused. 'I've agreed to send Joseph over to St Vincent again in the morning, but I think, reluctantly, that you ought to go along—for verification purposes. You'll have Howard's written authorisation, but you know what banks are like. They may become suspicious if Joseph attempts to withdraw any cash on Howard's behalf.'

Ruth pressed her trembling hands together in her lap. 'He wants some money—withdrawn?'

'Yes.' Her father frowned. 'He wants us to purchase him some clothes. I'm convinced that Joseph can attend to that, but it might be simpler if you spoke to Templar yourself.'

'I see.' Ruth felt a ridiculous sense of excitement at the prospect of the unexpected outing. 'What—what does he want us to buy?'

'You can leave that to Joseph,' replied Professor Jason firmly. 'I shall ask Howard to make a list. Your task is to explain the situation to Templar, and ensure that he treats the matter with confidence.'

Ruth nodded, but her expression hid the fervency of her thoughts. There were shops in Kingstown, shops that sold cheap clothes, and she was mentally calculating how she could make the housekeeping money her father gave her stretch to at least one new dress.

She hardly slept that night, she was too excited, and she was up and dressed as soon as it was light. It was almost a two-hour trip from Indigo to St Vincent, and she wanted to have plenty of time to do her shopping, after she had been to the bank. Joseph was easygoing. He wouldn't object if she went off on her own. And besides, he had his own instructions to follow.

Celeste was already up when Ruth entered the kitchen, and she gave the girl an appraising look as she lifted the coffee pot off the stove.

'You're just in time,' she declared, setting the pot on a tray she had already prepared. 'You can take this in to Mr Howard before you leave. I'se going to have my hands full while you off enjoying yourself in Kingstown.'

Ruth hunched her shoulders. 'Celeste, you know what Daddy says—'

'He say same thing yesterday, but that not stop you,' retorted the black woman tartly, pushing the tray towards her. 'Go on, give the man his breakfast. He ain't going to eat you.'

Ruth hesitated. 'Is Daddy up yet?'

'No.' Celeste shook her head. 'He still fast asleep. You and Joseph be long gone before he wake up. Hurry now—you ain't got all day.'

Dominic was awake when Ruth carried the tray into the bedroom, and his eyes widened when he saw her. He had been lying down, but now he struggled up on to his pillows, patting the bed beside him when she would have set the tray across his knees.

'I'll eat it later,' he said, the tawny eyes lazily intent as they surveyed her slender figure. 'You're up very early. I was expecting Celeste.'

Ruth straightened after setting the tray down on the bed, and returned his stare with difficulty. 'She— she's busy,' she said, noticing how much younger he looked with the growth of beard shaved from his chin. 'How are you feeling this morning?'

'All the better for seeing you,' he replied impudently, his eyes teasing her. 'Why didn't you come back yesterday? Did I say something to offend you?'

'Of course not.' Ruth felt uncomfortable. 'I had work to do, that's all. In any case, I can see that Celeste provided you with a razor.'

'Oh, yes.' He ran an exploring hand over his jawline. 'She takes good care of me.' He grimaced. 'I guess it's an improvement.'

Ruth didn't know how to answer that. 'You look —much better,' she conceded. 'I expect you feel— more yourself.'

'Indeed.' His tone was wry. 'I'm glad you like it.'

Ruth's smile was stiff. "Daddy used to have a beard once,' she volunteered irrelevantly. 'At least it saves you having to shave.'

'That's true.' He inclined his head. 'A very shrewd observation.'

Ruth pressed her lips together. 'You're being sarcastic, aren't you?' she commented, wishing she had more experience in these matters, and he quirked a mocking brow.

'Now why should you think that?' he countered, shifting to a more comfortable position. 'I thought I was behaving exceedingly well, considering the provocation of the situation.'

Ruth bent her head. 'I'd better go. Is there anything else you need—anything else Celeste can get for you?'

'I don't think so. Not right now.' The tawny eyes were narrowed. 'But you can tell me why you're in such a hurry to leave. I don't have the plague or anything, do I?'

Ruth's nervous system was not equipped to deal with this kind of conversation. 'I have to go,' she insisted, turning towards the door. 'I—I'm going to St Vincent with Joseph. He's probably waiting for me right now.'

Dominic frowned. 'You're going to St Vincent? Not your father?'

Ruth nodded. 'Daddy seldom leaves the island these days. As you've probably noticed, he's not well. He tires easily. He only goes to St Vincent when Doctor Francis sends him to the hospital there, for treatment.'

'I see.' Dominic looked thoughtful. 'So you're

going to speak to the bank manager?'

'That's right.'

'And are you going to buy the clothes I need, too?' he enquired dryly.

'No.' Ruth flushed. 'Joseph's going to do that.'

Dominic nodded. 'But you'll be with him?'

'I—I expect so.'

He crossed his legs beneath the thin covering of the sheet. 'Good.' His eyes held her startled ones. 'Buy yourself a new shirt and shorts while you're there.'

'I—I couldn't!' Ruth was horrified, but Dominic only shrugged.

'Why not? You tore your tee-shirt up to make a tourniquet, didn't you? I owe it to you.'

Ruth hovered in the open doorway. 'It's very kind of you, but it's not necessary, really.'

Dominic's mouth twisted. 'I know it's not necessary,' he declared impatiently. 'But I'd like to do it.'

Ruth only shook her head, and she was still shaking it after the door was closed and she was safely outside.

St Vincent's capital, Kingstown, was a lively and busy port, and Ruth always found the activity on the quayside a source of enchantment and wonder. Island schooners unloading bananas and yams, breadfruit and coconuts, were a constant fascination, and the market place, where farmers and small traders came to sell their wares, was a kaleidoscope of life and colour.

Ruth, waiting while Joseph secured their mooring,

stared about her with wide eyes. There was so much to see and absorb, and she was totally unaware of the admiring glances cast in her direction. Her attention was all on the trans-Atlantic freighter being loaded with crates of fruit and vegetables, and she didn't notice the inquisitive interest of the sailors hanging over the rail until a loud whistle alerted her to their attention. Immediately the hot blood stained her cheeks, and she was relieved when Joseph came to join her and she could get out of earshot of their insolent solicitations.

'You gotta get used to this sort of thing, Missy,' Joseph told her, with his lazy grin. 'Less'n you don't want to come to Kingstown no more.'

The International Bank stood in Grenville Street, and leaving Joseph to kick his heels outside, Ruth entered its imposing portals. She had been to the bank before. The income her father had from her grandmother's estate was transferred into Caribbean dollars at this branch, and Andrew Templar and her father had known one another for over ten years.

If some of the younger members of the bank's staff viewed the girl in the shabby tee-shirt and cotton skirt rather doubtfully, the older tellers did not, and almost immediately she was recognised.

'Miss Jason!' Edward Hollings, one of the senior cashiers, called her name. 'It's a while since we've seen you, Miss Jason. Is anything wrong?'

'Oh, no.' Ruth smiled at the elderly man behind the desk. 'As a matter of fact, I just wanted to speak to Mr Templar, if I could. Is he available?'

'I think he might be,' replied Mr Hollings, his eyes twinkling. 'You're a sight for sore eyes on this lovely morning, and no mistake. How is your father? I hear he still plays a mean game of chess.'

Ruth's laughter was spontaneous. 'You must have been talking to Doctor Francis,' she said, resting her arms on the counter. 'He's the only person I know who could make that kind of statement.'

'Yes.' Mr Hollings looked thoughtful for a moment. 'I suppose you don't see many people on that island of yours.'

'No.' Ruth sobered. 'Would you see if Mr Templar is free? It is rather urgent.'

Mr Hollings disappeared through the fluted screen door that divided the two sections of the accounting area, and Ruth straightened away from the desk. Did everyone think they lived a hermit-like existence? she wondered impatiently, realising she was becoming hyper-sensitive to that kind of comment. Just because a person didn't conform, there was no reason to imagine they were in any way extraordinary.

'Miss Jason!'

She swung round half guiltily, to find Andrew Templar at the cash-point, his lean, goodhumoured face creased into a smile.

'Won't you come through, Miss Jason?' he invited, swinging open the half door beside him, and with an embarrassed nod she complied. 'So,' he said, as they walked into his office. 'What can I do for you? Have you decided to open an account with us?'

The office he showed her into was large and impressive, with a high arched ceiling and a veined marble floor. The square desk that occupied the centre of the floor was impressive too, its tooled leather surface liberally spread with papers and files. There was an *In* tray and *Out* tray, the former bearing witness to the amount of work still waiting to be done, and several coloured telephones, that added colour to an otherwise businesslike formality.

Yet, in spite of these evident signs of industry, Andrew Templar seemed in no hurry to get down to business, and he insisted on ordering her coffee and asking about her father's health before pursuing the reasons for her being there.

But at last he broached the subject that was foremost in her thoughts, saying shrewdly: 'I suppose your visit has to do with the matter your father wrote me about three days ago. I have to tell you, that young man has caused us no small degree of difficulty.'

'You mean—Mr Howard? His transfer?'

'I presume you mean Dominic Howard Crown. Yes, it has created—problems.'

Ruth stared at him. 'Dominic—Howard—*Crown?*' she repeated slowly. 'You mean his name's not Dominic Howard after all?'

'Oh, yes,' said Templar patiently. 'His Christian names are Dominic and Howard. He just omitted to mention that he was James Crown's son.'

'James Crown?' Ruth felt she was being absurdly obtuse, but she couldn't help it. 'Who—who is James Crown?'

'Don't you know?' Andrew Templar stared at her aghast. Then he shook his head. 'No, no, of course you probably wouldn't. Although I doubt your father is that unworldly.' He sighed. 'Ruth—I may call you Ruth, mayn't I?' And at her nod: 'Ruth—

James Crown is the power behind Crown Chemicals, one of the most successful groups of companies in Europe!'

Ruth's tongue circled her lips. 'But why—'

'If you're going to ask why didn't your visitor give his real name, then your guess is as good as mine.' Andrew Templar made an aggravated gesture. 'Why do men like Crown like to keep their identities secret? I don't know. Unless, for publicity reasons, they prefer to remain incognito. I suppose that must have been his intention, although he must have known you were bound to find out.'

Ruth frowned. 'Not necessarily,' she murmured after a moment. 'I mean, how would we have found out?'

'Well,' said Andrew Templar reasonably, 'if he intended sending you here to collect his funds—'

'But he didn't,' Ruth interrupted quickly. 'Not originally. He—well, I suppose he would have collected them himself yesterday. If he hadn't been taken ill.'

'He's ill?' Andrew Templar looked concerned. 'Look here, Ruth, if there's anything seriously wrong with young Crown, I'd suggest your father gets him to the hospital in Kingstown immediately. His family aren't going to take kindly to any complications of that kind, even if he did deliberately set out to deceive you.'

'He's all right now,' Ruth hastened to reassure him, catching her lower lip between her teeth in sudden uncertainty. 'He was sick. His arm—I suppose Joseph explained that he had injured his arm—

well, it became infected, but Doctor Francis handled it without too much difficulty.'

'My God!' Templar shook his head. 'To think old John's been treating James Crown's son! Wait till I see him. I'll have a few words to say—'

'No, wait!' Ruth shifted uncomfortably. 'Daddy asked me to ask you to keep it in confidence.' She sighed. 'Those were Mr Howard's—Mr *Crown's* instructions.'

'What?' He stared at her. 'But I've already had your Mr Crown's friends on the telephone this morning, demanding to know where he is and what's going on.'

'And did you tell them?' Ruth held her breath.

'Not yet.' He ran frustrated hands over his scalp. 'I was waiting to hear from Crown again. Your father's instructions were implicit, and I respected that confidence. But now, with the Crowns breathing down my neck, I'm not so sure.'

Ruth was finding it extremely difficult to come to any decision. This was a contingency her father had not prepared her for, and despite what Mr Templar said she doubted he was aware of Dominic's real identity.

'I think you ought to do as—as Mr Crown suggests,' she averred at last. 'If he does want to keep his whereabouts to himself, I don't think you can do anything other than comply.'

Andrew Templar sighed heavily. 'You're right, of course. I can't reveal the information without his permission. But perhaps you can explain the situation to him and urge him to think again. It would certainly make things easier for me.'

Ruth nodded. 'Naturally, I'll do what I can.'

'And you're sure he's fit again?'

'Not entirely.' She tried to be honest. 'Doctor Francis says he's still very weak. It was blood poisoning, you see. But he's definitely improving.'

'I hope for your sake that you're right,' remarked Andrew Templar dryly. 'I'd hate to be in your shoes if anything happened to him.' He shook his head. 'I doubt if even Indigo would be remote enough to save you from the outcry that would evoke. Not to mention his father's wrath, of course.'

Ruth quivered. 'Are you trying to frighten me, Mr Templar?'

'No. No, I'm just trying to make you understand the situation, Ruth.' Andrew Templar studied her anxious face with some compassion. 'My dear child, you're dealing with people who can be completely ruthless, if it suits their purpose. Tell your father, explain the situation to him. I just don't want you to live to regret finding that young man on your doorstep.'

Ruth emerged from the bank feeling slightly dazed. Until then she had given very little thought to the reasons why Dominic might wish to keep his whereabouts to himself, but now she was faced with concrete facts. He was not some casual holidaymaker, but the son of a man Mr Templar obviously respected, a man whose power and influence stretched as far as these outposts of civilisation. He was obviously someone whose name was usually recognised, a wealthy man, a man to whom the loss of a yacht could be dismissed as of no account.

Joseph, noticing her tense expression, looked perturbed. 'Is something wrong?' he asked, touching her arm, and she looked at him blankly for a moment, unable to comprehend his question.

But then, as his dark face creased into anxiety, she found her voice. 'I—why, no. No, nothing's wrong, Joseph,' she got out jerkily. 'The sunlight blinded me for a moment, that's all. Shall we go?'

'Did you get the money?' Joseph was practical, and she looked down at the envelope clutched in her hand.

'Oh—yes,' she managed a faint smile. 'Yes, here it is. Now, what is it you have to buy?'

Joseph produced his list, and Ruth studied it with some confusion. 'Levis?' she muttered doubtfully. 'What are levis, Joseph?'

'They's denim, Missy Ruth,' he grinned, pointing a black finger down at his baggy pants. 'They's levis, denim trousers, see?'

'Oh, I see.' Ruth frowned. 'Are you sure that's what he wants? Aren't they rather casual?'

'They's what all the young folks wear,' Joseph assured her firmly, but Ruth couldn't help thinking that her father would not agree with him.

But now she sighed. 'Well, I suppose you know best,' she conceded doubtfully, her eyes darting up and down the street. 'Where do you intend to buy these things? I thought I might go to the market. Would you mind if I met you at the boat in, say—two hours?'

Joseph frowned now. 'You want to go off on your own?'

Ruth nodded, her smile appealing.

Joseph hesitated. 'I don't think your daddy want

me to leave you alone, Missy Ruth.'

Ruth sighed. 'Why not?' She made an impatient gesture. 'You said yourself I was growing up. I'll be perfectly all right.'

'You could get lost—'

'Then I'll ask my way.'

'Who from?'

'A policeman!' Ruth contained her temper with difficulty. 'Joseph, I'm not a child, and you're not my keeper. You go and get the things Mr—Mr Howard asked you. I'll meet you back at the boat at half past two.'

Short of using force, Joseph had no choice but to comply. He knew if he attempted to detain her, his actions could be misconstrued by others, and the last thing he wanted was to end up in the city jail. But he had one last warning for her.

'Don't you go speaking to no strangers, then,' he ordered. 'And you be sure and be back at the boat at two-thirty, or I's'll tell your daddy, and he won't let you come here no more.'

Ruth's face cleared. 'Oh, thank you, Joseph,' she cried, reaching up to press a grateful kiss on his cheek, and handing over the envelope she made good her escape, before he could change his mind.

It was quite exciting shopping alone, she decided later. Apart from anything else, she could spend as long as she liked looking in shop windows, and without Joseph to hurry her she was able to see and absorb so much more.

The models in the fashion stores along the main street of the town aroused her interest. They were dressed in a variety of clothes, from sleekly casual suits to elaboratedly designed evening gowns. Silks and chiffons, soft woollens and crêpes, their sophisticated elegance filled her with envy, though she doubted she could even walk in shoes with heels so high. She admired exotic scarves and delicately embroidered shawls, colours from blue-grey through to vivid cyclamen, shirts and sweaters whose price tags alone would have kept her and her father in essentials for a year, and supple hand-stitched leatherwork, as soft as her skin. There was even one window given over to a display of furs, in spite of their incongruity in St Vincent. Painted eyes and lips gazed disdainfully above collars of beaver and mink, the richness of sable making Ruth long to feel its folds about her. But such garments were not for this climate. They belonged to northern shores—like England—where the weather was much colder, and there was ice and snow and driving rain, all the things her father told her they had escaped from.

Inevitably, however, she was reminded of Dominic Howard—no, *Crown*, she corrected herself resolutely. Thinking of him destroyed her enjoyment somehow, and she turned away regretfully to find the more soberly priced stalls in the market place. He knew England, he knew those cold northern climes. He lived there. And he probably associated with women who looked and dressed just like the models in the shop window. However natural their lives seemed to them, she had to accept that he probably considered both her and her father eccentric in the extreme, and his attitude towards her seemed to substantiate that belief. He seemed to enjoy talking to her, but he did find her amusing, and

the conversations they had had must have given him
many a silent chuckle. She wondered what he would
tell his friends about her when he got back to Barbados, and felt curiously reluctant to anticipate his
reactions. Besides, what did it matter what he said
after he had left the island? she asked herself
severely. She was never likely to see him again.

Joseph was waiting for her when she got back to
the motor launch, pacing up and down, obviously
anxious at the delay.

'You know what time it is?' he demanded, when
she came sauntering along the quay towards him. 'It
after three o'clock already! I'se been waiting here
since a quarter after two.'

'I'm sorry.' Ruth was repentant. 'I forgot the
time.' She sighed. 'It was so nice being able to please
myself for once. Please don't be angry.'

Joseph's bluster evaporated. 'You get what you
wanted?' he asked gruffly, taking the bags she was
carrying from her. 'You get that soap and detergent
like Celeste tell you? These bags seem mighty light
for them heavy items.'

Ruth grimaced. 'Yes, I got the things Celeste
wanted,' she assured him, allowing him to take her
hand to help her aboard. 'What you're carrying are
one or two things I got for myself, that's all. I don't
have to spend all my money on household necessi-
ties, do I?'

Joseph's silence was eloquent, and she smiled as
she clambered to the back of the boat. She had had a
successful morning, and she relaxed contentedly as
the black man steered the small craft through the
moorings and out of the harbour.

'Did you buy the things Mr—Howard wanted?' she ventured, when he was able to give her his attention, and he inclined his head.

'Didn't take me more'n an hour,' he declared reprovingly. 'You had anything to eat?'

Ruth grimaced. 'No.' She shook her head. 'I never thought about it.'

'That's what I thought.' Joseph bent to extract a carrier bag from the locker below the steering gear. 'Here, I got you a sandwich and a can of Coke. I guessed you hadn't the sense to think about such things.'

Ruth grinned, only now becoming aware of the emptiness of her stomach as she opened the carrier to reveal a crusty roll stuffed with chicken and salad. 'Hmm, this looks gorgeous, Joseph. Won't you share it with me?'

'I've eaten,' he assured her dryly, tearing the ring off a can of beer. 'You enjoy it. Ain't no point in letting Celeste think you can't look after yourself.'

Ruth acknowledged his perception as she bit into the juicy roll and they exchanged a conspiratorial chuckle as they left the bustling port behind.

It was after five o'clock by the time they reached Indigo. Ruth had dozed during the latter half of the journey, curled up on the cushions in the stern of the boat, while Joseph lolled indolently behind the wheel, his clay pipe drooping from his mouth. He insisted on escorting her up from the harbour, ostensibly to carry her bags, but Ruth guessed he wanted an excuse to see Celeste. Despite his comments, he was obviously very fond of her, and Ruth wondered how he resolved his conscience when he went to

Confession with Father Andreas. His wife had borne him an armful of children, after all, and therefore must deserve better treatment. But his infatuation for his mistress apparently outweighed his loyalty to his spouse, and Ruth had to acknowledge that she was not experienced enough to make judgement in such matters. It seemed simple enough to her, but apparently it wasn't, and she concluded that sex outside the bonds of matrimony must be different from that inside.

Celeste was watching for them on the verandah, her face for once without its humorous cast. 'Where you been all this time?' she exclaimed, her reproving glance encompassing both of them before coming to rest on the girl. 'Your daddy been asking for you for more'n an hour. Go to him now. He's in his room.'

'Is he ill?' exclaimed Ruth, leaping up the verandah steps, but Celeste waved a reassuring hand.

'He just tired, that's all,' she declared, her attention all on Joseph now. 'You run along, you hear. Joe and me'll unpack these bags.'

Ruth had no alternative but to obey. Besides, she was eager to see her father and tell him what she had learned. Leaving them on the verandah, she walked quickly along the hall and opened the door of her father's bedroom.

Professor Jason's eyes were closed, but they opened at the sound of someone entering, and he smiled weakly when he saw who it was. 'Ruth, my dear,' he said, with evident relief. 'I was getting so worried about you.'

'There was no need, Daddy.' Ruth came round the bed and bent to kiss his dry cheek. 'Here I am, safe and sound. Mission accomplished, as they say.'

Professor Jason sighed. 'You saw Templar?'

Ruth nodded. 'Yes, I saw him. I had coffee with him, actually.' She moved her shoulders offhandedly, putting off the inevitable explanations. 'He asked how you were, and I told him about the storm. Apparently the roof was blown off the golf clubhouse—you know, along the highway north of Kingstown. But no one was hurt, thank goodness, although he did say some boats were damaged in the harbour.'

Professor Jason listened to her in silence, then he said: 'You did get Mr Howard's money, I hope?'

'Oh, yes.' Ruth moved restlessly about the room. 'I got it.'

'Good.' Her father was relieved. 'The sooner that young man has funds, the sooner he'll get off the island.' He closed his eyes again. 'And now if you don't mind, I'll rest. You'll excuse me from joining you for supper this evening, won't you, my dear? I really am extremely weary.'

Ruth turned, her lips parting in dismay. She had still to tell him about Mr Templar, and the mix-up over the names, but with Professor Jason's eyes closed she felt reluctant to disrupt his peace. Nevertheless, he had to be told, she fretted, trying to frame the words in her head in a way that would neither annoy nor alarm him, and then started when her father spoke again.

'Do leave the room, Ruth,' he exclaimed, waving a weary hand. 'I assure you, it's nothing to worry about, just a little tiredness. I'll be perfectly all right in the morning.'

'But Daddy—'

Ruth took an involuntary step forward, and her father gave a resigned lift of his fingers. 'Tomorrow, Ruth.' he said, with finality, and she left the room feeling as if she had deliberately deceived him.

CHAPTER SIX

Ruth slept fitfully, plagued by the knowledge of Dominic's identity. She had nightmares of him lying in a pool of his own blood, and herself and her father watching him die, powerless to do anything to save him. She saw jagged wounds, limbs hanging by a shred of skin, putrefying flesh—and awakened, bathed in her own perspiration, to find that the sky beyond the living room windows was gradually turning pink.

It was morning, and with a sigh of relief she got up off the couch. Normally she slept quite soundly, in spite of the hardness of her bed, but her dreams of the night before had coiled her body into a knot, and she stretched her aching limbs with real enjoyment.

Below the gardens of the bungalow the ground sloped away gradually towards the beach, and she shivered as she opened the shutters and felt the errant breeze against her heated flesh. The sea was translucent, shading from blue through green to palest amber, as the sun rose steadily above the horizon. Tiny clouds threaded the paling sky, and the air smelt fresh and clean, and unbelievably exhilarating.

Turning, she shed the cotton nightshirt, and rummaged through the clothes her father had installed in the cabinet behind the couch for a bathing suit. She had several bikinis, made by Celeste when her childish one-piece suits had become too small for her, and although her father had not been enthusiastic, he had allowed her the freedom, as no one else was likely to see them.

The bikini she chose had white spots on a blue background, and it complemented her olive colouring. The texture of her skin meant little to her, however. She was too used to it, and she had no idea that many girls of her age spent hours lying in the sun, trying to acquire just such an all-over tan.

Snatching up a towel, she let herself out of the bungalow, treading softly across the verandah and down the steps. Then, giving in to the surge of well-being that the morning evoked, she ran swiftly across the dunes and down on to the smooth damp firmness of the sand. Her hair, sleek and unconfined, streamed behind her, and she spread her arms and did a couple of pirouettes before becoming aware that she was not alone. A man was standing near the water's edge, looking her way, and she sobered rapidly as she realised he had been watching her. He was a tall man, lean and muscular, not a West Indian, but with darkly tanned skin that contrasted sharply with his light hair—

She put uncertain fingers to her lips. It was Mr Howard, she realised in amazement, or Mr *Crown*, as she had to get used to calling him. It was he who had been walking on the beach at this early hour of the morning, and as he began to stroll towards her she saw the bandage projecting from the turned-back sleeve of his shirt.

He looked different with his clothes on, she

thought, and then blushed at the connotation, but she hadn't realised he was so tall, or that a man could move so lithely. He had a co-ordinated indolence that was almost graceful, and the pants hanging low on his hips accentuated the powerful movement of his thighs. They must be the levis Joseph had told her about the previous day, and she couldn't help feeling that they were not quite decent. They moulded his legs like a second skin, hugging his hips and drawing her unwilling attention to the awareness of his un-doubted masculinity. Even his shirt, opened down the smooth expanse of his chest, was not like the shirts her father or Joseph or any of the men she knew wore. It was soft and expensive, like the clothes she had seen in the shop window in Kings-town, and the tawny silk matched the feline lightness of his eyes.

'Hello,' he said, when he neared her, his eyes narrowed now against the glare, and she was made instantly aware of the brevity of her own attire. His stare was as comprehensive as hers, and his voice was husky as he added: 'I guess you're going swimming. I wish I could come with you.'

Ruth moistened her upper lip, noticing as she did so that his skin was covered with a gilding of perspir-ation. In spite of his words and his apparent recovery, she guessed he was exhausted by his ex-ertions, and her first words mirrored her anxiety.

'Ought you to be up?' she exclaimed, forgetting her embarrassment in her concern for his welfare. 'Doctor Francis said—'

'I know what Francis said,' Dominic interrupted her flatly. 'And you didn't answer me.'

'Of course I intended to go swimming,' Ruth admitted. 'But I think I ought to get you back to the house—'

'I'm not an invalid,' he averred, sinking down on to the sand at her feet and spreading his long legs. 'Nor do I need you to tell me what to do. Go and take your swim. I'll watch you. I need a break from the monotony of those four walls.'

Ruth hesitated, looking down at him, and he reached up to tug the towel from her fingers. 'Go on,' he said, his eyes heavy with fatigue and something else she couldn't identify. 'I won't leave here, I promise you.'

Ruth shifted restlessly, scuffing her toe in the sand. 'I ought to talk to you,' she murmured, glancing sideways at him. 'When I went to the bank yesterday—'

'—they told you who I was, right?' Dominic shaded his eyes with one hand as he looked up at her. 'So—okay, you know now. Does it make any difference?'

Ruth sighed. 'Why did you lie? Why did you tell us the wrong name?'

'I didn't.' Dominic dropped his hand and fixed his gaze on the far horizon. 'My names are Dominic and Howard. I just didn't give you all my names, that's all.'

'You deliberately misled us.'

He shrugged. 'As you say.'

'And why don't you want anyone to know where you are? Mr Templar—he's the bank manager—he told me your friends in Bridgetown are frantic to know your whereabouts.'

'I can believe it.' Dominic's tone was uninterested. Then he looked up at her again. 'He didn't tell them?'

'No.' Ruth moved her shoulders. 'But he'd like to.'

'I'll bet!' he grimaced. 'I'll handle my—friends, in my own time.'

'But if anything had happened to you!'

The words burst from Ruth's lips, and his lips twisted. 'Yes? If anything had happened to me—what? It wouldn't matter, either way.'

'It would to us,' exclaimed Ruth indignantly, then flushed when he fixed her with a steady gaze. 'Well—' she defended herself, 'I can imagine your father's reactions if we'd let you die.'

'Oh, I see. You'd do that, would you? Let me die, I mean?' he teased, his mouth humorous now, and she shifted uneasily.

'You know what I mean,' she declared. 'Mr Templar said—'

'Oh, it was Templar, was it?' Dominic relaxed back on his elbows, wincing as he jarred his arm, and then silently daring her to say anything about it. 'I thought that didn't sound like you or your father. Believe me, that's only my family's way of putting on the pressure.'

'Putting on the pressure?' Ruth echoed blankly. 'What do you mean?'

Dominic shook his head. 'Go and have your swim,' he directed, studying the horizon once again. 'We'll talk again when you come out.'

Ruth was reluctant, but the sea was enticing and she was sticky from the terrors of the night. With an inconsequent shrug, she bowed her head, and without another word left him to take ever quickening steps into the ocean.

Despite her awareness of her audience, it was impossible not to find enjoyment in the chill translucency of the water. It was like silk against her skin, soothing her anxiety, and cooling her blood. She swam smoothly, effortlessly, her arms moving through the water in a measured rhythm, her legs kicking lazily in the buoyant, surging current.

She spent about fifteen minutes swimming and diving, and floating on her back, her face turned up to the strengthening rays of the sun, then she swam back to the shore and walked up the beach, squeezing the sea-water out of the slick coil of her hair. She felt clean and exhilarated, and a little intoxicated too when she encountered Dominic's strange enigmatic gaze.

He looked a little better after his rest, his pallor not so pronounced, and his expression was disturbing as he handed her the towel.

'I've never seen a mermaid disporting herself before,' he commented, as she towelled the moisture from her arms, and she didn't know what to answer when he held her gaze with his.

'You—you look better,' she ventured, biting her lower lip, and his expression underwent a change.

'Can't you forget about my arm for once?' he demanded, impatience darkening his irises. 'I offered you a compliment, not an excuse to discuss my health!'

Ruth concentrated on drying her legs, self-consciously aware of his appraisal. But Dominic

turned his attention from her, picking up handfuls of
sand and letting it drain away between his fingers,
and the silence between them stretched ominously.

'I—I suppose we ought to be getting back,' she
ventured at last, hoping for his compliance, and he
looked up at her broodingly.

'Why?' he demanded, his lids heavy. 'What's the
rush? Being shut up in that room all day doesn't
appeal to me, believe it or not, particularly when you
refuse to come and talk to me.'

Ruth bent her head. 'I—I have work to do—'

'*All* day?'

'I have to help Celeste.'

'So why don't you help me?'

'Help you?' Ruth looked down at him uneasily. 'I
don't understand—'

'No, you don't, do you?' he drawled, his expression softening slightly. 'Oh, hey, come here! Let
me do that for you.' And pulling the towel out of her
hands, he indicated that she should squat down in
front of him.

'I can manage,' she began, unwilling for him to
touch her, but the hardening line of his mouth persuaded her, and half apprehensively she subsided on
to the sand between his legs.

She had been drying her hair, but now his hands
took over, moving continuously over its thickness,
massaging her scalp and bringing a tingling awareness of his strength and gentleness. His fingers eased
her tension, they made her relax, and almost un-
thinkingly she yielded against him.

As soon as she felt the muscles of his legs against
her back, she straightened away from him. With

colour blooming in her cheeks, she would have hurriedly got to her feet then, but his hand on her shoulder stopped her.

'Don't get up,' he said, and his voice was curiously husky now. 'You're welcome to lean on me. Do it—it's very pleasant.'

Ruth swallowed. She supposed he was right. What harm could she do just resting against his chest? Her hair was only damp now, two skeins over her shoulders, and his skin was firm and reassuring against her shoulderblades.

Yet, in spite of her inexperience, she felt strangely guilty, sitting there, confined by the powerful curve of his thighs. Dominic seemed relaxed, but she sensed he wasn't, and the heat of his breathing was warm against her nape. She knew she ought to get up, in spite of what he said, but she was strangely reluctant to do so. It was an entirely new experience for her, and one that she could not deny excited her, though why this should be so was harder to understand.

'This is a beautiful place,' Dominic said suddenly, disturbing her anxious introspection. 'I can understand your father's attachment to it. And his reasons for keeping you here.'

Ruth bent her head, unknowingly exposing the tender curve of her nape to his gaze. 'We're happy,' she said, and her movements caused fine strands of black silk to brush his chest.

'Are you?' Dominic's response was abstracted. 'Maybe that's because you know of nothing better.'

Ruth half turned to look at him. 'And you do, of course. Know of somewhere better, I mean?'

His mouth was oddly twisted. 'I didn't say that,' he demurred, his tones harsh and uneven, and his eyes on her parted lips were almost a palpable intrusion.

It was a breath-constricting moment, and she could feel the air fighting to escape from her lungs. He was so close, closer than she had imagined, and her gaze lingered on the sun-bleached length of his lashes and the spasmodic jerking of a pulse in his temple. She knew the desire to touch him again, to stroke his lean cheek and run her palm along the beard-roughened skin of his jawline. She would have liked to slide her fingers through his hair and feel its heavy vitality between her fingers, but when his eyes lowered to the rounded swell of her breasts, thinly disguised by the damp swimsuit, she turned abruptly about so that he could no longer see them.

She was breathing quickly now, shallowly and unsteadily, endeavouring without too much success to assimilate what was happening between them. She didn't understand it. She didn't comprehend why his just looking at her should arouse such strong feelings. She only knew that when he looked at her she had wanted him to admire her body, and it was this as much as anything which aroused her sense of shame.

Struggling on to her knees, she reached for the towel that was lying beside him, and would have scrambled up if once again he hadn't prevented her.

'What's the matter?' he demanded, his eyes dark and searching now as they explored her distracted expression. 'Don't be alarmed. I'm not going to touch you. At least,' he amended dryly, acknowledging his present possession, 'not in the way you're afraid of.'

'I'm not afraid!' Ruth was stung by the underlying mockery in his words, and his brows arched inter- rogatively.

'No?'

'No.' she retorted, unaware that her breasts were rising and falling rapidly in her agitation. 'I just don't think you should look at—at me—at my body, as you were doing!'

His mouth compressed. 'Oh, I see.'

Ruth chin jutted. 'I'm not completely naïve. I have seen the way men look at women,' she declared.

'Oh. I believe it.' Dominic's expression was sober, but she suspected the bland way he was agreeing with her.

'I know you think I'm silly—and childish—and amusing,' she blurted, 'but you have no right to—to make me feel a fool!'

'Did I do that?' He raised his eyes heavenward. 'I'm sorry—'

'Oh, you—'

The humour lurking in the depths of his eyes in- furiated her, and without thinking, she wrenched herself away from him, completely overlooking the fact that it was his left hand that was holding her. Her sudden action jerked his arm, and she gazed down at him, horror-struck, as he rolled back on to the sand, groaning, and holding his injured arm to his chest.

'*Dominic!*'

She used his name without thinking, dropping down on to her knees beside him, touching him with fluttering, nervous hands. His eyes were closed, and he seemed to be in a great deal of pain, and she stared all about her desperately, before returning her attention to his evident distress.

'Oh, Dominic, what can I do?' she implored, leaning over him helplessly, at a loss for a way to relieve his agony. 'Please, say something, anything! Do you want me to go for Joseph?'

He spoke then, but it was barely audible, just a muttering in his throat that brought her head down to him.

'I can't hear you,' she protested, cradling his face between her hands, and then gasped in disbelief when he suddenly moved, rolling over quickly and imprisoning her beneath him.

Looking up into his tormenting face, she was tempted to scratch his eyes out, but she was too relieved to feel anything but a sense of reprieve. He wasn't hurt, she hadn't injured him, and her limbs felt weak with the knowledge of his returning strength.

'So you were going to walk away from me, were you?' he taunted, supporting himself above her. 'You see how dangerous it can be to think you have the upper hand.'

'I didn't think that,' she protested, avoiding his mocking gaze. 'But you were only teasing me, like you're doing now. And I didn't like it.'

'No, I gathered that,' he murmured, one hand stroking back her tumbled hair from her cheek. 'So what would you have me do with you? Take you seriously?'

Ruth's tongue appeared in unknowing provocation. Suddenly, there was less humour in the situation, and she was overwhelmingly aware of the denim-clad legs imprisoning hers against the sand, and the heavy weight of his body crushing her lower limbs. Yet she didn't want him to move. She found she liked the masculine angles of his body pressing down on hers, and she moved very slightly to accommodate his powerful frame.

'Would—would that be so impossible?' she asked now, as his fingers moved from her cheek to find the shell-like crevasses of her ear, and he looked down at her again, his mouth suddenly sensual.

'Oh, Ruth,' he muttered, and she wondered why his touching so commonplace a thing as her ear should cause such disruption inside her. 'Don't tempt me, there's a good girl. Right now you've caught me at a pretty low ebb, and I haven't got the strength to fight you.'

'To fight me?' She looked up at him confusedly. 'You mean your arm—'

'No, I don't mean my arm,' he retorted, and to her disappointment he rolled off her again. 'You're not old enough to understand,' he added, hauling himself up into a sitting position. 'And I'm not the one to teach you.'

Ruth sighed, remaining where she was, lying on the sand, drawing up one leg in unknowing provocation. 'I think you like making fun of me,' she said, half sadly, lacing her fingers through the sand, and he turned to look at her with sudden emotion.

'I'm not making fun of you, believe me,' he averred, and this time she believed him. 'You're a beautiful child, and I'm not unmindful of that fact. But you don't know what you're inviting.'

Ruth sighed, raising an arm to shade her eyes. 'I'm

not a child,' she exclaimed resentfully. 'I've told you—I'm seventeen!'

Dominic shook his head. 'All right, strictly speaking, you're not a child. But you are an innocent, and I'm not—as your father would be the first to tell you.'

Ruth lowered her arm. 'How does one become experienced, then?'

He uttered a short, disbelieving laugh. 'My God!' He gave her an impatient look. 'Ruth, get up! This conversation has gone far enough. I think we should go back to the bungalow.'

She didn't move, except to stretch out a daring hand and let her fingers brush his hip. It drew his attention back to her, as she had hoped it would, and she quivered beneath the deepening regard of that curiously angry gaze. He was looking at her differently now, all the humour had gone, and in its place was a smouldering impatience.

'I said let's go, Ruth,' he muttered harshly, but still she did not obey him. For the first time in her life she knew what it was to control a situation, and she also sensed that he was using his anger to disguise something else.

'I don't want to go,' she said, curling her toes into the sand. 'And you can't make me.'

'Ruth!' His voice was hoarse now, and almost unwillingly, he rested on his elbow beside her. 'Ruth, this has got to stop.'

'Has it?'

Her breathing seemed suspended. He was right— she didn't know what she was inviting, or what she wanted him to do. She only knew there had to be more to his sudden withdrawal than he was admitting, and she ached for him to show her what it was.

His fingers lightly brushed her shoulder, and she tensed as he lowered his head. The heat of his breath mingled with hers, filling her mouth, suffocating her, and her lips parted all unknowing, prepared, yet unprepared, for the touch of his.

It didn't happen as she expected. Instead, shamefully, she felt his tongue circling her mouth, and instinctively she stiffened. But he didn't stop, interspersing his exploration with his lips, rubbing them softly and sensuously against hers, inducing the lowering of her defences. Gradually, almost against her will, she began to enjoy it, and tentatively she tried to respond, letting her tongue emerge to meet his.

The intimacy this evoked left her weak, her bones dissolving into fluid. She felt something uncoiling inside her, something warm and sweet, that flooded her limbs and left them shaking. She was trembling so much, she knew he must be aware of it, and she put up her hand to draw him closer.

'God, *no!*'

At this point Dominic extricated himself from her clinging fingers, getting to his feet without a backward glance. Ruth's tremulous look up at him essayed the suspicion that he was as shaken as she was by what had happened, and she saw that the fingers that raked his hair back from his forehead were as unsteady as her legs.

Nevertheless she had to get up, and gathering the towel she scrambled to her feet. If he was aware of her doing so, he didn't acknowledge it, and feeling a sense of responsibility for what had happened, she lightly touched his sleeve.

'Are—are you angry with me?' she ventured, circling round to face him, and flinched at the angry glare he turned upon her.

'Yes,' he said grimly, 'I'm angry with you. Now will you please go back to the house and get some clothes on!'

Ruth hesitated. 'It—it's all right, really. I mean—I made you do what you—'

'Go home, Ruth!' he commanded, brushing her aside, and she stared after him unhappily as he walked away from her, down to the water's edge.

Trudging back to the bungalow, she tried once again to assimilate what had happened. It was her first experience of kissing, but it wasn't Dominic's, and she couldn't understand why he should feel angry when she didn't. On the contrary, she would have liked him to go on kissing her, it was a very pleasurable experience, even if it had left her feeling curiously flat afterwards. Perhaps that was what was wrong with him, she considered thoughtfully. Perhaps because he was so much more experienced, he didn't enjoy it quite so much.

She sighed. She could have sworn he was enjoying it. His breathing had been as laboured as hers. But she had felt his fists, clenched on the sand beside her, so perhaps he had been fighting her all along, as he had said.

It was an enigma, and one she wished she could explore more fully. If only there was someone she could ask, someone who would tell her why Dominic had got so angry at the end. There was always

Celeste, of course, but somehow Ruth was loath to share this particular problem with her. Which only left her father, and thinking of him, Ruth knew an intimation of why Dominic had behaved as he did. She also recognised her own culpability in ignoring her father's wishes and associating with a man he despised, and whose identity she had yet to reveal.

She heard her bedroom door close while she was in the bathroom, and guessed Dominic had returned. She wondered if he intended to join her and her father for breakfast, and anxiously anticipated the situation that would create. He might even tell her father about meeting her on the beach, and while she doubted he would betray all that had happened, she could imagine her father's reaction to this news.

She sighed again, dressing in her old skirt and tee-shirt, realising too late the construction her father might put on the new shirt and shorts she had bought the previous day. The last thing she wanted was to arouse his suspicions, particularly when any argument seemed to aggravate his condition.

Celeste, as usual, was busy at the stove when she entered the kitchen a few minutes later. However, the black woman glanced round provokingly when she heard the girl, and made her own contribution to Ruth's ever-increasing trepidation.

'You been with Mr Howard on the beach?' she queried, tilting her head on one side, and Ruth's features froze. 'I see him come back few minutes ago, and when I took in his breakfast he near snapped my head off!' Her lips twitched. 'What you been saying to the man? Seems like something ain't suiting him.'

Ruth seated herself at the kitchen table, avoiding the black woman's eyes, tracing the grain in its scrubbed surface with her fingernail.

'How do you know I've been on the beach?' she ventured at last, when Celeste had made it obvious she wasn't going to continue with what she was doing until she got a reply. 'I didn't see you when I came back. I might have been visiting Father Andreas.'

'Pigs might fly,' declared Celeste sharply. 'And I suppose that damp hair is through dipping your head in the font!'

'I took a shower,' said Ruth, playing for time. 'Where's Daddy?'

'Your daddy still in bed,' retorted Celeste shortly. 'And that's as well for you. But don't you go thinking you can fool Celeste like you fooling your daddy, 'cos it ain't going to happen!'

Ruth looked up then, her eyes wide and indignant. 'I'm not fooling him!' she protested.

'Ain't you?' Celeste stared piercingly at her. 'You mean to tell me your daddy knew about your date with Mr Howard?'

'It wasn't a date.' Ruth looked away again. 'We—we met by accident. How was I to know he'd be up at that time of the morning?'

Celeste studied her bent head. 'So what happened?' she probed. 'What he say to you? You can tell Celeste—you know it won't go no further.'

Ruth sighed. 'What do you think he said? We—talked, that's all.' She paused before adding: 'Nothing that Daddy couldn't have heard.'

'Is that right?' Celeste pulled out a chair with a

clatter and seated herself opposite. 'So you tell me. why Mr Howard like a bear with a sore head?'

It was harder to avoid the black woman's eyes when she was on a level with her, and Ruth stared at her mutinously. 'I've told you the truth. We talked! What did you expect us to do?'

Celeste's eyes narrowed. 'He didn't lay his hands on you. did he?' she demanded, and it was the hardest moment of Ruth's life to date to sustain that inimical gaze.

'No.' she said at last, the untruth torn from her. 'Why should he want to do that?' and saw from Celeste's expression that her suspicions were fading.

'You sure?' she persisted, but it was an academic question, she had already accepted Ruth's explanation. 'Well. you take care he don't, Missy. Is one thing to make conversation with the man, and something else to let him think you cheap!'

'Cheap?' Now Ruth detained her. 'What do you mean? I don't understand you.'

Celeste hesitated. 'Ain't no reason for you to know.' she declared at last. 'Ain't going to happen.'

'No. I want to know.' Ruth put her hand on the black woman's arm as she would have got up. 'Please. Celeste—tell me!'

Celeste sighed. but she allowed herself to be persuaded. 'Well.' she said slowly, 'it a word we use when a girl let a man have his way with her too easy.'

'Have his way with her?' Ruth was bewildered.

'You know what a man and woman does together, don't you?'

Ruth's face was burning. 'I think so.'

'You ain't let any man do that to you, have you?'

'No.' Ruth shook her head.

'So don't,' said Celeste simply. 'At least, not until you sure he intend to marry you.'

Ruth frowned. 'But you—'

'We ain't talking about me,' Celeste overrode her abruptly, getting to her feet. 'What I am, and what I do—that's my business.'

Ruth looked up at her. 'Are you cheap, Celeste?' she asked innocently, and then cried out in pain when the woman's calloused hand delivered a blow against her cheek.

'Don't you ever say that to me again, you hear?' Celeste almost screamed the words, and Ruth pressed her palm to the injured area.

'I didn't mean—'

'I don't care what you mean,' retorted Celeste, incensed. 'You too old to act the child. Your daddy going to have a heap of trouble on his hands, if'n he don't teach you what's what!'

Ruth sniffed, the pain in her cheek making her eyes water. 'I'm sorry if I was rude,' she articulated with difficulty, pushing back her chair. 'I'd better go and see how Daddy is. He may be wondering where I am.'

'Yes, you do that,' Celeste nodded brusquely, then as Ruth reached the door, she seemed to relent. 'I didn't mean to hit you so hard,' she muttered, with the nearest thing to an apology she was likely to make. 'Don't you go complaining to your daddy how I been beating you.'

'I won't.' It was too painful to smile. but Ruth managed a tearful grimace before she hurriedly left the room.

CHAPTER SEVEN

She stopped off in the bathroom before going to see her father, and spent some minutes bathing her face with cool water. Even so, the evidence of the blow was unmistakable, and she studied her reflection anxiously, wishing she had some make-up to disguise the revealing marks. But there had never been enough money for such luxuries, and in any case she didn't know how to use them, so she contented herself with drawing her hair forward, to hide the swelling.

In the event, her father hardly noticed her appearance. He looked pale and drawn in the light filtering through the shutters, and he confessed to having a pain in his chest that even his tablets would not erase.

'Francis is coming this afternoon,' he told Ruth weakly, when she expressed concern for his wellbeing, and she was relieved that Dominic's injury should require such assiduous attention. 'I'll have a word with him after he's examined Howard, and perhaps he'll be able to offer an alternative treatment.'

Ruth pressed her lips together. She knew she ought to tell him that Dominic's surname was Crown, not Howard, but now hardly seemed the right moment. Besides, was it really that important, in the circumstances? Dominic was improving. He would be gone soon. Then would be time enough to confess that their visitor had been more important than her father had thought. Not now, when such knowledge could well arouse concern and anxiety, conditions he had been advised to avoid.

She divided the morning between Professor Jason's bedside and the study. She read to her father for a while and then, when he fell into a shallow slumber, she returned to her studies, with a distinct lack of enthusiasm. It seemed as though the storm, and her discovery of Dominic's body on the beach, had been a turning point in her life, and now nothing and no one seemed the same. Even Celeste, who until now had always seemed a refuge in times of trouble, had been affected by Dominic Crown's entry into their lives, and Ruth's bruised face bore witness to a new and slightly frightening isolation. If—*when* her father died, she would no longer be able to depend on Celeste to cushion her against a hostile world. Those ties had been broken, destroyed by a single act of violence. In their place was a growing maturity, an increasing awareness, that she would be alone and self-dependent, and somehow she had to adapt to that fact.

She ate a solitary lunch in the dining room, served by a subdued Celeste. She thought perhaps the black woman regretted what had happened as much as she did, perhaps more, for Celeste was always volatile, but Ruth could not forget, though she would try to forgive.

'Mr Howard, he say he don't want no lunch,' Celeste remarked offhandedly, as she served a chilled fruit cocktail. 'He ain't eaten no breakfast either. What you think I should do?'

Ruth expelled her breath carefully. 'Doctor Francis is coming this afternoon,' she said, hiding the fact that the information had disturbed her. 'He's the one to ask.'

Celeste sniffed. 'It don't seem right. He eat okay yesterday. Why he not eat today?'

Ruth looked up, her hand concealing one side of her face. 'I don't know, Celeste,' she said quietly. 'Why don't you ask him? I can't think of any reason why he should refuse his food.'

'He say he not hungry,' persisted Celeste, hovering by the table. 'Maybe if'n you spoke to him—'

'Doctor Francis will deal with it,' replied Ruth firmly, concentrating on spooning an orange segment into her mouth. 'Don't worry, no one's going to blame you for his loss of appetite.'

Celeste still lingered. 'You sound as if you don't care,' she accused. 'You mad at me?'

'Oh, Celeste, please . . .' Ruth didn't think she could take much more today. 'I'm not mad, and I do care. But there's nothing I can do.' She drew a deep breath. 'Now, can I get on with my lunch?'

It was easy enough to sound indignant, but after Celeste had flounced out, Ruth's shoulders sagged and she put down her spoon. Truth to tell, her own appetite was practically non-existent, but she was determined Celeste should have no reason to complain about her. Picking up her spoon again, she tackled the rest of the fruit in her glass with grim resolution, and by the time she put it down again the glass was empty.

Doctor Francis arrived soon after three o'clock. Ruth kept out of the way when she heard his Gaelic brogue. and Celeste welcomed him into the house and accompanied him to Dominic's room.

There was silence for a while after that, and Ruth hovered in the study, feeling like an intruder in her own home. But she knew that nothing would prevent Doctor Francis's sharp eyes from observing the swelling over her cheekbone, and she was afraid of the explanations he would demand. She doubted whether the doctor would believe the story she had concocted, of hitting her face on the handle of a door, and she dreaded Celeste's careless tongue if her father ever foraged and found the truth.

Fortunately for her, the doctor did not come looking for her until after he had examined Professor Jason. Celeste had returned to the kitchen. Ruth could hear the clatter of cups and saucers as she prepared tea, and she positioned herself in a shadowy corner of the living room, so that when Doctor Francis came to find her, her puffy cheek was not immediately visible.

'So there you are,' he said, rather abstractedly, coming into the room, a thoughtful expression bringing a furrow to his forehead. 'I thought you must be out. when you didn't come to meet me. What are you doing, hiding away in here?'

'I'm not hiding away.' Ruth kept the tremor out of her voice with difficulty. 'How's Daddy? He's worse, isn't he?'

Francis came to sit near her, studying her anxious face with gentle concern. 'Now, Ruth, you know the situation as well as I do. Surely you're not trying to pretend it doesn't exist?'

Ruth shook her head. 'I remember what you told me.' she said. 'So what's the verdict? Can you help him?'

Francis sighed. 'There's only so much one can do, my dear,' he admitted regretfully. 'Your father's been in pain for a long time. Up till now the drugs he has had have succeeded in making it bearable. But I'm afraid, as his condition worsens—'

'—you won't be able to stop it?' Ruth's lips trembled.

'Not without his losing consciousness,' Francis replied heavily. 'My dear, you're going to have to accept that your father's time with us is limited.'

Ruth forgot her reasons for sitting in the shadow, leaning forward to bury her face in her hands. It was what she had expected, of course, but somehow today it was so much harder to bear. She felt the doctor's hand on her shoulder, accepted the handkerchief he stuffed into her hand, and gave in briefly to the intense feeling of loneliness his words presaged.

'Come along,' said Doctor Francis, after a few minutes. smoothing back her hair with a kindly finger. 'Things could be worse. I've managed to give your father something to ease the pain temporarily, and he's sleeping now. It may not be there when he awakens. Let's hope not.' He paused. 'Don't you want to know how my other patient is faring?'

Ruth drew away from him, and as she did so, a slanting ray of sunlight highlighted the bruised area around her cheekbone. In the shaft of brilliance, every swollen contour was visible, and the doctor sucked in his breath.

'Good lord!' he exclaimed, putting out a hand to touch the contusion, but instinctively she pulled back. 'How on earth did this happen? Who did it? Not—Curtis!'

'Daddy?' Ruth almost laughed, but it would hurt too much. 'Good heavens, no! Daddy wouldn't strike me.'

'I hope not.' Francis frowned. 'So how did it happen?'

Ruth licked her dry lips. 'It—it was carelessness. I was—kneeling, on the floor, and I turned, you know how you do? I'm afraid I hit my face on the handle of the door. Silly of me, wasn't it?'

Francis studied her anxious expression for several seconds, seconds that stretched into minutes in Ruth's imagination. Then, when she felt sure she couldn't sustain her composure any longer, he said harshly:

'Do you know something, Ruth? I originally heard that excuse when I was in my first year as a general practitioner.' He frowned. 'I heard it from a young woman, a young mother, actually, three months home from the hospital with a new baby.' He sighed reminiscently. 'The baby, I think it was a little boy, was fractious; you know how babies can be. He used to cry a lot, and the young woman's husband couldn't get any sleep.'

'Why are you telling me this?' Ruth was uneasy. 'What does it matter if someone else has done the same thing? I'm sorry, of course, but I don't see—'

'She didn't hit her face on a door handle,' Francis

interposed roughly. 'I only said that was her excuse.'
He considered his words carefully. 'As a matter of
fact, her husband had hit her—struck her, because
she couldn't keep the baby quiet. Now do you see
what I'm getting at?'

'You don't think I hit my face on the door either.'
Ruth endeavoured to appear calm. 'But that's ridiculous. Why should I lie?'

'Why indeed?' Francis sounded aggravated. 'To
think I defended that young man—'

'What young man?' Ruth stared at him. 'You
mean—Dominic?'

'Dominic? Is that what you call him?' Francis
snorted. 'Since when have you been on such confi-
dential terms?'

Ruth felt the colour pouring into her face. 'We're
not—I mean—we've talked together, that's all.'

'And did he do this?' Francis flicked a finger at her
face.

'No!' Ruth was horrified. 'I've told you, I did it
myself.'

Francis expelled his breath heavily. 'That's your
last word?'

'Yes. Yes!'

Ruth was stubborn, and the arrival of Celeste with
the tea tray was a welcome distraction. She wondered whether the black woman had overheard any
of their conversation, but whatever happened, Ruth
was determined her father should not be drawn into
it as he surely would be if she told the truth.

'So,' after the tea was poured and Celeste had left
them, she endeavoured to retrieve the situation,
'how—how is Dominic? You were going to tell me.'

Francis shrugged, helping himself to a second cucumber sandwich. 'He's improving—slowly,' he conceded. 'Not as quickly, as I'd like, perhaps, but steadily.' He paused. 'Did you encourage him to take that walk along the beach this morning? Because I have to tell you, he's overdone it.'

Ruth bent her head. 'I—I met him,' she admitted. 'But I didn't know he was down there.'

'No?'

'No.'

'And he didn't touch you?'

Ruth got to her feet then, pacing jerkily across to the windows. 'No,' she said, closing her eyes for a moment in a silent prayer for forgiveness. 'No, he didn't touch me, and—and I'd be grateful if you wouldn't—worry Daddy over any of this.'

There was silence for a moment, and then the doctor's large, square-fingered hands descended on her shoulders, startling her. 'Very well,' he said, and there was reluctant compliance in his voice. 'I won't tell Curtis, so long as you promise to tell me if—if it happens again.'

Ruth turned, her lips parting in protest, but the doctor had already left her, going across the room to collect his bag, and then making for the door.

'Take care,' he admonished her gently. 'I'll see you again tomorrow.' And before she could make any response, he was gone.

It wasn't until later, when she was sitting nursing a cold cup of tea, that she heard him leaving the house, and realised he must have gone back to check up on her father. Perhaps she ought to have accompanied him, if only to assure herself that he did not mention their conversation, she reflected, but it was too late now. In any case, she doubted he would do anything to upset her father, and telling him that he suspected Dominic had struck her would be nothing short of criminal.

Deciding that no good would come from sitting here moping, she carried their dirty dishes back to the kitchen, and then went to see her father. As Doctor Francis had said, he was sleeping, and she left him to rest, going out on to the verandah to enjoy the last of the day. The sun was sinking slowly behind the bungalow, spreading orange fingers over the garden, turning the sky to flame, and she leaned restlessly on the wooden rail, watching the seabirds swooping down towards the harbour. It was the time of day when the fishing boats came in, and they were never short of a feathered escort, their shrill cries plaintive on the evening air.

She became aware that she was no longer alone, almost by instinct. She hadn't heard anything. Dominic's bare feet had made no sound on the wooden slats below them. But she sensed his presence, and when she turned she was hardly surprised to find him leaning against the open door. Immediately one hand went protectively to her face, and she shook her hair forward about her shoulders as she met his hostile gaze.

'You know why I'm here, of course,' he remarked coldly, although his eyes had narrowed somewhat. 'I want to know what you mean by telling Francis I punched you in the face! God, I might have felt like it, but you know as well as I do that I didn't.'

'Oh, no!' Ruth stared at him apologetically. 'You

don't mean Doctor Francis came back to speak to you?' She shook her head. 'I didn't know, honestly. I thought he went to see Daddy.'

'Well, he didn't,' said Dominic harshly, straightening from the door jamb and coming towards her. 'But as I'm here, I might as well see what it is I'm supposed to have done—'

'No! Oh, please—' Ruth backed away from him. 'I didn't—that is—Doctor Francis got the wrong impression.'

'Like hell he did,' Dominic agreed, approaching her with all the persistence of a stalking cat. 'Dammit, Ruth, stand still, can't you? Don't I have a right to see the damage?'

Ruth came up against the corner of the verandah, and bent her head, putting her hand to her neck over the heavy curtain of her hair. 'It's nothing, really,' she whispered, begging his indulgence, but Dominic was determined to have his way.

Brushing her fingers aside, he lifted her chin, stroking back the hair from her face as he did so. Her eyes faltered as they met his, evading their tawny invasion, concentrating instead on the pallor of his cheeks, and the sheen of perspiration this persistent exertion was evoking. She did not observe his expression as he examined the purpling marks, or witness the tightening of his lips as he released her trembling chin.

'Who did do this?' he asked, his tone as mild and uninterested as if he was asking the time, and Ruth drew an uneven breath.

'I—I did it myself—'

'You walked into a door, I suppose?' His mouth curled.

'How did you know?'

'I didn't.' He made a sound of impatience. 'Ruth, that's the oldest excuse in the book.' He flicked his fingers at the swollen contusions. 'Come on, the truth, now. I mean to know. Was it your Father?'

'Daddy?' Ruth's eyes flashed. 'Daddy doesn't hit me. He never has.'

'Perhaps he should have,' remarked Dominic obscurely, but his eyes had darkened. 'Who hit you, Ruth? I'll make you tell me, if I have to.'

Ruth sniffed. 'How will you do that?'

'I can be ruthless, when it's necessary.' He paused, allowing his words to sink in. 'I could threaten to tell your father what happened on the beach this morning. Something tells me, he knows nothing about that either.'

Ruth's chin quivered. 'You wouldn't.'

'Wouldn't I?' Dominic brushed his thumb along her jawline. 'Do you want to put it to the test?'

Ruth held up her head. 'Why should you think I'd care?'

Dominic hesitated a moment longer, and then, as if his own exhaustion had achieved what her words could not, he shrugged. 'All right, I guess I know the culprit anyway. It has to be Celeste. I just wonder why.'

Ruth sighed, disturbed by the defeated note in his voice. 'If you must know, it was something I said, something that—offended her.' She made a helpless gesture. 'Now, don't you think you ought to go back to bed—'

'I'll decide when I go back to bed,' he retorted harshly. 'I'm not your father. I'm no invalid!'

'Then at least sit down,' begged Ruth uneasily, wishing he would move away from her. Celeste might appear at any moment, and the black woman's perception in these matters was too acute.

Dominic remained where he was. 'And how often does this happen?' he demanded, pursuing his theme. 'How often does Celeste administer corporal punishment?'

Ruth's tongue circled her lips. 'She doesn't. At least, I've told you—it was all my fault. Please—you won't mention this to Daddy, will you? I mean, she didn't intend to—to hurt me. She was angry, that's all. And Daddy gets so upset—'

Dominic's mouth compressed. 'If you say so.'

'I do say so.' Ruth's relief was almost palpable, but she shifted restlessly from one foot to the other. 'And now, won't you do as Doctor Francis advised you and rest? He—he didn't approve of your outing this morning, and I know he's only thinking—'

'Stop worrying about me.' Dominic was impatient. 'I'll be all right. It's you I'm concerned about. Do you realise how sick your father is?'

Ruth swallowed convulsively. 'I—I think so.'

'Do you know he's going to die?' he demanded brutally.

She drew back. 'Yes.'

Dominic's eyes narrowed. 'And what do you plan to do then?'

'What do you mean, what do I plan to do?' Ruth shrugged. 'This is my home. I'll stay here, of course.'

'Alone?'

'I shall be quite safe. The islanders are my friends.'

'Safe!' Dominic swung away from her abruptly. 'I

don't believe it. You can't seriously consider remaining here for the rest of your life?'

Ruth's palms dug into the wood of the verandah rail. *The rest of her life!* His words were unaccountably chilling. Was that what she was contemplating? A lonely existence here, with only Celeste for company?

'There must be an alternative,' muttered Dominic angrily. 'You must have relations—family—'

'I repeat—there's no one.' Ruth held up her head. 'You don't have to concern yourself about me. I'm quite capable of taking care of myself.'

Dominic was not convinced. 'What about this income you said you and your father lived on? It must come from somewhere. Your mother's family, you said. What about that?'

Ruth smoothed her damp palms down the seams of her skirt. 'That was from my grandmother, as I told you. But she's dead!' She dismissed the claim. 'Now—please—won't you go back to your room? I have work to do.'

Dominic expelled his breath on an impatient sigh. Then, as if reluctantly stirred to remorse, he said: 'You're all right, aren't you?' And at her startled response: 'I mean, of course, what happened this morning. I—' He broke off half irritably. 'I should apologise. I don't usually make such a fool of myself. I'm sorry.'

Ruth sucked in her breath. Inexperienced as she was of the ways of the world, she sensed the incongruity of his words. Somehow she knew that what had happened between them was not something one could dismiss with an apology. It reduced her to the ignorant adolescent she was, and destroyed her tentative bid for maturity.

'There's no need for you to feel responsible,' she declared at last, struggling to appear nonchalant. 'I'm not a child, I knew what I was doing.' She forced her stiff features into a semblance of a smile. 'Really, I'm not as naïve as you think.'

'Aren't you?' Dominic moved his shoulders in studied disbelief. 'Very well, so be it.' He turned towards the door behind him. 'As you say,' he added, half to himself, 'it's not my concern.'

Ruth ate supper alone in the dining room. Dominic did not put in an appearance, and her father was too weak to leave his bed. Celeste served her sullenly, apparently as troubled in her thoughts as Ruth was, and realising their unnatural relationship could not be sustained, Ruth endeavoured to mend the breach.

'Doctor Francis has prescribed some stronger medication for Daddy,' she volunteered, making a stalwart attempt at a friendly tone. 'Let's hope it makes him feel better. I think having a visitor in the house has been too much for him.' And when Celeste still didn't say anything, she added: 'Never mind. Mr—Howard will be leaving soon. Then perhaps we can get back to normal.'

The silence that greeted this statement left Ruth feeling utterly deflated. It wasn't like Celeste to bear a grudge, and usually their arguments were swiftly resolved. This uncharacteristic moodiness boded no good, and Ruth hoped the black woman was not going to cause more problems.

'Has—has Mr Howard had any supper?' she ventured, determined to provoke some response, and then flinched when Celeste speared her with a glare.

'What you been telling Mr Howard 'bout me?' she demanded, startling Ruth into dropping her fork. 'What tales you been blabbing to him?'

'Tales—' faltered Ruth blankly, and Celeste's palms supported her as she leaned across the table.

'That what I said,' she affirmed angrily. 'Seems like you can't wait to get Celeste into trouble, *bad* trouble!'

'That's not true—'

'Ain't it? You denying you went running to Mr Howard to show him what I'se supposed to have done to you?'

'I didn't—that is—' Ruth groped for words. 'Celeste, Doctor Francis—noticed. It was he who told Mr Howard, not me. He—Doctor Francis, that is—he thought Mr Howard had done it.'

Celeste's dark brows drew together. 'Why he think a thing like that?' she asked suspiciously.

'I don't know.' But Ruth's face was suffused with colour now, and Celeste's eyes narrowed. 'Anyway,' she went on quickly, 'I'm sorry if—if Mr Howard spoke to you about it—'

'He didn't.' Celeste sniffed, and Ruth gazed up at her uncomprehendingly. 'I see you together—on the verandah,' Celeste admitted carelessly. 'After the doctor leave. Celeste no fool. I got eyes.' She tapped her forehead significantly. 'Celeste know what going on.'

'There's nothing going on, Celeste!' Ruth got up ostensibly to pick up her fork, but also because sitting still left her at too much of a disadvantage. 'I don't know what you're talking about.'

'Celeste got ears, too,' the black woman insisted infuriatingly. 'I hear what Mr Howard say to you. But don't worry . . .' She straightened from the table and raised one hand in a conspiratorial gesture. 'I won't go telling tales, no, sir—'

'Celeste!' Ruth could hardly hide her revulsion at the knowledge that the other woman had deliberately eavesdropped on their conversation. 'You don't know—'

'Ain't no other way you going to get to be a woman, Missy,' Celeste interrupted her insinuatively. 'An' I guess Mr Howard is just the man for the job—'

'Be quiet, Celeste!' Uncaring that her words might rekindle the animosity between them, Ruth was compelled to silence her, but in this instance Celeste chose to be generous.

'One day,' she said, 'one day you'll remember what I said, and know I'm right.'

Ruth stared into her mocking face for several more seconds, and then, unable to think of any suitable response, she resumed her seat. With her hands clenched tightly in her lap, she silently conceded that she had no answer for her. But what hurt most was the knowledge that no one—not Celeste, nor her father, not even Dominic himself—behaved as if she had a mind of her own.

She looked in on her father on her way to bed, and was relieved to find he was sleeping peacefully. The lines of pain and weariness were ironed out a little in sleep, and he seemed more relaxed than he had done of late. Perhaps the stronger medication was all he needed. She prayed so. Right now, she needed him more than she had ever done before.

Notwithstanding the faint optimism she was feeling, sleep proved an elusive prey. In spite of the reassurance she had felt when she saw her father sleeping, her own metabolism was far too active to allow her to relax. She felt hot and restless, and her skin prickled every time she closed her eyes and thoughts of the day invaded her mind. So much had happened, so many experiences that were new to her, so many questions those experiences had left unanswered.

Not least was the uneasiness of her own body. She neither recognised nor understood the sensations she was made aware of, and the extreme sensitivity of her skin was a tangible distraction. The nightshirt she wore acted like an abrasive, and every part of her it touched, seared like a flame. Her whole body felt as if it was on fire, and she wondered, with sudden anxiety, whether she had contracted a fever.

But no. Her forehead was cool to her touch. Only her limbs burned with an inner heat, that manifested itself every time she allowed the memory of what Dominic had done to project itself. Over and over, she relived those moments on the beach, those moments when Dominic had kissed her. At least, she supposed it was kissing, even if it had been different from what she had imagined. Unknowingly, her tongue appeared, circling the lips that he had moistened, her breath suspended in sudden recollection. She felt again the flowering of emotion inside her, the sensual lethargy of feeling that evoked an actual

physical ache down low in her stomach, and the
curious desire she had had for a closeness she had
never experienced.

With fearful anticipation, her fingers suddenly
probed the contours of her body through the thin
cotton shirt. As she had half expected, her breasts
were engorged and swollen, the nipples hard and
thrusting against her palm. She knew instinctively
that that was how they had felt when Dominic
crushed her down upon the sand that morning, when
the hard muscles of his body had sought accom-
modation in hers . . .

CHAPTER EIGHT

Professor Jason insisted on getting up for breakfast the following morning, and he looked so much better, Ruth made no demur. On the contrary, she was delighted to see him on his feet again, even if his sharp gaze was quick to notice the lingering puffiness around her eye.

'You're not sleeping well on the couch,' he observed, fortunately misreading the signs, while a suspiciously amiable Celeste served them toast and coffee. 'I shall certainly get a date for Mr Howard's departure from Francis today. This situation can't be sustained any longer.'

'Really, Daddy I'm fine,' Ruth protested, buttering her toast with an averted gaze. 'It was a—a hot night, that's all. I did sleep badly. Please, don't concern yourself on my account.'

'But I do concern myself,' retorted her father, and becoming aware of Celeste's knowingly mocking gaze, Ruth forced herself to look up. 'I don't like this disruption to our lives,' Professor Jason continued severely. 'I'm constantly aware of how vulnerable you are when I'm incapacitated.'

Ruth's feelings of guilt at the memory of the thoughts that had kept her awake until the early hours multiplied. She was shameless, she castigated herself bitterly, wishing Celeste would hurry up and leave them. She felt evil, corrupt, an abandoned creature, unworthy of his regard. While her father spent his strength in worrying about her, she indulged in wanton licentiousness, in moral degradation, anticipating with excitement the things he stood in abhorrence of. And Celeste knew it. Or, at the very least, she suspected it, which was almost as bad.

'Thank you, Celeste. We have everything we need now,' Professor Jason remarked then, earning Ruth's gratitude, but after the black woman had reluctantly left the room, he returned to his theme: 'I'm going to spend the morning going over the translation you've been working at these past few days, but as soon as Francis appears, I want you to let me know.'

'Yes, Daddy.'

Ruth bit into the crisp bread in an effort to avoid further discussion, but her father wasn't finished yet.

'I see no reason why Howard shouldn't leave here today or tomorrow. He can be cared for just as satisfactorily at the hospital in Kingstown, thus relieving us of the responsibility for his welfare.'

Ruth put down the piece of toast she was holding, and wiped her mouth on her napkin. Now was her chance to explain who he was, she thought, but again her father forestalled her, pushing back his chair and rising to his feet.

'Let me know when Francis arrives,' he directed her once more, and walked out of the room before she could swallow the food in her mouth.

With the meal over, Ruth was obliged to carry the

plates into the kitchen, and Celeste turned to her with sardonic eyes. 'Poor baby,' she mocked. 'Ain't you sleeping these nights on that hard bed o' yours? Maybe you ought to consider sharing with Mr Howard.'

'As you do with Joseph, you mean?' Ruth was stung to retort, and Celeste's brown eyes opened wide in reproof.

'Ain't no need for you to take that tone with me, Missy,' she declared huffily, giving the girl her back, but Ruth was in no mood to trade insults with her.

'Have you given Mr—Howard his breakfast?' she asked determinedly, only hesitating over the name, and Celeste's plump shoulders quivered.

'One way of finding out, isn't there?' she responded, plunging her hands into soapy water, and Ruth expelled her breath in impatient acknowledgement.

Leaving the kitchen, she hesitated in the hall, listening for sounds of her father. But all that she could hear was the hens clucking in the yard, and the muted thunder of the ocean as it pounded the reef. The doors were open wide, and the scent of the flowering vine that grew in such profusion over the verandah was sweet and fragrant. The air was warm yet refreshing, a tantalising invitation to escape the confining limits of the bungalow, yet she had promised her father to wait and watch for Doctor Francis. She would have liked to get away, well away from the lingering anguish of deceiving her father, but for the present she was restricted and restrained.

Turning her head, she looked along the hall to

where her bedroom door remained firmly closed. Was Dominic in there, fretting as she was against the restrictions of these four walls? Was he aware of her father's desire to be rid of him? Would he welcome the freedom he was soon to be offered?

She guessed it was a futile question. Without doubt, he would welcome the chance to live his own life once again, independent of people he neither knew nor understood. His family and friends would probably find his descriptions of life here on Indigo quite amusing, and they would laugh about it afterwards, and pity him being forced to stay here. There might even be some girl he could regale with anecdotes about her own naïveté, or perhaps—and this was something she had not considered before—perhaps he was married, with a wife to share his experiences. Yet wouldn't a wife deserve to be told his whereabouts? Wouldn't a wife merit the kind of privileged information denied to everyone else?

'Did you want something?'

The coolly spoken remark nevertheless threw Ruth into a mild form of panic. She had not been aware of anyone's approach, and to be discovered hovering outside the door of Dominic's bedroom put her distinctly at a disadvantage. It was obvious he had been out again, without her knowledge, and she wondered how long he had been propped against the door frame, watching her.

'You look thoughtful,' he added, straightening, when she didn't answer him. 'What's wrong? Your father's not worse, is he?'

'Oh, no. No.' Ruth linked her fingers together

behind her back. 'How—how are you? You look much better this morning.'

'I feel better,' he averred, his expression still probing. 'I repeat—were you wanting me?'

'No,' Ruth shook her head. 'I—I—'

'You can't think of a suitable prevarication, is that it?' he suggested flatly, going past her to open the door of his room, and as she struggled to find words to deny this, he went on: 'Why don't you come right out and say it? You wanted to know where I was.' He shrugged. 'Well, here I am. So how about we stop playing games with one another and act like adult human beings, mmm?'

Ruth glanced behind her, half afraid her father might overhear him. But only a bee's humming disturbed the silence that followed this remark, and she allowed herself to breathe again.

'All right,' she admitted, coming to stand in the doorway. 'I was going to enquire how you were feeling this morning. But I can see, you're almost recovered.'

'I *am* recovered,' he assured her curtly. 'Not almost. So how do you feel about giving me a guided tour of the island? What was it you called that place where you said my yacht might have washed up? The Serpent's Tooth?'

'Teeth, actually,' corrected Ruth doubtfully. 'But that's right across the island. At least two miles.' She paused. 'Besides, Daddy has asked me to look out for Doctor Francis. He—he wants to speak to him.'

'About me, no doubt,' observed Dominic, with sharp perception. 'However, as your *friendly* doctor doesn't usually turn up until after lunch, I'd guess we could be there and back before he arrives.'

'I don't think so.' Ruth's face gained colour. 'Four miles, on foot. In this heat?'

'Don't you have any transport?' He stared at her.

'Only a bicycle,' Ruth confessed in embarrassment. And then: 'There are no roads.'

'Of course not.' Dominic frowned, as if this thought had just occurred to him. 'Okay. Do you have two bicycles?'

Ruth shook her head. 'In any case—'

'If you're going to tell me I can't ride a bike, then don't bother,' he muttered impatiently. 'Believe it or not, I get plenty of exercise back home in England. I'm in reasonably good shape, and cycling four miles isn't going to kill me.'

'Well, we don't have two bicycles,' declared Ruth firmly, moving away from his door as she heard Celeste crossing the tiled floor of the kitchen. 'I'm sorry, but we don't.'

Celeste emerged just as Ruth reached the door of the kitchen, but her shrewd gaze noted the open door along the hall and Ruth's flushed cheeks.

'I guess you found out for yourself, honey,' she remarked, in an undertone, and then assumed a beaming smile when Dominic reappeared. 'Well, hi there, Mr Howard,' she greeted him warmly. 'You enjoy your walk? You ready for some of my ham and eggs now?'

'Just eggs, Celeste, thank you,' Dominic assured her, casually following Ruth into the kitchen. 'Say, you don't know where I could borrow a bicycle, do you?'

Celeste glanced at her employer's young daughter, then frowned. 'Why, Missy Ruth—'

'I mean—other than Ruth's,' Dominic inserted smoothly. 'So she can show me a little of the island this morning.'

Celeste smirked. 'Is that so?' she murmured, giving Ruth a sideways glance. 'Well now, Mr Howard, ain't no other bi-cycle on the island not that I knows of.'

Ruth released her breath, but her relief was short-lived.

'You ever ridden a motor-cycle, Mr Howard?' the black woman went on, adding thoughtfully: ' 'cause my cousin Harold, he got one of them Japanese Sukis.'

'Suzuki?' suggested Dominic, with evident interest. 'And yes, I've ridden motor-bikes in my time. Do you think he'd lend it to me?'

'If'n I ask him to,' said Celeste smugly, but Ruth could not let this go on.

'I don't think Doctor Francis would approve of Mr Howard riding a motor-cycle, Celeste,' she declared forcefully. 'He might fall off.'

'Your confidence in me does wonders for my ego,' remarked Dominic, with a grimace, and Ruth's forehead furrowed as she struggled to understand him. 'Why should I fall off? Thanks to your ministrations my arm isn't paralysed or anything.' He flexed his wrist, curling and uncurling his fist. 'See! Everything's in working order.'

'I just bet it is,' Celeste inserted, grinning broadly, and Ruth's face burned with colour.

'I still think you ought to think seriously before

risking a relapse,' she insisted, realising there was no point in appealing to the black woman. 'How can you be sure you won't lose control of the bike? This isn't England. I've told you, there are no real roads here, only tracks. What if you hit a boulder?'

'What's going on here?' Professor Jason's impatient tones broke into the proceedings. 'Mr Howard.' He greeted the younger man without enthusiasm. 'So you're up and about again. I'm pleased to see it. No doubt you'll be leaving us now.'

Dominic's expression was wry. 'No doubt,' he agreed politely. 'How are you, sir? I understand from Ruth that you've been unwell yourself.'

Professor Jason met his daughter's anxious eyes. 'Yes,' he said at last. 'Yes, I do suffer a little indigestion from time to time. I'm grateful for your enquiry, but I'm quite well now, thank you.'

'Can I get you some coffee, Daddy?' Ruth asked, moving restlessly from one foot to the other, but her father shook his head.

'No. No, my dear, I just came to find out what was wrong. I was trying to work, but the—er—sound of your voices—'

'I'm sorry, Daddy—' Ruth began awkwardly, but Dominic overrode her apology.

'It was my fault, sir,' he assured the other man quietly. 'I was asking Celeste where I might hire some transport to get about the island, and your daughter was endeavouring to persuade me that it was foolhardy to attempt to ride a motorcycle.'

'I agree with her.' The Professor's mouth tightened. 'You'll be leaving here today or tomorrow, Mr

Howard. Could you not contain your—er—boredom until you get back to Barbados?'

'It's not boredom, sir.' Dominic stood his ground. 'I'm interested to see whether the yacht has surfaced on your coastline. To find out if there's anything worth salvaging.'

Professor Jason frowned. 'Is this a new idea, Mr Howard? Forgive me, but I don't recall your showing any interest earlier.'

Dominic shrugged. 'Had I been fit enough to leave soon after my arrival, I'd have organised a search to be made. As it is, what with the delay and so on, I thought I might take a look for myself.'

Ruth's father digested this in silence, then he shrugged. 'I can't forbid you to do whatever you think fit, Mr Howard, but it seems to me exceedingly reckless to attempt to ride a motor-cycle in your condition.'

Dominic expelled his breath heavily. 'Yes, sir.'

'So what do you intend to do?'

Dominic glanced thoughtfully at Ruth, then he moved his shoulders in an offhand gesture. 'I'll leave with Doctor Francis this afternoon,' he said, unknowingly sending Ruth's spirits plummeting to earth. 'I understand your feelings, Professor, and if any salvage operation is undertaken, I'll ensure that it causes you as little upheaval as possible.' He paused. 'I can't begin to thank you—and your daughter—and Celeste, of course—for what you've done for me, and I wish there was some way I could repay you. If there's anything you want—'

'There's nothing,' said Ruth's father firmly. 'We're glad to have been of service.' He paused. 'As to your boat, I must say I have grave doubts of its being washed up on our shores. It's much more likely to have been carried farther west, if indeed it survived the storm.'

Dominic absorbed this, his expression unreadable. Then, with a faint smile, he inclined his head. 'You're probably right, Professor,' he consented politely, but Ruth, meeting his enigmatic gaze, was less convinced of his sincerity. It seemed to her that her father was taking an unnecessarily pessimistic view of the situation, and that Dominic, for reasons best known to himself, was only choosing to endorse it.

'Good. Good.' Her father was evidently satisfied that he had convinced the other man of the futility of his quest. 'I think I will have some coffee now, Ruth. You can bring it to me in the study.' He paused, glancing significantly at Dominic, before going on: 'I'd like your help with these translations, my dear. I'm afraid you've made a lot of errors. We'll go over them together, shall we?'

Ruth knew she should feel relief at being rescued from a difficult situation, but shamefully, she didn't. In spite of herself, she found her exchanges with Dominic stimulating, and the excitement he generated alerted every nerve in her body. Knowing he was leaving that afternoon was like facing a gaping chasm, with no way round it, and no future in it. It was useless to pretend anything could ever be the same after he had gone. Suddenly she was aware of herself as she had never been before, and his departure would take something from her that could never be regained.

She left Dominic tucking into the plate of eggs Celeste had prepared for him, conscious of his eyes upon her as she made her way out of the door. She wondered what he was really thinking, and whether he believed what her father had told him. Whatever the truth of that situation, she was never likely to know.

Her father chose not to mention his conversation with Dominic. Perhaps he thought he had said enough, or maybe he was reluctant to bring up a subject which was obviously a source of contention. In the event, he concentrated instead on the chapters of Ovid Ruth had translated, showing her, whether he intended to do so or not, how disruptive this upheaval in their lives had been to her work.

Dominic joined them for lunch, but it was not a comfortable meal, with Ruth constantly aware of the antagonism between them, and reluctant to add to it by revealing Dominic's real identity. She had come to the conclusion that there was nothing to be gained by upsetting her father further, and as Dominic did not refer to it, neither did she.

After lunch, the weariness in her father's face was evident, and she suggested that he should rest for a while.

'I'll wake you when Doctor Francis arrives,' she promised, when he protested, and after a moment's consideration he gave in.

'Very well,' he agreed heavily. 'But I shall depend on you not to leave the house while I'm lying down.' His meaning was obvious, and as if to add to it, he went on: 'Perhaps you might like to correct the mistakes we discovered this morning. Your work has certainly suffered from a lack of concentration.'

Ruth nodded. 'All right.' She saw the sardonic slant of Dominic's mouth, but ignored it. 'Now do go and rest, Daddy. Doctor Francis will be here soon.'

Gathering their dirty dishes on to a tray ready for carrying into the kitchen, Ruth was aware she had Dominic's attention once more. He was still sitting at the table, observing her ministrations, making no effort to go and gather together the few belongings Joseph had supplied for him.

'So it's goodbye,' he remarked at last, toying with an unused piece of cutlery. 'I guess you won't be sorry to see me go.'

Ruth clattered a spoon on to the tray. 'I'm glad you're well enough to leave,' she murmured, her eyes downcast, and he made a sound of impatience.

'That's not what I meant, and you know it,' he said harshly. 'I just wish—' He broke off abruptly, tossing the fork he had been torturing aside. Then he pushed back his chair and got to his feet, his rubber-soled shoes blocking her path to the door. 'Ruth, you can't waste the rest of your youth playing nursemaid to that old man!'

Ruth stiffened, drawing back from him. 'That old man, as you call him, is my father,' she declared frigidly.

'I know that.' Dominic sighed. 'I have a father, too. And a mother, as it happens. But Jake and I, we don't always see eye to eye, and he knows it.'

'Jake?'

'My father, James Crown. You remember?'

'You call him by his Christian name?' Ruth was appalled.

'On occasion,' said Dominic irritably. 'It's what everybody calls him. I guess he likes it that way.'

'But don't you call him—Daddy?'

Dominic grimaced. 'Dad—sometimes,' he conceded dryly. 'But that's not important. We're getting away from the point of what I'm trying to say, and that is—parents don't *own* their children. They expect loyalty, of course, and respect, if they deserve it, but not blind, unthinking obedience!'

Ruth was shocked. 'I care for my father, Mr Howard—or Mr Crown—whatever your name is.' She took a deep breath. 'I don't consider my life wasted. I love my father. I'd do anything for him.'

'I know that.' Dominic shook his head. 'All I'm saying is, you can love someone without sacrificing yourself in the process.' He sighed. 'I'm not doing this very well, I know, but have you ever asked yourself who benefits most from your living here? How unselfish is he, depriving you of a normal adolescence?'

'I don't want to talk about this any more,' declared Ruth tautly, picking up the tray and holding it between them like a shield. 'Now, if you'll excuse me—'

Dominic hesitated, but eventually he stepped aside, watching her go, his hands pushed deep into the hip pockets of his jeans. Ruth brushed past him angrily, resentful of his ability to use words to confuse her. Obviously her father was right to mistrust him. He had few scruples, and absolutely no reverence for his parents—*so why did she still feel drawn to him, in a way that she instinctively knew could bring her nothing but pain . . .*

The afternoon wore on, but when Celeste came to find her with a jug of deliciously iced lime juice, Doctor Francis had still not made an appearance.

'What time is it, Celeste?' Ruth asked, eagerly gulping down the fruit juice before wiping her mouth on the back of her hand. 'Gosh, that was good! It's so hot in here!'

Celeste looked round the stuffy little room with distaste. 'What for you working on Mr Howard's last afternoon?' she demanded, with a scornful gesture. 'He leaving soon. Can't you at least *talk* nicely to him?'

Ruth sighed. 'I asked what time it was, Celeste. Is there no sign of Doctor Francis? He's usually here by now, isn't he?'

'It near five o'clock,' declared Celeste sulkily. 'And ain't no sign of that there doctor. Seems like he ain't coming today. Your daddy ain't going to like that.'

Ruth's pulses unaccountably quickened. 'Five o'clock?' she echoed, licking the lime juice from her upper lip. 'Is Daddy still resting?'

'Yes'm.' Celeste moved towards the door, the heated scent of her body musky in the afternoon air. 'You coming out now? Or is you going to hide in here for the rest of the day?'

'I'm not hiding,' protested Ruth indignantly. Then, aware of Celeste's scepticism, she said: 'All right. Where is Mr Howard? I'll ask him if he'd like some tea.'

'Mr Howard, he drinking a cool beer,' asserted Celeste with confidence. 'Sitting on that verandah, where he been all afternoon.'

Ruth acknowledged this with a nod of her head, and after Celeste had made a reluctant departure, she left her cubbyhole and emerged into the living room. It was cooler in the larger room, and cooler still in the hall, with the breeze drifting through the open doorway. She could see Dominic at once, seated in one of the basketweave chairs, his feet propped on the verandah rail, an empty can of lager hanging loosely from his fingers.

'Hello,' she greeted him, stepping out of the shadows, and with a lithe, easy movement he swung his legs to the floor and got to his feet.

'Hi,' he responded civilly. 'Finished studying?'

'For the present,' she conceded, walking to the rail and resting her palms upon it. 'It's been a beautiful afternoon, hasn't it?'

'Has it?'

He was not making it easy for her, and she glanced at him over her shoulder. 'Doctor Francis didn't come.'

'Apparently not.'

'I wonder why?'

'I guess he didn't realise it was that urgent,' he remarked brusquely. 'It looks as if you're stuck with me until tomorrow.'

Ruth half turned. 'I—we don't mind,' she murmured, but it was evident from his expression that he didn't believe her.

Ruth turned to look back at the ocean. She was guiltily aware that her father had not minced his words earlier, and it could not be pleasant being confined in a place where one felt one was not wanted. But her father was old—and sick—she excused him quickly, unwilling to indulge in any criticism of her parent, even if his reception of their visitor had been less than enthusiastic.

'So,' she persisted now, trying to act casually, 'what have you been doing all afternoon?'

'Well, not looking for the remains of my boat,' Dominic assured her dryly. 'I went for a walk, actually, but not too far. You should have come with me. I found a pelican's nest.'

'Did you?' Ruth turned eagerly to face him, resting her slim thighs against the wooden balustrade. 'Where was it? Along the beach? I know there's a colony there. You should see them diving for fish.' She laughed, forgetting for the moment to whom she was talking. 'They swoop down like meteors!' She made a swooping motion of her hand. 'They practically submerge themselves in the water.'

'I know.' Dominic's tawny eyes narrowed as they rested on the animated curve of her face, and she was momentarily hypnotised by his intent gaze. Then he looked abruptly away, moving his shoulders in a dismissing gesture and saying briefly: 'I spent some time in Florida last year. They're common enough there.'

She sensed his withdrawal, and was hurt by it. Somehow it was always like this between them, she thought, wishing she was more experienced, more *sophisticated*. Here she was, telling him things he could probably tell her, and more comprehensively. The trouble was, although she was well educated, she was not experienced, and she hadn't anything to say that was new or original.

As if aware of her confusion, he left her then, excusing himself to go into the house. She guessed he was going to seek the solitude of his room, and left, staring at an empty chair, Ruth felt an overwhelming sense of inadequacy suddenly. Compared to his, her life did seem pointless, somehow, and with insight she realised why her father objected so strongly to their association. He was afraid Dominic might influence her, and while she might argue against this, undeniably, he had.

Father Andreas arrived in the early evening, and with some relief Ruth invited him to stay for supper.

'Doctor Francis was supposed to come this afternoon,' she confided to the elderly priest, as they waited for her father to join them. 'But he didn't arrive, and I know Daddy would welcome your company.'

Father Andreas looked less convinced of this, but Professor Jason's attitude when he came to greet the priest was more enthusiastic than usual, and he was disarmed.

'Of course, stay to supper,' he urged, when he heard of Ruth's invitation. 'I'm sure our guest will be glad of alternative companionship, and it's some time since we shared a bottle of wine.'

Father Andreas smiled. 'As you say, Professor,' he affirmed, with quiet acceptance, and Ruth was relieved that the uneasy threesome of lunch was not to be repeated.

Dominic joined them soon after, and over dinner, he and Father Andreas discussed the Greek's homeland. It appeared that Dominic knew Salonika quite well, and he was willing to answer the priest's questions, and reassure him that the city had been completely restored to its former glory.

'So many Byzantine churches,' exclaimed Father Andreas, spreading his hands. 'So much beauty, so much devastation. The history of Salonika is the history of the world.'

'The city is called Thessaloniki now,' Dominic remarked ruefully, but Father Andreas was not to be moved.

'Salonika it will always be for me,' he declared staunchly, and Professor Jason scoffed a little.

'You don't move with the times, Andreas,' he commented provokingly. 'Like your religion, you're steeped in myths and legends: past victories, past glories; when are you going to accept that this is the twentieth century?'

Father Andreas was not offended. 'Perhaps I am a little old-fashioned,' he acknowledged, with a shrug of his thin shoulders. 'But so are you, or you would not be living here, allowing your undoubted talents as a teacher to go to waste.'

Professor Jason frowned, not caring for this turn of the conversation. 'Mine was a question of priorities,' he declared crisply. 'Not an inability to cope with a world gone mad!'

Father Andreas moved his head thoughtfully from side to side. 'Yes, yes,' he said, 'I suppose the world did go a little mad in 1940. But my faith did not falter.'

'Your faith!' Professor Jason shook his head. 'How can you believe in all that mumbo-jumbo!'

'Daddy!'

Ruth's protest was instinctive, but Father Andreas only smiled. 'Your father and I have had this argument many times, my child,' he told her gently. 'Unfortunately, he will only see what his eyes tell him is true. He does not allow the belief that man is not the all-powerful being he thinks he is. Yet without that belief man is only half alive.'

'Another half truth, Andreas?' enquired the Professor scornfully. 'A man of intelligence can distinguish between fact and fiction, can bring a scientific mind to bear. We all know where we came from—'

'—but it is where we are going that interests me,' retorted Father Andreas triumphantly, and Ruth, recognising the start of yet another theological debate, started to clear the table.

The kitchen was empty when Ruth carried in the tray, and she was unloading the dirty dishes into the sink when she heard footsteps behind her. Glancing round, she found Dominic depositing two tureens on the table, and she forced a nervous smile when his eyes encountered hers.

'Daddy's lecturing on his favourite subject,' she explained, half apologetically. 'He and Father Andreas always get around to religion sooner or later.'

Dominic straightened, pushing his hands into the low waistband of his jeans. With his shirt unbuttoned at the collar to expose the brown column of his throat, his smooth silver-fair hair brushing the neckband at his nape, he emanated the kind of sexual attraction Ruth had hitherto never encountered, but that didn't prevent her from responding to it. On the contrary, she had never been more aware of him than she was tonight, and just watching him brought a disturbing unsteadiness to her knees.

'Where's Celeste?' Dominic asked now, keeping his opinion of her father to himself, and Ruth shrugged.

'I don't know,' she admitted, leaving the dishes to soak and drying her hands. 'Is there something you want? Perhaps I can get it for you.'

'I don't think so.' Dominic looked thoughtfully round the kitchen, and as he did so they heard a squeal of excitement from outside. It was unmistakably Celeste, and Ruth beat Dominic to the door by only a hair's breadth. He came up hard behind her as she halted uncertainly on the threshold, and she didn't know which disturbed her most, the sight of Celeste, her skirts high above her knees on the back of her cousin's motor-cycle, or the compelling pressure of Dominic's muscled frame behind her.

It was obvious that the black man in charge of the motor-cycle had coasted the last few yards. There had been no sound, and a motor-cycle's engine would have carried to the house. Clearly, Celeste had taken no notice of her employer's dictates, and she scrambled off now, giggling as she exposed more of her plump thighs.

'There, you see,' she said, speaking to Dominic, as he put Ruth firmly aside and went to join them. 'Didn't I tell you my cousin'd do anything for me?'

Harold, for that was who it must be, Ruth guessed, grinned, showing broad white teeth. 'If'n you want to borrow this m'chine, Mr Howard, sir, you're mighty welcome.'

Dominic cast a speculative glance back at Ruth, and then inclined his head. 'Two-fifty,' he remarked. 'It's a powerful little motor. It must be ten years since I rode one of these.'

'You're not going to ride it—are you?' Ruth spoke urgently at first, and then tempered her protest with a question. 'I mean, it's dark. Wh-where could you go now?'

Dominic grimaced. 'I don't know. You tell me.' He turned back to Harold, who was getting off the machine. 'Has it got fuel?'

'Gas? Yes, sir. I filled it up m'self.'

'Good.'

Dominic hesitated only a moment before taking the bike from him and swinging his leg across the saddle. Then, straddling the machine, he tested it for weight and control. It was light, and manoeuvrable, and he gave the three of them a whimsical look.

'Okay,' he said, wheeling it round in a semi-circle. 'I'll give it a go. Anyone want to come with me?'

Celeste looked at Ruth, her dark eyes slightly malicious. 'You want to go, honey?' she enquired in a silky voice. 'Or you going to let Celeste ride pillion?'

Ruth's mouth felt dry. 'My father—Father Andreas—' she began, but Celeste only scoffed.

'What they doing?' she demanded. 'Arguing, as usual? Hell, ain't no one going to miss you for half an hour. Leave it to Celeste.'

'Perhaps you ought to stay here.' Dominic remarked now, flatly. 'As you say, we wouldn't want to upset your father, would we?'

Ruth's fists clenched at her sides. 'I—I've never ridden a motor-cycle before,' she exclaimed, in her own defence, and Celeste snorted.

'Ain't but only one way to learn, Missy,' she taunted. linking her arm with Harold's. 'Ain't that so?'

'Are you coming or aren't you?'

Dominic was getting impatient, and Ruth shifted uneasily. She didn't want him to go, but if he insisted on disobeying her father's instructions, she could not prevent him. But to go with him—that was something else, something she knew without a shadow of a doubt her father would forbid.

And yet she wanted to go. Where was the harm? she asked herself. As Celeste said, her father need never know. No matter how culpable that made her feel. this was her last chance of being alone with Dominic.

'All right,' she conceded, rather breathlessly, and stepped forward uncertainly, not quite knowing how to proceed.

'Climb up behind me,' Dominic directed, supporting the bike with a foot on the ground at either side. 'Now, swing your leg across—that's right. And hold on to me.'

Ruth endeavoured without much success to keep her skirt at a respectable length, conscious all the while of Dominic's lean form in front of her, timid to hold on to him as he had suggested.

'You want to follow the track down to the harbour.' said Celeste's cousin now, coming forward.

'If'n you want, you can freewheel all the way down to the harbour, then start your engine when ain't no fear of being overheard.'

'Good idea,' Dominic remarked laconically, but Ruth could not see his face. 'Then where would you suggest? You'd better give me some directions.'

'There a track over by Guarder Rock,' Celeste told him, frowning. Then she looked at Ruth. 'You know the way, Missy. You can show him.'

Ruth nodded, rather jerkily. 'We—we won't be long. If Daddy misses me—'

'—I'll tell him you're taking a bath,' declared Celeste, shortly. 'Have a good time. It's the only way.'

Ruth wondered, and as Dominic pushed the bike towards the rise leading down to the village, she half wished she had stuck to what she knew was right. This was totally against her nature, behaving in this clandestine way, and she wondered what Dominic was thinking as the momentum sent them rolling, ever more quickly, down the uneven slope.

Her own thoughts were soon taken up with the need to keep her seat. With the wind rushing through her hair, streaming out behind her like an ebony banner, and the speed of the bike increasing every second, she was compelled to put her arms around Dominic's waist and cling to him for dear life. She had no experience in such matters, no understanding of balance or the centrifugal force that would keep her on the machine. She only knew a moment's blind panic, when she felt sure she was about to be lifted bodily from the smooth leather, before she gave in to the desire to hold on tight, so that she might enjoy this exhilarating feeling of speed.

Dominic slowed the bike at the foot of the hill, turning to look at her in the pale illumination cast by the moon. 'You all right?' he asked, and she was forced to release him to allow his free movement, nodding wordlessly in answer to his query.

With a shrug, he turned back again, starting the engine, and this time the powerful throb of the motor added to the sense of elation she was feeling. They followed the track that wound up from the harbour, and round the shoulder of the headland. Despite her fears, the way was quite smooth, ironed out by years of use. With the moon's light and the powerful beam of the headlight, there was no danger of losing their way, and Ruth determinedly forgot her anxieties and began to enjoy herself. She had never done anything like this before, never travelled so fast, or so excitingly, never disobeyed her father quite so deliberately.

CHAPTER NINE

Below them, the curve of the bay followed their progress, moon-gilded and romantic in its secretive shadow. It was a time of the evening that Ruth had never enjoyed before, and she realised in passing how much she had still to learn.

Dominic brought the motor-cycle to a halt on a grassy knoll overlooking a deserted stretch of sand. A tussocky slope gave on to palm-strewn dunes, and beyond, the surging waters of the Caribbean drifted in continual motion. The line of foam that marked the ocean's passage was silver-tongued and melodious, and the murmur of its intrusion softly played along the shore. On either side of this sheltered inlet, rocky bastions jutted for almost half a mile, and Dominic kicked down the metal strut that supported the bike and dismounted with lazy precision.

'Is that the Guarder Rock Celeste was talking about?' he enquired, and Ruth pushed her skirt over her knees, remaining where she was.

'It's Garde du Roc, actually,' she said, correcting him. 'And yes, this is the bay.'

'And where are the Serpent's Teeth from here?'

Ruth swallowed hard. 'Not far. Perhaps a mile.'

'Is that right?' He came to the bike to stand with his hands on the petrol tank, supporting himself. 'How about taking a look?'

Ruth licked her dry lips. 'We've been gone about fifteen minutes already.'

Dominic's mouth hardened. 'You want to go back?' he asked flatly and she shifted uncomfortably. 'Sh—shouldn't we?'

He shrugged, and then nodded rather resignedly. 'I guess so.'

Ruth bit her lip. 'We could go down to the beach for a few minutes, if you want to,' she offered.

'Why?' He was very direct.

'To—to stretch our legs,' she ventured. 'It's such a lovely night.'

'You noticed!' he remarked, making no attempt to hide his sarcasm.

'Of course I noticed,' exclaimed Ruth indignantly, trying to wriggle her leg over the bike without exposing herself as Celeste had done. It was not a successful attempt, but she faced Dominic bravely as he watched her futile efforts, finally giving up the struggle for modesty, and allowing him a glimpse of a slim brown thigh. 'Well, shall we do that?' she demanded, standing beside him, tall and slender as a reed in her faded skirt and cotton shirt, and with an indifferent gesture he complied.

She left her sandals on the seat of the bike, preferring to walk barefooted on the sand. It was cool beneath her feet, sliding between her toes, slightly abrasive where particles of coral had been ground to a fine powder. It was threaded with shells of every shape and size, their colours muted in the moonlight, a necklace of sea-pearls lacing the shore.

Dominic walked beside her, his hands thrust deep into the pockets of his slacks, saying nothing; yet she was aware of him with every fibre of her being. She wished she could say something—*anything*—to break this impasse, but no matter how she tried to compose her words, they all sounded silly and child-ish inside her head.

She glanced sideways at him, pressing her lips together in helpless frustration. What would Celeste do in circumstances like this? she wondered, and then coloured hotly at the inevitable answer. One thing was certain, she would not be tongue-tied and nervous. Celeste knew what she wanted, and went out and got it. The trouble was, Ruth didn't honestly know what she wanted. She only knew her time with Dominic was slipping away, and he seemed hardly aware of her.

With extreme daring, she put out her hand and touched his arm then, drawing his eyes to her. His skin felt cool and firm to her touch, the muscles hardening to resist her grasp, but she slid her fingers round his sleeve, linking her arm with his.

Dominic halted, removing her fingers with elo-quent firmness, his brows drawing together above the mild impatience of his features.

'Don't do that, Ruth,' he said, his tone cool and offhand. 'If you want to go back, just say so. I didn't ask you to come down here.'

'I don't want to go back!' Ruth protested reck-lessly, meeting the narrowing darkness of his eyes. 'I just wanted you to remember I'm here, that's all. I might as well be invisible for all the notice you take of me.'

There was a strained silence after this outburst. Ruth was appalled at her own audacity, and she guessed Dominic was as embarrassed by it as she was. She didn't know what had come over her, and she turned away abruptly, feeling ready to die of shame.

'You're wrong,' Dominic said at last, but she had the feeling the words were being dragged from him. 'Of course I'm aware of you, Ruth, although I doubt you know what that really means.' He paused. 'I told you once before—you're a beautiful girl. I couldn't help being aware of you, even if I wanted to. So stop feeling so sorry for yourself and let's go back.'

Ruth turned slowly, her hair swinging silkily almost to her waist. 'You really think I'm beautiful?' she echoed disbelievingly. 'But that day on the beach, you seemed angry when you told me so.'

Dominic pushed back his hair with a restless hand. 'I wasn't angry—at least, not with you. With myself, maybe.'

'Why?' She was puzzled.

'Ruth, let's go back,' he said flatly. 'This kind of conversation is going to get us nowhere.'

'Then why are you getting angry again?'

'I'm not getting angry.'

'You are.' She frowned. 'I can tell. I know—'

'You know me so well, is that it?' he demanded harshly. 'Come on, Ruth—'

'Don't be angry,' she begged. 'You're going away tomorrow. Can't we at least remain friends?'

'We are friends,' he assured her grimly. 'Good lord, you saved my life. And if there was something I could do for you, some way I could repay you, I would. But your situation here—well, it precludes any help I might wish to give you.'

'Help?' She looked faintly apprehensive.

'Yes, help.' He sighed. 'The chance to offer you something you obviously couldn't afford.'

'You mean you want to *buy* me something?' she exclaimed disbelievingly, and Dominic made a sound of impatience.

'You're taking me very literally.'

'What, then?'

He hesitated. 'An education, maybe,' he suggested. 'A university education. If your father would only let you come to England—'

Ruth drew back from him. 'I am educated,' she declared tremulously. 'I may seem inexperienced to you, but I'm not ignorant!'

'I never said you were,' he amended mildly. 'Don't you see? If you went to university—'

'I see that you seem determined to define me as a student!' she retorted stiffly, twisting her hands together. 'You're just like my father. You won't see me as anything more than a child!'

'I am *not* like your father!' he countered, with some heat. 'I don't think like your father, I don't act like your father, and God knows, I don't *feel* like your father!' He took her by the shoulders then, when she persisted in avoiding his gaze, his thumb bruising her throat, forcing her to lift her chin. 'Be sensible, Ruth,' he snapped, 'and don't invite difficulties. Believe me, I can be nothing but trouble to you.'

'Trouble?' Ruth frowned then, her blue eyes wide and uncomprehending between the dark silky lashes. 'I don't know what you mean.'

'I think you do,' he informed her brusquely, and

she was intrigued by the sudden harshness of his mouth, and the erratic beating of a pulse just below his jawline. His lips were slightly parted, and the wine-scented odour of his breath came to her in uneven waves of sweetness, mingling with hers in a curiously disturbing coalescence. It was an intangible merging, a pervasive intrusion, that left her feeling weak and strangely vulnerable.

Yet she did nothing to break that aggressive contact, that tenuous embrace that Dominic was sustaining almost against his will it seemed. Even when his hands moved with controlled impatience against the thin cotton of her shirt, and strong fingers moulded the bones beneath the material, before tightening with painful intensity, she remained motionless as his breathing quickened to a laboured oscillation. Then holding her startled eyes with his, he jerked her towards him and bent his head to hers.

It was not like that other occasion when he had played with her lips, without any real satisfaction. This time, the hungry pressure of his mouth on hers was an unexpected assault, and the tongue that forced her lips apart was a moist and sensual invader. Every bone in her body seemed to melt beneath that passionate possession; she sagged heavily against him, depending on his support.

His hands slid round her waist, drawing her against him, and she could feel the hardening muscles of his thighs surging against her. She knew, instinctively, what that meant, but any resistance she might have offered was being negated by the searching pressure of his mouth against her neck. His hands threaded through her hair, drawing it across his lips, crushing it within his fist, caressing it and stroking it, until Ruth felt it almost had a life of its own.

But when his hands slid upwards, over her waist and the taut skin that covered her rib cage, to the swelling fullness of her breasts, a cry of protest broke from her. Allowing him to kiss her might be wrong, letting him press his aroused body close to hers might be wrong, but they were things she could excuse. This was not. Somehow, she didn't know when, he had released her shirt from the waistband of her skirt, and those long brown fingers she had watched combing his hair, and massaging his arm, and eating his food, were now curving around her naked breast, beneath the concealing covering of her shirt. What was more, they were caressing her, kneading her firm softness, plucking at the roseate peak that surged against her shirt in shameless vanity.

'Please—you mustn't,' she begged, trying to push his hand away, but Dominic's eyes were dark and unyielding.

'Why mustn't I?' he demanded, in a shaken voice. 'Why mustn't I touch you? You know you want me to. Unbutton your shirt, and let me see.'

'No!' Ruth's tongue circled her lips in innocent provocation. 'Dominic, we have to go back. It's getting late. Please—you must listen to me!'

'I'm listening,' he said, but as he did so, he slid the offending shirt off one shoulder, exposing the creamy skin to his urgent gaze. With his tongue, he traced the tender outline of the bones beneath her skin, then beat a searing path up the side of her neck, to bite the shell-like lobe that framed her ear. By the time he had explored the hollows beneath her ear,

Ruth felt as if she was on fire, and she turned her face eagerly towards him, seeking the sensuous pleasure of his mouth.

She realised that her shirt was unbuttoned, and the body hair that formed a fine mat on his chest was abrasive against her breasts. Yet it was not an unpleasant abrasiveness, and for the first time, her hands went involuntarily to him, seeking to feel the texture of his skin. He had unfastened his shirt to the waist, and her fingers slid beneath its softness, spreading against the smooth tautness of his back. She felt the tension in him, the coiled spring of emotion that was rapidly getting out of control, and knew a curious satisfaction that she was the cause of it.

'Ruth,' he groaned, against her mouth, 'I want you. I want to make love to you. Are you going to stop me?'

Ruth quivered, her whole being aroused to such a pitch that his words were hardly comprehensible. 'You—you are making love to me,' she breathed, and he made a strangled sound, deep within his throat.

'No, I'm not,' he said, swinging her off her feet suddenly and into his arms. He looked down at her passionately, then bent to rub his lips against hers. 'I want to,' he added, his breath filling her mouth. 'I want to be a part of you. However, I've no intention of seducing a virgin. That can be far too hazardous!'

Ruth looked up at him, her lips parted, the delicate curve of her body outlined within his grasp. 'Dominic?' she pleaded, half confused even now, and his eyes closed against the unconscious appeal of her.

'Home,' he articulated at last, through clenched teeth, setting off across the sand. 'Back to sanity. Back to your father.'

Ruth struggled in his grasp. 'Put me down,' she protested. 'I—I'm too heavy. Your arm—'

'My arm can make it,' he retorted dryly, his features taut, and then swore angrily when he stumbled over an exposed root. The impetus of his momentary loss of balance was too much for him, accentuated as it was by her weight in his arms, and they pitched together on to the sand, collapsing in an ungainly heap. 'Hell, I'm sorry,' Dominic exclaimed, as constricted sounds escaped Ruth's lips, but his contrition turned to anger when he found she was not crying, as he had at first thought, but laughing.

'I could have broken your neck,' he exhorted her harshly, leaning over her as she lay prostrate on the soft dunes. 'My God, that would really have been something to tell your father, wouldn't it?' His hand brushed back the dark hair from her forehead. 'He'd never have forgiven me for that either.'

Ruth captured his hand, drawing it with intuitive sensuality to her mouth. 'I'm sorry,' she whispered. 'But you were so certain that you could make it.'

Dominic's eyes dropped the length of her, lying relaxed beside him, and they darkened imperceptibly. 'Oh, I could make it,' he averred, unable to prevent himself from seeking the pointed thrust of one rounded breast, seizing it between his lips, his tongue coaxing it to wild abandon. 'You were made for a man's delectation, but not mine—*not* mine.'

Ruth's body seemed to have a mind of its own, shifting beneath him, arching towards the thrusting hardness of his with all the instinctive eagerness of untried youth. Her hands found his nape, gathering handfuls of his hair to pull his mouth back to hers, parting her lips and letting her tongue entwine with his as he had taught her to do.

Dominic was not proof against such unknowing sensuality. She sensed his arousal in the uneven pounding of his heart, thudding against hers, in the slight tremor of his limbs as he hovered above her, in the hungry desperation of his gaze as he strove to keep his head. His brain was telling him one thing, but his eyes told another story, and the lissom form that strained towards him demanded his possession.

With hands that were not quite steady, he un-fastened the button on her skirt, then bent his head to trail a path of kisses across her midriff and down to her navel. There was innate gentleness in his touch, and she was hardly aware of what he was doing until she felt the coolness of the night air against her heated flesh, and his hand probing the inner softness of her thigh.

'Oh, Dominic . . .' she breathed, as he eased her legs apart, and his mouth silenced any protest she might have tried to make.

With growing urgency he removed the rest of his clothes, releasing the pulsating evidence of his man-hood. Poised above her, he knew a moment's agony before he sought their consummation, but it was too late then for him to draw back. He wanted her, he was astounded at how badly, and with a groan of submission, he gave in to his body's demands.

Ruth, despite her arousal, was not prepared for that ultimate invasion. When he lowered himself upon her, she panicked, and her fists battered against his chest in blind terror.

'No—no, you mustn't!' she breathed, turning her head this way and that, but Dominic captured her quivering chin between his fingers.

'I must,' he told her huskily, his lips calming the words of protest that spilled from her tongue, and the momentary shock of his entry was softened by his warm mouth.

The pain, and there was pain to begin with, brought the tears to Ruth's eyes, but Dominic's tongue captured them and soothed her childish fears. 'Relax,' he said, caressing her fluttering lashes, and cautiously, incredulously, she let herself acknowledge the intimacy they were sharing. Celeste had not been lying, she thought disbelievingly. All her stories had been true, and it was not the furtive, sordid thing she had foolishly imagined. It was a wonderful feeling of belonging and sharing, of being completely whole for the first time in her life, and she wanted the moment to last.

When Dominic started to move inside her, she was half inclined to protest. She didn't want him to move, she didn't want him to leave her, she wanted to prolong these minutes of intimacy that they might never share again. Yet almost immediately she sensed that he was not drawing away from her. His movements compelled a response that sent the blood like liquid fire through her veins. He was exciting her, and as he did so, an enveloping warmth began to surge through her, searing her in its heat and enfolding her in a wave of fiery emotion that made her want to move with him, to arch herself against him, and promote a closer fulfilment yet. A kind of wildness gripped her, and the low moan of pleasure that reached her ears came from her own throat. Unable to think of anything but him, she wound her arms around his neck, raking his back with her nails, twisting and turning beneath him, urging him on and on until a frenzied explosion burst within her. She glimpsed Dominic's sweat-streaked features in the moment before he buried his face in her hair, and then a delicious languor spread to every nerve and sinew, replacing the frantic emotions of minutes before. She felt her balled fists uncoiling in the sensuous aftermath of feeling, and it was at that moment she realised exactly what she had done.

Nothing could protect her from the sense of chill that swept over her then. With an objectivity she had not known herself capable of, she saw herself as her father might see her, and was appalled. Wanton; shameless; abandoned; she was all of those things and more, she thought sickeningly, and yet nothing could deny she had wanted Dominic's love, and the passionate assuagement of his possession.

Dominic's body was a heavy weight upon her, and wriggling urgently, she endeavoured to free herself from him. It wasn't easy. He didn't want to let her go, and he protested lazily when she tried to thrust him away from her.

With a feeling of panic, Ruth eventually had to voice her frustration, and her plea at last had some effect.

'Please,' she begged, 'let me go. I—we—I have to get back. Daddy will be desperate to know where we are.'

Her words seemed to achieve her objective, because after a moment's hesitation Dominic rolled away from her, spreading his hands in a gesture that implied she was free to do as she liked, but making no attempt to join her.

Ruth scrambled to her feet, avoiding looking at his unashamed nakedness. But all the while she struggled into her clothes, she was aware of his lean, muscular form stretched on the sand beside her, and knew a feeling almost of incredulity that only seconds before they had shared a closeness she had innocently assumed could only be found in marriage. And yet even that wasn't entirely true. She had not believed two people could share such sensations, and for a fleeting moment she recalled the way he had made her feel in nerve-tingling detail. She had not known such feelings existed; but she also perceived with sudden insight that maybe only Dominic could make her feel that way.

She turned to look at him then, meeting his lazy gaze with troubled eyes. If it were true that only Dominic could give her such pleasure, might it not then follow that only she could please him?

Licking her lips, she sought for words. 'Dominic—'

But before she could say any more, he sprang abruptly to his feet and began to pull on his jeans. He presented his back to her as he zipped himself into the close-fitting pants, and then bent to pick up his shirt before turning to look at her.

'I know,' he said heavily at last, buttoning the shirt with impatient fingers. 'We have to get back. I guess we've only been away a little over an hour. Maybe

Celeste has managed to stall your father.'

'Stall?' Ruth was confused, but Dominic only shook his head.

'Come on,' he said, shoving his feet into canvas shoes, and brushing the sleeve of his shirt down over his bandaged arm. 'Can you manage? I'll go and start the motor.'

'No—that is—wait!' Ruth caught his sleeve, and then dropped her eyes before the penetration of his. She sighed. 'Dominic, I—I just wanted you to know, it—it was good.'

Dominic's eyes narrowed. 'Ruth,' he muttered, half angrily, 'I don't think we should discuss this.'

She looked up then. 'Why not?'

'Why not?' he echoed, taking a deep breath. 'Why not?' He shook his head. 'Well, how about because it should never have happened?'

Ruth hesitated. 'But it did.'

His long fingers raked the hair at the nape of his neck. 'Goddammit, I know that.'

'Dominic, I just wanted to tell you that it meant a lot to me—'

'Ruth!' He spoke in a driven tone, obviously disturbed by her innocent attempt at reassurance. 'Ruth, it happened. It was good. But it's over! And the sooner we both forget it, the better.'

'Forget it!' Ruth was astounded now. 'Forget it? Dominic, how can you say that? It—it was the most wonderful thing that ever happened in my life—and you tell me to forget it?'

Dominic scuffed his toe in the sand. 'Ruth, oh, Ruth, what can I say to you? You were an innocent, and I took advantage of you. Some gratitude for

saving my life, wasn't it?' His tone was bitter. 'I'd
have served you better dead!'

'No!' Ruth was appalled. 'No, that's not true—'

'It is true,' he muttered savagely. 'You don't seem
to understand, Ruth. What happened—I never intended to happen. I knew it could. I knew there was
always the danger, particularly when you showed me
that day on the beach exactly how responsive you
were. But I hoped I'd have more will power, more
sense! Instead of which, I let my senses rule my head,
and lost my mind completely.'

'But you wanted to make love to me. You said so.'

'I know I did. And it's true. You've been a constant temptation. Even now—' His eyes darkened.
'Ruth, let's stop this. Go back to the bike. I have to
think.'

She was puzzled. 'But, Dominic, why can't we talk
about it? I mean—we have to talk about it, don't we?
It—it happened.' She paused. 'It was meant to happen.'

Dominic stared at her, then he shook his head. 'I
doubt that,' he said heavily at last. 'I doubt that very
much.'

Ruth licked her lips. 'You mean, you wish it
hadn't?'

He sighed. 'Yes—and no.' He shifted restlessly.
'Ruth, you must know how I feel. Try and understand. I don't want to hurt you, but—'

'Hurt me?' Somehow, she managed to hide the
sense of shock his words were generating. She had
known that what they had done was wrong. In that
first aftermath, she had tasted the bitter flavour of
her own betrayal. Yet, even then, she had fought

back the painful suspicion that all was lost. In reliving those moments, she had justified them, temporarily at least; but now Dominic's words were reviving the frightening awareness of her own vulnerability.

'Ruth, if there was some way I could show you—'

'Don't bother.' Her response was choked now, broken, strangled by the effort to control her feelings, but when he would have touched her she drew stiffly away.

'I'm not so immature,' she continued, and the longer she spoke, the stronger her tone grew. 'Don't imagine I expect you to—to marry me or anything. I don't. In fact, I have no desire to marry anyone.'

'Ruth—'

His use of her name was a groan, but she ignored him, continuing doggedly: 'As a matter of fact, I should be grateful to you. Until—' her voice shook, 'until tonight, I was naïve. I know that. Celeste— Celeste is always telling me so—'

'*Celeste!*' Dominic repeated the black woman's name with a savage intonation, but again Ruth would not be deterred.

'She—she said I should learn one day, and I have—' she continued, but this time Dominic would not let her go on.

'Stop it!' he muttered, grasping her arms, resisting her frantic struggles and thrusting his face close to hers. 'You're not like Celeste!' he snapped. 'Don't ever imagine you are.' He expelled his breath frustratedly. 'Ruth, you're a brave and beautiful young woman. Any man would be proud to ask you to be his wife. Unfortunately,' and now his face twisted in an ugly grimace, 'unfortunately, I do not have the right to claim that privilege. You see, I'm already committed to marrying someone else!'

CHAPTER TEN

Dominic awakened with a pounding head and a sour taste in his mouth. It was difficult to focus on the face of the clock on his bedside table, but gradually the hands swam into view, and he groaned at the awareness of how late it was. He could already hear his father's scathing admonitions ringing in his ears, as he rolled on to his back, and he closed his eyes again against the shaft of sunlight filtering through the blinds.

It was no use lying here, however, he thought wearily, pushing back the bedcovers and swinging his long legs to the floor. But the pounding in his head increased as he endeavoured to stand up, and he dragged himself dispiritedly to the end of the bed, to gaze, red-eyed, at his haggard reflection.

He looked a mess, he thought disgustedly, noting the lines of sleeplessness above his cheekbones. His face looked gaunt, and with a night's growth of stubble on his chin, he had a distinctly debauched appearance. Evidence of the amount of alcohol he was consuming lately, he decided grimly, and reaching for the wine silk dressing gown tossed carelessly over the bedrail, he groped to put it on.

The sudden tapping at his door brought his head up, and guessing it to be his mother he called: 'Come in.' But the face that appeared tentatively in the

aperture was Ginny, his mother's secretary, and as
he struggled to cover his nakedness, she giggled a
little behind her hand. She was a plump, pretty girl,
in her early twenties, a little immature, Dominic
surmised, but his mother seemed to like her. She
made no secret of her attraction to her employer's
son, and Dominic suspected she would not be averse
to a more intimate relationship. But he had no interest in her, though her attempts to draw his attention
amused him.

'Good morning, Mr Dominic,' she said now, after
he had secured the cord of his robe. 'Mrs Crown
asked me to tell you she would like to speak to you
before you leave for the office.'

'Oh, would she?' Dominic inclined his head,
guessing his mother would not expect Ginny to come
to his room. But Ginny, as usual, chose to be provocative, and she lingered now, even though she had
delivered her message.

'It's after eleven,' she volunteered, as if the time
had some bearing on her errand. 'You're late again,
Mr Dominic. Would you like me to fetch you some
breakfast?'

'No, thank you.' Dominic was polite but firm. 'I'll
have some coffee with my mother. I'm not hungry.'

'You really should eat something,' Ginny persisted, lingering in the doorway. 'I read somewhere
that breakfast is the most important meal of the day.
Puts a lining on your stomach, it does. Are you sure
you wouldn't like some toast and marmalade?'

'Thank you, Ginny, I only want to get dressed,'
Dominic retorted shortly. 'If you don't mind.'

'I don't mind, Mr Dominic.' Her eyes flirted with

his. 'It's just so good to have you home again. You were so lucky fetching up on that island, weren't you? I don't know what your mother would have done if anything had happened to you.'

'Well, nothing did,' observed Dominic dryly. 'Thank you, Ginny.'

'Your arm's fully recovered now, isn't it?' she persisted. 'Mrs Harrington says you'll always have the scar, but I suppose that's nothing compared to what might have happened.'

'Ginny—'

'I've never seen a scar like that. Could I see it?'

'Not now,' Dominic informed her shortly, and crossing the room determinedly, he took charge of the door, leaving her no alternative but to step outside.

Half an hour later, showered and shaved, and tastefully attired in a silver-grey business suit, with a matching waistcoat and silk shirt, Dominic presented himself at his mother's sitting room. This room was on the first floor of the spacious Georgian town house his parents owned in Curzon Terrace, and like the rest of the building it bore witness to Isobel Crown's taste in design and furnishing. Tall darkwood cabinets framed an elegant Adam fireplace. Sofas, upholstered in delicately-woven tapestry-work, echoed the print that hung in silken panels on the walls, and rose silk curtains at the long windows billowed dangerously near the matching bowl of tea-roses that provided a feast of colour on the polished surface of the piano.

Isobel was seated at her writing desk, an inlaid escritoire, that did not look out of place among the heavier pieces, dictating her correspondence to Ginny. As she was the chairperson of a number of charitable societies, and the organiser of garden fêtes and coffee mornings, Isobel's life was a busy one, and Dominic knew she enjoyed being the centre of so much activity. At present she was arranging a ball to be given in support of a fund for homeless families, but she looked up cordially at her son's appearance, and dismissed Ginny in pursuit of some refreshment.

Ginny was reluctant to go, but she knew better than to disobey Mrs Crown's instructions, and Isobel permitted herself a moment's impatience when the door closed behind her.

'Really,' she exclaimed, getting up from her chair, 'there are days when that girl is so trying!' She sighed. 'I hope you don't encourage her, Dominic. Mrs Harrington tells me she saw her coming out of your room half an hour ago.'

Dominic grimaced. 'Hardly coming out,' he amended. 'She was hovering in the doorway, delivering your message.'

'You must know I didn't expect her to find you in bed,' retorted his mother shortly. 'I wasn't even sure you were still in the house. What earthly time did you get back last night?'

'Late,' said Dominic noncommittally, flinging himself into an easy chair and looking up at her wryly. 'Was that what you wanted to talk to me about? If so, relax. I'm moving back to the apartment today.'

'Oh, Dominic!' His mother looked at him disappointedly. 'Must you? I was hoping you'd be here for dinner this evening. I've invited the Marsdens, and as Barbara is still away I thought you might even the numbers.'

Dominic flicked a speck of dust from his boot, then looked up at her whimsically. 'You know and I know that the Marsdens' coming for dinner is purely incidental,' he remarked. 'You're hoping Dad and I will get together. That's your real ploy. And if that's why you brought me here, you're wasting your time.'

'Dominic! Be reasonable—'

'I am being reasonable. I just object to being treated like an imbecile, that's all.'

'James doesn't treat you like that!'

'He tries,' retorted Dominic broodingly. 'Look— all my life, I've done what he wanted. Home, school, university; hell, I even let him decide what degree I should take—'

'You wanted economics,' his mother inserted appealingly, but Dominic wasn't listening to her.

'I've even agreed to marry the girl he would have chosen—'

'But you love Barbara!'

'Barbara and I get along well enough, I know,' snapped Dominic shortly, getting abruptly to his feet again. 'But it would have been all the same if we didn't. Your husband is only interested in furthering his own ends, Mother, and I've had it with trying to humour him.'

'Don't say *your husband* like that, Dominic. James is your father. Good heavens, isn't it obvious enough? You're so alike, you're constantly on a collision course.' She sighed. 'Delay your removal for one more day, please. You know how I worry about you.'

'Mother, Kingston told you I was fully recovered.'

'But are you?' Isobel looked anxious. 'Oh, I know your arm has healed, but you're so thin. You don't eat enough, and—and—'

'—I drink too much?' he finished for her, momentarily sorry for upsetting her like this. But living in the same house as his father for the last six weeks had been a mistake, and he couldn't wait to be his own master again. Putting a sympathetic arm about her shoulders, he gave his mother a brief hug now, and said gently: 'I'll compromise with you. I'll attend your dinner party—but I'll go home afterwards.'

'This is your home.'

'No, it's your home,' Dominic corrected her firmly. 'So? Is that all? Because I think I ought to go before James releases any more adrenalin into his blood.'

Isobel caught his arm as he would have turned away. 'Actually, no,' she said, looking up at him doubtfully, a slim attractive figure in her well-cut shirt and pleated skirt. 'I mean, that wasn't all I had to say to you, darling.' She hesitated, as if reluctant to go on. 'As a matter of fact, I wanted to ask you something.'

'Yes?'

Dominic's eyes narrowed, the long, gold-tipped lashes shielding his expression, and Isobel made a play of straightening his tie. 'Tell me, darling,' she said, 'why did you ask Tim Connor to investigate that girl's background? I was talking to his wife yesterday evening, and she let it slip that—'

'What girl?' Dominic spoke deliberately harshly, and his mother moved her shoulders apologetically.

'You know. There's only one girl who might qualify for that description. Ruth, wasn't that her name? Ruth Jason?'

Dominic removed himself out of reach of her agitated fingers. He should have guessed Tim Connor couldn't keep anything from Marcia, he thought violently. He was completely dominated by his wife, and Dominic knew Marcia had been intrigued when she ran into him coming out of Tim's office three days ago.

'I was curious, that's all,' he answered his mother now, thrusting his hands into his trouser pockets. 'A girl like that, whose father is dying. I wondered if she had any relatives.'

'But didn't you tell me she hadn't?' asked his mother in surprise. 'I thought—'

'Her father says she hasn't,' remarked Dominic flatly. 'I wanted to be certain, that's all.'

Isobel sighed. 'But why? What difference can it make? There's nothing you can do for her. I'm grateful for the way she and her father cared for you, of course, although I can't help feeling a little resentful that they didn't think fit to give us your whereabouts—'

'Mother, that was my decision.'

'Not initially, it wasn't. Didn't you tell me you were unconscious?'

'They didn't know who I was,' Dominic retorted impatiently. 'Professor Jason thought I was a beachcomber, I think. In any event, they were not to blame for my idiosyncrasies.'

His mother shuddered. 'When I think of how worried I was when Trevor telephoned—' She broke off with evident distress. 'I know we've discussed this before, but how could you take a boat out in such weather? You must have been drunk!'

'Maybe,' responded Dominic laconically, and his mother gazed reproachfully at him.

'You said you hadn't touched a drop,' she protested, and a wry smile twisted her son's lean mouth.

'You said I must have been drinking,' he reminded her mildly, and she made a sound of frustration.

'Nevertheless, it was reckless.'

'Agreed.'

'So why did you do it?'

'I've told you—I was bored.'

'But Barbara was there!'

'So?' Dominic expelled his breath heavily. 'Can I go now?'

'I suppose so.' Isobel spread her hands distractedly. 'If you must. Where is that wretched girl with the coffee? She's never here when I want her.'

As if on cue, there was a light knock on the door, and Dominic, going to open it, reflected on the premise that Ginny had been standing outside eavesdropping. Certainly her face was flushed as she carried the tray into the room, and he was tempted to confront her with his suspicions and see how she reacted.

But a glance at his wrist watch advised him it was nearing twelve, and bidding his mother farewell for the present, he made his escape, breathing more freely when he was descending the steps to the pavement outside.

It was a beautiful morning, the warm sunshine more than making up for the frost the night before. Already the blossom was out on the trees in the park across the way, and despite the gusty north-east wind, it was comparatively mild on the unshaded side of the street.

It was a good fifteen minutes' walk to his father's office in Holborn, but despite the fact that he usually made the journey on foot, this morning Dominic walked to the end of the terrace and hailed a cab. The sooner he put in an appearance at the offices of the Crown Chemical Corporation the better, although he felt little real compunction at his lateness. He had spent the previous three evenings working until well after eleven, and he deserved a break. James Crown was a demanding employer, and in his eyes his son merited little, if any, leniency. Nevertheless, Dominic would have chosen to avoid the inevitable confrontation with his father, if he could have helped it, knowing as he did what stress their arguments put on the older man. If only his father would accept that Dominic had a mind—and a life—of his own. Instead of which, their present familiarity only added to the contention, putting a strain on both of them.

Even so, as the cab wove through the busy West End traffic, it was not his father who filled Dominic's thoughts. Annoyance at Tim Connor's incompetence was uppermost in his reasoning, and irritation with himself for instigating the enquiry in the first place. He knew he had had no right to ask Connor to look into Ruth's affairs, but it was doubly galling to have to explain his motives.

Yet nothing could alter the fact that he did feel a sense of responsibility towards her. He didn't want to feel it. He had tried hard since he came home to dismiss the interlude on the island from his mind. But no matter how he endeavoured to justify himself, he could not forget the look on Ruth's face when she had tried to feign indifference.

The memory of that night on the beach haunted him still, even though it was more than six weeks since he returned to London. Deep inside him, he knew that irrespective of how eager Ruth had been, she could not be held accountable for his behaviour, and ultimately the blame for what had happened was his. She was an innocent—he had known that. He had even teased her about it. He had had no right to violate the trust she had placed in him, and leave her to face the consequences.

Shifting moodily in his seat, he raised one booted foot to rest on the bar of the pull-down seat opposite. As always, his thoughts left a distinctly unpleasant taste in his mouth. He was thirty-two years old, and all his life he had enjoyed the company of the opposite sex. But for the first time in his life he found himself at a disadvantage, and he did not like it.

The cab slowed to a halt in the Charing Cross Road, snarled up in a stream of traffic, and Dominic settled back moodily, realising he might have done better to walk after all. It was too late now, however, and unwilling to join the press of humanity on the pavements, he resigned himself to the delay—and to further introspection.

He decided he was a fool to involve himself further. It wasn't as if Ruth would welcome any help from him. On the contrary, the epilogue to that affair on the beach had been that she had sworn him to silence over what had happened. Her earnest face convulsed with anxiety, she had threatened him with actual physical violence if he dared to reveal one word of what had happened to either her father or Celeste, and while he had not taken her vow of retribution seriously, it had appeared an unnecessary caution. Only in retrospect did he question his own integrity, and the willingness with which he had accepted that easy solution.

Yet what could he have done? he argued now. What possible good could have come from admitting his guilt to the old man? It might have killed him. Certainly it would have abused the faith he had in Ruth, and made a mockery of their relationship. Nothing he, Dominic, could have done for them would have compensated for that loss, so why was he tormenting himself like this? There had been no suspicion. On the contrary, their return to the bungalow had gone unremarked. Professor Jason and the old priest, Father Andreas, were still engrossed in their discussion on comparative religions, an extension of their original theme, and as Celeste and her cousin were nowhere about, the pitfalls of discovery had all been erased.

· He sighed now, as the cab began to move again. It wasn't as if he hadn't offered her anything. The following morning, just before the doctor's arrival, he had attempted to speak with her, to make the proposal that should there be anything— should she *need* anything—she should contact him through the International Bank in Kingstown, but she wouldn't listen to him. She wanted nothing from him, she had told him contemptuously, and Dominic's mouth compressed impatiently in remembrance of his impotence to get through to her. She had been remote, scornful, aloof beyond her years—yet pathetically noble, in her faded shirt and shorts. She had been desirable too, he recalled now, with an unwilling quickening of his senses. He remembered well the wide, innocent guilelessness of her eyes, her nose, small and yet delightful, the soft vulnerability of her mouth. He could still feel that responsive, lissom body beneath him, the surging upthrust of her breasts, and the yielding sweetness of her thighs. Their lovemaking had been everything he had imagined and more, and he wondered, with a sudden pang, whether if things had been different he might have considered bringing her back to England. There had been a certain novelty in being the first man to invade her honeyed sweetness, and they had been good together—But he soon dismissed this flagrant proof of his own foolishness. He must be mad, to be even contemplating such an idea, he thought disgustedly. Whatever else she might be, she was seventeen, and he was fifteen years older; she was shy and inexperienced, he was already cynical; she was naïve, ingenuous, immature, while he was jaded with the fruits of success. They had nothing in common. She would bore him silly, and he would probably frighten her. It would have been a disastrous union, and he was wasting his time even considering the consequences.

Nevertheless, he felt distinctly raw when he got out of the cab, and he was in no mood to respond to the provocative smile bestowed upon him by the receptionist who occupied a desk in the entrance hall of the Crown Building. With the briefest of nods, he crossed the veined marble floor to the lifts, pressing the button with an impatient finger.

His office was on the fourteenth floor, but he had barely stepped out of the lift before Andrea Bell, his secretary, came hurrying towards him along the corridor.

'Oh, there you are, Mr Crown,' she exclaimed, with some relief. 'I was just coming to meet you. Your father's been ringing for you this past hour. He's waiting for you upstairs.'

Dominic adopted a resigned stance. 'Do you know what he wants, Andrea?' he asked wearily, and the redheaded girl made an apologetic face.

'No,' she responded regretfully. 'He wouldn't say. Just to ask you to go up and see him, the minute you came in.'

Dominic nodded. 'Okay, you can tell him I'll be right there. Oh, and get me Tim Connor on the phone, would you? Tell him I'll meet him in the Alexander for a drink at one o'clock.'

'Yes, Mr Crown.'

Andrea made a note on the pad in her hand, and with a wry smile Dominic stepped back into the lift and pressed the button for the penthouse floor, two floors above.

James Crown's suite of offices incorporated the boardroom of the Crown Chemical organisation, in addition to the penthouse apartment which he used for himself, as well as for entertaining, and the huge digital computer that stored every detail of both the corporation and its employees. Dominic sometimes thought his father was a little like the computer. He, too, analysed every action, before putting it into motion.

His father was waiting for him in the large panelled office belonging to the chairman of the board. It was an austere room, with its dark panelling and mahogany furniture, an intimidating room, to those who came here under duress, and yet a beautiful room for all that, in its elegant simplicity. When the Crown Chemical Corporation had moved from its smaller offices in Deansgate to these more spacious premises in Malta Square, James had had his apartments furnished to his own design, and entering the office now in response to his father's summons, Dominic briefly acknowledged that his parent had good taste.

'Good morning,' James acknowledged, in answer to his son's greeting, glancing significantly at his pocket watch. The hands hovered a centimetre from their midday position, and the silent bid for sarcasm was not lost on Dominic.

'I overslept,' he said, before a word of admonishment could be spoken. 'I'm sorry I'm late, but you owe me the time.'

'Do I?' James Crown's lips thinned. 'Because you choose to spend your nights at Daly Tanners, I'm to overlook a matter of some two and a half hours' absence, is that it?'

Dominic sighed. 'If it's two and a half hours you're worried about, deduct it from the five hours' extra time I worked last evening,' he suggested laconically, tucking his thumbs into his waistcoat pockets.

His father, who had been conducting the interview

from the high-backed leather chair behind the desk, rose to his feet. 'I consider the extra hours you've been working lately some small recompense for the six weeks when you didn't put in an appearance at all,' he remarked tersely. 'And before you tell me that it wasn't your fault, I'll remind you that had it not been for your recklessness, you wouldn't have half killed yourself in the first place.'

Dominic conceded the truth of his father's words, but he was in no mood to say so. 'Maybe if you'd allow me a little more responsibility around here, there wouldn't be this conflict between us,' he averred instead. 'You don't want a son, Jake, you want a robot, a toy, some mechanical device you can move around to your own choosing.' He paused, realising what he had to say next could blow the argument sky-high. 'Perhaps it would be better for both of us if I left Crowns. You don't need me. Any accountant could do my job, and I guess I—'

'You're not just an accountant!' snapped his father now, with angry emphasis. 'And what's the point of leaving Crowns, when it will all be yours when I retire?'

'When you retire,' remarked Dominic dryly. 'You mean when they carry you out of here in a wooden box!'

'Not necessarily.' James subsided into his chair again, and Dominic, receptive to every nuance in his father's voice, knew a sudden chill. Was it his imagination, or did the old man's face have a slightly greyish tinge? He was so used to looking at those features, so like his own in shape and colouring, that he seldom examined them objectively. At sixty-two,

James Crown was as active as he had ever been, but now Dominic noticed the slight stoop to the broad shoulders, the whiteness in hair that had previously been only grey. Was he imagining it, or was his father ill? Somehow that possibility had never entered his head.

Moving to the desk, he rested his palms on its polished surface and appraised the older man thoroughly. 'Tell me,' he said, and all trace of indifference had gone from his voice and his manner, 'exactly what was the essence of that remark?'

An hour later Dominic entered the crowded bar of the Alexander Hotel in Tavistock Gate. The hotel was near Tim Connor's office, and was full of eager young executives and their secretaries, all crowded round the bar, eating crisps and drinking beer. It was an 'in' place, and Dominic knew Tim came here most lunchtimes, to enjoy a sandwich and a couple of gin and tonics. It was one of the few occasions when he could pry himself free of Marcia's clinging tentacles, and Dominic could rely on his being alone.

He was seated in the corner as usual, studying the *Times* crossword, and munching on a wedge of ham and cheese. He looked up half irritably when Dominic came to stand over him, but when he realised who it was, he quickly folded his paper and made room for him on the padded bench. Dominic deposited the two gin and tonics he had collected from the bar on his way over on the table, then shook the frosted droplets of condensation from his fingers. 'How are you, Tim?' he enquired mildly, and the other man relaxed and emptied the dregs in the glass in front of him.

'Can't grumble, Dominic,' he asserted comfortably, reaching for the drink Dominic had provided. 'As a matter of fact, I was going to ring you today, but you beat me to it.'

Dominic studied his companion's florid face without enthusiasm. Although he was only about ten years older than Dominic, Connor had the puffy eyes and broken veins of a much older man, and too much good food and too many hard drinks had left their mark upon him. Perhaps he ate to compensate, Dominic reflected now, then raised his own drink in dismissal of that particular train of thought.

'How's Jake?' Connor was asking now, observing the formalities. 'Marcia was talking to your mother at that charity auction yesterday evening. She said Isobel thinks he works too hard.'

'He does,' said Dominic flatly, without elaborating. 'So—you had something to tell me?'

Connor looked slightly disconcerted now, but he managed to maintain a façade of good humour. 'I thought you wanted to speak to me, Dominic, old boy,' he protested, taking another sip of his drink. 'Age before beauty, as they say.' He chuckled.

Dominic's mouth was a thin line. 'No, you first, Tim,' he insisted without expression, and with a discomfited sigh Connor complied.

'That matter you asked me to look into,' he began slowly. 'About Miss Jason?' Dominic nodded impatiently and he went on: 'You were right. She does have relatives—well, one relative, at least. An aunt, a woman called Davina Pascal. Have you heard of her?'

Dominic frowned. 'Should I have?'

Connor hesitated. 'That depends. She's wealthy enough, goodness knows. Her father was Henry Pascal. He was a famous art collector in his day.'

Dominic shook his head. 'The name doesn't mean anything.'

'No, well, it's some years since old Henry died. His wife preceded him.'

'And this woman—Davina—is his daughter?'

'That's right.' Connor was beginning to enjoy himself. 'It's quite an interesting story really. Henry Pascal was an art collector, as I said, but he didn't really have the money to indulge his hobby. So he found himself a wealthy heiress, the daughter of some mill owner from Yorkshire, and she financed his business.'

'I see,' Dominic nodded. 'And I assume Ruth—that is—Miss Jason's mother, was his daughter too.'

'That's right.' Connor fumbled for his cigar case. 'There only were two daughters, no sons. Davina inherited everything.'

Dominic looked thoughtful. 'Do you know why? I mean, why should Miss Jason's mother be ignored? Was she the younger daughter?'

'No. As a matter of fact, Helen was the eldest.' Connor offered his cigars to Dominic and when he refused, extracted one from the case. 'I suppose it's the classic situation. Helen married a man her father didn't like, so he cut her out of his will.'

Dominic was sceptical. 'And you learned all this from documentation.'

'No.' Connor sniffed defensively. 'As a matter of fact, it was common knowledge in 1944. Your Miss Jason's father was a conscientious objector, and you know how well liked they were.' He put the cigar between his teeth and lit it with some effort. 'Old Henry nearly had a fit when his little girl left home to marry a conchy.'

Dominic put up a hand to massage the back of his neck, trying to assimilate what he had heard. No wonder Jason had chosen to keep Ruth apart from the other members of her family! He had had no intention of allowing any of them to influence his daughter, even if he was not averse to living on the allowance his wife's mother had left her.

'I guess that clarifies the situation, doesn't it?' Connor was saying now, puffing away at his cigar and creating a blue haze about them. 'Poor little rich girl, hmm? Are you going to tell Miss Pascal she has a niece?'

'I imagine she knows,' retorted Dominic absently, remembering that Ruth had been born in England. Then, tersely; 'It's really nothing to do with me.'

Connor nodded. 'I see.' He paused. 'I was just going to add that that adopted son of Davina's might have something to say about it.'

'Adopted son?' Dominic stared blankly at him. 'But you said—*Miss* Pascal.'

'That's right.' Connor was enjoying his importance. 'But there is an adopted son. I've seen the papers. Some boy, whose parents were killed when he was little more than a baby. Davina adopted him. I imagine she decided that even if she wasn't about to get married, there was no reason why she shouldn't enjoy the delights of motherhood.'

Dominic shook his head. He had never expected anything like this. His enquiry had been instigated by a desire to reassure himself that if—*when*—Professor Jason died, Ruth would not be destitute. He had never imagined there might be more reasons than her father had given her for living on the island, and instead of this information reassuring him, it did quite the opposite.

'Is there anything else I can do for you?' Connor asked now, triumphant in his success; and remembering why he had contacted the man in the first place, Dominic nodded.

'Yes,' he said flatly, and ignoring Connor's expectant expression, he went on: 'You can refrain from discussing my affairs with your wife.'

'I didn't!' Connor's face turned crimson, as he struggled to defend himself. 'If Marcia has said anything—'

'Marcia has said plenty,' returned Dominic, finishing his drink and getting to his feet. 'And it won't do your reputation any good, Tim, if it's commonly known that you can't respect a client's confidence.' His lips twisted half in sympathy then, as the older man collapsed, deflated. 'I'd advise you to forget I ever asked about Ruth Jason.' He grimaced. 'After you've sent me your account, of course.'

CHAPTER ELEVEN

Dominic left the office early that afternoon, and took a cab to his apartment in Tressilian Square. He occupied the penthouse suite of a tower block, whose position in part made up for the phenomenal rent he paid. He would have preferred a town house, like that belonging to his parents, but it seemed an unnecessary encumbrance, commuting as he invariably did between his home and the house in Curzon Terrace. Besides, in summer he enjoyed driving down to Marlin Spike, a sprawling country residence his father had bought about thirty years ago, and where Dominic had spent much of his childhood. His old nurse, Miss Bainbridge, still lived there, now ostensibly acting as housekeeper, but as there had been no other children since his younger brother's death in infancy, his mother preferred the more active life in town.

The apartment was cool, and quieter than Curzon Terrace. The spacious living room, with its split-level elevation and silk-screened walls, was a delightful change from his mother's home, despite its elegance. This room was aggressively modern, with plate glass windows, wall-to-wall carpeting, and the kind of squashy leather sofas that Dominic could stretch his length upon. There was a stereo and hi-fi system, television and video equipment, and plenty of space for entertaining, or simply being untidy.

A man came into the living room from the direction of the bedrooms while Dominic was standing at the long windows, enjoying the view. He was a neat man, short and dapper, with a balding pate and a small moustache. Dominic, sensing his presence, glanced round without surprise, nodding at the man and giving him a wry smile.

'I didn't think you'd be here, Shannon,' he remarked, turning away from the windows and unfastening his tie. 'Did you collect my belongings already? I thought you might run into some difficulties with my mama!'

'Mrs Crown did say she had tried to persuade you to stay a little longer, sir,' Shannon responded politely, picking up the tie Dominic had discarded, and viewing his employer with evident satisfaction. 'Still, it's nice to have you back, sir. It's not the same, cooking for myself.'

Dominic's smile was rueful. 'Thanks, Shannon. It's nice to be back. But I'm afraid I shan't be eating at home this evening. My mother insisted that I make up her numbers for dinner, and in the circumstances I didn't like to refuse.'

'I understand, sir.' Shannon helped him off with his jacket. 'Shall I run your bath, or will you be taking a shower?'

'Neither one, right now,' replied Dominic tersely. 'I want to speak to Hector Greenslade on the telephone, and then I have some work to do. I'll take a shower later, Shannon. Just get me a drink, there's a good chap. I badly need it.'

Shannon hesitated. 'Mr Greenslade, sir? Isn't he

the specialist your father saw last year?'

Dominic nodded, flinging himself on to one of the low couches and looking up at the manservant resignedly. 'Right.'

'There's nothing wrong with you, is there, sir? I mean—' Shannon hastily qualified the question, his accent pronounced in his agitation. 'Sure and there are no complications to your recovery, are there?'

'My recovery? Hell, no.' Dominic watched while the little man dropped ice into a glass, before covering it with a measure of Scotch, then took the glass from him gratefully. 'I learned today that my father was warned last year that he had a heart condition. Unfortunately he chose not to tell anyone else.'

Shannon's lips parted. 'What do you mean? Mr Crown is ill?'

'He will be if he doesn't slow down,' Dominic declared flatly. 'He had some pain last week and he made another appointment with Greenslade. He got the results of the tests they ran on him this morning.'

'And?'

'And—he's been advised to take a rest, a long rest.'

'To retire, you mean?'

'I guess that's what it adds up to,' agreed Dominic, swallowing a mouthful of his drink, and then staring down broodingly into the glass. 'He's called an extraordinary meeting of the board for tomorrow. He's asked me to attend.'

Shannon nodded. 'I can guess why.'

Dominic looked up. 'So can I. The point is—do I want it?'

'Do you want it?' Shannon made a sound of disapproval. 'Man, how can you even ask such a question? And you kicking your heels these past few years, just waiting for a chance to take over!'

Dominic grimaced. 'Maybe I was more ambitious then. Right now, it seems a hell of a responsibility.'

The telephone bell interrupted their exchange and waving Shannon away, Dominic reached for the receiver. 'Yes?' he said impatiently, in no mood for diplomacy, and then gasped aloud when a feminine voice teased: 'What a way to welcome someone home!'

'Barbara!' Dominic sat forward on the couch, spreading his legs, the hand holding his glass hanging loosely between. 'When did you get back? I thought your father told me you weren't due home until the weekend.'

'I wasn't,' Barbara agreed lightly. 'But Jane's all right now. The baby's thriving, and she has a perfectly good nursemaid. Besides,' she paused, 'I wanted to see you, darling. These past two weeks have seemed positively endless! Have you missed me?'

Dominic slumped back against the cushions at her words, feeling abominably guilty. In all honesty, he had had little time to miss his fiancée, and recalling the content of his conversation with Tim Connor at lunchtime, he felt even worse. Barbara was so eager, so accommodating, exactly the right sort of girl to become Mrs Dominic Crown. The trouble was, he knew, he simply didn't appreciate her.

Now, however, he found the right words to placate her. 'Of course I've missed you,' he told her gently. 'When can I see you? It's been much too long.'

'How about tonight?' Barbara suggested breathily, his words effecting their purpose. 'Daddy's going to a business dinner this evening. Why don't you come over? We'll have the place to ourselves?'

Dominic sighed. 'I can't, not tonight.' And he went on to explain the situation. 'It will have to be tomorrow evening. I'm sorry, but you should have warned me you were coming home.'

Barbara sounded disappointed. 'Couldn't you come here after dinner tonight?' she appealed. 'Daddy won't be back until late, and we've hardly been alone together since we got back from Barbados, what with one thing and another. I want to see you, Dom. I want to *be* with you. Couldn't you try and get away early?'

Dominic chewed absently at his lower lip. 'Okay,' he said at last. 'I'll try. But I can't promise. You know what these dinner parties of Ma's are like— they go on for ever.'

'Well, do your best,' pleaded Barbara urgently, and after further protestations of her eagerness, she rang off, leaving Dominic feeling decidedly contemptible.

In the event, Dominic was able to excuse himself from his parents' guests at about a quarter to ten, and he levered himself behind the wheel of the silver-grey Porsche with some relief. He had driven himself to Curzon Square to give him freedom of movement afterwards, but now, instead of heading towards Barbara's home in Kensington, he turned into Park Lane and drove north towards Regent's Park.

After his conversation with Hector Greenslade

that afternoon, he had purposely searched the telephone directory for Davina Pascal's address. Hers was not such a common name, and the designation when he found it—Pascal, Miss Davina—was unmistakable. Her address was given as 2, Wellington Mews, and a consultation with the map had elicited the information that it was among that maze of streets and squares between Gloucester Place and the Edgware Road.

It wasn't easy to find at night, despite the street lighting. He suspected he might have found it easier on foot. But eventually he turned into a small square, with Wellington Mews opening off it, a narrow cul-de-sac, approached beneath a stone arch. It was certainly private, and after parking the car and taking a look, he was reluctantly impressed. There appeared to be only the one house opening into the mews, despite the number, and it was tall and narrow, flanked on either side by what looked like stables and garages. In the pale illumination from a pair of carriage lamps, he could see geranium-filled window boxes below windows with ornamental shutters, and a heavy door with a fluted fanlight, above whitewashed steps. There were lights at an upstairs window, and he wondered who was at home. He wondered what reaction he might get if he rang the bell and introduced himself, if he informed Miss Pascal of her brother-in-law's illness, and reminded her of the existence of her niece. How might she receive the news of her sister's child? Surely a woman who had adopted a son rather than remain childless might welcome a surrogate daughter.

However, Dominic knew he could not intrude. If,

after her father was dead, Ruth contacted him, if she asked for his assistance, then, and only then, could he explain that she was not without a family of her own. With a sigh, half of impatience, half of frustration with himself for once more getting involved, he turned back to the Porsche, sliding behind the wheel and starting the engine. Ruth would never contact him, he thought broodingly. He was the last person on earth she would turn to. And if her own father chose to keep her ignorant of the facts, it was not his prerogative to interfere.

Nevertheless, driving back to Kensington, Dominic knew it would take more than self-justification to put Ruth out of his mind. Like it or not, he could not forget her, and he would have to hope that time, and events, would achieve what willpower could not.

Barbara's home was a Victorian residence near Holland Park. Her father, Gerald Symonds, was a politician, and although his constituency was in some industrial district of the north-west, he found it easier to have his base in the capital. Besides, he had various business interests that demanded his time, and he enjoyed the social life at Westminster.

Barbara's parents were divorced. Her mother, who had been unaware of her husband's political aspirations when she married him, had found the life of a politician's wife too much for her to handle. She was basically a quiet woman, content with her home and her family, and in consequence she had chosen to remain in Cumbria, while her husband made his life in the capital. Of course, it hadn't worked, and when she discovered that her husband had found himself a mistress, Mrs Symonds had filed for divorce.

Barbara had been in school at that time, and the scandal had not affected her. Later, when she and her sister Jane, who was a year younger, returned home, they had had mixed feelings, and eventually Barbara had chosen to live with her father, while Jane, already involved with a young farmer, opted for the rural life, like her mother.

Barbara opened the door of the house almost before Dominic had parked the Porsche at the kerb. She stood, framed in the light emanating from the hall behind her, and Dominic thought, as he had done many times in the past, what an attractive girl she was. Her hair was short and curly, a bubbling red-gold aureole around her pointed face. She was small and vivacious, if anything inclined towards plumpness, but in the right clothes from the right fashion houses, she was every bit as elegant as girls inches taller. Just now, she was wearing a loose-fitting caftan, that only hinted at the contours of her figure, but the light from behind her cast her voluptuous curves into silhouette.

'Dominic!' she exclaimed, as he climbed out of the car, and paused a moment to turn the key. 'Oh, Dominic, you came! I was beginning to think you weren't going to.'

Dominic circled the car and came towards her indolently, slipping his keys into the pocket of his mohair jacket. 'How could I disappoint you?' he teased, bending to take her eagerly proffered lips.

'Dom,' she breathed, the evocative perfume she wore drifting to his nostrils. 'Oh, darling, it's been so long! Why did I agree to go and stay with Jane?'

'Because she needed you,' replied Dominic, straightening, and urging her into the house. 'How is Jane, by the way? And your mother? I expect the Lake District is quite beautiful at this time of the year.'

'Oh, it is,' Barbara agreed willingly, closing the door behind them, and linking her arm with his. 'But Kensington is better. Don't you agree?'

She led the way into a high-ceilinged drawing room, and then turned to him, her face upraised. With her lips slightly parted and her eyes half closed, it was an open invitation, and Dominic would have been less than human if he had not reached for her.

'Darling, darling,' she whispered, drawing his hands to her breasts, letting him feel the hard peaks beneath the fine silk of the caftan. 'Do you realise you haven't made love to me for more than six weeks! Not since before you took off for that crazy stunt on the yacht.'

Dominic caressed the side of her neck with his lips. 'You know why,' he murmured evasively. 'My arm—'

'I know, I know.' Barbara was endearingly generous. 'I'm not blaming you exactly. I just wish that affair had never happened.'

'So do I,' responded Dominic tautly, wishing she had not chosen to bring it up. With a determined effort he drew back from her, and forced a faint smile. 'Do you think I could have a drink, honey? My mother watches my intake like a hawk, and I'm positively dying of thirst.'

Barbara sighed regretfully, but she went to do his bidding, lifting the bottle of Scotch from the table in the corner, and pouring a generous measure into a glass. Dominic, meanwhile, sought the comfort of the buttoned-leather sofa, loosening his jacket, and draping one leg casually over the arm.

'Daddy won't be back for hours,' Barbara told him, as she handed him his drink and subsided beside him. 'You can stay the night, if you want to. Mrs Laurence will make you up a bed.'

Dominic took a mouthful of the drink, and then shook his head. 'If I know Mrs Laurence, she's probably tucked up in bed by now,' he remarked dryly. 'And in any case, Shannon would never forgive me if I wasn't home for breakfast in the morning. This is my first night back at the apartment. He wasn't exactly overjoyed to learn I was dining out, and I couldn't disappoint him again.'

'But you can disappoint me, is that it?' Barbara suggested, tensely, her long nails beating a tattoo against the dark brown hide, and Dominic heaved a sigh.

'Honey, it's not just a question of where I sleep. You know as well as I do that your father wouldn't approve of me spending the night here. Besides,' and he knew an involuntary pang as he realised he was making excuses, 'I'm not really very good company this evening.'

Barbara's arched brows ascended. 'No?'

'No.' Dominic examined the contents of his glass with studied concentration. 'Barbara, it looks as if Dad's going to retire at last.' He paused, as she sucked in her breath in anticipation of what was coming next. 'He wants me to take his place—on a temporary basis, at least.'

'Oh, *Dominic!*' Barbara's irritation disappeared beneath a wave of enthusiasm. 'Why didn't you tell me straight away? Oh, this is so exciting! You're going to be the head of the corporation! Honestly, I can hardly believe it!'

She wrapped her arms around his neck, careless of the glass in his hand, covering his face with kisses. Her delight at the proposed appointment was ex- uberant, and Dominic had to hold her off eventually, saying flatly: 'You haven't asked why my father is giving up the reins. Surely you realise he wouldn't have done it without good reason.'

Barbara's jubilation gave way to a puzzled frown. 'But I thought—I mean, I assumed he had decided the time was right—' Her voice trailed away. 'He's not been taken ill, has he?'

Dominic disentangled himself from her hands, and got restlessly to his feet. 'Not exactly,' he conceded, smoothing his ruffled hair. 'But he's not a well man, and the doctors have finally persuaded him he'll kill himself within a year if he goes on as he is.'

'Oh!' Barbara pressed her lips together now, look- ing up at him anxiously. 'I'm sorry, Dom. I had no idea.' She made a helpless movement of her shoulders. 'And here was I, thinking you were crazy not to be jumping for joy.'

'Mmm.' Dominic swallowed another mouthful of his drink. 'Jumping for joy?' He paced broodingly across the screened fireplace. 'What if I were to tell you I'm not entirely convinced I'm the right man for the job? That quite honestly the responsibility of it scares me silly?'

Barbara moved to the edge of the sofa, holding out her hand towards him. 'Don't say that, Dom,' she exclaimed, half impatiently. 'You know you're the *only* man for the job. Your father made that company. He built it up from nothing. When your grandfather died, it was just a string of little pharmacies, getting their supplies from one of the larger chemists. If Jake Crown hadn't had the vision to realise that drugs were going to be big business, if he hadn't created his own laboratories, his own wholesale organisation, Crown Chemicals would never have come into being.'

'I know that.'

Dominic expelled his breath harshly, but Barbara wasn't finished yet. 'You know the organisation inside out. You've worked in the laboratories, you've spent time in the factories, you've studied economics, and business management; it was even your idea that Crowns began producing health foods. For heaven's sake, Dominic, you can't turn your back on it now. It needs you, and you need it.'

'Like I need a hole in the head,' Dominic retorted grimly, and Barbara rose to her feet, standing before him, small and determined.

'It's a challenge, can't you see that?' she exclaimed. 'And I can help you. Just like I've helped Daddy.'

Unbidden, an image of Ruth as his wife flashed before his eyes. She was not like Barbara. He suspected she was more like Barbara's mother. The idea of being the chairman's wife would probably terrify her. She was a child when it came to such things. But then she *was* just that, he thought bitterly. A child! And he was a despicable swine, for violating her as he had.

'Dominic, what are you thinking about now?'

Barbara's slightly peevish voice came to him as if from a distance. 'I'm sorry,' he said, blinking. 'Did you say something?'

'I asked what you were thinking,' she retorted, plucking at his sleeve. 'Dominic, you're not really serious about this, are you?'

'About what?' Dominic's mind was suddenly blank, and it took some seconds for recognition to return to him. 'Oh—you mean about the corporation.' He shook his head. 'I guess not. How can I? Jake owns fifty-one per cent of the stock.'

'So you'll have control!' Barbara could hardly contain her excitement. 'Oh, Dominic, I can't wait to tell Daddy.'

Dominic grimaced. 'I'm glad you're pleased,' he conceded flatly. 'Can I have another drink? And then I think I'd better go.'

Much to Barbara's regret, he left before midnight, and her fingers lingered on his lapels when he was kissing her goodbye. 'Tomorrow night,' she made him promise, pressing herself against the muscled strength of his thighs. 'You won't get rid of me so easily then. We'll eat at the apartment, and *I* won't refuse an invitation to breakfast.'

As it happened, Dominic ate dinner alone the following evening, at a hotel in Berne. He had a meeting the next morning with his father's Swiss bankers, and during the following days, he visited all the European divisions of Crown Chemicals. It was necessary, his father said, to make his presence felt, and certainly at the end of that first week Dominic felt better equipped to handle the operation. No amount of telecommunications could take the place of a personal appearance, and he had to acknowledge that Jake knew what he was talking about.

The hectic activity of Dominic's first week as nominal head of Crown Chemicals precluded any chance of seeing Barbara again, and their contacts were limited to the medium of the telephone. She was disappointed, she said, and Dominic had no doubt that she was: but she was also ambitious, and she had not overlooked the position she would occupy once they were married. It was worth the separation to know that come September, she would take his mother's place, and rather cynically Dominic wondered what she would have done had he refused the obligation his father placed upon him. She cared for him—or so she said. But would she care for a humble economist equally as well? He guessed he would never know, and decided that too much introspection was bad for his morale.

He arrived back from Cologne at the end of that first week feeling utterly exhausted. Too many hours looking at files and dossiers, listening to the various heads of departments outlining their plans for the coming year, eating scratch meals and drinking too much, combined with many hours of waiting around at airports, had robbed him of any enthusiasm he had started out with. He felt he wanted to sleep for at least forty-eight hours before facing another balance sheet, and telling Shannon he was taking no calls, he fell into bed without even taking a shower.

Around midday, approximately fifteen hours later, Shannon ventured into Dominic's room with a breakfast tray. His employer was still dead to the world, but when he jerked the cord of the blind, releasing daylight into the room, Dominic stirred. He groaned, rolled on to his back, and then squinted up at the little Irishman with dour impatience.

'I said—no calls,' he muttered, scowling. 'And close those blinds, can't you? I don't want to know what time it is.'

Shannon set down the tray on the bedside table, and stood firm, not at all perturbed by this show of acerbity. Dominic was seldom at his best in the mornings, and Shannon was not offended.

'Sure, and it's noon, sir,' he informed his employer brightly, folding his hands. 'I'd be wishing you good morning, only the clock has already struck the hour.'

'So what?' Dominic grimaced at the tray beside him. 'You can take that away as well. I'm not hungry, just tired. Go away and leave me alone.'

'Ah, well, I would do that, sir, but your father's been calling since ten o'clock, and I promised him you'd be up at midday.'

'Did you?' Dominic gazed up at him in exasperation. 'And who gave you permission to tell my father that?'

'It's a lovely day, sir,' said Shannon, beaming. 'Doesn't it make you wish you were up and out in it?'

Dominic acknowledged this evasion, and heaved a sigh. 'You mean out of here and into my office, don't you?' he suggested, with some irony. 'Oh, all right, pour me some coffee. I suppose I'll have to make a move.'

Shannon nodded his approval, and bent over the tray, while Dominic struggled up on the pillows. It was twelve-fifteen, he saw, with some amazement. He had not slept so long since he was a child.

There was a copy of *The Times* on the tray beside the coffee pot, and while Shannon added sugar to the cup of aromatic black liquid he had poured, Dominic flicked through the pages. The headlines didn't interest him. The current industrial action being taken by one of the larger unions had appeared in all the continental papers, too, but as it didn't directly affect the corporation, he was not involved. He was more interested in the share prices in the city, and the political unrest in South America where they were hoping to expand.

He saw to his relief that the latest siege in Central America had ended without bloodshed, and he was about to toss the paper aside and take the coffee cup Shannon was holding out to him when a picture on one of the inner pages caught his eye. He doubted he would have noticed it at all, had the name Pascal not been in evidence, and even then he stared at it for several seconds without really believing what he was seeing.

'Your coffee, sir.' Unaware, Shannon was becoming mildly impatient, and Dominic looked up at him almost aggressively.

'All right,' he exclaimed, taking the cup and in so doing slopping half its contents into the saucer. 'Did I ask you to wait?'

Shannon sighed, and removed the cup from his employer's hand again, bustling through to the bathroom to attend to the spilt liquid, and Dominic, temporarily relieved of an audience, gave in to his own exclamation of impatience. Then, discarding any pretence at indifference, he read the blurb below the picture with narrowed hostile eyes.

It was not a particularly good picture. Without the accompanying blurb and the individuality of her aunt's name, Dominic could have been forgiven for not giving it a second glance. Certainly he would never have recognised Ruth without some added assistance. In what appeared to be a well-cut shirt and jacket—the picture was only small, he could see no more than her head and shoulders—her hair either cut or confined in some way, she looked much different from the way he remembered her. She looked uncertain, too, or maybe that was just the way the camera had caught her, and Dominic felt his emotions stir with a mixture of feelings. There was disbelief, of course, and incredulity, but there was anxiety, too, and another emotion far less easy to identify.

'There you are, sir.'

Shannon had returned with a clean saucer, and having topped up the cup was now offering it to his recalcitrant employer. This time Dominic took it broodingly, but without any aggression, and Shannon inclined his head with evident relief.

'You won't forget the time, will you, sir?' he ventured, viewing Dominic's apparent absorption with the paper with some disapproval, and the younger man looked up almost abstractedly.

'What?'

'Your father, sir,' prompted Shannon with a sigh. 'You haven't forgotten—'

'Oh, no. No.' In point of fact, Dominic had, but he refused to give Shannon that satisfaction. 'I'll get up in a few minutes. If my father phones again, you can put the call through here.'

'Yes, sir,' Shannon nodded, and took a step towards the door. Then, as if compelled to reassure himself that Dominic was all right, whatever the consequences to himself, he hesitated. 'There—er—there's not bad news in the paper, is there, sir?' he enquired intrepidly. 'I mean, I couldn't help noticing—'

Dominic slumped back against his pillows and regarded the Irishman resignedly. 'No,' he said, after a few moments. 'No, it's not bad news exactly. Just something I didn't expect, that's all.'

Shannon still lingered. 'It wouldn't have to do with that picture of Miss Pascal and her niece on page five, would it?' he suggested, and Dominic stared at him with an astonishment that turned rapidly to irritation.

'What the hell do you mean?' he demanded, thrusting the half empty coffee cup back on to the tray and dragging himself upright again. 'What do you know about Miss Pascal?'

Shannon was not abashed. 'It's an unusual name, sir. And I found it on the pad beside the phone last week. You'll forgive me for glancing through the paper now, I'm sure, and when I read the young lady's name—'

'You put two and two together,' muttered Dominic dourly, pushing the paper aside. 'All right—as you've probably read it yourself, Davina Pascal is Ruth Jason's aunt.'

'And it seems her father has died,' put in Shannon sympathetically. 'Sure, the young lady's lucky to have relatives like that.'

'Yes.' Dominic now found he was not so sure. Seeing Ruth's picture like that, reading that her father had died, and that her aunt had brought her back to England, threw all that had happened between them into sharp perspective. He didn't know why, but he felt a curious kind of resentment towards both Ruth and her aunt, and although he kept telling himself that this was what he had wanted for her, what he had hoped for, it didn't quite ring true.

'Seems like the young lady's father died soon after you came home, sir,' Shannon was saying now, and Dominic watched with ill-concealed frustration as the Irishman picked up the paper and turned to the picture again, and its accompanying article. 'Poor girl! Sure, London must be quite a frightening place for her.'

Dominic pushed the bedclothes aside, and got out of bed. 'She'll survive,' he remarked, a little brutally, and Shannon looked up at him reprovingly.

'I thought you owed the young lady your life,' he exclaimed, as Dominic strode across to the bathroom. 'Sure, and it might be a kindness to show your face at Wellington Mews, mightn't it?'

Dominic hesitated in the bathroom doorway. 'You don't miss a trick, do you, you old reprobate?' he demanded, half amused, in spite of himself. 'I suppose you got the address from the phone pad, too, did you?'

'Ah, no. That I looked up for myself,' admitted Shannon with a sigh. 'It's not far from here. Just across the park—'

'I know where it is,' retorted Dominic shortly, and slammed the bathroom door before the Irishman could say anything else.

Nevertheless, later in the day, with the immediate de-briefing with his father completed, Dominic found his thoughts irresistibly drifting to what Shannon had said. Ruth and her father had saved his life, he acknowledged grimly, stabbing impatiently at the blotting pad with a paper knife. He did owe her that much. And regardless of how callously he had behaved, there was a bond between them. Even if she didn't want to see him, he ought to make the effort to see her, for courtesy's sake. He could always offer her his help if she needed it—to find a place to live or get a job. Doubtless her aunt was taking care of all of that, but he should assure himself of her well-being.

With a smothered exclamation he got up from his desk and walked restlessly across to the windows. How the hell could he do it? he asked himself savagely. What if she hadn't told her aunt about him? There was no real reason why she should, and his own family had taken pains to keep the story out of the papers. How could he present himself at her aunt's home, without giving any explanations? Particularly as Ruth was unlikely to welcome his appearance.

Expelling his breath on a heavy sigh, he turned back to survey his office. It was not the office he had previously occupied, but it was not the chairman's office either. His father still occupied that. He was not quite yet ready to give up all responsibility, and it had been agreed that there should be a six-month period, during which time Dominic was expected to ease himself into his father's shoes. In consequence, he had been given an office on the penthouse floor, and the use of his father's secretary, Mrs Cooke, who had been with Crowns almost as long as Jake Crown himself.

One thing Dominic had learned in these first few days of power, and that was that his father had avoided delegation of duty. In all aspects of the business, Jake had kept his own finger on the pulse of the organisation, and not one of his executives had been given a responsibility he himself could shoulder. Dominic suspected this was not the way. In a small business, perhaps, with time to oversee all departments. But in a corporation like Crowns, to expect to absorb all aspects of the organisation was madness. What was more, it was physically impossible, and it was this, as much as anything, which had ultimately destroyed his father's health.

Now, Dominic paced back to his desk and pressed the call button that connected with the secretary's extension. 'Mrs Cooke, could you come in here for a moment?' he requested shortly, and released the button to resume his seat behind the desk.

He wondered, as Adelaide Cooke entered the room, whether in fact she had ever been married. Despite her courtesy title, he had never heard her mention her husband's name, and certainly his presence had never prevented her from working the outlandish hours his father had often demanded of her. Tall and thin, with horn-rimmed spectacles and tightly-drawn greyish hair, Mrs Cooke exuded competence and efficiency, and a total dedication to duty that Dominic sometimes found irksome.

'Yes, Mr Dominic?' she said now, holding her notebook and pencil firmly between both hands. He was invariably addressed as Mr Dominic, to distinguish him from his father, but today that too was a source of irritation he tried hard to conceal.

'I'm leaving now, Mrs Cooke,' he informed her politely, getting to his feet once again. 'There's nothing urgent awaiting my attention, is there?'

Mrs Cooke looked slightly scandalised. It was only half past four, after all. Mr Crown seldom left before six o'clock, and Mr Dominic had not put in an appearance until after one o'clock.

Now, however, she consulted her notepad, before lifting her head. 'There was a call,' she declared, frowning slightly. 'While you were in the chairman's office. It was from—Miss Symonds. I explained that you were in conference, and she said she would call back.'

Dominic's lips tightened. 'You didn't tell me, Mrs Cooke.'

'No.' Mrs Cooke looked slightly discomfited now. 'As it was a personal call, I didn't think it was urgent. And as Miss Symonds said she would call back—'

'In future, I'd like a list of any calls that come in while I'm in conference to be left on my desk, Mrs Cooke,' Dominic interrupted her crisply. 'Personal or otherwise. I'll decide if they're important.'

'Yes, Mr Dominic.'

Mrs Cooke inclined her head, and briefly he felt contrition. It was not her fault, after all. His father wouldn't have welcomed that kind of information, particularly when it had nothing to do with the corporation.

'Right.' Dominic inclined his head rather more agreeably. 'Was there anything else?'

Mrs Cooke shook her head. Then: 'Shall I tell Mr Crown you're leaving? He may wish to speak with you before you go.'

'Be that as it may,' Dominic's lips twisted rather ironically, 'I don't intend to give him the opportunity,' he asserted dryly. 'Tell him he can ring me later, if there's anything urgent.' He massaged the back of his neck with weary fingers. 'I doubt if I'll be going out this evening.'

'And Miss Symonds?'

'Barbara? Oh, yes.' Dominic's hand dropped to his side. 'If she calls again, tell her I'll ring her this evening. Right now, I need a drink—a strong one!'

Mrs Cooke did not look as shocked as he had expected now. Instead, she permitted herself a faint smile, and he realised she had humour, after all.

'Until tomorrow, then, Mr Dominic,' she said politely, and he left his office feeling distinctly less brittle.

CHAPTER TWELVE

Barbara rang again while he was in the shower, and Shannon came into the bathroom waving the extension.

'Shall I be plugging it in here?' he asked, when he had attracted his employer's attention, and Dominic gave a resigned nod, before wrapping a thick towel around his hips and stepping out of the cubicle.

'Darling, would you mind if I changed our arrangements?' Barbara exclaimed, when she heard his masculine tones. 'Daddy's sprung this dinner party on me, right at the last moment. One of those awful political things, that he really couldn't avoid. So could you have dinner here this evening, instead of me joining you as we planned? I know it's short notice, and I do want to see you, but I simply can't let Daddy down.'

Dominic eased himself against the wall, lifting one leg to rest the ball of his foot against the tiles behind him. 'I don't think I feel up to attending one of your father's political rallies this evening, Barbara,' he said at last, with flat finality. And at her cry of protest he added: 'Honey, I've had it with dinner parties. For tonight, at least. You and me—that was something different. But I've just spent the last eight days attending one conference after another, and quite frankly, I'm talked out. I'm sorry, but that's the way it is.'

'Oh, Dominic!' Barbara made a sound of evident annoyance. 'Dominic, there were people I wanted you to meet—friends of Daddy's. People who could help you, who could help Crowns!'

Dominic felt a sudden constriction in his stomach. It was a feeling he had had before, whenever his father had attempted to coerce him into doing something *he* wanted. It was a gut feeling, a painful tightening of his stomach muscles, that produced a totally negative response.

'You mean I'm invited to this dinner party?' he enquired with apparent mildness, and Barbara confirmed that this was so.

'Of course you're invited. When Daddy suggested it, I couldn't help but agree.' She paused, and when he didn't say anything, she went on: 'Won't you come, darling? For me? I promise you won't regret it.'

'I thought you said your father sprang it on you at the last moment.'

'Well, he did. But naturally he expects you to attend. He knew you were expected back yesterday, and when he learned that you and I planned to have dinner at your apartment—'

'—he decided to use the situation,' finished Dominic expressionlessly.

'Not—use, exactly,' confessed Barbara reluctantly. 'But naturally, there are people he'd like you to meet. After all, as the nominal head of—'

'No, Barbara.' Dominic's tone was final, but she would not accept it.

S.—H

'You—you can't mean that,' she stuttered, scarcely believing he would disappoint her, but he was adamant.

'I'm tired, Barbara,' he said implacably. 'And what's more, I don't intend to spend my evenings furthering your father's career.'

Barbara gasped. 'That's a rotten thing to suggest!'

'But relevant, don't you think?' suggested Dominic coldly. 'Gerald and I have hardly been friends, up to this point.'

'Daddy and your father have always—'

'I'm not my father!' retorted Dominic tersely, and then, realising he was behaving boorishly, he shook his head. 'Look, Barbara, I don't want to quarrel over this, and if you choose to change your mind and come and take dinner with me, then that's okay. But so far as me joining your father's dinner party is concerned, forget it.'

Barbara was silent for a few moments, and he thought at first she might have rung off. But then the unmistakable sounds of her sobs reached him, and the constriction inside him balled into a hard core.

'For God's sake, Barbara,' he muttered, clenching his fist beside him, straightening away from the wall. 'It can't be that important to you!'

'I—I'll ring you to—tomorrow, Dominic,' she sniffed, but still she didn't ring off, and Dominic's mouth compressed.

'All right,' he got out at last, and it was almost a snarl of self-disgust at his own weakness. 'All right, I'll be there!' he told her, giving in to her deliberate appeal to his sympathy, and rang off before he was tempted to change his mind again.

Shannon entered the bedroom as he was dressing to go out, and viewed his employer's velvet dinner suit with some concern.

'Are you not eating at home this evening after all, sir?' he exclaimed, brushing a speck of dust from Dominic's sleeve. 'Haven't I got a rack of lamb roasting this past hour, and a dish of smoked salmon cooling in the freezer?'

Dominic expelled his breath heavily. 'I have to go out,' he said flatly, meeting the Irishman's offended gaze. 'I know I said I'd be eating at home—but now I find I'm not.'

Shannon frowned. 'Would you be eating dinner with Miss Pascal and her niece?' he asked with a meeting of his brows. 'Sure, you took my advice and spoke to the young lady.'

'No, I didn't.' Dominic's response was brusque, but he couldn't help it. 'I'm having dinner at the Symonds'! I'm sorry if you've gone to a lot of trouble unnecessarily, but there it is.'

Shannon turned and left the room without another word, and Dominic couldn't blame him. He was put out, and quite rightly, but then so was Dominic, and he was frustratedly aware that he had been manipulated. His father would be very amused if he ever learnt that his son had been persuaded by a woman's tears, particularly when he suspected they had been deliberately turned on for his benefit.

He turned away from the mirror and picked his wallet up off the bed, and as he did so, an image of Ruth, as he had last seen her, flashed before his eyes. It wasn't the black and white photograph he envisaged, but the flesh and blood female that she was, standing on the verandah, watching him walk away down to the harbour with Doctor Francis. If she had shed tears, would he have turned back? If she had spoken with him, if she had appealed with him to stay, might he have been persuaded then?

He walked into the living room, where Shannon had already switched on the lamps. The warm glow from their amber shades contrasted sharply with the crystal-cold darkness beyond the long windows. The lights of London glittered with an icy brilliance, and he wondered how Ruth was reacting to the chill of an English spring.

The beige telephone on its polished table mocked his introspection. There was one way of finding out, an inner voice derided. He had only to pick up the receiver and dial her aunt's number. Ruth herself might answer. As soon as he heard her voice he would know how she was feeling. Her tone was very expressive.

He glanced at his watch. There was still half an hour before he need leave for the Symonds'. Plenty of time to call a friend and enquire after her health. Only Ruth wasn't a friend, he told himself savagely. To her, he was an enemy, and to him, she was the manifestation of his own bestiality.

He flung himself on to the couch beside the phone and viewed its simple lines with dislike. In God's name, why was he tormenting himself like this? She wasn't in danger any longer. She wasn't alone or abandoned. She had an aunt and an adopted cousin of her own. So why was he plaguing himself with responsibilities that were not—and could not—be his?

He got to his feet again, and went and poured himself a Scotch. The raw spirit was soothing, and he poured another before returning to his seat, staring into his glass as if all the secrets of the world might there be revealed.

He was still sitting there when the telephone rang, and for a moment he wondered if some method of thought transference had induced Ruth to ring him. This idea was quickly abandoned, however, when his father came on the line, and at the end of their conversation he felt more morose than ever. Jake wanted him to go to the United States the next day, to attend a conference of Western industrialists in New York, and the possibility that it might be another week before he was back in London filled him with impatience. He didn't feel like packing up and leaving again, and he had been tempted to tell his father to find someone else to take his place. He didn't think Barbara would be too thrilled either, and he slumped back against the soft leather with a feeling of acute depression.

Finishing his drink, he eventually hauled himself upright, sitting in a hunched position, legs apart, his hands holding his glass hanging loosely between. This was no good, he told himself severely. He was allowing Ruth to occupy too large a place in his thoughts. Like anything remembered, he was exaggerating his responsibility towards her out of all proportion, and there was only one way to discard it.

Putting the glass aside, he reached for the phone, and after only a second's hesitation dialled the number of the house in Wellington Mews. There might be no one in, he consoled himself, as the tone purred. He could hardly blame himself for not getting in touch with her if there was no one in, and by the time he got back from New York he might have succeeded in shaking off this melancholy.

'Miss Pascal's residence!'

The aloof female tones were too precise to be those of Davina Pascal herself, and Dominic drew a deep breath before saying harshly: 'Is Miss Jason there? I'd like to speak to her.'

There was a moment's silence, and then the voice continued: 'Who shall I say is calling, sir?' and Dominic's teeth jarred together.

'I'm—a friend of hers,' he said at last, with reluctance. 'Please ask her to come to the phone.'

There was another silence, longer this time, and Dominic's long fingers sought the tense nerves at the back of his neck. For God's sake, he muttered silently, what was going on?

When Ruth's voice came on the line, his reaction was more powerful than even he had expected. It was such a delightful voice, soft and faintly husky, and evidently anxious as to who might be calling her.

'Ruth?' His own voice had suffered from the delay, and came out more roughly than he could have wished. 'Ruth, how are you? I read about your father in the paper. I'm terribly sorry.'

'Dom—Mr Crown!' she choked, obviously recognising his voice without effort. Then, more coldly: 'What do you want?'

'What do I want?' Dominic expelled his breath impatiently. 'What do you think I want? I want to know how you are. Whether you're happy. What you think of London.'

'I'm very well, thank you.' Her response was clipped. 'Thank you for calling—'

He knew she was going to ring off, and it was suddenly imperative that he should stop her. 'Ruth! Ruth—wait!' he exclaimed, overriding her polite rejoinder. 'Ruth, please—talk to me!'

There was another of those nerve-racking silences, when he half suspected she had rung off already, and then she said quietly: 'We have nothing to say to one another, Mr Crown. I—I don't know why you bothered ringing me. I'm perfectly all right. Aunt Davina is very kind, and Martin and I are good friends already.'

'Martin?'

Dominic couldn't prevent the automatic echo of the name, and Ruth explained, 'My cousin Martin. Or at least, my adopted cousin. He's Aunt Davina's adopted son—'

'Yes, yes.' Dominic was impatient now. He didn't want to hear about Martin Pascal, whatever the boy's name was, he wanted to hear about Ruth, and the gulf between them had never seemed wider. 'So, how long have you been in England? I've been away—' He didn't stop to explain, but hurried on: 'I saw your picture in *The Times* this morning. I—I didn't even know your father had died.'

'Why should you?' Ruth was very cool, very detached. 'As a matter of fact, I've been in England a little over two weeks. Daddy died just a few days after—after—'

'After I left?' asked Dominic abruptly, and she

made a sound of confirmation. 'So what happened? How did you find out you had an aunt?'

'It's a long story,' said Ruth flatly. 'It's not important now. The important thing is that—I'm here, and—and I'm happy. That's all you need to know.'

'Ruth!' His use of her name was strangled. 'Ruth, can't we at least speak civilly to one another? For God's sake,' he broke off savagely, and then continued, in a driven tone: 'Ruth, I want to see you. Will you meet me for—for breakfast tomorrow? I'd say lunch, but by then I'll be on my way to New York.'

'You can't be serious!' Ruth sounded shocked now, and he half regretted his impulsive invitation. But somehow he had to satisfy himself that she was well and happy, and he couldn't do that through the medium of the telephone.

'I am serious,' he said heavily. 'Ruth, don't you think you owe it to me to—'

'I don't *owe* you anything!' she retorted chokingly, and this time there was no mistaking the fact that she had broken the connection.

Dominic replaced the receiver with controlled impatience, and then remained where he was for several minutes just staring at the instrument. Bitterness, resentment, anger—he felt all of those things, and an almost insane desire to get in his car and drive to Wellington Mews, and force his way into her aunt's house.

'What time are you leaving, sir?'

Shannon's entry had gone unnoticed, and now Dominic looked up at the manservant sourly. 'What?'

'I said—what time are you—'

'I don't know,' Dominic interrupted him, proving that he had registered what Shannon had said, getting up from the sofa and pacing moodily about the floor. He glanced again at his watch. 'I should have left five minutes ago, does that answer your question?' he demanded arrogantly, and the little Irishman gave an involuntary shrug of his shoulders.

'Sure and I only asked,' he murmured, making for the door, but this time Dominic halted him.

'I did as you suggested,' he said unpleasantly. 'I phoned Miss Jason. I just hope you're satisfied now.'

Shannon hesitated. 'Wasn't the young lady at home?'

'Oh, yes. The young lady was at home,' declared Dominic dourly. 'Unfortunately, she didn't want to speak to me.'

'No!' Shannon sounded surprised. 'Ah, well, perhaps it's just as well.'

'What do you mean?' Dominic glared at him, and the Irishman shifted uncomfortably.

'I don't think Miss Symonds would approve of you making overtures to another member of the opposite sex,' he opined sagely, and Dominic felt a rising sense of frustration.

'Don't you?' he enquired, the sarcasm evident in his voice. 'Well, it's a little late to tell me that now.'

Shannon shrugged. 'Why? You said the young lady didn't speak to you. There's no harm done.'

'Isn't there?' Dominic didn't bother to correct him, and with a cursory inclination of his head he strode out of the apartment.

Behind the wheel of the Porsche, he felt his nerves

tightening again. The last thing he needed now was a dose of Gerald Symonds' political dogma. The man might have been useful to his father in the past, but Dominic had no desire to get involved in party politics, and without really considering the consequences of what he was about to do, he turned into the Marylebone Road.

Wellington Mews was easier to find, now that he knew the way, but he parked the Porsche outside the narrow entry, and walked the last few yards to the door. The knocker was brass and highly polished, and the sound it made echoed round the enclosed yard long after he had let it fall. It had an ominous ring, and it momentarily daunted the determination that had brought him here. What was he doing? he asked himself impatiently, then stiffened as the door was opened.

An elderly woman waited inside, and he guessed this must be the individual he had spoken to earlier. Stepping into the light shed by the carriage lamps, he forced a faint smile to his lips, and then, at her enquiring stare, said: 'My name is Crown, Dominic Crown. I'd like to speak to Miss Pascal.'

'Miss Pascal is not at home this evening, sir,' the woman replied, in the carefully modulated tones he remembered. 'If you would like to leave a message . . .'

Dominic inwardly cursed. Then, coming to a decision, he said: 'Miss Jason—I believe she is at home. May I speak with her instead?'

Now, the housekeeper—for she was surely too old to be anything less—looked doubtful. 'I'm not sure that Miss Jason is expecting any callers, sir,' she said dubiously. 'I think she may have gone to bed.'

'At half past seven?' Dominic observed sceptically. 'Isn't that a little early?'

The woman looked uncertain. 'Does Miss Jason know you, sir?'

Dominic sighed. 'Yes.'

'Then perhaps you'd better come inside, while I find out if she can see you,' remarked the housekeeper consideringly, and Dominic hesitated only fractionally before stepping into the house.

The hall was warm and mellow, its illumination coming from a cut-glass chandelier at the foot of the stairs. Seasoned panelling, a russet and gold carpet underfoot, delicate prints of a bygone era—it was evident that Davina Pascal was a woman of substance, and Dominic looked about him in frank appraisal as the housekeeper ascended the curving staircase.

He had approached a daguerreotype of an old Model T Ford, and was examining it in detail, when he heard hurried footsteps on the stairs. He glanced round, half surprised that the elderly housekeeper should be able to move so swiftly, and then felt a sudden jolt at the sight of the girl, who had halted, nervously, on the curve of the staircase. In a simple but evidently expensive dress of some soft woollen material, its cowl collar framing her determined little chin, and her hair bound securely round her head in a coronet of braids, she looked far older, and infinitely more sophisticated, and he knew a sudden pang for the innocent adolescent she had been. Even her eyes seemed to hint at a new experience, and his opinion of himself reached a new, and all-time, low.

'What do you mean by coming here?' she exclaimed now, in a hushed voice. 'You have no right to be here. Please—go away!'

'Ruth—' He crossed the hall to the foot of the stairs, and stood looking up at her with a feeling of frustration. 'Ruth, for heaven's sake, I wanted to see you. I wanted to talk to you. Surely you knew, I had to make sure you're all right.'

'Well, as you can see, I am,' Ruth said huskily, glancing anxiously up the stairs behind her. 'Now, will you go? Aunt Davina is likely to come back at any time. I don't want her to find you here.'

'Why not?' Dominic wished she would come down the stairs. 'Oh, I see. You haven't told her about me yet. Never mind, she's bound to find out sooner or later—'

'No!' Ruth's response was instinctive, and Dominic's mouth compressed.

'No?'

'There's no reason why Aunt Davina need be told. She—I—that's in the past. I don't even want to think about it.'

Dominic could feel his patience wearing thin, and endeavoured to control it. 'At least come down and speak to me,' he persisted flatly. 'I promise I won't embarrass you if your aunt appears. I'll tell her I'm selling tickets for one of my mother's charitable organisations.' He exhaled heavily. 'Don't make me have to come up and fetch you.'

Ruth was shocked. 'You wouldn't dare!'

'You know I would,' he told her politely, and with a helpless gesture, she gave in.

'You'd better come up,' she said tautly. 'The sitting room is on the first floor. If you'll follow me—'

Dominic did so, his eyes irresistibly drawn to the long slender legs, now sleekly encased in sheer silk. Following her, he was aware of the perfume she was wearing, and the faint trace of perspiration she exuded, as if the cool exterior she presented belied an inner conflict.

They crossed a wide landing, passing the figure of the elderly housekeeper, who had apparently been awaiting her mistress's instructions. Ruth bade her leave them, and as she went heavily down the stairs again, the girl led the way into a tastefully furnished drawing room. She stood back to allow him to walk into the centre of the room, evidently intending to leave the double doors open. But Dominic firmly took possession of the handles, and closed the gap deliberately before allowing her to speak.

Ruth stood on the hearth before the fireplace. There was a fire in the grate, whose warming glow highlighted the darkened corners of the moulded ceiling, but she was scarcely aware of it. She was obviously ill at ease, and nervous, and Dominic could not entirely deny his own coiling tension.

'So,' he said, coming towards her, 'you're a young lady of leisure at last. I'm glad. I've thought about you a lot since I got home.'

'Have you?' She sounded sceptical, and his lips tightened.

'Yes,' he insisted, halting a few feet from her and pushing his hands into the pockets of his dark blue velvet jacket. 'Believe it or not, I was worried about you. And I'm sorry to hear that your father is dead. Do you want to talk about it?'

'I don't want to talk about anything with you,' Ruth asserted shortly, holding up her head, and a feeling of exasperation gripped him.

'Why not?' he demanded. 'You used to enjoy talking to me.' He sighed, looking down at the polished toes of his boots. 'About what happened, Ruth—'

'Oh, please.' She half turned away from him then. 'Don't you think this is all a waste of time? What happened, happened. It was all my fault. I—I don't blame you for it.'

'Ruth!' Dominic's lean face darkened with sudden colour. 'Ruth, you've got to let me make amends—'

'How?' She turned to look at him then, and he moved his shoulders helplessly.

'I don't know.' He looked at her. 'Is there anything you need? Somewhere to live, somewhere of your own. Money—'

Ruth coloured now. 'As you can see, I'm quite well provided for, thank you,' she responded coldly. 'Aunt Davina has taken care of everything, and Martin gives me anything I need.'

'Martin?' Dominic's jaw hardened. 'Your cousin.'

'My adopted cousin,' she corrected him firmly. 'I think—I know Aunt Davina hopes that we—'

'You can't be serious!' Dominic overrode her now, his voice harsh and incredulous. 'You haven't known him above a couple of weeks! For God's sake, Ruth, don't be stampeded into a relationship you're neither prepared nor ready for!'

'As a matter of fact, I've known Martin and Aunt Davina for a lot longer then two weeks,' Ruth replied coolly. 'They flew out to the islands a few days after Daddy died. It was they who helped me to—to deal with everything.'

Dominic's eyes narrowed. 'You told me you had no relations.'

'I did believe that.' Ruth bent her head. 'It's what Daddy always told me. It was as much a surprise to me as anyone else.'

'So your father did tell you, before he died?'

'No.' Ruth shook her head now. 'No, as a matter of fact, Aunt Davina told me herself.' She paused. 'When—when Daddy died, the income he had had from Mummy's estate had to be transferred to me. As soon as Aunt Davina learned I was—alone, she made arrangements to fly out at once.'

'I see.'

Dominic couldn't help feeling Davina Pascal's intervention had been slightly out of character. She had known of the girl's existence for years without contacting her, yet as soon as her father was dead she immediately appeared to claim her niece. He frowned. Of course, he could be doing the woman a rank injustice. She must have known Curtis Jason before he left England, and no doubt she also realised he was unlikely to approve of his daughter associating with her mother's relatives. All the same, she could have written to the girl from time to time, if she felt any affection towards her, and not simply allowed her to grow up in ignorance of her rightful heritage.

'So you see everything has turned out perfectly,' Ruth was saying now, her voice still a little jerky, in spite of herself. 'You don't need to concern yourself on my behalf any more.' She paused, her darting glance evading his, and then added reluctantly: 'Your—your arm? It's properly healed now, I suppose. You—er—you don't seem to have any stiffness with it.'

'No.' Dominic moved the arm he had injured freely. 'No, it's as good as new. Thanks to you and your father—and Doctor Francis, of course.'

'Yes.' Ruth pressed her lips together. 'Good.'

'Good,' he echoed dryly, and exhaled rather heavily.

There was a silence after that, a pregnant cessation of sound, during which he could hear the uneven tenor of her breathing. She was trying hard to appear calm and casual, but he sensed the struggle she was having to sustain that composed façade. He wondered what she was really thinking, whether she really found his presence as objectionable as she professed—and why he was asking himself that question, with Barbara waiting impatiently for his arrival at Farleigh Terrace.

The remembrance of his fiancée made him suddenly aware of the time. He was already late for the dinner party, without an adequate excuse, and it was obvious he was wasting his time by remaining here. He had done what he came for. He had assured himself that Ruth was well and happy. He need no longer feel responsible for her. *But he did!*

'Ruth—' he began helplessly, but this time she interrupted him.

'I think you'd better go,' she declared huskily. 'I—it—it was good of you to come,' she finished politely, and his stomach muscles tightened in a sudden wave of frustration.

'Ruth,' he muttered, pulling his hands out of his pockets and capturing her wrist between his fingers. 'Ruth, my telephone number is in the book. Promise me you'll ring if you need anything, anything at all.'

Ruth endeavoured to release herself from his grasp, but when she couldn't, she didn't struggle. Instead she looked up at him squarely, and said very clearly: 'Wouldn't your fiancée have some objections if I did?'

Dominic's senses stirred. He couldn't help it. She was so proud, so courageous, so utterly desirable in every way. He realised he had forgotten how lucid her eyes could be, how delicate the curve of her cheekbone, how soft and vulnerable her mouth. As he looked at her, all thoughts of Barbara faded from his mind, and he wondered how he had lived for almost eight weeks without her. His searching gaze recognised the moment when she became aware of the intensity of his regard, and his eyes lowered to the thrusting evidence of her arousal. Beneath the fine material of her gown, her hardening nipples were outlined in sensuous detail, and his body throbbed with an answering excitement.

She tried to free herself then, realising how dangerous the moment was, but Dominic would not let her go. Against her will she was impelled towards him, and his mouth sought hers with burning urgency. Her lips were pressed tightly together, forbidding his hungry assault, but anger hardened his resolve. She was not as indifferent as she would have

him believe, he told himself fiercely, yet still she
resisted his demands.

At last he drew back his head to look into her face,
and saw her features contorted with indignation, her
eyes brilliant with unshed tears. But she was determined he should not have that satisfaction, and he
felt a sense of disappointment out of all proportion to
the situation. She didn't say anything—or perhaps
couldn't, was nearer the truth—but her feelings had
never been clearer. What he saw in her eyes chilled
his blood, and with a gesture of impatience he released her, raking tormented fingers through his hair
to his scalp.

'I think you'd better leave,' she got out at last,
putting up a shaking hand to the now uncertain
coronet of braids. 'I don't think we have anything more to say to one another. It's all been
said.'

Dominic's brows drew together. 'Oh, Ruth,' he
muttered, in a driven tone. 'All right, I'll go. But at
least tell me you won't forget that I'm here if you
need me!'

Ruth bent her head. 'And will you tell your fiancée
about what happened between us—as you told
Daddy?' she asked suddenly, and his lips parted.

'What?'

Ruth repeated what she had said, adding with
difficulty: 'You swore you wouldn't tell him, but you
did.'

Dominic was totally confused. 'Tell him? Tell him
what?'

'About us. About what happened,' she exclaimed
tearfully, her emotions getting the better of her in

spite of herself. 'If—if you hadn't told him, he might still be alive. Doctor Francis said—'

'Wait a minute.' Dominic could feel the adrenalin flowing inside him. 'What is it I'm supposed to have told your father? That I made love to you? That I took you down to the beach and seduced you?' His lips twisted. 'I didn't. You know I didn't. My god, what kind of a bastard do you think I am?'

Ruth gazed up at him. 'You—didn't? But you must have. How—how else did he find out?'

'I don't know.' Dominic ran a restless hand inside his jacket, over the ruffled silk of his shirt front. Then he shook his head. 'Did you really believe I would do a thing like that? My God, what would have been the point?'

Ruth turned away in confusion. 'I—I don't know. What am I supposed to think? He knew. Somehow, he knew. No one else could have told him.'

'How about Celeste?' suggested Dominic shortly. 'She didn't exactly treat you with kid gloves, did she? Maybe she wanted to stir up trouble. Perhaps she was still aggrieved over the way you'd treated her.'

Ruth shook her head. 'Celeste didn't know—'

'You mean you didn't tell her,' Dominic corrected cynically. 'Oh, Ruth, you're an innocent, but Celeste's not. Do you think she didn't guess what had happened?'

'Was it so obvious?' Ruth's face burned with colour, and Dominic knew an almost overwhelming desire to comfort her. But this time he suppressed the emotions she aroused. He had no right to demand anything more of her, when he had no intention of breaking his engagement. Still, he consoled himself, there was no reason why they should not be friends, and he put out his hand to run the back of his knuckles down her averted cheek.

He felt a moment's irritation when she flinched away from him, but he refused to be deterred. 'You do believe me, don't you?' he asked, determinedly keeping his voice gentle, and she pushed the tips of her fingers across her damp cheeks.

'Does it matter?' she countered, giving a sniff, and his patience wavered.

'Of course it matters,' he said, between his teeth. 'Ruth, I'm sorry—for everything. But isn't it possible for us to—to start again?'

'Start again?' She looked at him blankly. 'What do you mean?'

Dominic sighed. 'We were friends once. I'd like us to be friends again.'

'Oh, no!' A faintly hysterical note had entered her voice now. 'Dominic, you can't be serious!'

'Why not?'

'Why not?' Ruth spread her hands. 'Because we can never be friends. You're going to marry—your fiancée, and I—I shall very probably marry Martin.' She took a deep breath. 'End of explanation.'

Dominic's impatience flared. 'I suggested you take a little more time before deciding you want to marry anyone,' he retorted bleakly. 'Whatever you say, you can't be sure that Pascal, or whatever he calls himself, is the right man for you. Give yourself more time. Go out and meet people. Don't tie yourself down again!'

Ruth shook her head. 'I've met lots of people since I left the island,' she asserted. 'Aunt Davina took me to New York before we came to London. I met people there, young and old.' She paused, before adding, deliberately, he thought, 'None of whom I liked as much as Martin.'

Dominic could feel the anger building up inside him. It was ridiculous. He had no reason to care what she did with her life. But nonetheless he was involved.

'I want you to think very carefully, before you agree to anything,' he averred roughly. 'Don't let gratitude to your aunt blind you to the facts of life. You're still an innocent, Ruth, whatever you think. So, keep your independence. Have some fun!'

'As you do.' She suggested, looking up at him through her lashes, and Dominic felt the hairs lifting along the back of his neck. He couldn't help it. She was infuriating—but as he felt the quickening of desire coursing through his blood again, he knew he still wanted her.

With a feeling of impotence he abruptly turned away from her, walking towards the door, eager to put himself beyond temptation. But now she came after him, moving with a lissom grace, in the high-heeled sandals she had learned to wear, and which complemented the slender curve of her ankles. She came up behind him as he reached the doors, and her hand touched his sleeve.

'Dominic . . .'

He halted, aware of her with every nerve of his being, and then forced himself to face her expressionlessly. 'Yes?'

'I do thank you,' she said softly, and his hands clenched at his sides. 'For coming, I mean. And—

and for reassuring me about Daddy. I do believe you, if it means anything.'

Dominic could feel the blood pounding in his ears, and he knew he had to get out of there before he did something he would almost certainly regret. With a curt nod, he bowed his head, and then wrenching open the door, he bounded down the stairs, without even looking back.

Behind the wheel of the Porsche his pulses slowed, and the blood receded from his temples. The recollection of Barbara's dinner party, now surely well into its second course, was a sobering thought, and he inserted the keys in the ignition. He badly needed a drink, but that would have to wait. Right now, he had to think of a reason for his late arrival, and somehow he sensed that whatever he said, Barbara was unlikely to forgive him.

CHAPTER THIRTEEN

Ruth awakened to the noise of the milk float clattering around Wellington Grove. She was still not accustomed to the normal sounds associated with early morning in London, and she invariably awoke long before the rest of the household.

Even her bed was a source of annoyance at times. She was used to a much harder mattress, and the minimum amount of covering; the linen sheets and soft woollen blankets that her aunt's housekeeper had provided seemed weighty and confining, yet without them she shivered in the early morning chill.

The climate in England was still cold to her, although not as unpleasant as her father had led her to believe. It did not rain every day, as she had expected, and Aunt Davina had told her that they seldom had a lot of snow, even in the depths of winter. Just now, it was spring, and the flowers in the Park delighted her, as too did the ducks on the pond, and the dozens of small children, and their mothers, who flocked to feed them. She liked the mellowed old buildings, and the shops, although the press of people who used them frightened her a little, and as she was learning to drive, she was looking forward to being able to drive out of London and see more of the country where she had been born.

It was strange how she had lived so many years without knowing of Aunt Davina's existence. Now, it seemed she had always known her, and the affection the older woman had shown her filled her with warmth and gratitude.

Gratitude!

Her lips clung together in sudden uncertainty. She wished she had not thought of that particular word, and her skin prickled at the images it evoked. Why had Dominic come to see her? Why had he come here, when she had succeeded in convincing herself that she should never see him again? Why had he appeared and destroyed her fragile shell of indifference?

Her breath escaped on a tiny sob, and she turned to bury her face in the pillow. For weeks now, she realised, she had been practising a kind of self-deception. Ever since Aunt Davina had arrived like a fairy godmother, to solve all her problems, she had endeavoured to forget what had happened to her. Her father's sudden death, the awful solemnity of his funeral, her subsequent feelings of raw bereavement—these things had served to keep other thoughts at bay. A kind of numbness had gripped her, and she had welcomed it. If Doctor Francis had suspected anything, he had kept his own counsel. His opinion had been that Professor Jason's death had been a mercy, and there had been nothing left for her father but pain and distress. Ruth had embraced that reassurance, and tried to live with it.

Dominic's reappearance had probed a nerve, alerting her once again to an awareness of her own weaknesses. Although she might regret what had happened between them, she could never forget it, and she was very much afraid that given the same circumstances, it could happen again.

She fumbled for the handkerchief she had taken to bed with her the night before. She had stuffed it under her pillow, before crying herself to sleep, and now she scrubbed its still damp folds across her cheek. Why was she so vulnerable where Dominic was concerned? she asked herself bitterly. Why couldn't she condemn him completely for what he had done? He was unscrupulous. He was quite prepared to conduct an affair with her, and still maintain a façade of respectability with his fiancée, yet when he kissed her as he had kissed her last night she had found it desperately hard to resist him. That she had succeeded was due in no small part to his lack of persistence, and she knew that had he continued his assault on her senses, she would have succumbed.

It was humiliating, and she was overwhelmingly relieved that Aunt Davina had not been there to witness her niece's distress after his departure. That would have been utterly degrading, and she doubted if even Martin would have forgiven her.

Thinking of Martin, Ruth pushed back the covers and got determinedly out of bed. There was no point in lying there, brooding over what might have been. It hadn't happened. She had not given in to him. And somehow she had to make sure it never happened again.

The room heaved as she moved away from the bed, and a feeling of nausea gripped her. She remembered, belatedly, that she had eaten next to nothing of her dinner the previous evening, and Mrs

Radcliffe had viewed her lack of appetite disapprovingly. Obviously she was hungry, and although the thought of food was not entirely acceptable to her, she determinedly went into the bathroom to wash and clean her teeth.

She dressed in corded pants and a silk shirt, briefly admiring her slender figure as she passed the long cheval mirror. Having a full-length mirror was an unexpected delight, and although she seldom spent long in front of it, being able to see herself from every angle was a novelty.

Her hair she secured as usual in the braids her aunt preferred. Davina, she knew, would have had her hair cut in New York, had Ruth been agreeable, but when the girl demurred, she had compromised by insisting that she keep it confined at least. Ruth complied, but she didn't altogether like the severity it brought to her face, and in bed, and in the privacy of her bedroom, she determinedly left it loose.

It was barely seven-thirty when she descended the stairs from her second-floor bedroom. The house in Wellington Mews was large and sprawling, spreading over the now-unused stables and carriage houses beneath. Aunt Davina kept a Daimler for her own use, and Martin had his Lamborghini, but apart from that the garages were empty.

Ruth had found such a surfeit of space intimidating when she first came here. Used to the bungalow, where all the rooms had a purpose, she found the idea of so much emptiness disturbing, and she was sad that the library and the music room had so little use, and spent most of their days silent, behind slatted blinds. But then everything had been strange to begin with, not least the idea of having relatives she had never met.

Aunt Davina never referred to the reasons why her father had lost contact with her mother's sister. In the beginning, she had explained that distance had separated the two families, but as Ruth began to comprehend what a wealthy woman her aunt was, she couldn't help wondering why she had never taken the trouble to fly out and see them. She suspected it had to do with Professor Jason's blank denial of any other living relative, and because she was loath to appear critical of her father, she had remained silent.

Nevertheless, she had been amazed to discover that she had an inheritance of her own. The income they had lived on which came from her grandmother's estate, had not been the pittance she had always believed. On the contrary, it was quite a considerable allowance, and because of her father's parsimony, it had mounted up in the bank, and accrued interest. In consequence, she could have lived quite comfortably on her own, had Aunt Davina not chosen to offer her a home.

The island, too, was hers. She doubted it was worth much, but in any case, she had no desire to sell it. Somehow, just knowing it was there made her feel more secure, and she had promised Father Andreas that he need not fear for his home again. In return, he had promised to tend her father's grave, a small plot in the shadow of the church Professor Jason had so staunchly opposed in life.

Ruth entered her aunt's morning room to find the elderly housekeeper laying the breakfast table. Mrs

Radcliffe, she knew, had been with Aunt Davina for years, and was really too old to continue as house-keeper. But her aunt was fond of the old woman, and Ruth had made friends with her. She was not at all like Celeste, but Ruth could talk to her, and she smiled now, as the girl came through the door, and straightened to put a supporting hand to her spine. 'You're an early bird, and no mistake,' she re-marked, by way of a greeting. 'When are you going to learn to sleep till midday, like Mr Martin?'

'Never, I hope,' declared Ruth, with a grimace. 'It's no good. The milkman always wakes me. And besides,' she rubbed her flat stomach vigorously, 'I feel a bit empty.'

'That's no surprise,' observed Mrs Radcliffe dryly. 'You eat like a bird, too. It's time you started tucking in to a good old English breakfast. Ham and eggs, sausages and bacon, topped up with toast and mar-malade—'

'Oh, don't!' Ruth had turned quite pale at the thought, and the housekeeper viewed her anxiously.

'You feeling all right this morning?' she ex-claimed, coming round the table towards the girl. 'You look proper pasty, now I come to look at you. Come along with me to the kitchen, and I'll give you a nice hot cup of tea.'

Ruth hesitated, but as the nausea receded, she nodded. 'I think I must be very hungry,' she said, following the housekeeper down the stairs. 'But just toast and marmalade, I think. None of those other things.'

By the time Aunt Davina put in an appearance Ruth was feeling much better, and as Davina invariably ate breakfast in bed, she was now ready to deal with her correspondence. In the two weeks since they had arrived back in London, Ruth had taken to joining her aunt at this time, and helping her with her letters, scribbling her replies on scraps of paper, ready for typing later. At present Davina typed her own letters, but Ruth was thinking of suggesting that she might learn to do them, and in that way repay her aunt a little for the time and patience she was expending on her.

This morning, however, her aunt suddenly looked up from an invitation she was scanning, and subjected her niece to a piercing stare. Davina had a very penetrating stare when she chose, from eyes of a much paler colour than Ruth's, and in consequence able to freeze at a glance. Combined with high cheekbones, and a prominent nose, and the kind of regal bearing Ruth had hitherto only associated with royalty, Davina could be quite a daunting figure, and this morning Ruth was made acutely aware of it.

'Mrs Radcliffe tells me you had a visitor last evening,' she remarked, without expression, and Ruth felt the tell-tale colour fill her cheeks. In her hurry to dispel the sense of nausea she had been feeling, she had completely forgotten her earlier intention to ask the housekeeper not to mention Dominic's visit, and now she was nonplussed by this unexpected challenge.

'I—well, yes,' she got out at last, and Davina tilted her head at the angle which denoted she expected her to continue her explanation. 'It—it was someone selling tickets for—for a charity ball,' she added in mortification, and Davina's pale eyelids narrowed her accusing stare.

'Someone selling tickets for a charity ball?' she repeated at last, and Ruth nodded. 'Who was selling them?'

Ruth inwardly groaned. 'I—I think he said the name was Crown,' she said, unable to dissemble any further, and almost miraculously her aunt's face cleared.

'Crown? Did you say Crown?' she exclaimed, without any of the condemnation Ruth had expected. 'Of course! Mrs James Crown is well known for her work for charity. I wonder who came selling the tickets. Some voluntary worker, I suppose. Did you buy any?'

'Buy any?' Ruth almost choked. Obviously, Mrs Radcliffe had not mentioned Dominic's name. 'I—why, no. No. I—I didn't think you'd be interested.'

'Oh, one always subscribes to worthy causes,' replied her aunt, patting her hand. 'But of course you weren't to know that. Perhaps it was a little naughty of Mrs Radcliffe, letting him in. After all, one never knows who one is letting into one's home these days.'

Ruth's lips formed a faint smile, but she was shaken, and she hoped her aunt would not notice.

'Anyway, enough of that,' said Davina, tossing the invitation she had been holding aside and reaching for another envelope. 'I shall probably be contacted from another source.' She frowned. 'Now, let me see, have you got your notepad ready? Good. Shall we begin?'

Martin appeared as one of the maids who came in daily to help Mrs Radcliffe arrived with a midmorning tray of coffee. He came into his mother's sitting room yawning widely, and then gave them his sheepish grin as Davina glanced pointedly at the clock.

'I know I'm late,' he apologised, bending to kiss his adopted mother's cheek, before bestowing a similar salutation on Ruth's temple. 'But I'm not meeting Jarvis until one o'clock, and I needed a good night's rest before going out on the track.'

His mother grimaced, and even Ruth looked a little doubtful at his words, but Martin ignored them, helping himself to a cup of coffee before lounging on to the couch. Sitting there, sipping at the coffee, he had a decidedly boyish air, and Ruth could quite see why Aunt Davina found it so hard to deny him anything. A little above average height, slim and attractive, with russet-coloured curly hair, and a mischievous grin, he was easily the most easy-going person Ruth had ever met, and this, combined with his amusing personality, made him a very likeable character. That he was inclined to be lazy, too, was usually overlooked, and Ruth had initially been amazed that he did not have a regular occupation. Her father had insisted on keeping busy, even when illness had made concentration difficult, but when she had broached this premise with Martin, he had only laughed.

'Ruthie,' he cajoled, using his pet name for her, which she personally abhorred, 'What possible point would there be in me getting a job, and depriving some other poor bloke of the privilege? I don't need to work. I don't need the money. Why should I waste my time and energies in some dull office, when I can enjoy myself far more satisfactorily out in the open air?'

And it was true that Martin did spend a lot of time out of doors. He was an enthusiastic golfer and yachtsman, he played tennis and squash, he liked swimming and skiing, and he was a founder member of a club, for something called hang-gliding, which he had explained to Ruth consisted of hanging by a kind of harness from a parachute-like device. It had all sounded rather silly to her, but Martin obviously enjoyed it, and he had said he would teach her, too, if she was interested.

At the moment, however, his interests lay in an entirely different direction. A friend of his with connections in the motor trade had got him involved in motor racing, and this afternoon he was joining something called the production car trials at the track. Ruth knew Aunt Davina did not approve of him racing. She thought it was too dangerous. But somehow Ruth sensed that Martin was unlikely to be in any real danger. He was simply not the type to take unnecessary risks. Life was much too sweet to him as it was.

'I hope you realise I shan't have a moment's peace until you're home again,' Aunt Davina said now, abandoning her correspondence to pour herself more coffee. 'Why don't you take Ruth with you, then she can ring me if anything goes wrong? You can't rely on that man Jarvis to do the right thing. He's a thoroughly unfavourable influence.'

'Oh, Mother!'

Martin swallowed the last of his coffee and balanced his cup precariously on the arm of his chair.

while Ruth endeavoured to retrieve the situation.

'I am going with him, Aunt Davina,' she reassured the older woman firmly. 'I'm looking forward to it. Why don't you come, too?'

'Oh, no!' Her aunt shuddered convincingly. 'I can think of nothing more boring than watching a bunch of noisy vehicles chasing one another around a track.' She paused, glancing back at the letters with a thoughtful eye. 'You know, I ought perhaps to ring Mrs Crown about those tickets?' And as Ruth's mouth dried up completely, she went on: 'I wouldn't like her to think I had refused to buy any.'

'What tickets?' Martin was curious, and his mother explained about Ruth's unexpected visitor. 'Of course, it's possible I may be contacted again,' she added, 'but I shouldn't like to offend her.'

'Mmm.' Martin was thoughtful. 'I wouldn't mind knowing the Crowns. Do you know, they sponsor racing events? It's all advertising, I suppose. They make products for cars and car maintenance. Jarvis told me about some sealer he'd heard of for radiators that—'

'Oh, really, Martin, I'm not interested in the products that are available to the motor trade,' retorted his mother irritably. 'I doubt if Mrs Crown concerns herself with such mundane matters. Since her younger son died, she's become well known for her work helping the underprivileged, and it's in that capacity that we're speaking of her.'

While Martin and Aunt Davina argued over the relevant merits of Dominic's mother, Ruth experienced a temporary release from tension. Aunt

S.—I

Davina's words about Dominic's younger brother had touched a chord inside her, and she wondered when he had died, and why. It was strange, but because Dominic was involved it seemed important that she should know, but she could never ask, not without arousing unnecessary suspicion.

'I think perhaps I should call at the house,' Aunt Davina said suddenly, and Ruth's attention was speared once again. 'The telephone is such an impersonal instrument, I always think.'

'*Let me!*' Before she could prevent herself, the words had spilled from Ruth's lips, and both her aunt and her cousin turned to look at her in surprise. 'I could go,' she hastened on, committed to her cause, now that she had started. 'I mean, it was I who turned the—the man away. And—and you have enough to do, Aunt Davina.'

'Hey, that's a good idea,' Martin endorsed her suggestion, and went on enthusiastically: 'I'll drive you.' He gave a wicked grin. 'That way, I may get to meet her husband.'

'Oh, don't be so silly, Martin.' It was Aunt Davina who squashed his proposal. 'If Ruth gets to speak to Mrs Crown's secretary, she'll be lucky.' She frowned, before adding almost irrelevantly: 'In any case, her husband has retired, I believe. I did read something about his having a heart condition, and the son taking over the business.'

Ruth bent her head, hoping the revealing colour that stained her cheeks would be attributed to the hot coffee she had just swallowed. Did that mean that Dominic had now taken his father's place? Unless there was another son, and as she remembered

Mr Templar had not mentioned one, it seemed extremely likely.

'Well, Ruth?' Aunt Davina was speaking to her now, and with an effort she lifted her head. 'Magnus can take you round to the Crowns in the Daimler, apologise for the interruption, and explain that I was out yesterday evening.'

Ruth, if anything, felt even worse. What was that saying about tangled webs and deceptions? Now she was committed to calling at Dominic's home and making up some tale about someone selling tickets, and goodness knows what they might make of that.

She consoled herself with the thought that it was better that she should be involved, rather than anyone else, and it was always possible that there really was a charity event, as Dominic had suggested, that she could buy tickets for. Whatever, she had saved Aunt Davina from any embarrassment, and secured herself a little more time to find a solution.

'I think you should go right away,' Aunt Davina decided thoughtfully. 'Before lunch.' She scanned her niece's casual attire with an appraising eye. 'But get changed first. I think a skirt suit would look most suitable.'

'Oh, Mother, honestly!' Martin got to his feet then, and surveyed his adopted cousin with approval. 'Ruth looks perfectly all right as she is. As you said yourself, she's unlikely to get past Mrs Crown's secretary. What on earth's the point of her getting dressed up?'

Ruth looked doubtful. She liked herself in trousers too, and the wine-coloured corded pants and matching silk blouse were flatteringly feminine.

There was a jacket to match the pants, and this she suggested she could wear now, earning her aunt's reluctant endorsement.

'Oh, very well,' she said. 'If Martin thinks you look well enough. But do remember, if Mrs Crown invites you in, don't stand with your hands in your pockets, as you're doing now.'

Ruth immediately pulled her hands out of the hip pockets, and Martin gave her a sympathetic grin behind his mother's back. Aunt Davina never got the better of him as she did of everyone else, and Ruth wished she possessed a little more of his flippancy.

Nevertheless, her knees were knocking by the time Magnus, her aunt's chauffeur, had driven her to the Crowns' town house in Curzon Terrace. In spite of her aunt's instructions, she hadn't any real plan of what she was going to say, and her throat felt so dry she had difficulty in breathing. What if they turned her away? What if they imagined she was trying to gain entry under false pretences? What if Mrs Crown rang her aunt and demanded to know what was going on?

Magnus brought the old-fashioned Daimler to a halt by the kerb, but she forestalled his efforts to assist her by pushing open the door as soon as he stopped, and climbing out herself.

It was a mild sunny morning, and the trees planted at intervals along the terrace were all in blossom, but Ruth paid no attention to them. Her objective was the tall, elegant, cream-faced residence, with several painted steps leading up to its shady porch.

Realising there was nothing to be gained from delaying any longer, and unwilling to arouse

Magnus's curiosity, she crossed the pavement and mounted the steps. But as she lifted her hand to touch the bell, the door opened, and she stepped back in confusion. She thought for one moment that her approach had been apprehended, and her lips parted to form the words she had rehearsed as she climbed the steps. But they were never spoken. The sight of the man coming out of the house, closely followed by a woman a few years older, caused her tongue to cleave to the roof of her mouth, and she stood there like a doll, frozen to the spot.

Dominic recognised her at once, she knew that, but those curiously tawny eyes were swiftly guarded. She was mortified at the thought of what he must be thinking, and wondered, with a sickening sense of humiliation, whether he imagined she had come here to confront him. She had not expected to see him. Hadn't he told her on the phone the night before that he was going away? He was carrying a briefcase, but his dark grey business suit did not necessarily denote his intention to travel. He could be on his way to his office or, she quivered, meeting his fiancée. He looked cool and controlled and sophisticated, while she felt hot and sticky and embarrassed. Yet, even so, she could not prevent the instinctive reaction she had every time she saw him, the disruptive awareness of his masculinity, and the disturbing remembrance of what they had shared. This man had actually possessed her body, she thought with incredulity, even if he was looking at her now as if he didn't know her.

'Can I help you—'

The older woman was stepping forward to speak

to her, and Ruth realised that although it had seemed like an age since she came up the steps and Dominic opened the door, it had only been a few seconds. It was strange, because she had a curious sense of disorientation, as if she wasn't really standing on the steps at all, but floating some inches above them, and Dominic wasn't looking at her in that mocking way, but actually showing some concern for her welfare. As if from a long way off, she heard her own voice, but it wasn't saying the things she wanted it to say. Instead of explaining why she was here, she was actually groping for the handrail, and the words she heard were: 'I—I'm afraid I don't feel very well—'

Ruth came round to find herself lying on a sofa in an attractive green and gold painted sitting room. There was a window open nearby, and the breeze it admitted was cool and refreshing, restoring her strength and dispelling the feeling of giddiness which had preceded her loss of consciousness. Someone had removed her jacket, but she appeared to be alone in the room, and she expelled her breath unevenly, feeling the tears of pain and embarrassment prick her eyes. How could she have been so stupid? she asked herself bitterly. To faint on Mrs Crown's doorstep! It was so humiliating. She wanted to die with the shame of it all. What must she be thinking? What must Dominic be thinking? And what would Aunt Davina say when she found out?

With a sob of despair she tried to sit up, only to find herself pressed back again with a not ungentle firmness. 'Stay where you are,' Dominic told her harshly, coming round the couch to stand looking down at her. 'I'm sorry if my appearance shocked you, but how the hell was I to know I'd find you here?'

Ruth lay on the cushions, because it was easier to do so, but she moved her head anxiously from side to side. 'You don't understand,' she exclaimed. 'Aunt Davina sent me here. I—I'm supposed to buy those tickets you were supposed to be selling!'

Dominic came down on the edge of the couch beside her, and she had to shuffle herself as far across the soft leather as she could, to avoid contact with his hips. 'What was that?' he exclaimed, staring at her narrow-eyed, and with a feeling of helplessness she repeated what she had said.

'You—you see, Mrs Radcliffe told Aunt Davina some—someone had called, and I—I couldn't think of anything else.'

Dominic's expression grew brooding, as with an almost involuntary hand he smoothed the errant strands of hair back from her forehead. 'Why didn't you just tell her the truth?' he asked, his voice low and disturbing, and Ruth felt her response to his gentleness stir in the base of her stomach.

'You—you know why,' she got out chokily. 'I told you. There's no need for Aunt Davina to know about —about you—'

'So now you're getting yourself deeper and deeper into deception by concealing it?'

Ruth sighed. 'Not—not necessarily. As—as you're here, you could just sell me some tickets, if—if there are any available. I said they were for a ball, but they don't have to be. I mean, I could pretend I'd made a mistake. So long as your mother doesn't know anything anything about it—'

'But she does,' he interrupted her dryly.

'She does?' Ruth was puzzled. 'You mean you've told her I'm here?'

'I didn't have to tell her. She saw for herself,' replied Dominic impassively apparently unable to resist the urge to tidy the silky strands from her nape, too. 'She spoke to you. Didn't you hear her?'

'You mean—you mean the woman behind you— that was your mother?' Ruth was horrified.

'I'm afraid so.'

'But—but,' Ruth struggled to recall what she could of the woman she had seen, 'she—she didn't seem old enough!'

'I'm sure she'll be very flattered to hear it,' remarked Dominic, with a wry smile. 'But I assure you that was the person you apparently came to see.'

'Oh, *heavens!*'

Ruth put up her arm to shade her eyes, trying desperately to cope with this new development. He was right; she should have told her aunt the truth. But that episode in her life was still too raw, too sensitive; and she had been unwilling to expose her own vulnerability. It had been easier to say nothing, to try and forget it, and in so doing erase the evidence of her childish infatuation.

'Stop it!'

Dominic's voice had deepened, and when she removed her arm to look up at him she saw the darkening emotion in his eyes. It didn't reassure her. She was too conscious of his power over her, but although she put out her hand in protest, his fingers moved purposely from her nape to follow the open neckline of her shirt.

'What am I going to do about you?' he demanded in a driven tone, his sensual touch probing beneath the clinging silk, to find the throbbing peak of her breast. His hands were cool and possessive on her skin, yet urgent as they parted her shirt to expose the swollen nipple, and Ruth, still weak and shaken, found it incredibly difficult to drag the two sides of her shirt together again.

'Your—your mother,' she articulated with difficulty, and his mouth assumed an ironic slant. 'Where —where is she? I—I must speak to her.'

'She's gone to get you a glass of water,' Dominic intoned flatly, watching as her shaking fingers struggled to fasten the buttons. 'Believe it or not, but she was concerned about you. She thinks you're rather sweet.'

Ruth completed her task, and shuffled up on the cushions, trying to get her bearings. Heavens, Mrs Crown could come in on them at any moment, and she must look an absolute sight. A hand at her nape assured her that her braids were still coiled in place, but she guessed her face was flushed, and the evidence of Dominic's outrageous behaviour was there in her eyes, if anyone chose to look for it.

'I—I thought you were supposed to be going to— to New York,' she said now, glancing about her for her jacket. Aunt Davina would be so shocked if she could see her, and six weeks of obedience to her aunt's dictates could not be shrugged aside.

'I was,' returned Dominic indifferently. 'I was on

my way to the airport when you chose to drop at my feet.' His mouth twisted. 'Why are you wearing your hair like that? I don't like it.'

Ruth ignored this, concentrating her attention on his earlier statement. 'But you must have missed your flight!' she exclaimed, and he inclined his head laconically, as if it wasn't important.

'Oh, but that's awful!' she persisted, trying to keep her thoughts away from the warmth of his thigh against her leg, the long fingers resting only inches from her hand. 'I mean—what must your mother be thinking?'

Dominic shrugged his shoulders, and as he did so Ruth heard the sound of the door opening behind them. She guessed she was soon to find out for herself, and she was not surprised when Dominic got up from the couch to give his mother a faintly ironic glance.

Isobel Crown came round the couch to face the girl, and Ruth coloured anew at the ignominy of her position. However, Dominic's mother did not seem at all perturbed, and her smile was warm as she held out a glass of water.

'How are you feeling?' she asked, taking the seat her son had just vacated. 'I'm sorry if I appeared a little slow in recognising you, but Dominic had omitted to mention that you were in London.'

'Dominic,' echoed Ruth faintly, taking the glass and turning her face up to him. 'I'm afraid I—I don't understand—'

'Unlike you, I did tell the truth,' remarked Dominic lazily, his eyes meeting her startled ones in mocking audacity. 'Why not? My mother knows your name. What she didn't know was that you were Davina Pascal's niece.'

Ruth pressed her lips together to prevent them from trembling, and Isobel Crown shook her head sympathetically. 'You must not let my son upset you, Miss Jason,' she assured her, removing the untouched glass from her shaking hand. 'But of course we did know about you, and what you and your father did for Dominic, and I'd like to express our gratitude.'

Ruth didn't know what to say, and she looked reluctantly at Dominic again, seeking his assistance. How much had he told his mother? she wondered. What reason had he given for her being here? And now that Isobel Crown knew her identity, might she not reveal the truth to Aunt Davina?

'I told my mother that I didn't think your aunt was aware of our—association,' Dominic inserted now, with a wry grimace. 'I also admitted that I called on you yesterday evening, to assure myself of your—wellbeing.'

Ruth's tongue circled her lips. 'Did you?'

'Yes,' said his mother firmly. 'And I'm pleased to see that you've told your aunt at last.'

As Ruth cast another anxious look in Dominic's direction, he interceded again. 'She hasn't,' he said flatly. 'Quite the contrary, in fact. She told her aunt that I went to the house selling tickets for one of your charity balls!'

Isobel Crown looked astounded now, and Ruth felt terrible. 'I'm sorry,' she muttered uncomfortably. 'I didn't mean to—to involve you in any of this. And—and my aunt didn't think that—

that Dominic, I mean, Mr Crown, himself came to
the door—'

'For God's sake, don't start calling me Mr Crown,'
muttered Dominic grimly, before exchanging an impatient glance with his mother. 'She lied,' he
declared shortly, thrusting his hands into his jacket
pockets. 'She was put on the spot, and she said the
first thing that came into her head.' He sighed. 'It's
my fault. I shouldn't have gone there in the first
place.'

Isobel Crown surveyed both of them with faintly
reproving eyes. 'I would agree with that,' she confirmed dryly. Then, to Ruth: 'Why didn't you tell
your aunt the truth in the first place, my dear?
Dominic's quite respectable. No one would have
raised an eyebrow, you know. Not with your father
as chaperon.'

'I don't think it matters why she did or she didn't,'
Dominic retorted harshly. 'Either you're going to
respect her confidence or you're not. Which is it to
be?'

Ruth felt dreadful. She was responsible for the
way Dominic was speaking to his mother, and she
felt terribly guilty.

'I'm so sorry you've been involved in this, Mrs
Crown,' she began unhappily, but now Isobel shook
her head.

'No, Dominic's right. It's no business of mine why
you chose to keep the matter to yourself.' She
smiled. 'How old are you, my dear? How long is it
since you last came to England?'

Ruth moved her shoulders a little jerkily. 'I
don't remember how long ago we left England, but

—but Daddy never came back. And—and I'm seventeen.'

'Mother!'

Dominic sounded exasperated now, raking back the silver-blond hair with agitated fingers, but his mother gave him a benign smile. 'Isn't it time you were leaving for the airport, darling?' she suggested, glancing at her wrist watch, and as Ruth acknowledged this with some surprise, Dominic explained.

'There is a later flight,' he informed her shortly. 'Come with me to the airport, and wish me a good trip.'

'I don't think that's a very good idea, Dominic,' his mother interceded smoothly. 'Didn't you invite Barbara to see you off? I hardly think—'

'Ruth knows about Barbara, Mother,' Dominic interrupted her sardonically. 'And no, I did not invite Barbara to the airport. As you may recall, we didn't part last evening on the best of terms.'

Isobel folded a pleat in her skirt, and gave Ruth a rather apologetic look. 'These young people,' she murmured, with a sigh. 'Always kissing and making up.'

Dominic's mouth had hardened perceptibly. 'All right,' he said, 'I'll go. I promised Jake I'd make that meeting in Newport tonight, and I will.' He paused. 'But you will ensure that Ruth gets home safely, won't you? And with a satisfactory explanation, hmm?'

'You can depend on me,' affirmed his mother, lifting her face for his kiss. 'Look after yourself, won't you, darling?' Her lips trembled for a moment. 'You're all I've got.'

Dominic squeezed her shoulder as he bent to kiss her cheek, and Ruth averted her gaze from the intimacy of their farewell. Then she forced a smile to her lips. as he strode towards the door, and wished with a foolish sense of regret that he had kissed her too.

CHAPTER FOURTEEN

There was a car parked in the Mews when Ruth returned from her driving lesson. It was a sleek grey sports car, and she guessed it belonged to one of Martin's friends. She could think of none of her aunt's associates who would drive a car like that, and she passed it admiringly as she approached the door. Perhaps, after she had passed her driving test, Aunt Davina would allow her to buy a car, although she doubted it would be anything as elegant as the silver-grey Porsche.

Entering the house, she slipped her key back into her pouch bag and began to remove her jacket as she climbed the stairs. She guessed Aunt Davina would be resting. She often rested in the afternoons, and Martin had gone to the race track again that morning, and was unlikely to be home yet. It was a week now since his first visit to the track, and his enthusiasm was wearing. Ruth knew her aunt hoped that familiarity would serve to blunt his devotion to the sport, but so far there was no sight of it waning.

Ruth had not been impressed when she accompanied him on that first occasion, but she acknowledged she had had other things on her mind. Her visit to Dominic's home had been exhausting, and her nerves were in no state to respond favourably to the sustained noise and confusion in the pits. She had

still had that decidedly lightheaded feeling, and a
rather disgruntled Martin had brought her home
sooner than he would have liked. He had not invited
her to accompany him again, and she couldn't
honestly blame him. In any case, she had no desire to
repeat the experience, and appeased her conscience
by listening politely to his experiences every evening,
and sympathising when all did not go well.

Leaving the jacket of her velvet suit draped carelessly over the banister, Ruth entered the sitting
room without hesitation, halting in confusion at the
sight of her aunt seated on the couch, serving tea to
her visitor. The sight of her aunt was surprising, but
the identity of her visitor overshadowed all else, and
Ruth had difficulty in preventing his name from spilling from her lips. For a week now she had struggled
to put him out of her thoughts, but now here he was
again, assaulting her emotions, and tearing aside her
defences.

All the strength drained out of her, and she hardly
heard her aunt's formal introduction. 'Of course,
you know Mr Crown, don't you, Ruth? You met him
last week at his mother's. He has very kindly called to
assure himself that you're feeling better.'

Ruth clung to the door handle, aware that
Dominic had got politely to his feet and was waiting
for her to come and join them so that he could sit
down again, but she didn't move. His audacity in
coming here should not have amazed her, particularly after what his mother had told her, yet she
found it hard to believe that he could do such a thing
to her. Didn't he care what Aunt Davina might think
—what his fiancée might think? And why was he

pursuing her, when there were so many other girls in London?

'Ruth!'

Aunt Davina sounded a little impatient now, and Ruth endeavoured to compose herself. 'I'm sorry, Aunt Davina,' she apologised hastily. 'I—I thought you'd be resting.' She took a deep breath. 'Good afternoon, Mr Crown. How—how kind of you to call.'

Dominic's mouth compressed at the conventionality of her greeting, but he inclined his head in acknowledgement, and as Ruth was obliged to close the door and come and join her aunt on the couch, he resumed his position opposite.

'I was just asking Mr Crown to thank his mother for looking after you, Ruth,' Aunt Davina said pleasantly, glancing at her niece. She had had to be told what happened; Magnus had been far too inquisitive to be put off with anything less. 'But you know what young girls are like, Mr Crown,' she added, turning to him again. 'Always thinking of their figures. I'm sure Ruth doesn't have to worry on that account.'

'Aunt Davina!'

Ruth was embarrassed by her aunt's frankness, and even more so when Dominic remarked: 'You were saying your niece was brought up in the West Indies, Miss Pascal. I suppose that accounts for the darkness of her skin.'

Ruth was appalled that he could discuss her as if she wasn't there, but Aunt Davina was unperturbed. 'That's right,' she nodded. 'My brother-in-law bought a small island out there, but he died recently, so my son and I quite naturally invited her to come to England and make her home with us.'

Dominic hesitated. 'So I imagine Miss Jason will know few young people in London,' he murmured, as if considering the point. He smiled. 'Perhaps I could arrange some introductions for her.'

Ruth's eyes widened at this further proof of his arrogance, and even Aunt Davina looked a little taken aback now. 'I'm sure you realise I appreciate your offer, Mr Crown,' she replied, rather stiffly, 'but my son and his friends have made Ruth feel at home, haven't they, my dear?'

'What?' Ruth's lips parted. 'Oh! Oh, yes.' She coloured. 'Yes, Martin's been marvellous!'

Aunt Davina's somewhat thin lips relaxed. 'So you see, Mr Crown, although it was very good of you to offer—'

'I'm sure we can compromise,' Dominic overrode her smoothly, and Ruth realised her aunt would not have the easy passage with him she had with other people. 'My fiancée and I are giving a party for some friends on Saturday evening. Perhaps Miss Jason—and your son—might like to join us. It's very informal. Just an excuse to drink wine, and enjoy some good music.'

'I don't know—'

Davina was in a cleft stick, Ruth could see. She obviously would have preferred to refuse his invitation, but the awareness of his background, and how useful his mother might be as an associate, caused her to hesitate.

'I'd have to ask my son, of course,' she said at last, and Ruth clenched her small fists.

'And me.' she inserted, rather rudely, so that Davina's expression quickly became reproving.

'It would be an opportunity for you and Martin to meet some new friends,' she declared tersely, and Ruth guessed that her cousin would jump at the chance. 'I—I'll ask him to let you know, Mr Crown. If you'll leave your phone number . . .'

'Of course.' Dominic pulled out his wallet and handed her a square of pasteboard. 'My card,' he said, with a wry smile at Ruth, and she felt the strength of his personality vanquishing her weaknesses.

'And now I must be going,' he said, getting to his feet, and Davina remembered her manners and raised her eyes from the card.

'I'll get Mrs Radcliffe to show you out,' she said, but Dominic forestalled her.

'Miss Jason will show me out,' he averred firmly, ignoring Ruth's expression of dismay. 'I shall look forward to hearing from you, Miss Pascal. Goodbye.'

Davina had little choice but to accept the situation, and short of being downright rude, Ruth could not thwart him. With a nervous smile at her aunt she preceded him from the room and ran down the stairs ahead of him, as if the devil himself was at her heels.

She opened the door for him, and stood aside for him to go out, but instead of doing as she expected, he took hold of her forearm and compelled her to accompany him out into the Mews. Only when they reached his car did he release her, and she stood indignantly, rubbing her arm and glancing anxiously at the upper windows.

'Don't alarm yourself.' Dominic commented

dryly. 'Your aunt is unlikely to risk being seen peering down at us. Besides, what could she see? I was very discreet.'

'Discreet!' Ruth allowed all her pent-up emotion to escape in that low disapprobation. 'You don't know the meaning of the word! I don't know how you dared to come here, after—after coming here before. Didn't Mrs Radcliffe recognise you?'

Dominic sighed. 'Your housekeeper is an old woman, and it was dark when I came before. She wouldn't recognise me. And even if she thought she did, I should deny it.'

'Yes, you would, wouldn't you?' exclaimed Ruth bitterly. She expelled her breath unsteadily. 'Why are you doing this? What did you come here for?'

Dominic turned to face the car, turning his back on the house as he said quietly: 'To see you, of course. What else? How was I to know you'd be out taking driving lessons?'

Ruth shook her head. 'But you told your mother—'

'I know what I told my mother. However, I found I had to see you.' He shrugged, looking sideways at her. 'Have you missed me?'

Ruth's face suffused with colour. 'Missed you?' she gasped. 'How—how could I miss you? I—I don't know you.'

'You know me,' he insisted huskily, his eyes on her mouth. 'Oh, Ruth, come with me now. Let me take you for a drive. I need to talk to you.'

'No!' Ruth took a step back from him. 'You—you have no right—'

'Oh, don't preach to me about rights!' he snapped

savagely. 'I know what's right and what isn't, and right now, I'm going quietly out of my mind!'

'Dominic!' She glanced behind her apprehensively, half afraid Mrs Radcliffe might come to see why the door had been left open, and overhear his impassioned words. 'Dominic, this is crazy!'

'Yes, isn't it?' he agreed, his long fingers curling tightly over the frame of the car door. 'I have to confess, I don't like it any more than you do.'

Ruth sighed. 'Dominic, you know I can't see you.'

'Why not?'

He was not looking at her, but at some point in the wall of the stables opposite, and she wished she was not so conscious of watching eyes.

'You know your mother wouldn't approve of this,' she said at last, and he turned to look at her then, his face twisting angrily.

'What the hell does my mother have to do with it?' he demanded. 'I'm over twenty-one. I don't have to account to anyone but myself!'

Ruth held up her head. 'So she told me.'

'What do you mean by that?'

She hesitated. 'She said—she said there were always girls in your life—'

'Did she?'

'—and that you were inclined to be reckless at times.'

'Really?'

'Yes.' Ruth swallowed convulsively, before continuing: 'But that—that you really loved your fiancée —I believe she said her name was Barbara Symonds —and that I shouldn't read more into your—your interest than there actually was.'

'The hell she did!' Dominic was incensed. 'And you believed every word, I suppose?' He shook his head angrily. 'What if I was to tell you that the reports of my exploits have been vastly exaggerated?'

Ruth pressed her lips together. 'It's nothing to do with me,' she insisted, and heard his harsh intake of breath.

He said a word then that even she understood was not polite. It was just a short word, a succinct little ejaculation, that was brutally explicit, and her teeth ground together tightly in expectation of some further profanity. But it never came. Without saying anything else, he jerked open the car door and levered himself behind the wheel, and as she stepped back uncertainly, he started the engine and drove away with a viciously protesting squeal of the tyres.

It was incredibly difficult to turn then, and go back into the house. Climbing the stairs on legs that were still like jelly, she dreaded what Aunt Davina was going to say, and she felt too drained to argue with her after that exhausting scene with Dominic.

Aunt Davina, however, was in a curiously thoughtful frame of mind. Her eyes when they met Ruth's across the room displayed a vaguely worrying expression, and she was especially affectionate towards her niece as she offered her some tea.

'Did you have a good lesson, darling?' she asked, offering Ruth one of Mrs Radcliffe's home-made scones. 'I haven't had a chance to speak to you yet, what with that man turning up and everything.' She patted the girl's hand apologetically. 'You know, I was just about to go upstairs when he arrived, and I couldn't do anything other than offer him tea, could I?'

Ruth managed a mouthful of scone before replying. 'I'm sorry you were disturbed,' she murmured, rather awkwardly. 'I—I never imagined—'

'Of course you didn't,' her aunt reassured her warmly. 'I'm not blaming you, Ruth. It wasn't your fault. Obviously his mother was curious about you, and sent him round here to find out about us.'

'Yes . . .' Ruth hid her face behind a teacup, and her aunt went on:

'Really, he tired me out. Speaking with him was quite exhausting, didn't you think so? He's obviously used to getting his own way. Being an only son, I suppose.'

Ruth put down her cup. 'I thought you were saying he had a brother the other day,' she ventured cautiously. 'But he died.'

'That's right, I was.' Her aunt glanced at her quickly. 'Did the Crowns mention him to you?'

'Heavens, no!' Ruth made an expressive gesture. 'I—we—we didn't talk about personal things at all.'

'No, no,' her aunt nodded, 'of course you wouldn't.' She smiled at her niece. 'And now, somehow, we've got to extricate you from this party invitation.'

Ruth bent her head. 'Yes.'

'You don't want to go, do you?' demanded her aunt sharply, and Ruth quickly made her denial. 'I—I was just wondering what Martin would say,' she said evasively, instinctively choosing the right diversion, and Aunt Davina clicked her tongue.

'Yes, I know what you mean,' she said. 'Martin's

bound to see this as an opportunity to become friendly with the circle the Crowns move in.' She sighed. 'We must just think of a way to avoid it.' She paused, then added thoughtfully: 'It might be a good idea if you and Martin went away for the weekend. You haven't had much time alone together since we came home, and I know he'd welcome the opportunity to have you to himself.'

Ruth coloured. 'Aunt Davina—'

'No, no, I insist. Young people need time alone together. And you and Martin—well, you know my feelings about that.'

Ruth licked her suddenly dry lips. 'Aunt Davina, I'm not sure—'

'What are you not sure about?' Her aunt frowned.

Ruth shook her head. 'I don't know. I mean—not really. I like Martin so much, you know that, but—I don't know if I'm ready—'

'For a serious commitment?' Aunt Davina lifted her chin. 'No one's suggesting that you are, Ruth.' She assumed a faintly injured air. 'Goodness knows, I don't want to rush you into anything. You've hardly had time to get accustomed to our ways yet—I know that. But, Ruth—' She broke off abruptly, and then continued again, more gently: 'I just want you to know that there are no two dearer people in the world to me than yourself and Martin.'

Ruth felt despicable. Aunt Davina had shown her so much kindness, flying out to the island, when her whole world seemed to have fallen apart, taking charge of everything, offering her a home, with the family she had never known she had. How could she disappoint her now, simply because a man she ought to loathe and despise was making demands upon her he had no right to make? What was wrong with her, that she allowed him this control over her? He had no integrity, no decency, no respect—either for her or his fiancée. It might be easier if she was married to Martin. That way, she would be beyond his reach once and for all.

She and Martin went to a disco party that evening, and as he made no mention of Dominic's visit, nor did she, guessing correctly that his mother had reserved that information. It was easier if she too put Dominic right out of her mind, but when they got back to the house she was reluctant to face the inevitable isolation of her own bedroom.

'Let's have some coffee,' she suggested, when Martin flung himself lazily down on to the couch in his mother's sitting room. 'I'll make it. You put on a record.'

Martin grimaced goodnaturedly. 'Okay,' he conceded, dragging himself up again, and Ruth pattered down the stairs to the kitchen to plug in the percolator.

When she carried the tray upstairs, she found Martin had chosen a low rhythmic blues sound, and taking the tray from her and putting it aside, he pulled her eagerly into his arms. With her hands looped behind his neck, and his hands on her waist, they moved sensuously to the music, enjoying the freedom from restraint after the press of humanity at the party.

'Mmm, you smell nice,' Martin murmured, nuzzling her ear. 'What is it? Something I gave you? It must be. I only buy perfumes that turn me on.'

Ruth looked slantingly up at him. 'Do I turn you on. Martin?' she asked, unconsciously seeking reassurance after her doubts of this afternoon, and he cupped her face between his hands and brought his lips to hers.

'You know you do,' he said huskily, but there was no real passion in his kiss, and Ruth realised that Martin was simply not capable of strong emotions— about anything.

'You know you're very sweet,' he whispered, kissing her again, and Ruth tried to infuse his kisses with a little of the excitement she felt when Dominic touched her. 'I've known lots of girls, but none of them as sweet as you. I really think I've fallen in love with you.'

Ruth drew back to look at him. 'Have you, Martin?' she asked, biting the lips he had just caressed. 'How—how do you know? How do you know when you love someone?'

'Hey. you know. you shouldn't be asking me that,' he reproved her, tapping her nose with a playful finger. 'When you love someone, you just know. You don't have to ask. You think about them a lot. Mostly, all the time. You want to look after them. care for them. share your life with them. You want to be with them more than with anybody else.'

Ruth looked anxious. 'Is that how you feel about me?' she probed, and Martin gave a low chuckle.

'Don't you believe me?'

Ruth frowned. 'I don't think you care that much about anybody.'

Martin assumed an offended air. 'Ruthie. Ruthie.'

he protested, feigning distress, 'how can you even suggest such a thing?'

Ruth's lips twitched. Martin was irrepressible. He could never be serious about anything for long, and she doubted if it was in his nature to feel really strongly about anyone. In his way, he did love her, she believed that. Just as she cared for him. They had fun together, and they laughed a lot. But was it enough?

'You're looking very solemn, suddenly,' he commented now, going to help himself to a cup of coffee. 'Has Mother been talking to you?'

'Aunt Davina?' Ruth turned away. 'No. Why? Has she been talking to you?'

'She's suggested we fly to Switzerland for the weekend,' he conceded dryly, and Ruth turned to him in surprise. 'Why?'

'For the skiing, I guess,' Martin replied, tasting his coffee. 'Isn't that what people usually go to Switzerland for?'

Ruth shook her head. 'But isn't it too late?'

'There are places in Switzerland where you can ski all the year round,' remarked Martin, with a shrug. 'It's only a question of getting up high enough.'

Ruth hesitated. 'And do you want to go?'

'I don't mind. Do you?'

Ruth considered. If it meant taking her out of reach of Dominic's influence, she ought to be eager. But deep inside her she knew she wasn't.

However, that had nothing to do with her decision. 'Of—of course I'd like to go,' she determined, keeping her voice light with an effort. 'I can't remember ever seeing snow before.'

'Okay.' Martin smiled. 'I'll make the arrangements. If we leave on Friday morning, that will give us two full days and three nights. I'll have to come back on Monday. I have a session at the track on Monday afternoon.'

Ruth tried to look eager. 'I'll look forward to it.' She shrugged. 'I know Aunt Davina will be pleased.'

'Yes.' Martin conceded the truth of this, and Ruth went to bed, determined not to think any more about Dominic's invitation.

CHAPTER FIFTEEN

On Thursday afternoon it rained, and Ruth, who had arranged to have another driving lesson, viewed the sudden downpour with gloomy eyes. She didn't like London in the wet. She didn't like the bedraggled buildings, or the choked-up smell of oil and diesel, and she particularly didn't like the feeling of claustrophobia that the lowering skies evoked.

As she had some shopping to do for Aunt Davina, she had arranged to meet her instructor at the offices of the driving school, and by the time she came hurrying along Bond Street, her head and feet felt soaked. She should have carried an umbrella, she supposed, but she was always afraid she might put someone's eye out with the perilous spokes, and the hood of the waterproof coat she was wearing refused to remain in place.

She was late, and her whole attention was concentrated on reaching her objective, so that when someone suddenly stepped into her path she practically cannoned into them. She gasped an apology, groping for the handbag that had nearly been knocked to the ground, and then realised that the man who had halted her headlong dash had not released her. She looked up anxiously, apprehensive that she might be being accosted, and blinked disbelievingly at her rescuer.

'Dominic!' she breathed, his name sounding husky on her lips. 'Dominic, what are you doing here?'

His expression took on an ironic cast. 'Would you believe coincidence?' he enquired, but as she continued to look at him blankly, he added harshly: 'What do you think? I've been waiting for you, of course.'

'Waiting for me?'

Ruth tried to absorb what he was telling her, but it didn't seem to make sense. How did he know where she would be this afternoon? How had he known what driving school she attended?

Raindrops sparkled on his long lashes, and on the silvery fairness of his hair, and she suddenly realised he was not wearing a raincoat. He had turned up the collar of his jacket, against the drops of rain that ran from his hair down the back of his neck, but his shoulders were dark with wetness. Added to this was the reluctant awareness that he did not look well. There were dark rings around his eyes, and his cheeks seemed to have hollowed out, giving his face a haggard appearance. It hardly seemed possible that it was only two days since she had seen him. What had happened to him?

Glancing round helplessly, she said: 'We can't talk now. I have a driving lesson. I'm already ten minutes late.' She sighed, concerned in spite of herself. 'Don't you have an overcoat? You're getting soaked!'

'I expected you'd be on time,' he retorted grimly, as she stepped back from him. 'And my car's parked just round the corner. Forget the driving lesson. Come with me!'

'Dominic!' She gazed up at him aghast. 'I can't do that.'

'Why can't you? No one need know. You can tell them you were ill or something.' He paused, and then went on heavily: 'Ruth, please! Don't send me away again.'

Ruth bent her head. She didn't know what to do. She knew what she *should* do, but his appeal was compelling. How could she walk into the office behind her, and ignore him? Could she do that, knowing he had waited in the rain to see her? She didn't owe him anything, she argued with herself unhappily, and yet she knew that when he had driven away and left her two days ago she had suffered the same conflict of conscience she was experiencing now.

'Dominic,' she began slowly, and his lids lowered to half cover his eyes. 'Dominic—we have nothing to say to one another.'

'Don't we?' He moved his shoulders wearily. 'Well, if that's your final decision—'

'Oh, Dominic!' Common sense warred with the emotions he always evoked, and as he turned away she caught his sleeve. 'All right,' she said, regretting the words almost as soon as they were spoken. 'All right—I'll miss my lesson.'

He didn't say anything in response; not 'Good' or 'Thank you' or any of the things she might have anticipated. Instead he took a firm hold of her arm and propelled her around the corner to where the sleek grey sports car awaited their possession. He put her into her seat before striding round the bonnet to get in beside her, shedding his jacket as he did so, and tossing it into the back. Then, after settling himself to his satisfaction, he determinedly took her shopping basket from her and deposited it in the back as well, along with his coat.

Ruth glanced at the narrow gold wristwatch Aunt Davina had bought her as he started the car. 'I—I only have three quarters of an hour,' she began doubtfully, and turned her face to the streaming windows when he made no reply.

She didn't know where he was taking her. In the rain it was impossible to read street names. She could only look at the direction boards they passed, and realised after a few minutes that they were heading towards the outskirts of the city.

'You—you said you wanted to talk to me.' she reminded him at last, when they had been driving for about fifteen minutes, and Dominic gave her a sidelong look.

'I know.'

'So why don't we talk?' she exclaimed. 'I should tell you, we'll have to be going back soon.'

'No.'

His denial was low and without emphasis, but a denial nevertheless, and Ruth stared at him. 'Yes, Dominic.'

'Do you think now I've got you to myself, I'm going to deliver you back to your aunt without us having some time alone together?' he demanded, in a tortured voice, and she trembled. 'I didn't stand a half hour in the rain just to spend a miserable forty-five minutes with you,' he added, slowing for some traffic lights. 'I need you, Ruth, and you know it.

Now, relax and enjoy the drive. I've got somewhere I want to show you.'

Ruth fumbled for the handle of the door as the Porsche slowed to a standstill, but the car was locked and she couldn't get it open.

'Don't be melodramatic, Ruth,' he told her, as the lights changed and the car began to move again. 'Jumping out into the rain isn't going to solve anything. You know that and I know that, so stop fighting me!'

'I'll never stop fighting you,' she declared childishly. 'I should have known. I shouldn't have trusted you. I should have realised you were entirely without integrity!'

'Oh, for God's sake!' With a squeal of brakes Dominic turned the car, skidding into a layby and bringing it to an abrupt standstill. 'All right,' he said, raking back his damp hair with unsteady fingers, 'I'm a swine and I'm a bastard. What else do you want to say?'

'I don't want to say anything,' she mumbled, through shaking lips, as he pulled down his tie and loosened the top button of his shirt. 'I—I just want you to take me back to—to my aunt's. Or—or let me take a bus or something.'

'A bus!' Dominic sighed, resting both elbows on the steering wheel and propping his head in his hands. 'Ruth, I'll take you back if you really want to go. And apologise to your aunt as well, if you want me to.'

Ruth pressed her lips together. 'Dominic, you shouldn't have done this—'

'It was the only way I could think of to see you

alone,' he replied simply, and she shook her head.

'But how did you know—I mean—how did you find out where I was learning to drive?'

'Oh,' he grimaced, turning his head on his hands to look at her, 'that was easy. I asked your aunt.'

'Aunt Davina?' Ruth was shocked.

'Yes. Why not? When I asked where you were and she told me you were taking a driving lesson, it was not unreasonable to ask who was teaching you.'

'Oh, you mean on Tuesday?' Ruth nodded. 'I see.'

'As to the time . . .' He shrugged. 'I had someone make enquiries.'

'Who?'

'My secretary.'

'Oh!' Ruth bent her head.

'A Mrs Cooke,' he told her flatly. 'She used to be my father's secretary, actually, but now she's mine.'

Ruth's tongue circled her upper lip. 'My—my aunt said she'd read that your father has retired.'

Dominic nodded. 'That's right, he has. Or at least, he's trying to.'

'And—and you're in charge?'

'Nominally,' he agreed dryly. 'For a trial period.'

'Do you like it?' Ruth was interested, in spite of herself.

He moved his shoulders in a dismissing gesture. 'I don't know,' he said at last. 'It's a big responsibility.'

'Is that why—I mean—' Ruth stopped in some confusion, and then, realising she had to finish, she went on: 'You look—tired. I thought—I wondered—'

'—if I was losing sleep over the company?' Dominic's mouth twisted in self-mockery. 'Oh, no, I don't lose any sleep over Crown Chemicals.' He paused. 'Only over you.'

'Me?' Ruth stared at him, wide-eyed. 'But you can't! I—I don't believe you!'

He straightened, reaching for the ignition. 'I'll take you back now,' he said heavily, starting the engine, and Ruth gazed at him helplessly, not knowing what to say next.

'Wait,' she articulated at last, as he drove to the end of the layby, and prepared to pull out. 'Dominic —Dominic, where were you taking me?'

'Does it matter?'

He was cold and detached now, and she couldn't bear it. 'It—it might,' she ventured, preventing him from putting the car into gear. 'Dominic, please, I—I'd like to know. Don't—don't be angry with me.'

His eyes darkened before he could prevent her seeing it, but his voice was still chilling as he said shortly: 'I was taking you to Marlin Spike. Now will you let go my arm?'

Ruth sighed, gazing up at him. 'Then take me there,' she said huskily, and when he gave her a suspicious look, she added: 'I'll ring Aunt Davina. I'll tell her I'm staying in town to do some shopping. Really. I like seeing new places. Is it a town or a village?'

Dominic shook his head. 'Marlin Spike is the place where I was brought up,' he said heavily. 'It's a house—my house. Now, do you still want to come?'

Ruth hesitated. A house! A place where they might be completely alone! Her legs felt like jellys.

'A-all right,' she got out jerkily. 'Is—is it far?'

'Not too far,' he conceded, estimating the speed of

a slow-moving lorry, and pulling out ahead of it. 'Well? Do we go on—or turn back at the next round-about?'

'We go on,' she murmured huskily, and slumped in her seat with sudden exhaustion.

She had wanted to see more of England, and she was seeing it. With the sprawling suburbs of London giving way to acres of fields and woodlands, with only villages to break up the landscape, she began to relax. She had not realised the country lay so close to the town, and even though some of the villages were evidently extending their boundaries rapidly, to accommodate the outflow from the urban districts, they still had beauty and character. There was light and space, and when the sun pushed its way through the clouds, to cast a watery brilliance over every-thing, there was colour, too. It was as if the day was trying to show her that she had made the right de-cision, and her spirits rose as the sun's warmth grew.

She would have liked to take off her coat, but it was still damp and clinging to her, and her hair felt heavy about her ears. She contented herself with kicking off the high-heeled suede shoes she had been wearing, and wriggled her toes delightfully in their new-found freedom.

Marlin Spike stood on the outskirts of Great Missenden. It was a grey brick house, set in park-land, with a winding gravel drive leading up to circular forecourt. It was much bigger than Ruth had expected, and yet its creeper-hung façade was not intimidating, its long lead-paned windows sharing a friendly intimacy.

'I was born here,' remarked Dominic, leaning on the wheel for a moment before getting out. 'Do you want to see where?'

Ruth's lips quivered. 'If you want to show me,' she murmured, watching his mouth, and his expression was strangely diffident.

'I do,' he said, thrusting open his door, and she struggled to find her shoes as he came round the bonnet.

'Come on,' he said, pulling open her door, realising what she was doing. 'I'll carry you,' he added, lifting her out without effort, and her heart hammered heavily as he strode across the crunching stones.

The door opened as they approached, however, and a grey-haired woman came to the top of the steps. She was small and round and buxom, with lines that hinted at her age, but her cheeks were rosy, and her eyes were bright, and her lips parted in a smile of welcome when she saw who it was.

'Dominic!' she exclaimed, as he mounted the steps, and he put Ruth down on the threshold, to bend and embrace the old lady. 'Why didn't you let me know you were coming?' she exclaimed reprovingly, her gnarled hands fragile against his muscular shoulder. 'Whatever am I going to give you to eat?'

Dominic glanced humorously at Ruth, then smiled at the old lady. 'We didn't come here to be fed, Bridie,' he assured her dryly. 'I wanted to show Ruth the house, that's all. Now, let me take off her coat before I introduce you.'

Ruth pulled the buttons apart, as Dominic eased
the coat off her shoulders, supremely conscious of
his hands against the fine material of her shirt. It was
a matching outfit of an amber silk shirt and a wrap-
around skirt, and she could feel the vibrant warmth
of him through the thinness of her clothes.

Dominic introduced the old lady as Miss Bainbridge, and explained that she had been his nurse
many years ago. He explained Ruth as the young
lady who with her father had looked after him when
his yacht capsized, and if Miss Bainbridge thought it
was strange that Ruth should now be living in
England, and evidently continuing her association
with her erstwhile patient, she kept her opinions to
herself.

They entered the house through a wide sunlit entrance hall, with a long straight staircase running up
one wall. The walls themselves were panelled in a
light oak, and the floor, too, was polished wood,
glowing with the patina of years. Obviously, Miss
Bainbridge took her present duties as housekeeper
very seriously, and there wasn't a speck of dust any-
where, on window ledges, or in the niches that
gleamed at either side of the softly-piled stair carpet.
It was evidently a labour of love and when Dominic
complimented her on it, she only shook her head
dismissingly.

Doors opened to left and right, and Dominic
opened one of these into a high-ceilinged reception
room, eerie now, with the curtains drawn and dustsheets shrouding all the furniture. 'The drawing
room,' he remarked half mockingly, tugging one of
the sheets aside, and Ruth caught her breath in

admiration at the sight of the dusty pink velvet sofa he had revealed.

'I think you ought to go and get changed first, Dominic,' Miss Bainbridge remarked from the doorway, noticing the traces of dampness that still lingered on his shoulders and at the bottoms of his pants. 'Your room is prepared for you, as usual, and it won't take me long to make up a bed for Miss Jason—'

'Oh, no,' began Ruth automatically, and Dominic left the couch to put his hands on the old lady's shoulders.

'We're not staying, Bridie,' he insisted, giving her a gentle shake. 'I told you, I've just brought Ruth to see the house. We'll be leaving before dinner.'

Miss Bainbridge's rosy face lost a little of its animation. 'Couldn't you at least spend the evening here?' she enquired hopefully. 'I seem to remember there are some steaks in the fridge, and some of my home-made lentil soup.'

Dominic glanced thoughtfully at Ruth, and then determinedly turned away. 'I'm sorry, Bridie,' he refused blankly. 'Miss Jason can't spare the time. Another day, perhaps.'

Miss Bainbridge sighed, but she had to accept it, and Ruth knew a momentary pang. There never would be another day, she thought regretfully, and wondered why this intelligence depressed her so.

'I'll make some tea, then, shall I?' The old lady was endearingly eager, and Ruth looked anxiously at Dominic. 'You'll not refuse a cup of tea, will you?' she added. 'Not after coming all this way?'

Dominic smiled. 'No, I won't refuse a cup of tea,'

he agreed gently, and after bidding him once again to get changed, she hastened away to prepare it.

'This is a lovely room,' commented Ruth, when they were alone, and Dominic went to jerk back the heavy velvet curtains. She pulled another of the dustsheets aside. 'Oh—a piano!'

'Do you play?' asked Dominic, coming back to her, but she only shook her head.

'We didn't have any musical instruments,' she confessed ruefully. 'Daddy wasn't madly keen on music. I was, but—' she broke off suddenly, as if he might imagine she was complaining. 'I—do you? Play, I mean?'

'Occasionally,' said Dominic absently, standing beside her, stroking her shoulder with a disturbing finger. Then: 'Come on, I'll show you the rest of the house, while Bridie is making the tea.'

The remainder of the ground-floor rooms were swathed in dustsheets, like the drawing room, but even without taking all the shrouds aside, Ruth sensed this house meant something special to him. It wasn't like his home in London, which had seemed very gracious, but formal, at first impression, and it certainly wasn't like Aunt Davina's house, which was treated more like a hotel. This house had warmth, it had an atmosphere, and Ruth guessed he had been happy here.

Upstairs, there were eight bedrooms, several with their own private bathrooms. The master bedroom, which Dominic said no one used these days, was large and impressive, and it was here, in the huge four poster, that he had been born.

'Yes. I first saw the light of day on this mattress,'

he said mockingly, bouncing up and down on the blue and gold quilt. 'To James and Isobel Crown, a son, Dominic Howard, eight pounds six ounces.'

Ruth smiled, her toes curling in the soft cream pile of the carpet. 'I imagine you were quite a handful,' she commented, meeting his eyes, and he sobered immediately, and got off the bed.

She would have recognised his room without the evident absence of dustsheets. It was spare and masculine, even austere, the only touch of luxury the king-size proportions of the bed.

'Come in,' he invited, when she hovered in the doorway. 'I'd better do as Bridie suggests, and get changed anyway, and I shouldn't like her to be shocked if she comes looking for us.'

'I'll go downstairs,' said Ruth doubtfully, glancing behind her, before recognising the look of impatience in his face. 'All right, I'll stay,' she conceded huskily, closing the door, and he turned away abruptly to his dressing room.

She heard the sliding sound as a door was rolled back in the small room adjoining, and moved automatically towards the dressing table. She was appalled at the tumbled reflection that confronted her. The rain had washed what little make-up she had been wearing from her face, and her hair drooped lopsidedly over one ear. Wisps had come loose, and were curling damply about her ears, while a whole strand lay damply against her neck.

With a feeling of impatience she pulled the hairpins out of her hair, letting the braids tumble down to her shoulders. Then, with urgent fingers, she unplaited the hair and picking up Dominic's brush, ran

it eagerly through it. It would dry far more quickly
loose, she consoled herself firmly, ignoring the reluctant awareness that she wanted to please Dominic.

Maybe it was thinking of him that caused her to
turn her head sideways to look into his dressing
room, or maybe it was simply a desire to see again the
muscular strength of his body. Whatever the truth of
it, she did turn her head, and Dominic, naked to the
waist and wearing only the briefest of underpants,
glanced up from the slacks he was preparing to put on.

Ruth put down the brush with a clatter, her tongue
seeking to moisten her suddenly dry lips. 'Oh,
Dominic,' she breathed, unable to prevent herself,
and he dropped the slacks and covered the space
between them.

'Ruth,' he groaned, his hands curving at her nape,
and with a whisper of submission she leaned against
him, allowing the whole length of her body to mould
to the masculine hardness of his.

Her lips parted in anticipation of the possession of
his mouth, opening wide beneath his, admitting the
sensual invasion of his tongue. She had been a child,
inexperienced, unaware, when he kissed her on the
island; now she was a woman, and she knew exactly
what she wanted of him.

'Ruth,' he said unsteadily, his hands parting the
fastening of her blouse, exposing the ripened peaks
to his urgent gaze. 'Oh, Ruth,' he muttered again,
capturing her breast with delicious savagery, 'Ruth,
don't stop me now, for God's sake!'

'I won't.' she breathed, and knew that it was true.
Whatever happened, whatever came after, she
should have this to remember, and surely even

Barbara would not begrudge her the memory.

The shirt slid unheeded to the floor, followed swiftly by her skirt. She was close against him, compellingly aware of his arousal, wanting, and needing, and eager to please him.

Her fingers probed the band of his trunks, delighting in the intimacy, and with a moan of satisfaction he swung her up into his arms and carried her to the bed. Tearing the covers aside, he deposited her on the dark brown sheet, removing the rest of her clothing without shame or embarrassment, then sliding on to the bed beside her, to cover her mouth once again.

Only once did she make any objection, and that was when she remembered Miss Bainbridge. 'She won't disturb us,' Dominic told her huskily, his mouth beating a trail across her midriff, and down, over her flat stomach. 'Mmm, you're beautiful, Ruth, do you know that? Beautiful, and warm, and responsive— Oh, darling, relax. That's right. Relax, and let me—'

Ruth's whole body felt as if it was aflame. His mouth was everywhere, exploring the secret places of her body, stroking her and caressing her, awakening the strong sexual urge inside her. Her nails curled against his chest, against the crispness of his body hair, raking a passage of their own across his shoulders, clasping, and clinging, and holding him closer. Her lips opened against his jawline, against the strongly-corded column of his throat, and he moaned softly in his throat as he sought her mouth again, searching and exploring, hungrily intimate.

His kisses were getting deeper, more passionate, draining any lingering trace of resistance. He drank from her lips, drugged with the taste of her, arousing the instinctive response of her unconscious sensuality. She shifted beneath him urgently, arching towards his possessive hands, allowing an eager exploration of her body. She was learning how to please him, as he was pleasing her, and the low sounds of pleasure he made then told her she was having success. It didn't matter that the curtains were undrawn, or that a watery sun was only just beginning its slide into the west. She was oblivious to the world outside this room, oblivious to everything and everyone but Dominic.

She wanted him to take her. She wanted to feel him inside her, loving her, possessing her, probing the very essence of her being. And when his own hunger overcame all else, and he sought that ultimate satisfaction, it was almost a relief to wind herself about him.

'Dear God, Ruth,' he muttered, winding the dark coil of her hair around his fingers, drawing her face to his. 'You're the most important thing in my life. How, in the name of all that's sacred, could I ever have imagined otherwise?'

Ruth silenced his groan of anguish with her mouth. She didn't want to hear this. She didn't want to be reminded of all the other women he had made love to, or of the woman who would eventually bear his name. It was enough to know that he was with her now, a part of her, sharing with her the most intimate relationship two people were capable of. She loved him desperately—oh, yes, in those sensitised minutes, she could admit the truth—but neither he, nor anyone else, should ever know it.

The hungry possession of his body became all-consuming, and she felt the soaring crescendo building inside her. With his tongue, Dominic explored every contour of her lips, and she was helpless in the grip of a feverish rapture, that tore human limitations aside, and transported her to a pinnacle of emotion. If it were possible to think coherently, she would have acknowledged that her deeper awareness brought a deeper satisfaction, and she wound her arms around his neck, to cover his sweat-streaked face with kisses. Their wild abandonment exploded in a pulsating flowering of sweetness, that left them weak and clinging to one another; and Dominic buried his face between her breasts until the shuddering aftermath of appeasement left him, sighing in contentment when Ruth's fingers threaded through his damp hair.

'I love you,' he groaned, turning his lips against her neck, and Ruth trembled at the awareness of his vulnerability in those moments. There was no doubt that the experience had left them both in a state of mild intoxication, but somehow she knew when that bemused state left him, he would regret that carelessly spoken confession.

But for now, she said nothing, feeling amazingly mature in her new-found philosophy. The pain would come later, but for the present she refused to allow it to intrude on these precious minutes with him.

'Ruth?' His thumb probed her chin, turning her face to his. 'Ruth—don't go back tonight. Stay with me!'

Her breathing quickened in spite of the delicious

lethargy his lovemaking had left her with. To stay with him, to spend the night here, to *sleep* with him; she could think of nothing she would like better, but she could not do that to Aunt Davina. It was simply out of the question.

'I can't,' she breathed, with a shaky sigh. 'Dominic, I have to go back. You know I do.'

'Why?'

'Why?' She wriggled up on the pillows to look at him, completely unselfconscious with him now. 'You know why. Aunt Davina—'

'To hell with Aunt Davina,' he muttered huskily, caressing her breast with angry possession. 'I need you, Ruth. Far more than Aunt Davina.'

'And you've had me,' she pointed out softly, submitting pleasurably to the hungry pressure of his mouth this evoked. 'Oh, Dominic, I'd like to stay, you know I would. There's no point in my denying something that's so obvious. But I can't. I owe Aunt Davina too much to treat her so carelessly.'

Dominic sighed. 'All right,' he conceded heavily. 'But compromise. Stay for dinner.'

'How could I do that? What could I say?'

'I'll think of something,' he promised, heavy-eyed. 'Hmm, come here. You're irresistible. God, I want you again.'

'Dominic!' she breathed, half protestingly, but when his eager lips possessed hers again, she had no will to resist him.

If Miss Bainbridge thought they had spent rather longer exploring the house than she would have expected, she made no comment, except to compliment Ruth on the loosened curtain of her hair.

'I used to have long hair when I was young,' she confessed, as they took tea together, and Ruth was overwhelmingly conscious of the lazy satisfaction in Dominic's eyes as he looked at her, too.

'By the way,' he declared provokingly, 'We've decided to stay for dinner, after all, Bridie. That is, if you've no objections, of course.'

'Heavens, no.' Bridie was evidently delighted. 'Oh, I'm so glad. It's so seldom I have visitors,' she hesitated, and then added regretfully: 'You don't come here like you used to, Dominic.'

'No.'

His response was clipped, and Ruth wondered if he had any regrets in bringing her here. Yet, when he looked at her, she could only read warm emotion in his eyes.

When tea was over, Dominic took her outside to show her the gardens. It was a deliciously warm evening after the rain, and they left their coats indoors, Dominic looking young and relaxed in a pair of beige corded pants and dark brown velvet sweater. Since he came to meet her that afternoon, the lines of gravity and weariness had been erased from his face, and Ruth consoled her conscience with that knowledge.

Hand in hand, they tramped across the now-empty paddock to the woods beyond, and Ruth gasped in delight at the clumps of bluebells and violets that grew among the long grasses. She had never seen such simple beauty, and she knelt to bury her face in their fresh sweetness.

'You like the country, don't you?' Dominic commented, pulling her up into his arms, and she looped her arms around his neck as she nodded.

'I like it here.' she said innocently. 'I love your home. Dominic. I love everything about it. But mostly. I love the peace and the silence. It's so *quiet!*'

'And me?' he prompted softly. rubbing his tongue against her lips. but she avoided an answer by pulling away from him. and darting mischievously away between the trees.

They were both ravenous by the time they came back to the house, and Ruth's face was glowing with health. She had never looked lovelier. and Dominic was not unaware of that fact.

'I must ring Aunt Davina.' she said. as soon as they came into the house. 'I—I should have done it sooner. I'm an awful coward.'

'Let me do it.' said Dominic abruptly. 'I'll explain how I met you. and where you are.'

'Oh. no.' Ruth shook her head. 'I—I have to do it. Where—where can I phone?'

'In here.' said Dominic flatly. leading the way into the book-lined library. where a cream telephone resided on the desk against the far wall. 'There you are.' he indicated shortly. and went out again and left her. closing the door heavily behind him.

Her aunt was just beginning to be concerned about her. she said. 'I wasn't absolutely certain of the time of your driving lesson.' she went on brusquely. 'but I guessed you'd have some shopping to do for your trip tomorrow—'

The trip!

Ruth's immediate reaction was of stunned disbelief. Until her aunt mentioned it. all thoughts of the trip to Switzerland had been forgotten in the excitement of being with Dominic. But now it all came back in sharp detail, and she was shocked at her own negligence.

'Oh, Aunt Davina,' she began, half apologetically, only to break off in embarrassment, when she realised her aunt was still talking.

'Is Martin with you?' Aunt Davina was asking irritably, and when Ruth hastily denied it, she went on bitterly: 'You young people can be so thoughtless! Are you completely indifferent to the feelings of your parents?'

'Aunt Davina, I—'

Ruth tried to get a word in, but her aunt wasn't listening to her, and as the older woman went on, criticising the heedless arrogance of the youth of today, she realised that it was Martin who had provoked this tirade.

'He's at the track, I know it,' declared Aunt Davina harshly. 'I've tried to ring him there, but I can get no answer, and I have no idea of the number of that man Jarvis.'

Ruth hesitated. 'I—isn't his number in the telephone book?' she ventured doubtfully, but her aunt had apparently thought of that already.

'Do you know how many Jarvises there are in London?' she demanded, her voice rising shrilly. 'Where the devil is he? Why can't he simply pick up a phone?'

Ruth didn't know how to answer her, but as she sought about desperately for something to say in reassurance, she heard the sound through the phone of a door slamming.

'Wait a minute—'

Aunt Davina put down the receiver with a clatter, and Ruth heard her go out of her sitting room and on to the landing. There was a shouted exchange of words, then her aunt came back to the phone, breathing rather heavily.

'He's home,' she declared, with evident relief. 'Thank God for that!' She paused, before adding: 'Get home as quickly as you can, my dear. I shan't be here. I have that reception at the gallery to attend, but Martin will take care of you—won't you, darling?'

To her astonishment, her aunt rang off then, without even asking her whereabouts, and Ruth didn't know whether to feel relieved or disappointed. She had been prepared for accusations and recriminations, but instead she was left with the certain awareness of her own dispensability.

She came out of the library feeling slightly bemused, and found Dominic in the drawing room, standing by the windows, drinking from a glass containing some amber-coloured liquid. She guessed it was Scotch, and wished she dared to have one. Right now, she felt she needed something to restore her sense of balance.

She expected Dominic to ask what her aunt had said, but he didn't. He acknowledged her presence by turning to face her, and then, waving the glass in his hand, asked if she would like a drink.

'Yes, please.' she said, catching her lower lip between her teeth. Was no one to behave predictably? Didn't he care what happened to her any more?

Dominic approached a cabinet, and indicated its contents. 'What would you like?' he enquired politely. 'There's Scotch and gin and brandy; or a fruit drink, if you'd prefer it.'

'I'd like a Scotch, and—and soda,' she declared firmly, causing him to look at her doubtfully, before conceding to her demands. She noticed he poured only a small measure of Scotch into her glass however, and topped it up liberally with the colourless effervescent.

It was still quite powerful for someone unused to alcohol in any form, but she sipped it determinedly, ignoring his speculative stare. Since the call to her aunt, the atmosphere had cooled perceptibly, and now she wished she had not agreed to stay to dinner. It was obvious he was regretting bringing her here, and the inevitable connotations her visit would have for him. But once he was married to Barbara, they would no doubt occupy the master bedroom when they came to visit, so no lingering memories of his recklessness need mar his future occupation.

'Well?' he said, when she had almost given up thinking about the call, and she looked at him blankly. 'Did you speak to your aunt?' he asked harshly, and her fingers tightened on her glass as she hastily nodded her head. 'So?' he persisted. 'What did you tell her? That you had met a friend of your father's, after your driving lesson? Or that the driving school's car had had a puncture, and you were forced to delay your outing? Didn't she think it was a little strange that you should be so late? Or did you think of another convincing argument?'

Ruth was flushed by the time he had finished, and her lips quivered as she struggled to reply. 'As—as a matter of fact, I didn't have to tell her anything,' she retorted huskily. 'Mar—Martin was late, and she was worried about him. She—she didn't even ask where I was. So far as Aunt Davina is concerned, Martin has precedence.'

Dominic thrust his glass aside and came towards her. 'You mean she didn't even want to know who you were with?'

'I—I expect she might do, later. But right then, she was more concerned about Martin's whereabouts. As a matter of fact, he came in as we were talking. He'd probably been to the track. He does some amateur racing, you know. Did—did Aunt Davina mention—'

'I'm not interested in your cousin,' snapped Dominic fiercely, taking her by the shoulders, and when she looked anxiously up at him, he jerked her towards him. 'Dammit, Ruth, you should know how I feel.' He shook his head. 'You're all I care about. And it infuriates me that Davina Pascal should be so bloody selfish!'

Ruth felt a little of the coldness ease inside her. 'I—I thought you might be relieved,' she began, only to break off again at the darkening anger in his face.

'I'm not relieved,' he muttered. 'I'm glad you didn't have to lie about it—but that woman's attitude is inconsistent, to say the least. I can hardly believe it's the same woman who flew out to Indigo like a mother hen, the minute she apparently discovered you were on your own.'

Ruth shook her head. 'It doesn't matter—'

'It matters to me.' he retorted, his hand caressing her nape. and she yielded weakly against him.

'I thought you were regretting bringing me here,'

she whispered shakily, and he pressed her closer against him.

'Regretting it?' he groaned. 'God, don't you know I'd like to keep you here, like Rapunzel, in her tower, with myself holding the only key!'

Ruth tipped her head back wonderingly. 'You're jealous!' she breathed, and his lean face hardened.

'Oh, yes,' he conceded grimly, 'I'm jealous. As jealous as hell, of anyone who gets near you.'

'Dominic!'

His lips twisted. 'Didn't you know? You should. I can't keep away from you. And that woman—your aunt—I don't trust her.'

Ruth arched her brows in puzzlement. 'Why not?'

'The Doctor Fell syndrome, I guess,' he muttered harshly. 'Oh, God, I don't want anyone else taking care of you but me.'

His mouth sought hers, warm and passionate, and incredibly sweet. She responded to him eagerly, too bemused to resist, and then broke away from him in dismay when there was a discreet cough behind them.

'Er—dinner's ready,' Mis Bainbridge announced, not without some embarrassment, and Ruth walked quickly towards her, avoiding Dominic's enigmatic stare.

CHAPTER SIXTEEN

'Miss Symonds is on the line again, Mr Dominic,' Mrs Cooke informed him ruefully, coming into the office at his summons, and giving him a sympathetic look. 'Shall I put the call through now, or do you want me to speak to her? I explained that you were up to your eyes in contracts, but she simply refuses to believe me.'

Dominic sighed, pushing a pile of folders aside, and reaching up to tug his tie away from his throat. He had shed his jacket over two hours ago, and now he unbuttoned the collar of his shirt before making a gesture of resignation.

'Okay,' he said, 'put her through. I might as well break for fifteen minutes. Is there a cup of coffee going, do you think? I could surely do with something reviving.'

Mrs Cooke smiled. 'I'll get Jennifer to make you one,' she affirmed crisply. 'And what about Mr Grenville? Will you have time to see him today, or shall I ask him to come back on Monday?'

'Grenville? Grenville?' Dominic massaged the muscles at the back of his neck. 'Oh, yes, Grenville.' He frowned. 'I'd forgotten all about him. Has he been waiting long?'

'About half an hour, Mr Dominic. He said he didn't mind waiting. I explained that you were busy, but he was determined to stay.'

Dominic nodded thoughtfully. Then, almost immediately, he gave an exclamation. '*You* see him,' he said, extending a hand towards her. 'You deal with him, Mrs Cooke. Goodness knows, you know as well as I do why he's come here.'

'Oh—I couldn't!' Mrs Cooke looked nonplussed. 'I mean, it's you he wants to see, Mr Dominic.'

'Correction, it's my father he really wants to see,' retorted Dominic dryly. 'But as he can't, I've no doubt you could handle the preliminary discussions.'

'I don't think your father would agree to that, Mr Dominic,' murmured Mrs Cooke doubtfully. 'He always saw the customers himself.'

'I know he did.' Dominic lay back in his chair. 'But you were more often than not present, Mrs Cooke, and with your background and information, you know how to handle it.'

The woman looked absolutely confounded, and Dominic's hard face creased into a smile. 'Relax, Mrs Cooke! It's not the end of the world. I'm not asking you to sign away the Crown millions! All I want you to do is see Grenville, find out what he wants, and tell him I'll see him next week.'

Mrs Cooke shook her head, saying nothing, and Dominic gave an impatient sigh. 'If it's a rise you want,' he declared abruptly, and she caught her breath in indignation.

'I—I never thought of such a thing!' she exclaimed, and he knew she hadn't. But just now he was in no mood to be diplomatic.

'Relax,' he said, straightening up in his chair before getting to his feet. 'I know I can rely on you to do the right thing, or I wouldn't have asked you.' He pulled a wry face. 'You and I may both win our spurs together, Mrs Cooke. Think about that, when you're dealing with Harry Grenville.'

Mrs Cooke left him, still in something of a state of shock, he feared, but recovering rapidly. He had every confidence in her. In the three weeks since he had taken over the bulk of command, she had proved her worth a dozen times over, and he could quite see why his father had depended on her judgement. Unfortunately, so far as his father had been concerned, she was female, and while Jake Crown had always enjoyed the company of the opposite sex, he deplored their promotion in business. The idea of giving his secretary the kind of responsibility she deserved would never have occurred to him, and in one thing Mrs Cooke was probably right, Dominic acknowledged; Jake would not approve.

He heard the click as the outside call was switched through to his office, and resuming his seat again, he lifted the receiver. 'Barbara?' he asked, bracing himself. 'How are you?'

'I'm all right. How about you?' she countered shortly, confirming his suspicions. 'Where were you last evening? Didn't Shannon tell you I called?'

'He did,' Dominic admitted dryly, smiling his thanks to the young typist who had just brought in his coffee. 'But it was late when I got home, and I couldn't ring you then.'

'You could have rung this morning,' insisted Barbara, and Dominic had to concede that he could. 'Where on earth were you? Daddy brought the

Trade Secretary to dinner, and I wanted you to meet him!'

Dominic sighed. 'Then it's just as well I was out,' he remarked flatly. 'Anthony Barras and I hate the sight of one another!'

'Oh, don't be silly, Dominic.' Barbara was impatient. 'I know you mean because he used to bully the younger boys at school! Good heavens, you left Winchester fourteen years ago!'

'I'm aware of the time lapse,' retorted Dominic mildly, stirring several spoons of sugar into his cup. 'But I have no intention of humiliating Crowns by courting his support.'

'Your father always understood that one should never mix business with personal likes and dislikes,' exclaimed Barbara, controlling her temper with evident difficulty. 'Tony could be useful to you. He understands your problems—'

'And I understand his,' countered Dominic, without heat. 'He's a junior Minister, with a name to make for himself, and he thinks he may do it riding on the back of Crown Chemicals!'

Barbara gasped. 'Oh, that's ridiculous!'

'Is it?'

'Of course.' She cast about for words of repudiation. 'He's a charming man, sincere and intelligent. I'd say he was a man most likely to succeed.'

'You're probably right.' Dominic was bored by this conversation. 'However, I don't propose to provide the springboard to his eventual canonisation.'

Barbara made a sound of annoyance. 'You're hopeless!' she maintained. 'Here am I, doing what I can to improve your standing with your father, and all you do is run my efforts down!'

Dominic put down his spoon, feeling a reluctant twinge of ingratitude. It was true. Barbara was only trying to help. So why did he feel this sense of resentment at her efforts?

'Look, Barbara,' he said quietly, 'I have to run Crowns my way. Not your way, or Jake's way, but my way. It may not be the best way, I'm not denying that. But it will be the best I can do.'

Barbara sniffed. 'It's not just a question of running Crowns, Dominic,' she declared. 'Being the chairman of a big company like Crowns is important, of course, but one has to look to the future.'

'The future?' Dominic frowned. 'In what way?'

Barbara hesitated. Then she said carefully: 'Everyone knows the world is sliding into recession. Oil is running out. Chemicals depend on oil, don't they? Sooner or later, Crowns themselves may be eaten up by some even bigger conglomerate. Isn't it sensible to have a second string to your bow? If you gained influence in Government circles, if you showed you were interested in politics—'

'Like your father, you mean?' Dominic's voice had hardened considerably, and Barbara hastened to appease him.

'Not like Daddy, no,' she argued. 'Daddy's constituency is small, unimportant. You could choose somewhere else, somewhere near London—'

'You must be crazy!' Dominic was angry now. 'My God, I don't even agree with your father's politics, let alone anything else!'

'But of course you must do,' protested Barbara disbelievingly. 'In your position—'

'In my position, nothing,' Dominic interrupted her harshly. 'My God, I can't believe this!'

'Well, Tony says—'

'I don't give a damn what Tony says,' Dominic retorted violently. '*Tony!* Bloody hypocrite!'

There was silence for a few moments after that, and he raked his scalp with weary fingers. It had been a lousy day, and now this! He felt drained of all compassion.

'Dominic?'

Her tentative use of his name invited a response, and with a heavy expellation of his breath he said: 'I'm here.'

'I'm sorry,' she apologised, evidently unwilling to ring off without an attempt at conciliation. 'That wasn't really why I rang. But I get annoyed when you're so indifferent to people who—'

'I thought that wasn't why you rang,' Dominic overrode her curtly. 'As a matter of fact, I wanted to speak to you, too. Are you free for dinner this evening?'

'I suppose so.' Barbara's reply indicated her resentment at his tone. 'Unlike you, I do not disappear without leaving word of my whereabouts.'

Dominic looked down into his cup. 'I was at the house last night,' he said flatly. 'Marlin Spike. I had dinner with Miss Bainbridge.'

'You what!' Barbara sounded incensed. 'You went all the way down to the country to have dinner with that old woman!'

'That old woman, as you call her, was my nurse,'

Dominic reminded her woodenly. 'And it's not that far—only a little over thirty miles.'

'Thirty miles!' Barbara was scathing. 'It's more like fifty. I can't imagine why you like going there. It's miles too far from town. I don't know why your father doesn't sell it, and buy a villa in the South of France or somewhere.'

'If he sells it, I shall buy it,' Dominic replied flatly. 'I like it. I was brought up there. And contrary to your opinion, I do not consider it's too far from town. On the contrary, it occurs to me that if I gave up the apartment I could live there and commute.'

'You have to be joking!' Barbara's mood was still too volatile to allow that particular piece of information to go unchallenged. 'What? Live at Marlin Spike? What kind of a social life do you think we'd have there?'

Dominic shrugged, and then realising she could not see him, he said: 'Is a social life so important to you, Barbara? I should have thought that was the least of our worries.'

'Well, I wouldn't,' Barbara contradicted him vehemently. 'Oh, this conversation is getting us nowhere. I wanted to talk to you about the party, but you insist on being awkward. Call for me this evening. You may be in a more amenable frame of mind by then.'

'Don't bank on it,' retorted Dominic dourly, and waited until she had rung off before replacing his receiver.

His coffee was half cold, but he drank it anyway, and was still sitting brooding over his exchange with Barbara, when Mrs Cooke came in. Her face was flushed, but she had a definite air of confidence about her, and Dominic thrust his own problems aside to give her a lazy grin.

'You look pleased with yourself,' he observed, pushing his empty cup aside. 'I gather it wasn't as bad as you expected.'

'Not really,' she agreed, a little breathlessly. 'He objected at first.' She gave a nervous laugh. 'He said he wanted to speak to the butcher, not the block.'

Dominic gave a humorous grimace. 'Harry always did have a colourful turn of phrase,' he remarked dryly. 'I hope you put him straight.'

'Oh, I did,' Mrs Cooke nodded. 'I explained that you were tied up and that if he didn't talk to me I couldn't guarantee him seeing you before the last date on the present contract.'

'Very aptly put,' Dominic complimented her. 'This calls for a drink—and I don't mean coffee. What's your poison?'

'Oh, I couldn't drink in working hours, Mr Dominic,' she protested vehemently, but he wasn't listening to her.

'Here,' he said, handing her a Scotch and soda. 'If you're going to become my personal assistant, you have to get used to drinking with the customers. I can't have my representative falling about after only a couple of gins.' He raised his glass. 'Success!'

'Success,' she echoed doubtfully, tasting the contents of her glass almost experimentally. 'I—I don't know what your father would say.'

'I do,' declared Dominic laconically. Then: 'Is it good?'

'It's quite—palatable,' she conceded daringly, and

Dominic couldn't help laughing at the astonishing spectacle of the staid and proper Mrs Cooke enjoying a double whisky in the middle of a working day.

But when she had gone again, to continue with her usual duties, Dominic sought the chair behind his desk with a narrowing gaze. Barbara's call had reminded him of the invitation he had issued to Ruth, and her cousin, and with irresistibly quickening pulses, he switched to an outside line and dialled the number of the Pascal residence. Even the thought of hearing her voice again filled him with anticipation, and he waited impatiently as the dial tone seemed to go on for ever before the call was connected. He wondered what her aunt had said to her this morning about her unexpected outing, and his stomach muscles tightened at the awareness of the developing crisis of conscience he was going to have to face.

He had driven Ruth home quite early last evening, on her insistence, and then spent the rest of the evening at his club, drinking himself into a mindless stupor. The idea of returning to his apartment, to spend the rest of the evening wondering what Ruth was doing and who she was with, had been anathema to him, and he knew the present situation could not be allowed to continue.

It was Davina Pascal herself who eventually answered the call. Dominic could have wished for a more favourable advocate, but he concealed his chagrin, and said courteously: 'This is Dominic Crown, Miss Pascal. Could I speak to Miss Jason?'

'Oh, Mr Crown!' Davina sounded positively gushing. 'I was just about to ring you. You're calling about the party, of course, and you must think me very impolite not having contacted you before this, but what with one thing and another—'

'Don't give it another thought,' Dominic interrupted her civilly. 'I know how busy you must be. My mother—'

'Oh, yes, your mother—such a charming lady. And so generous.' Davina sighed. 'We should all take an example from her.'

'Yes.' Dominic's tone was dry now. 'Well, if I could just speak with Miss Jason—'

'Oh, you can't—'

'I can't?' Dominic's stomach muscles contracted in disbelief. 'Miss Pascal, I—'

'She's not here,' Davina inserted smoothly. 'That was what I was going to ring you about. Neither of them are here. Not Ruth or Martin. They've gone away for a few days—'

'Gone away?' Dominic was incredulous. Ruth had said nothing about this.

'Yes.' Davina sounded smug. 'They've gone skiing. That's what I was trying to tell you. I should have rung you sooner. I'm afraid they'll miss your party.'

Dominic sucked in his breath. He would have liked to tell Davina Pascal what she could do with the accursed party. Why hadn't Ruth told him she was going away? Why had she deliberately kept this information from him?

'Are you still there, Mr Crown?'

Davina's voice had an edge of satisfaction to it now, and Dominic knew she had arranged this deliberately. The scheming old bitch, he thought savagely, and then struggled to control his anger.

'Yes, I'm still here,' he affirmed in a clipped voice.

'Thank you for your time. I'm sorry to have troubled you.'

'That's perfectly all right.' Davina could afford to be generous. 'Do give my best wishes to your mother, won't you? And thank your fiancée for the invitation. It was kind of you to think of it, but as you can see, Martin and Ruth lead quite a hectic social life.'

Dominic made some civil rejoinder before ending the call, but once the receiver was replaced, he pressed both hands painfully against the sides of his neck. He sat like that for several moments, feeling the blood draining out of his head, then allowed his arms to fall on to the desk, feeling the weight of depression bearing down on him.

Why had she done it? he asked himself again, staring broodingly across the room. Why hadn't she told him what they had planned? Why had she let him find out in this most humiliating way? In God's name, she had had plenty of time the night before to tell him. What kind of a selfish game was she playing? What kind of man did she think he was?

He slumped back in his chair, closing his eyes against the images that came to torment him. Where was she right now? What was she doing? What did she really think of Martin Pascal? And what the hell was he going to do about it?

Pushing back his chair, he got abruptly to his feet, reaching for his jacket and pulling it on carelessly. Then he pressed the intercom and looked up moodily as Mrs Cooke came in. 'I'm leaving,' he said, without preamble. 'I've had enough for today. Take all my calls for me, will you? I'll come in in the morning, if there's anything urgent.'

Mrs Cooke looked concerned. 'Is anything the matter, Mr Dominic?' She hesitated. 'You don't look very well, if you don't mind my saying so. You've been working too hard.'

Dominic's mouth curled. 'No, I haven't. I haven't been working hard enough.' He adjusted the collar of his shirt, sliding his tie back into place. 'See you on Monday, hmm?'

'Would you like me to come in in the morning?' she enquired anxiously. 'I don't mind. I have nothing else to do.'

Dominic paused, momentarily stirred to an instinctive compassion. 'Don't you?' he asked probingly. 'I thought perhaps—Mr Cooke—'

'There is no Mr Cooke,' she declared, moving her shoulders in a gesture of dismissal. 'There was, but he left me fifteen years ago. Does that answer your question, Mr Dominic?'

He sighed. 'I'm sorry.'

Mrs Cooke shook her head. 'I'm not. I'm glad to get it off my chest. Your father—well, he never asked me.'

'He wouldn't,' averred Dominic dryly. 'So long as you did your work to the best of your ability, that was all he was concerned about.'

'I know that.' She gave a tentative smile, before saying impulsively: 'But I'm glad you did. I—we— I'm sure you're going to make a success of your job, Mr Dominic, if it's not presumptuous of me to say so.'

Dominic grimaced. 'I wish I could believe that,' he commented wryly. But all the same, his hard features

S.—L

softened. 'I think the whisky must have gone to your head, Mrs Cooke,' he added, yet he couldn't deny the faint stirring of optimism he felt as he walked towards the lifts.

The doorman hailed him a cab, and Dominic gave the address of his parents' home in Curzon Terrace. Then he settled back, and waited rather impatiently for the driver to reach his destination. He felt hot and irritable, and he would have liked nothing better than to go straight to the apartment and take a shower. But he wanted to talk to his father, and this was as good a time as any.

However, when he walked into his mother's sitting room to find her strumming idly at the piano, she quickly disabused him of his expectations.

'Your father's not here,' she told him, her tone half apologetic in the face of his frustration. 'He's playing golf with Alan Harmer. It's nothing urgent, is it, Dominic? I don't like to ring him at the club— you know how agitated he becomes if he gets an unexpected phone call.'

Dominic swore softly, then flung himself resignedly into an armchair. 'What time do you expect him back?' he asked, resting one ankle across his knee. 'I didn't know the old man even liked the game.'

Isobel's brows arched in faint disapproval, but she forbore from commenting on his lack of parental reverence. Instead she said: 'You should have told him you were coming. I'm sure he'd have much preferred a chat with you, to advertising his handicap to Alan Harmer.'

'I doubt it,' remarked Dominic dryly, then moved his shoulders indifferently. 'Oh, well, I guess I can wait. Providing you can supply me with something long and cold and thirst-quenching.'

'Lager?' suggested his mother, getting up from the piano stool, and Dominic inclined his head.

'If you've nothing stronger,' he agreed, as she rang the bell for Ginny, and Isobel firmly shook her head.

Ginny showed a distinct inclination to linger, but Isobel dismissed her sharply before seating herself near her son. Then, when he had emptied half his glass, she lay back in her chair, curled her hands over the arms, and said bluntly:

'Why did you take that girl down to Marlin Spike? You must have known that we would find out sooner or later.'

Dominic found himself at a disadvantage. It was the last thing he had expected his mother to ask, and he took some time drinking the remainder of the lager in his glass, before giving her any reply.

'How did you find out, just out of interest?' he said at last, disappointed that Bridie should have deliberately betrayed him, but his mother unwittingly restored his confidence.

'It was through Barbara, actually,' she admitted flatly. 'She rang me about half an hour ago. She said she'd been speaking to you.'

'But Barbara didn't—'

'—know? I'm aware of that. However, when she told me where you'd been I rang Bridie to apologise for your inconsiderateness in turning up like that.'

Dominic bent his head. 'And that's when she told you.'

'Eventually,' conceded his mother dryly. 'You know what Bridie's like. She thinks the sun shines

out of your—well, we won't go into that. Sufficient
to say, that she accidentally mentioned that she had
made dinner for three. Naturally, I insisted on knowing who had accompanied you.'

'Naturally,' observed Dominic, with some sarcasm, and his mother gazed at him with unveiled
irritation.

'Do you know what you're doing?' she demanded,
'taking that girl there? Have you any idea how
Barbara would react if she found out?'

Dominic sighed heavily. 'I get the picture.'

'Do you? Do you?' Isobel's voice rose a little, and
she quickly controlled it. 'Dominic, I don't know
what's come over you. Ever since that trip to Barbados, ever since you met that girl—'

'Oh, no.' Dominic would not have that, and his
tawny eyes were hard as they encountered hers. 'Not
just since I met Ruth, Mother. Before that—long
before that.'

His mother made a little helpless movement of her
fingers. 'I don't understand you. I—we—your father
and I—we've done everything for you. Since
Michael died—'

'I know, Mother, I know.' Dominic rested his
head back against the soft upholstery, feeling the
churning tide of frustration rising inside him again. 'I
know you mean well—'

'Mean well? Mean well?' His mother's voice rose
again. 'Is that all it's ever meant to you?'

Dominic groaned. 'No. No, of course not.' He
lifted his head to look at her again. 'But try and be a
little more reasonable. I know you care about me. I
know that since Michael died you've channelled all

your emotions in my direction. But don't you see? I can't be held responsible for all your thwarted ambitions for him as well as me!'

Isobel's lips trembled. 'That's a cruel thing to say, Dominic!'

'But true,' he averred, resting his arms along his thighs, leaning towards her. 'Mother, listen to me—'

Isobel shook her head, fumbling for her handkerchief, and defeated once again, he lay back against the cushions. It was always like this, he thought wearily. Michael's death lay like a weight across his shoulders.

'This girl,' his mother said at last, when he made no attempt to continue the conversation, 'how did you come to take her to Marlin Spike? Does her aunt know about your relationship?'

'No!' Dominic was emphatic. Then, answering her other question, he said: 'I knew she was taking a driving lesson yesterday. I met her outside the school.'

'You—arranged to meet her?' Isobel probed, and Dominic shook his head.

'No. It was all my idea,' he replied briefly. He paused, before adding bitterly: 'She didn't even want to come.'

His mother was amazed. 'You mean you forced her?'

'Not exactly,' he conceded dryly. 'I—persuaded her.'

'But what is she to you?' demanded Isobel fiercely. 'Are you attracted to her? Do you have a—a physical relationship?'

'I don't think that's any of your business. Mother,'
he retorted flatly. bringing an unbecoming darkening of colour to her cheeks. 'As to what she is to me,
perhaps you ought to ask what am I to her?'

'What do you mean?'

'She left for Switzerland this morning. with her
aunt's adopted son. She omitted to tell me she was
going.'

Isobel looked slightly relieved. 'So—so you think
she's involved with this—this cousin of hers?' she
ventured faintly. and then drew back when Dominic
made a strangled sound.

'If she is. I'll kill him.' he responded grimly. and
she clasped her palms together in a gesture of stunned incredulity.

CHAPTER SEVENTEEN

Martin soon got bored with Ruth's inexperienced efforts on the nursery slopes, and she could tell from the way he knocked first one fist and then the other into his palms, and stamped his feet, that he was growing restless. Towering above them, the challenging slopes of the Grensberg glacier were a constant temptation, and she guessed he was envying those expert skiers who took the chair-lift up the pass.

'You don't have to stay with me, you know,' she told him, over dinner their first evening. 'I'm quite willing to join Herr Ferrier's class. You go and enjoy yourself. I know you're dying to try your skis.'

Martin grinned, reaching for her hand across the table. 'Am I so transparent?' he sighed ruefully. 'I must confess, the higher slopes are appealing.'

'Then go ahead,' Ruth suggested, letting her fingers lie pliant within his. 'I'd like to try my hand at skating, actually, so why don't we both do what we want?'

Martin sighed. 'Somehow I get the feeling my mother wouldn't approve,' he brooded doubtfully. 'This weekend was supposed to throw us together.'

Ruth sipped her wine. 'We'll have every evening,' she pointed out reasonably, and she could see Martin was attracted by the prospect of some exciting sport.

In consequence, Ruth passed Saturday morning in company with a crowd of other would-be skiers, learning the rudimentary rules of the exercise, and after lunching alone at one of the ubiquitous pastry houses, spent the afternoon touring the shops. The richness and variety of the goods on sale quite took her breath away, and she spent a long time admiring a chunky cream sweater, patterned in shades of blue and green and yellow, thinking how attractive it would look on Dominic. She had tried very hard not think of him. She had determined that once she left England she would put him out of her mind. But this morning, after a restless night tossing in the comfortable hotel bed, she had felt so sick and miserable she had realised that she was fooling herself by imagining that distance would achieve what proximity could not.

She went back to the hotel around five, changed into her bathing suit, and took a swim in the pool. She and Martin had used the pool the night before, but she was still a little nervous about doing things alone. Nevertheless, it was all part of her intention to prove herself independent, and she swam the length of the pool a couple of times before climbing out on to the side.

'It's Miss Jason, isn't it?'

She looked up in surprise at the friendly question, then relaxed as she recognised Herr Ferrier. The young ski instructor was obviously just on his way to take a swim, and she smiled politely at him as she returned his greeting.

'You're leaving?' he asked, with some regret.

'What a pity! I should have welcomed your company.'

Ruth knew Herr Ferrier was an Austrian, but his English was very good, and his smiling attention was just what she needed. 'I'm sorry, too,' she answered, loosening her hair from its knot, so that it fell silkily about her shoulders. 'Excuse me—I have to go and change.'

'Later—' he said, as she started to walk away, and she looked back at him puzzlingly. 'Join me for a drink later,' he amended. 'In the *après-ski* lounge. 'We could share a dish of *fondue*, no?'

Ruth hesitated. 'I don't know—'

Herr Ferrier frowned. He was very good-looking, square-shouldered, and muscular; very athletic. He was evidently used to having success with the girls he selected, Ruth guessed shrewdly, but she was not offended by his persistence.

'Please,' he said. 'I shall be there in—thirty minutes. Do not disappoint me.'

Ruth smiled. 'My cousin may have other plans.'

Herr Ferrier shrugged. 'Bring her with you,' he declared expansively, and Ruth's lips twitched.

'I'll bring—*him*, shall I?' she suggested, and with the lightning courtesy of his race, the Austrian performed a little bow.

'It will be my pleasure,' he assured her gallantly, and Ruth went to put on her towelling robe, with a certain lifting of her spirits.

In the event, it was an entertaining evening. There proved to be quite a number of young people gathered together in the lounge, and as they all seemed to know the young Austrian, Ruth and Martin were absorbed into their group. Dinner was a casual meal, taken buffet style, from the dish of *fondue* they all shared. Squatting on cushions, dipping squares of bread into the cheesy concoction in the centre, interspersing it with glasses of chilled white wine, Ruth relaxed for the first time since Dominic had driven her home, and the enormous log fire that blazed merrily in the wide hearth brought a glow of health and vitality to her cheeks.

'You are enjoying yourself, yes?'

She became aware that Martin had moved away to talk to some people he had been skiing with that afternoon, and his place had been taken by the Austrian. Herr Ferrier was looking at her very intently, his blue eyes bright in the glow from the fire, his fair good looks accentuated by the healthiness of his tan. It was strange, she thought inconsequently, how much different two fair-haired people could be. Herr Ferrier's hair was golden-blond, not silver, and his eyes were Nordic blue, not amber; but most particularly, his skin was fair, tanned a golden brown, while Dominic's was sallow, and darkly pigmented. Yet, despite the Austrian's classical beauty, it was Dominic she preferred, and his hard, lean body was infinitely more disturbing than Herr Ferrier's rippling muscles.

'You are not enjoying yourself?' he enquired now, when she didn't answer him, and she hastened to restore his opinion.

'Oh, yes,' she said, cradling her glass between her palms. 'I'm having a lovely evening, thank you, Herr Ferrier.'

'My name is Johann,' he told her softly. 'And your

name, I know, is Ruth. Surely we can omit the formalities for once. I would very much like you to use my name.'

'All right—Johann,' Ruth smiled. 'I'm not used to ceremony either. Tell me, do you live here?'

'In Grensberg? No,' he shook his head, 'my home is in Innsbruck. My father has a printing business there. But me, I like to ski, and I am afraid my family despairs of me.'

Ruth was interested. 'But one day you'll go back, won't you? To the printing business, I mean.'

'Perhaps.' He shrugged. 'When I am no longer young. When I cannot ski the glacier.' He paused. 'And you? What do you do? Do you live in London?'

Ruth hesitated. 'London, yes,' she conceded slowly. 'And I'm afraid I don't do anything, not right now, anyway. But—but I hope to.'

'Ah, I see. You have just left school, no?' Johann nodded, and Ruth decided to let him think so. 'It is good to be young, and have one's whole life in front of one.' He glanced at Martin. 'But Mr Pascal, your cousin, he is your friend, no?'

'My friend?' Ruth frowned. 'Yes, Martin and I are friends. Why do you ask?'

'Ah, you misunderstand me,' declared Johann quietly. 'In my way, I am asking whether he is your lover also.' His eyes caressed her. 'But I am persuaded that he is not.'

Ruth was glad the heat of the fire hid her blushes, and she was relieved when Martin came to join them. His presence precluded any further intimacies, and when he yawned and said he was ready for bed, she eagerly went with him.

As they went up to their rooms, however, Martin had other matters to concern him. 'Did you see that tall blonde girl in the red and white catsuit?' he asked her earnestly. 'The one with the huge gold hoops in her ears? I was skiing with her and her brother this afternoon, and she's really terrific!'

'Is she?' Ruth glanced wryly at him, and he gave her an involuntary hug.

'She's a terrific athlete,' he exclaimed enthusiastically. 'A natural on skis. You should come and watch her tomorrow. You could go up and down on the lift—I'd take care of you.'

'No, thanks.' Ruth shook her head. She had had experience of Martin's taking care of her at the racetrack near London. His ideas of looking after someone amounted to taking them where he wanted to go, and then leaving them to their own devices for hours on end. She had no desire to spend a freezing couple of hours up on the high slopes, with nothing between her and the valley but empty wastes of tree-scattered snow. 'I told you, I want to try the ice rink. You go with—with—'

'—Val and David,' Martin put in for her, and she nodded.

'Yes, you go with Val and David,' she acknowledged lightly. 'Don't worry about me.'

'I think that Herr what's-his-name fancies you,' interjected Martin suddenly. 'You watch yourself with him. I don't trust these professional sportsmen.'

'Nor do I,' returned Ruth mischievously, looking at him, and Martin gave her a punishing slap on her tail, before she disappeared into her room.

Sunday was much like Saturday, except that Ruth

slept longer in the morning, and awakened feeling
decidedly unwell. She guessed the altitude didn't
agree with her, and making her own way to the
coffee shop, refused everything but milk and wheat
flakes.

After breakfast, she felt much better, and collect-
ing her gloves and parka, she made her way across
the busy square to where the ice rink was attracting a
small crowd. Several of the professional skaters from
the hotel were giving a small display, but after they
were finished and the audience had applauded, the
ice was given over to the amateurs, and Ruth went to
hire some skates.

'May I accompany you?'

It was Johann Ferrier again, at her elbow, his
smiling face full of confidence. She guessed he must
have been waiting for her to join his skiing class, but
when she didn't turn up, he had decided to look for
her.

'I'm only going to *try* and skate,' she exclaimed
reluctantly. 'I've never been on skates before. I'm
sure you'll be awfully bored.'

'Allow me to be the best judge of that,' he declared, taking her arm. 'Come, I have some skates I
can lend you over here. There is no need for you to
stand in line.'

Ruth submitted to his eager ministrations, calculating that nothing untoward could happen on an ice
rink. Afterwards, she intended going straight back to
the hotel, and Herr Ferrier could find someone else
to charm.

It was a little scary on the ice. Her feet kept running away with her, and she clung desperately to the

railings that surrounded the rink, refusing Johann's pleas to her to trust him.

'You will never learn how to skate by hanging on to railings!' he exclaimed impatiently. 'You must let your body go where your feet will take it. Learn how to balance on your own two feet. See—it is easy!'

'For you, maybe,' Ruth insisted, glancing about her unhappily. 'I can't keep my balance. It's no good.'

'Did you never have the—what do you call them? —roller skates, when you were a little girl?' he demanded incredulously, and Ruth's brows drew together.

'Roller-skates?' she echoed blankly, and Johann raised his eyes skyward in evident exasperation.

'Where have you been living?' he exclaimed, half in humour, half in irritation. 'On a desert island?'

Ruth felt the hot colour surge into her cheeks, and misunderstanding her reaction, Johann apologised. 'I am sorry,' he said, 'I should not have said that. It is only that you are—how shall I say?—so timid!'

Timid! Ruth's teeth clamped together. Was that really what she was—timid? She took a deep breath. If someone who had only known her for a little over twenty-four hours thought she was timid, how could she expect Aunt Davina, who knew her so much better, to consider her capable of being independent?

'What do you want me to do?' she asked now, cautiously removing one hand from the railings and putting it on Johann's sleeve.

'Ah, that is better,' he approved, grasping her hand in his and drawing her resistingly towards him.

'Now—so—come to me,' and seconds later she was gliding over the ice and into his arms.

It was a not unpleasant sensation, and excited by her own success, she did not object too strongly to his enveloping hold. On the contrary, by leaning on him, she found she could move steadily round the ice, and instead of clinging like a schoolgirl to the railings, she glided smoothly over the icy surface.

'It is fun, is it not?' he breathed, his lips against her hair, and she had to admit it was. Compared to her childish attempts at skiing, and her earlier stubbornness on the rink, this was exhilarating, and in no time at all she could balance holding only his hand.

'Thank you,' she said breathlessly, as they circled the ice for the umpteenth time, and she began to appreciate the time he was devoting to her, and Johann skated closer.

'You can thank me this evening,' he said, touching her cheek with a gloved finger. 'There is to be music and dancing at the hotel, and I am reserving the right to your company.'

Ruth made no objection. After all, she and Martin were going home tomorrow. It was good to relax and let oneself go. She would think of the future when she got back to London.

The accident happened as they were leaving the ice. Johann was skating ahead, pulling her after him, when a pair of skaters coming too fast, collided with them. The impact tore Johann's hand from Ruth's grasp, and she found herself spinning backwards across the ice, groping and flailing, and desperately trying to regain her balance.

She didn't. She came down heavily on to the ice,

twisting her wrist and cracking her head, and sliding several feet farther, as the momentum carried her on.

Mouthing curses, Johann reached her first, kneeling beside her and chafing her hands in his. 'Ruth, *liebling*,' he muttered in his distress. '*Ach, die Idioten, sie haben kein Verstand!*'

'I'm all right, really.' Ruth sat up gingerly, rubbing her head. 'It was just the shock I got.' She looked up at him ruefully. 'And after all your good work!'

Johann shook his head impatiently, and helped her to her feet. '*Idioten!*' he said again, glowering angrily at the two boys who had caused the accident, standing anxiously on the edge of the gathering group of skaters. 'They are so reckless. You could have been knocked senseless!'

'But I wasn't,' Ruth reassured him firmly. Nevertheless, she did feel decidedly unsteady, and she allowed him to remove her skates before they walked back across the ice. Her back still hurt, her head was starting to ache, and she wanted nothing so much as to lie down for a while, and she was grateful that Johann took her straight back to the hotel and advised her to rest for the afternoon.

'I will see you this evening,' he promised, bidding her goodbye at the foot of the stairs, and Ruth managed a smile before making her painful way upstairs.

She missed lunch, feeling too stiff to make the effort to go downstairs again, and when Martin returned in the late afternoon he came looking for her.

'What happened?' he exclaimed, examining her pale features with anxious eyes, and after she had told him: 'Have you seen a doctor?'

'A doctor?' Ruth looked incredulous. 'Honestly, Martin, a doctor, after falling on the ice!'

'Why not after falling on the ice? You could have done yourself some damage. Slipped a disc or something.'

'Oh, you're very reassuring, aren't you?' she exclaimed impatiently. 'My back just feels stiff, that's all. And I have a headache. I don't need a doctor.'

'I'm not so sure.' Martin regarded her thoughtfully. 'I know Mother would insist on it.'

'Your mother's not here.'

'No, but I am. And I'm supposed to be looking after you,' retorted Martin severely, obviously anticipating what his mother's reaction might be if she learned that Ruth had had an accident on the skating rink, while he was enjoying himself on the steeper slopes.

'Oh, all right.' Ruth gave in. In actual fact, she thought she would welcome something to get rid of her headache, and she didn't want to spoil their last evening. 'Call the doctor. Cover all possibilities.'

Martin pulled a face at her sarcasm, but he was evidently relieved to be able to summon professional advice, and within half an hour a Doctor Kaufmann presented himself at her door.

'I understand you had a skating accident, *fraülein*,' he said, coming over the the bed where she was lying. 'I think I had better do a thorough examination. That young man of yours is most concerned for your welfare.'

Ruth didn't trouble to explain that Martin was not exactly her young man, but her cousin. It wasn't important what Doctor Kaufmann thought, she decided, struggling to unfasten her sweater. Like Johann, he could form his own opinion.

Some minutes later, Ruth was beginning to wish Martin had never started this. The doctor's examination was certainly comprehensive, she thought disagreeably, resenting his professional hands upon her body, prodding and probing, and making her feel uncomfortable.

However, when Doctor Kaufmann straightened, and told her she could replace her clothes, his face was rather solemn, and mild panic flared inside her. Surely she didn't need hospital treatment? she thought anxiously. Surely the ache in her spine was only muscular? Why was he looking at her as if she was to blame?

'Is—is everything all right, doctor?' she asked at last, unable to bear the suspense any longer, and he turned away to replace his stethoscope in his bag.

'You have been lucky this time, *fraülein*,' he told her, snapping the bag shut. 'But I suggest you refrain from taking such unnecessary risks.'

Ruth breathed a sigh of relief. 'I know. I'd never skated before, you see,' she explained hurriedly. 'Then these two boys collided with me—' She shook her head. 'I lost my balance.'

'Yes, well, I would advise you not to do anything so reckless again,' remarked the doctor, softening a little. 'Young women in your condition are usually more concerned for themselves, but I suppose, like everything else, they object to the limitations put on them by their sex.'

He moved politely towards the door, but Ruth could not let him go like that. His words had not

made sense to her, and she put a hand to her throat as
a thought occurred to her. 'Is—is something wrong
with me, doctor?' she asked, her voice squeaking a
little over the last words, and his dark brows descended in mild impatience.

'Wrong with you? No, nothing is wrong. It should
be a perfectly normal pregnancy, so long as—'

'A—*what!*'

Ruth swung her legs to the floor then, and stared at
him in wild disbelief. She didn't really need him to
repeat it to know what he said, but the reality of it
was so stunning, she needed those few moments to
restore her sense of balance.

Doctor Kaufmann frowned, however. 'Did you
not know, Miss Jason?' He shook his head. 'Hah,
you must have done!' Ruth moved her hand in a
helpless gesture of denial, and he came abruptly
back to her. 'You did not know? But how could you
not know? Have you not missed at least two—how
do you say it?—the periods, no?'

Ruth's lips parted. Had she? *Had she?* She
couldn't think. When she lived on the island, she had
seldom thought about it, accepting the slight discomfort naturally when it came, and dismissing it
from her mind at other times. She had never studied
its regularity, or marked the date on the calendar.
Living with her father, she had no one to discuss it
with but Celeste, and even she had never paid it a lot
of attention.

But now, sitting here in this Alpine hotel bedroom, she acknowledged that she could not remember having any discomfort since she came to live with
Aunt Davina, and the inevitable conclusion to that

awareness turned all her bones to water. *Dominic*, she thought faintly; she was going to have Dominic's baby. And fast on the heels of this thought came another—*she could never tell him!*

'Well, *fraülein*? I am right, am I not?' Doctor Kaufmann was studying her anxious expression. 'And I suppose that young man outside is responsible.'

'Oh, no—no—that is—' Ruth put an unsteady hand to her head. 'I—I'd really rather not discuss it.'

Doctor Kaufmann shrugged. 'Very well, it is your decision. But I must impress upon you, the necessity to—how shall I say it?—curb your natural impulsiveness. Another fall as you had this morning, and I cannot guarantee you would not lose your baby.'

'No. No, I see.' Ruth was finding it almost impossible to think coherently. 'No, of course I won't do anything silly.'

'Good.' Doctor Kaufmann permitted himself a slight smile. 'And don't worry. You are a perfectly healthy young woman. Having a baby is the most natural thing in the world.'

'Thank you, doctor.' Ruth slid gingerly off the bed, to find that apart from the lingering stiffness, she felt much better.

'*Nichts*,' responded the doctor dismissingly, and opened the door into the hall outside, where Martin was hovering. 'Your girlfriend is perfectly all right, Herr Pascal,' he reassured him politely, and walked briskly away towards the stairs.

Martin grinned as Ruth came to lean weakly against the door frame. 'All present and correct?' he asked teasingly, and she managed a faint nod.

'That's good. I had visions of having to tell Mother how it happened!'

Aunt Davina! Ruth swallowed rather convulsively. What would she say when she discovered what had happened? She would have to be told, and Ruth mentally anticipated the battle that would ensue. She had few doubts that her aunt would be furious, and not without good reason, but she determined that on no account should she betray what had happened to Dominic. He was going to marry his fiancée. It was all arranged for September—Mrs Crown had told her that. She had also told her what a wonderful wife Barbara would make. The last thing Ruth wanted was for Dominic to feel compelled to marry her, when his whole future depended upon him making the right choice.

Ruth ate in her room that evening, despite Martin's pleas to the contrary. She felt she could not face Johann's eyes upon her, excusing herself on the grounds that she still felt slightly groggy. Martin did not object too strongly, and she guessed he had made arrangements to meet Val and David again. He had spoken enthusiastically of the day they had had out together, and Ruth was glad he was not there to probe her still vulnerable incredulity.

Her mirror image was reassuring, however. Without the doctor's testimony she would not have guessed there was another life growing inside her, although now she came to think of it, it explained so many things—her occasional nausea in the mornings, the hunger that gripped her at unusual times of the day, and the faint she had had the morning she went to see Mrs Crown.

Thinking of Mrs Crown brought her thoughts back
to Dominic, and a feeling of cold reality replaced her
earlier wonder. No matter how miraculous the
thought of having Dominic's child might be, she had
to face facts. She was pregnant, and she was un-
married; with little likelihood of being otherwise, she
acknowledged with a pang. She was young and
healthy, and she had the money her father had left
her, along with the allowance from her grandmother's estate, but she knew there was no way she
could have this baby in England without Dominic
finding out about it.

They flew back to England the next morning.

Johann Ferrier was waiting in the hall as they were
leaving, and he regarded her departure with accusing
eyes. 'You did not join us yesterday evening as you
promised,' he reproached her, while Martin was
organising the loading of their cases into the cab.
'You are angry because I let you fall.'

'Oh, no, no.' Ruth shook her head apologetically,
pressing her gloved hands together. 'It was just—
easier this way, that's all,' she assured him gently.
'I—we—are parting friends.'

Johann nodded. 'I understand,' he said, transfer-
ring his gaze to Martin, but she doubted he did. 'Be
happy,' he added, turning away, and she wished it
was that simple as she climbed into the back of the
car.

Her opportunity to speak to Aunt Davina came
sooner than she had expected.

Their return was greeted with much enthusiasm by
her aunt, although some of that effusiveness turned

to impatience when she discovered Martin intended
to go out on the racing circuit that afternoon. She
had things she wanted him to do, she said, without
specifying, and Ruth left them arguing together
when she went upstairs to get changed.

Over lunch, however, Aunt Davina was brittly
talkative, asking about the trip, insisting on hearing
all the details, despite Martin's obvious chagrin.
However, at three-thirty he managed to make his
escape, and Ruth and her aunt were left sitting over
the coffee cups in the morning room, each of them
regretting Martin's departure, but for different
reasons.

Ruth had been turning over in her mind how best
she should phrase what she had to say. It was not
going to be easy to broach such a subject, particularly when she had no intention of confessing who
the father of her child was, and she blessed the
reticence she had evinced earlier in keeping
Dominic's identity to herself. Her aunt would never
make the connection without that previous knowledge.

'Aunt Davina—'

'Ruth—'

They both spoke at once, and Ruth drew back
automatically. 'Please,' she said, 'What were you
going to say? What I·have to tell you can wait.'

The older woman hesitated a moment, then she
conceded, 'Very well. But it's not important really. I
was merely going to mention that Dominic Crown
called me while you were away.'

Ruth felt as though someone had delivered a blow
to her solar plexis, but she managed to hide the worst

effects of her reaction, and moved her shoulders offhandedly. 'Did he?' she asked, trying to appear only casually interested. 'What did he have to say?'

'It was about the party, naturally,' Aunt Davina stated calmly, her eyes unnecessarily intent. 'Of course, I explained that you and Martin were away, but I think at first he didn't believe me.'

Ruth made an involuntary gesture. 'I wonder why.'

'Yes,' Aunt Davina's lips thinned, 'I wondered that myself.'

Ruth's fingers curved over the handle of a fork. 'I—I expect he thought we should have—have rung him.'

'Perhaps.' Her aunt inclined her head. 'Or more reasonably, I think, he thought *you* should have told him.'

'Me?' Ruth's voice came out like a squeak, but she quickly controlled it. 'Me?' she said again. 'How could I have told him?'

'I imagine when you had dinner with him on Thursday evening,' observed Aunt Davina coolly. 'It was Dominic Crown you spent the evening with, wasn't it?' she persisted. 'You've been seeing him regularly since you arrived in England, haven't you?'

Ruth was flabbergasted. This was the last thing she had expected, and her brain was working furiously, as she tried to assimilate what it might mean.

'Come along.' Aunt Davina was getting impatient. 'I know all about him turning up half-drowned on the beach at Indigo. His mother told me. I had quite a long conversation with her this morning.'

'Did you?' Ruth could hardly believe this was happening.

'Yes, I did. And it explained a number of things, not least that ridiculous story you spun me about him coming here selling tickets for a charity ball!'

Ruth expelled her breath heavily. 'Did—did Mrs Crown tell you about that too?'

'Why wouldn't she? She's as embarrassed by this whole business as I am.'

Ruth could believe that. Dominic's mother had left her in little doubt as to where she considered his loyalties lay.

'You may be wondering why I troubled to make these enquiries,' her aunt continued now. 'The truth is, Ruth, I was concerned about you.'

'About me?'

'Yes.' Aunt Davina frowned. 'There had to be a reason for your reluctance to admit your affection for Martin. I know you said you needed more time, and I respect that, but I am not prepared to stand back and let Dominic Crown ruin your life.'

Ruth bent her head. 'Aunt Davina, I—'

'No, don't say anything, Ruth. I know you're going to defend the man, and—and perhaps I can understand that. He was in your care for a little while, and naturally you've conceived a kind of childish infatuation for him. It's not a unique situation, goodness knows. He—well, I suppose he is an attractive man, if you like the combination of that fair hair and swarthy skin. Personally, I prefer a more conventional make-up, but there you are.' She paused. 'In any event, we both know that so far as you are concerned he's bad news, and I should hate

to see a promising debut marred by insinuations of
an illicit association with Dominic Crown. It's not
fair to you, and it's certainly not fair on his fiancée.'

'I know that, Aunt Davina.' Ruth managed to
intervene at this point. 'I—as a matter of fact, I have
no intention of seeing Dominic again—'

'I'm pleased to hear it.'

'—but, unfortunately, there's a complication to—
to my debut, as you call it.'

'What kind of complication?'

Ruth took a deep breath. 'I'm going to have a
baby.'

'*No!*'

Aunt Davina stared at her then as if she couldn't
believe her ears. Her eyes dilated, and her face lost
colour, and for an awful moment Ruth thought she
was going to pass out. It took her several minutes and
an obvious effort of will-power to sustain the shock-
ing information, but gradually the blank look that
had briefly scared her niece gave way to a white-
lipped concentration.

'I'm sorry.'

It was inadequate, but Ruth could think of nothing
else to say, and after a few minutes her aunt slowly
put her thoughts into words.

'Does—does anyone else know about this?' she
demanded faintly, and Ruth hastened to reassure
her.

'If you mean Dominic—no,' she told her flatly. 'I
only got to know myself yesterday.'

'Yesterday?' Her aunt looked horrified again, and
Ruth quickly explained.

'I had a fall,' she said. 'On the ice. When the

doctor examined me afterwards, he thought I would know about it.'

'And Martin?'

'No.' Ruth made a negative gesture. 'Only me.'

'So apart from this doctor, you and I are the only ones who know about it?'

Ruth nodded.

'Thank God!'

Aunt Davina gave heartfelt thanks, and Ruth could only assume she had been afraid of the scandal which would ensue if this ever came out.

'You can't tell Dominic Crown, of course,' her aunt said at last, and Ruth conceded the point.

'I had no intention of doing so,' she said tightly, and Aunt Davina nodded, before getting up from the table to pace restlessly across to the windows.

She was evidently trying to assess what this might mean to her social position, and Ruth's shoulders sagged with sudden relief. It had not been half so bad as she had expected, and although Aunt Davina was probably still in a mild state of shock, she would get over it.

'The marriage will have to be brought forward!'

Her aunt's amazing statement brought Ruth's head round with a jerk, and as she stared at her wide-eyed, Davina went on: 'Yes. Yes, of course, that's the answer. All our problems solved at one stroke.'

Ruth swallowed. 'Marriage?' she echoed. 'What marriage? You mean—Dominic and Barbara's?'

'Dominic and Barbara's?' Her aunt looked at her aghast. 'No. No, of course not.' She strode back to the table to look down at her niece with penetrating eyes. 'I assume you are about—what?—two months pregnant?'

'Something like that,' Ruth nodded. She had yet to make the exact calculations.

'So if you and Martin got married right away, no one need ever suspect.'

'If Martin and I got married!' Ruth was astounded. 'I can't marry Martin now. You don't seem to understand, Aunt Davina. I'm going to have Dominic Crown's baby!'

'I know that. I'm not stupid.' Aunt Davina sighed in frustration. 'It's you who are not listening to what I'm saying, Ruth. If you and Martin got married—next week, say—everyone would assume the baby was his.'

'Martin wouldn't,' exclaimed Ruth stubbornly, but her aunt waved her objections aside.

'He will, if you don't tell him otherwise,' she retorted, bringing a wave of horrified colour to Ruth's pale cheeks. 'My dear girl, Martin's no mathematician. If you tell him it's a seven-month baby, he won't dispute it.'

Ruth was appalled. 'But I couldn't do that to him!'

'Why not? You want a father for your child, don't you? You don't want it to be labelled illegitimate!'

'Well, no, but—'

'No buts,' declared Aunt Davina firmly. 'Think about it. You'll see that I'm right. Now all I have to do is persuade Martin that an early confirmation of your relationship would be—advisable.' She frowned, catching her lower lip between her teeth. 'I might even be able to use Dominic Crown's apparent interest in you to good advantage.' She nodded thoughtfully. 'If I could make him jealous—'

'Stop it!' Ruth had had enough of this. 'You can't do it, Aunt Davina. I won't let you.' She got up from her chair, but she was shaking so much she could hardly stand. 'If—if my baby has to be illegitimate, then so be it. I have no intention of allowing you to make Martin a dupe on my account.'

Aunt Davina faced her angrily. 'So this is how you repay me?'

'No.' Ruth shook her head. 'I know I can't stay here—I've thought about that. I want to go back to the island. I want to have my baby there.'

'And after the child is born, what then?'

Her aunt was regarding her with eyes filled with dislike, and Ruth wondered what she had done to make Aunt Davina so angry. Surely she could see how wrong it would be for Ruth to take advantage of Martin like that, even had she wanted to. Perhaps she meant well, but how could she say she loved him and then condemn him so readily? She realised how little she really knew of either of them at that moment. It was almost as if these weeks of their relationship had been wiped away, leaving a curiously unnatural void between.

'I don't know,' she said now. 'I—I may come back to England. You brought up a child alone, Aunt Davina. I can do the same.'

Her aunt seemed to be having a battle inside herself, but finally she said: 'Very well. As you insist on blinding yourself to the practicalities of the situation, I wash my hands of you. I brought Martin up alone, it's true. But my father was still alive in those days. I had him to lean on. Who will you lean on, Ruth, when your body gets heavy, and you find it tiring to get about; when your legs begin to ache, and your ankles swell in the heat? And what about when you have the baby? When the pains start coming, and you've no one to care for you, or give you encouragement. What will you do then, Ruth? When your body feels as if it's being torn apart!'

Ruth turned away. Her aunt's words were frightening, as they had been intended to be, but still she clung to her own beliefs. She would not force Martin to father another man's child, nor would she force her child to be brought up in a relationship founded on deceit. She did care for Martin. She might even have come to love him in time. But she refused to use him, which was what Aunt Davina was asking her to do.

CHAPTER EIGHTEEN

The house in Wellington Mews seemed deserted when Dominic rang the bell, and he waited impatiently for someone to answer the door. When he rang earlier, only the housekeeper had been at home, but she had said that her mistress was expected back around four, and it was exactly that time now.

The door remained obstinately shut, and Dominic went down the steps and looked up at the windows before mounting them again. All the blinds were drawn at the upstairs windows, and no sudden movement betrayed a person's presence. Whoever was at home was either stalling or dead, and his temper boiled as he realised the time he was wasting.

He pressed the bell again, keeping his finger on the button, hearing its chimes ring through the house. Surely to goodness someone could hear that, he thought angrily, tempted to try the windows, then expelled his breath heavily as the door at last swung inward.

'Oh, Mr Crown.' It was the housekeeper, her face somewhat flustered. 'Can—can I help you? I—I'm afraid Miss Pascal is not at home.'

'Is she not?' Dominic's mouth hardened. 'I thought you said she'd be back at four o'clock.' He shrugged. 'Never mind, I'll wait.'

'You can't!' Mrs Radcliffe's denial was involuntary, but she followed it up with an apologetic wave of her hand. 'I mean, there would be no point. Miss—er—Miss Pascal is not coming back today. She—er—she's gone away—'

'The hell she has!' Dominic refused to be put off any longer, and brushing the housekeeper aside, he strode into the hall. 'All right,' he demanded, 'Where is Miss Jason? And don't tell me she's gone away, too.'

'She has.' The voice came from somewhere above him, and for a moment it had a disembodied sound. Then he looked up and saw Davina Pascal descending the stairs towards him. 'What a persistent man you are, Mr Crown! Pestering Mrs Radcliffe with phone calls, bursting into my house without invitation—'

'Where's Ruth?' demanded Dominic, without ceremony. 'I want to see her. I want to speak to her. If you don't tell me where she is, I'll make your life very much more difficult, believe me!'

'Really?' Davina descended the remainder of the stairs, dismissing the housekeeper with a flick of her fingers. 'I'd advise you not to make idle threats, Mr Crown. I, too, have friends in high places.'

Dominic controlled his temper with difficulty, thrusting his hands into the pockets of his jacket and regarding her with brooding malevolence. 'I only want to see Ruth,' he declared, his tawny eyes unblinking. 'Now do you tell me where she is, or do I force you to do so?'

'I doubt if you could force me to do anything, Mr Crown,' Davina retorted scathingly. 'As to Ruth's whereabouts, that's her concern. If she'd wanted you to know where she was, no doubt she would have told you.' She paused. 'She is not an item for your amusement, Mr Crown. I suggest you pay less attention to my niece, and more to your fiancée—'

'Will you tell me where she is?' Dominic overrode her harshly, and Davina moved her thin shoulders dismissingly.

'I don't know where she is.'

'What do you mean? Of course you know!' Dominic looked as if he might physically demand a response, but he restrained himself. 'Where's your son? Is she with him? I intend to find her, Miss Pascal, so you might as well accept it now, and save us both a lot of unpleasantness.'

'I don't know what you mean.' Davina's nostrils flared, and Dominic swore violently.

'All right, Miss Pascal,' he said grimly. 'Shall we start with your motives for bringing Ruth back to London? Do you think they'd make flattering reading in the gossip columns of the popular press?'

Davina's face stiffened. 'My reasons for bringing Ruth back to England would bear any investigation. She *is* my niece, Mr Crown, and I have a strong sense of family.'

'Oh, yes?' Dominic's lips curled. 'Particularly where your adopted son is concerned, Miss Pascal.' He paused, before continuing cruelly: 'What a pity he wasn't *your* son, Miss Pascal, *your* flesh and blood. If that were so, we might not be having this conversation at all.'

Davina's jaw assumed a stubborn tilt. 'I don't know what you're talking about, Mr Crown. Please leave. If you don't, I shall call the police and have you forcibly ejected!'

Dominic shrugged. 'That's your prerogative, of course. However, before you do, let me remind you that all wills are made public.' He paused. 'Even your father's, Miss Pascal.'

Davina stared at him, her cheeks paling in the amber light, shed from the glittering chandelier. She looked suddenly old and apprehensive, and despite what she had done, Dominic felt his pity stir.

'You think you're very clever, don't you, Mr Crown?' she got out at last, and Dominic shook his head.

'Not particularly.' In all conscience, he felt the responsibility for what he was doing weighing heavily upon him. 'I only want to find Ruth, that's all. Where's your son? Perhaps he'll tell me, if only to protect you.'

Davina made a negative gesture. 'Martin—Martin knows nothing of all this,' she exclaimed agitatedly. 'He—he's away, driving in some motor rally. Ruth's not with him.'

'No?' Dominic was sceptical.

'No.' Davina looked at him squarely. 'Martin—Martin is not involved. You've got to believe me.'

Dominic hunched his shoulders. 'Ruth,' he said heavily. 'Where's Ruth?' and her answer left him completely confounded.

'But she can't be,' he protested at last, and Davina regained a little of her imperiousness as she answered him.

'But she is,' she declared, with evident satisfaction. 'She left London two days ago. We've both been spurned, Mr Crown. It seems she wasn't happy in England, so she's gone back to the island . . .'

Ruth rested both her arms on the rail of the motor launch, supporting her chin on her hands. It had been another beautiful day, and already she could feel the peace and tranquillity of the islands seeping into her bones. The noise and the bustle of London seemed very far away from St Vincent, and Indigo, and here at least she would not have the constant fear of meeting Dominic unforeseen. She couldn't even read about his activities in the newspapers, or see his picture in one of the society magazines to which her aunt had subscribed. She need hear nothing about him—not his power or his influence, not the success he was having with his father's business, and most particularly, she would not be torn to pieces by reading about his forthcoming marriage.

It was almost a week now since she had left Heathrow in the dampness and hustle of an April afternoon. Her flight had been late in departing, and the airport had been crowded, and she had climbed aboard the wide-bodied jet with a feeling almost of detachment. It had been so hard to leave England, to know that she was severing the tenuous bonds between her and Dominic, to acknowledge that if they ever met again, he would already have a wife.

There had been times, during those last days, when she had been tempted to call the number he had left with Aunt Davina. She had even argued the justice of his right to know she was expecting his child. But always she came back to the same assessment: he had never questioned the possibility of her being pregnant, therefore he forfeited all rights to the information.

Turning her head, she studied Joseph lounging, with his customary indolence, behind the wheel. Despite what Doctor Francis had told her that morning, she could not honestly find it in her heart to condemn the man, and instead she deliberately recalled the other occasion when he had taken her to St Vincent. She had not realised then, when she visited the bank and learned the truth about Dominic, that Joseph was going to play such a significant part in her life. Yet, in spite of what had happened, like Celeste, he was still an integral part of her existence, and as such, worthy of her respect.

She gazed out over the blue water again, picking out the tiny atolls she had known since childhood. Sunbaked mounds of coral, they rose out of the water like so many tiny castles, mounting their defences, and guarding their inner secrets—just as she was doing.

Celeste knew, of course. She had guessed at once. The minute she had seen Ruth walking up to the bungalow, she had sprung up from her chair on the verandah and embraced her, making Ruth overwhelmingly glad she had permitted the woman to stay there.

'Honey, I just knew you'd come back!' she declared, her huge brown eyes moist with tears. 'Ain't no one else can take care of you like old Celeste. Isn't that what your daddy always used to say?'

Of course her father had not. But then he had not known that Aunt Davina would descend from the heavens in her helicopter, churning up the sand on the shoreline, sending all the crabs scuttling for cover. If he had guessed, perhaps he might have had more sympathy with the black woman.

Still, in spite of everything, it had been good to feel herself wanted again. And Celeste had done everything in her power to make Ruth feel at home. Indeed, she had even curbed her tongue on the subject of the baby's father, although Ruth suspected that was only a temporary reservation, not intended to be regarded as permanent.

Doctor Francis had voiced his own reservations concerning Celeste's capabilities, when Ruth had had her interview with him this morning. But then he had voiced so many reservations she could hardly remember them all.

His prime target had been her isolation on the island. If anything should go wrong, he said, if she should have a sudden miscarriage, she was fully two hours from the mainland, and any kind of professional help. Celeste was all very well in her way, but he would not trust her in the delivery of a baby, and her methods of nursing left a lot to be desired.

Ruth knew he was referring to her indifference in providing Dominic with the means of his own destruction. If he had fallen off the motor-bike, Doctor Francis said, if he had sustained another infection in his arm, he could easily have lost it.

Ruth had been shocked, she couldn't deny it. But then she had also been shocked to learn that the doctor knew about the motorbike. That was something she had not expected to hear, and to discover subsequently how Doctor Francis had acquired that information had left her feeling slightly bewildered. Only now did she realise that it successfully removed any lingering suspicion from Dominic, and she felt a twinge of conscience for the way she had accused him.

Thinking of Dominic did not contribute to her peace of mind, however, and determinedly she tried to focus her thoughts on something else. Doctor Francis's suggestion that she might come and stay with him and his wife during the final weeks of her pregnancy had to be considered, and realising how much she wanted this baby, she was certainly tempted to submit. She had no doubt that Mrs Francis would see she had the best of care, but she was virtually a stranger to her, and right now she was in no state to decide. Too many strangers had played a part in her life recently, too many people wanting to control her future. There was plenty of time to make the arrangements; when she felt more capable of doing so . . .

Celeste was waiting for her, when she wound her way wearily back to the bungalow. It had been a long day, and she was tired, but she suffered the black woman's ministrations, and gratefully accepted a cup of tea.

'Well?' prompted Celeste eagerly. 'What Doctor Francis say? Ain't no reason why you shouldn't have a healthy baby, is there?'

'No reason at all, Celeste,' Ruth conceded a little flatly. Then: 'It's good to be home again. The temperature in St Vincent was in the high eighties.'

'Maybe there going to be a storm,' Celeste remarked offhandedly, pouring more tea. 'It don't matter none. You and me's as snug here as two fleas in a blanket.'

Ruth gave a wry smile at Celeste's turn of phrase, but thinking of storms brought her thoughts irrevocably back to Dominic. Was it only a little over three months ago that she had found him on the beach? So much had happened since then, it made the rest of her life seem dull and pointless.

Such speculations were vaguely disloyal, she decided, finishing her tea and getting up from her chair. A shower and a change of clothes was what she needed, and then a lazy dinner with Celeste, hearing about the latest happenings amongst the varied members of the black woman's family.

It was still quite early when she went to bed. As Celeste had predicted, lightning was flickering like wildfire on the horizon, and from time to time a low rumble of thunder vibrated the cosmetic jars on her dressing table. It didn't rain. It was only an electric storm. But the heat and her own restless thoughts kept her awake, and she lay wearily on her back, wondering if this was the pattern of things to come. Until today, actually being on the island, remote from the problems she had created for herself in London, had been enough. She had eaten well, and slept well, and anaesthetised herself against a mental breakdown. Now, however, with the memory of what Doctor Francis had said to distract her, and the disturbing atmosphere of the storm all around her, she felt the depressing awareness of what she would never have, bearing down upon her. Oh, Dominic! she breathed, silently into the night, and buried her face in the pillow to silence her racking sobs.

She must have slept for a while, because she awakened with a fast-beating heart, evidence that something—or someone—had disturbed her. Yet the bungalow seemed as silent as ever. Perhaps it was one of Celeste's midnight suitors, stumbling over his own feet, she speculated doubtfully, then tensed again when she heard a muffled curse.

It had definitely come from the verandah, and sliding out of bed, she reached for the cotton wrapper that matched her sprigged cotton shift. She was curiously unfrightened. They had never had an intruder at the bungalow, and if someone was prowling about, Celeste would surely hear him, too.

Pulling open her bedroom door, she padded silently along the passage. There was little light, the low-hanging clouds concealing the moon, and casting shadows in dark corners. It crossed her mind, with a prickling of her flesh, that her father had died in the bungalow, and she had given no thought to her visitor being of anything less than physical origins, but remembering the muttered curse, she discarded such a fanciful notion.

Then, when she saw the shadow beneath the door, moving purposely towards her, her courage almost gave out on her. Someone was out there, on the verandah, someone who must know by now he was in the wrong place. Her hand went to her mouth, and a scream rose in her throat, but it was never uttered. The loud rat-a-tat on the panels dismissed all suspicion of a stealthy intruder, and she stumbled quickly towards it, pulling the door wide.

'Joseph!' she exclaimed, gazing weakly at the black man, 'what on earth—oh, my God! Dominic!'

Ruth was as near fainting then as she had been that morning at the Crown house. Seeing Joseph like that, she had immediately assumed that something was wrong. Her father had been called out on occasion, to tend some feverish child, or to administer first aid to an injured seaman, and her first thoughts on seeing Joseph ran along those lines. It was only when her eyes moved to the second man, standing right behind him, that she realised she must be mistaken, and she gripped the door frame painfully in an effort to overcome the shock.

'Hallo, Ruth,' Dominic said now, stepping forward. 'I'm sorry if we disturbed you, but—'

'Mr Howard, he come with my cousin Wesley, from Kingstown, Missy,' Joseph interrupted him quickly, casting an indignant look over his shoulder. 'He say you be pleased to see him, but me, I ain't so sure. You want I should send him 'way, Missy, till the morn—'

'Just try it,' drawled Dominic pleasantly, and Ruth rapidly came to her senses. The last thing she wanted was a fight to develop, here, on her verandah. She knew Dominic well enough to know that when he set his mind on something, he was unlikely to be deterred from getting it, and although his sudden appearance had set her pulses racing and her head throbbing, she could not ignore him.

'It's all right, Joseph,' she said now, struggling to find words to hide her confusion. 'Mr—er—Dominic can come in. But—but thank you, anyway, Joseph. I appreciate your concern.'

'You sure you don't want me to wait out here till he's ready to leave?' Joseph suggested hopefully, but

Ruth shook her head. Whatever had brought
Dominic all this way, he was unlikely to be inhibited
by Joseph's presence—but she would be! If Dominic
had somehow learned about the baby, if he had come
here to make some obligatory offer, the last thing she
wanted was for Celeste to hear of her refusal, and if
there was to be a row, better it should be in private.

'I—I'm sure Mr Howard can find his own way back
to the harbour, Joseph,' she assured him now, and
Dominic politely inclined his head.

'Thanks for the escort, old man,' he remarked
dryly, and then stepped purposely forward as Ruth
retreated.

In the revealing light of the living room, she faced
him bravely, her hands linked tightly together. With
her eyes focussed somewhere near the dark blue
knot of his tie, she addressed him stiffly, realising
that this interview could well be the most significant
of her whole life.

'How did you find me?' she asked tautly, and
Dominic moved his shoulders in an offhand gesture.

'Your aunt told me.' He took a step towards her.
'Ruth, you have no idea—'

Ruth took an involuntary backward step, then
stiffened herself again. 'What—what exactly did
Aunt Davina tell you?' she persisted, avoiding his
eyes, and Dominic made a sound of impatience as he
searched for a reply.

'What did she tell me?' he echoed. 'What do you
think she told me?' He sighed. 'She said that you had
told her you weren't happy in England. That you
wanted to return to the island, of course. What else?'

'What else?' echoed Ruth faintly, the weakness of

relief almost robbing her of the strength in her legs.
Of course—Aunt Davina would not have told
Dominic the truth. She still held out hopes that at
some future time Ruth would change her mind about
Martin.

'Ruth, I had to see you!' Dominic took another
step towards her, expelling his breath with unsteady
urgency, but now she knew where she stood.

'You realise, of course, that the whole island will
know about this by the morning, don't you?' she
declared tautly. 'If you have no thought for yourself,
you might at least have spared a thought for me!'

'For you?' he repeated, gazing at her blankly, and
she nodded.

'Of course. I—I—this is my home. I have to live
here. What kind of a person will they think I am,
inviting callers into my home at—at—' she glanced
anxiously at the clock, '—at midnight!'

Dominic's expression took on a cynical twist. 'Is
that all you have to say to me, Ruth? I travel—I don't
know—four thousand miles, and all you can do is
worry about your reputation!'

Ruth bent her head. 'It—it may not seem important to you—'

'Of course it's important,' he interpolated impatiently. 'I've been left in no doubt as to the importance you place on reputations. But I'm hoping what
I have to say may alter your opinion of mine!'

Ruth could not allow this to continue. 'Dominic,'
she said, and her tone was less defensive now,
'Dominic, you shouldn't be here. You're wasting
your time—'

'Am I? Am I?' He came towards her then, and

although she stepped back, she came up against the front of the cabinet, and could go no farther. 'Ruth, I love you, and I think you love me. Can you honestly stand there and tell me that I mean absolutely nothing to you?'

Ruth moved her head jerkily from side to side. 'I—I—I admit, we did have some—some good times together—' she began, seeking an escape, but Dominic would not let her get away with it.

'Good times?' he echoed savagely, placing his hands on the cabinet at either side of her. 'Good times? I don't believe you, Ruth. They were more than just—*good times!*'

Ruth's nervous gaze darted up at him then, and the sight of his thin, haggard face was almost her undoing. Whatever he had been doing since she last saw him, it had taken every ounce of flesh from his cheeks, and his eyes were dark-rimmed and slightly bloodshot, yet burning with an intense brilliance.

'You don't understand,' she got out unsteadily, 'You don't understand! I—I can't go on as we were doing. I can't stand the pace. I—I know you think you care for me, but your kind of loving and mine differ, and—well, it's better if we just—just forget one another.'

'Can you forget me, Ruth?' he demanded fiercely, pushing his face close to hers. 'Can you forget this— or this—' And suddenly he was kissing her, over and over again, kisses that rapidly changed from an angry salutation to a bruising caress, kisses that brought her up close against him, and subsequently destroyed any hope of resisting him. He was so much stronger, so much more determined, and for a time she gave herself up to the mindless possession of his mouth.

'Ruth—oh, Ruth,' he breathed, in a shaken voice. 'When I found you'd left me, I nearly went out of my mind!'

It was these words that brought Ruth abruptly to her senses. For a while, the searching seeking pleasure of his mouth had acted like an intoxicant upon her, muddling her thinking and blinding her to the obvious recklessness of what she was doing. Nothing had changed, she realised desperately. She had known Dominic wanted her before she left England. But he was going to marry Barbara, and she was still pregnant!

With a concerted effort she freed herself from him, taking advantage of his sensually-induced weakness, putting the width of the couch between them.

'It's no good,' she declared breathlessly, wrapping her arms close about her. 'I won't be your mistress, Dominic, however I may feel.'

'My mistress!' He turned, lounging against the cabinet, a look of intense weariness crossing his face. 'My mistress,' he said again, massaging his temples. 'Dear God, Ruth, do you think I'm going to give you up now?'

Ruth's lips trembled. 'What do you mean?'

'What do you think I mean?' he demanded, straightening. 'I didn't come here to find a mistress. I came to claim a wife.'

'A wife?' Ruth couldn't help it, but she could not take this in. 'Dominic, don't tease me—'

'Tease you—God! I'm in no mood for teasing.' He

unloosened his tie and breathed out heavily. 'You're not listening to me, Ruth. I want you to be my wife.'

Ruth turned abruptly away, putting up a hand to her hair, tugging absently at the lapels of her wrapper. Could it be true, what he was saying? Could he seriously mean what he had said? Was her own desperate need to believe him playing tricks with her, or had he actually said he wanted to marry her?

'I—I found out today how—how Daddy found out about us,' she said suddenly, needing to keep her head, even though her heart was pounding. 'It—it was Joseph, you know. Joseph who told him. Oh, not intentionally, I suppose, but he did it just the same.'

'Ruth!'

'It was the day after. The day you left.' She licked her dry lips. 'Joseph has a soft spot for Celeste, you know. Oh, he's married, and his wife has several children, but Celeste—well, he's always been fond of her.'

'Ruth, look at me—'

'You remember Harold, don't you? The young man who lent you the motorbike. Celeste's *cousin*! Well, apparently he spent the night with Celeste, and Joseph was furious. He went to Daddy and actually complained!' She stifled a half hysterical laugh. 'Yes, he complained, and he mentioned that Harold had lent the motorbike to us, just to give his story weight, I suppose. Anyway, Daddy was shocked, as you might imagine, and—and he told Doctor Francis. It was Doctor Francis who told the story to me.'

'I'm sorry.' Dominic sounded weary, but Ruth had to go on.

'It's all right. He didn't know what had really happened, you see. I mean—when he reproached me, I thought—I thought you'd told him, but you hadn't, and he didn't know—not everything, anyway.'

'I'm glad.' Dominic spoke with sincerity. 'Perhaps you can forget it now.'

'Yes.'

Ruth bowed her head, then she felt him behind her, his hands sliding about her waist, drawing her back against him. 'Ruth,' he said, rubbing his lips against her neck. 'Your father need not have worried. You bewitched me, almost from the first moment we met.'

'I don't—I mean, I can't—' Ruth was finding it hard to speak, with his hands sliding up over her rib cage, moulding the swollen fullness of her breasts. 'Dominic—that's not true.'

'It is true,' he insisted huskily. 'You don't know this, but I knew all about Aunt Davina long before I saw your picture with her in the paper. I actually had someone look into your family history, to ensure myself that you wouldn't be alone if anything happened to your father.'

'But—but that's not the same thing—'

'Isn't it?' Dominic's tone was wry. 'Oh, love, don't you know I was so eaten up with remorse for leaving you, I found it incredibly hard to think of anyone else?'

She shook her head. 'But if I hadn't come to London—'

'—I'd have ended up here, sooner or later,' Dominic told her gently.

'But what about Barbara?' Ruth persisted, turning in his arms to face him. 'Dominic—'

'Barbara and I were having problems even before we went to Barbados,' he replied honestly. 'Why do you think I took the yacht out in the storm? Why do you think I didn't want anyone to know where I was?' He sighed, and then went on huskily: 'Ruth, my father chose my fiancée for me. It was to be what you might call a suitable match. I wasn't madly keen at first, but I had no radical objections, and we just—drifted into it, I suppose.' He shook his head, as she slanted her gaze up at him, and added: 'That may sound weak to you, but until I met you I'd never encountered a woman I could imagine spending the rest of my life with.'

'And—and Barbara?'

'Oh, Barbara's ambitious. I knew that. Just how ambitious for me, I learned later.'

'But after you got back—'

'After I got back to England, Barbara went away. Her sister had just had a baby, and we decided it would be good for both of us if we had a break. Unfortunately, so far as I was concerned, it didn't work.'

'But you didn't break your engagement.'

'At the beginning, no.' He compressed his lips for a moment. 'You have to understand my position—'

'There's no need,' she began, but he removed her silencing finger.

'There's every need,' he insisted, and then could not resist covering her parted lips with his, when her tongue appeared in unknowing provocation.

'Anyway,' he continued at length, somewhat

thickly, 'it all has to do with my brother Michael.'

'The one who died?'

'You know about that?'

'Aunt Davina mentioned it.'

Dominic nodded. 'I see. Well—yes, it has to do with him.' He paused. 'He was killed, you see. He fell from his pony when he was just seven years old. My mother was desolated.'

'I can believe that.' Ruth was shocked. 'How terrible for her! Where did it happen?'

'Can't you guess?' Dominic nodded at her look of awareness. 'Yes—Marlin Spike. That's why she never goes there now, why there are no horses in the paddock.' He shrugged. 'She can't bear to think of it.'

'Poor woman!'

Dominic agreed, touching her cheek tenderly. 'So you see,' he went on, 'I became the most important thing in her life.' He said this without conceit, and Ruth understood. 'It's very touching, but also very wearing. And naturally, I've always tried to fall in with their wishes—my parents', I mean.'

'Yes, I see.' Ruth looked doubtful now. 'So how—'

'Give me time,' he reproved her, kissing her nose. 'Much as I long to make love to you, I want you to know that breaking my engagement to Barbara was not the traumatic thing you might expect.' He shrugged. 'We had a row, of course, but then we've had a number of them lately, and I think we were both realising that our marriage simply wouldn't work.'

Ruth bit her lip. 'But your mother—'

'I know, I know. I know my mother spoke to you

about us. She confessed that she'd suspected there
was something between us, and she didn't want you
to be hurt.'

'Me?' Ruth's eyes widened.

'Well, that's her story, and she's sticking to it,'
remarked Dominic wryly, and Ruth's lips quivered
into a smile. 'After all,' he said, 'you're going to be
her daughter-in-law, and she has visions of becoming
a grandmother before too long.'

Ruth's face coloured then, but fortunately
Dominic did not make the association. 'So,' he continued, 'after speaking to my father, and gaining his
blessing, if you like, I couldn't wait to see you.' He
sighed. 'Unfortunately, as you know, you were away
—for a few days, your aunt told me. So instead of
driving myself frantic, wondering where you were
and what you were doing, I took myself off to the
north of England, to visit our plant in Cumbria. By
the time I got back you'd already left the country.'

'Oh, Dominic!'

'Oh, Dominic, indeed,' he muttered, his hands on
her hips, pressing her against him. 'And that aunt of
yours wouldn't even come to the phone! When I
eventually went to the house, she actually threatened to have me thrown out!'

'But why?' Ruth was horrified. 'What did you say
to her? Were you rude? Why wouldn't she speak to
you?'

Dominic hesitated. 'I suppose she doesn't like
me.'

'No.' Ruth frowned. 'No, I thought that. But then
you didn't like her either.'

'No,' Dominic conceded dryly. 'However—'

'So how did you get to speak to her?' Ruth persisted. 'How did you find out where I was? Did Martin tell you?'

'Martin wasn't there,' said Dominic flatly. 'She said he was on some rally or something.'

'Oh, yes,' Ruth smiled. 'Martin is very keen on motor-cars, at the moment.' She gave Dominic a teasing look. 'I'm very fond of Martin. He was very kind to me, and he needn't have been, in the circumstances.'

'What circumstances?' Dominic frowned.

'Well—' Ruth considered her words carefully, 'I was the usurper, wasn't I? I mean, not every son would welcome a stranger into his home, particularly not someone on whom his mother was spending a lot of money. Money that he might conceivably regard as his one day.'

'Oh, I see,' Dominic nodded. Then, as if coming to a decision, he said: 'Yes, I suppose you're right. Martin isn't such a fool as I thought.'

Ruth linked her arms around his neck. 'Are you sure—'

But Dominic had covered her mouth with his again, successfully silencing her, and she could only cling to him weakly, lost to the rapture of his kiss.

It was some time later before either of them felt like talking again. In the faintly luminous glow before dawn, Ruth awoke sleepily to find Dominic nuzzling her nape with his lips, while his hand strayed disturbingly down over her still-flat stomach. It was the first time she had actually slept with him, and there was a tingling delight in feeling his warm hard body close to hers beneath the sheet that covered them, one leg sprawled possessively across her thighs. In the eager hunger of their lovemaking, she had had no time to think of other things, but now the simple pleasure in knowing he was not going to leave her again made her move ever more urgently against him.

'You know,' he mused huskily, capturing her breast between his lips and stroking the rosy-gold aureole with his tongue, 'I think you've put on a little weight in this region, my darling. And I like it. Mmm, yes, I like it.'

Ruth's caressing fingers instantly stilled, and he moaned in protest, bringing her hands to him again. 'Don't stop,' he muttered, shifting to accommodate her. 'What do you want to do? Drive me crazy?'

Ruth's mouth opened under the passionate pressure of his, her resistance as always overwhelmed by his ardent nature. But when he released her mouth, to bury his face in the silky cloud of dark hair that surrounded her, she managed to find the words to still his eagerness.

'Dominic—Dominic, there's something else. Something I haven't told you.' She faltered. 'Something I couldn't tell you before . . .'

He drew back a little then, so that he could look into her face, and her gaze fell before his. There was such a look of concern in his eyes, and for the first time she realised he might misunderstand.

'Well?' he said, his anxiety giving his voice an impatient harshness. 'Ruth, for God's sake, what is it? You're not going to leave me now. Whatever it is, I won't let you.'

Ruth's lids lifted and she looked into the narrowed

tawny eyes, glittering now with the urgency of his passion. 'I'm going to have a baby,' she told him simply, and watched the look of incredulity come over his face.

'A baby!' he breathed, his eyes dropping to the shadowed contours of her body. 'A baby! Are you sure?'

'I—I'm af-fraid so.' She found she was stumbling over her words now, in her eagerness to get them out. 'I—I've seen two doctors, one in Switzerland, and one here. Doctor Francis, you remember? I saw him only this morning—or I should say yesterday morning, actually, and he said—' She broke off suddenly, and clasped one of Dominic's hands in both of hers. 'Oh, you don't mind, do you? I mean—you know, it's yours—'

'God, *Ruth!*' His hand turned her face up to his, silencing her nervous tongue with his thumb across her lips. 'Do you mean to tell me you came away because you were expecting my child?'

Ruth quivered. 'Partly.'

'Why in the name of all that's holy didn't you tell me?'

'And—and have you marry me, because you—you felt you had to?' she breathed unsteadily, and he gathered her closely against him.

'Oh, my darling,' he was finding it difficult to articulate, and Ruth breathed more freely in the knowledge of his reaction. 'Don't you know that nothing and nobody would have kept me away from you, if I'd known? I've known I had to have you, right from the start, and if I'd dreamed—if I'd suspected—' He broke off, and looked down at her again, his eyes warm and compelling. 'It must have been that night here, on the island,' he murmured thickly. 'God knows, I was in no state to prevent such a thing from happening.'

'So—so you don't mind?' she whispered, and he chuckled softly.

'Mind? Of course I mind,' he retorted. 'I wanted you to myself for much longer than a few months. But never mind, I'm sure Bridie can be prevailed upon to offer us her services.'

'Miss Bainbridge,' murmured Ruth contentedly. 'Do you think she would?'

'I'm sure of it. Particularly when I tell her I'm thinking of using the house at Marlin Spike again. The house needs children, and who knows, maybe my mother will learn to forget when she has a grandchild to cradle in her arms.'

'Well, of course, we couldn't live at your parents' home,' said Ruth thoughtfully. 'And I love Marlin Spike.'

'I do have an apartment as well,' Dominic reminded her gently. 'And an Irishman called Shannon, who takes care of me.'

'Oh, dear.' Ruth looked anxious, and Dominic frowned.

'What is it?'

'He may not like me,' ventured Ruth doubtfully, but Dominic only laughed.

'My darling, it was partly due to him that I found you again. If he doesn't like it, he has only himself to blame.'

Ruth's son was born a few weeks before Christmas,

and in February she met Aunt Davina and Martin
again, at the christening of baby James. The whole
family had gathered at Marlin Spike for the occasion,
and Dominic's mother, who had visited the house
several times since the wedding, came up to Ruth as
she was bidding Shannon to fetch some more champagne.

'Wasn't he good, darling?' Isobel smiled, watching
with envious eyes as Dominic's father held his grand-
son with obvious pride. 'He didn't cry once, not even
when Mr Collings poured that water over his head,
and I'm quite sure so much enthusiasm wasn't necessary.'

Ruth smiled, slim and composed in her lime-green
suede suit. Marriage, and motherhood, evidently
suited her, and she had adapted admirably to her
new role as the chairman's wife.

'Mr Collings was delighted to see you in church
again,' she assured her mother-in-law smoothly.
'Oh, here's Martin. You have met my cousin,
haven't you?'

Isobel nodded, but presently she drifted away,
drawn as if by a magnet to her husband's side.
Both Ruth and Martin watched her abortive attempts to gain the baby's attention, and then smiled
at one another in a mutual sharing of understanding.

'I was a fool, do you know that?' Martin remarked
now, surveying her with evident admiration. 'I
should have snapped you up before you had time to
meet Crown again! And I don't just mean for the
obvious reasons, that Dominic has no doubt told
you.'

Ruth frowned. 'Obvious reasons?' she echoed, feeling a faint twinge of alarm. 'What obvious reasons?'

'Didn't Dominic tell you?' Martin sounded surprised. 'No, well, I guess he mightn't at that. He's a much worthier fellow than I am. I'd have put him down any way I could.'

'Martin, you're not making sense.' Ruth could see Aunt Davina watching them with some apprehension, and it occurred to her that she must find out, before her aunt had chance to come and interrupt them. 'Please—what could Dominic have told me? Martin, I want you to tell me. You can't leave me in suspense.'

'About your grandfather's will, of course,' Martin retorted, helping himself to more champagne, and Ruth realised that it was due in part to the amount of champagne he had consumed that he was speaking so freely now. 'You remember old Henry Pascal, don't you? Mother told you of the relationship. About your mother being his eldest daughter, and how he cut her out of his will.'

'Yes, yes.' Ruth was getting impatient. 'But what has that to do with me? What has it to do with Dominic?'

Martin sighed. 'It's the inheritance factor, you see. I'm not Davina Pascal's real son, I'm only adopted. And the will says that if Davina dies childless, your mother's offspring are to inherit.'

'And—and Dominic knows this?' Ruth was amazed. He had never mentioned it. He had never told her that her aunt's main interest in her stemmed from the terms of her father's will. So that was why she had pushed Ruth and Martin together, why she had wanted them to marry . . .

'How do you think he persuaded Mother to tell him where you were, when you ran off back to the island? He was pretty mean, I can tell you. We assumed he'd blow the gaff the minute he laid eyes on you. Imagine our surprise when we got an invitation to the wedding!'

Ruth turned away, dazed by what she had learned, and as she did so, her husband's arm came around her. 'Hey,' he murmured, and his strength enveloped her like a welcoming shield. 'What is it? What's that bastard been saying to you? If he's said anything to hurt you—'

Ruth shook her head, looking up at him adoringly. 'He—he told me about—about the will. Oh, Dominic, why didn't you tell me? Why didn't you let me see what an awful woman Aunt Davina really is?'

Dominic sighed, drawing her into a corner, and concealing her from the rest of the gathering with his body. 'Honey, there was no need for you to know,' he told her gently. 'At least, not while your aunt was alive anyway. She's the only relative you've got—'

'So you were prepared to put up with her, invite her here, knowing she'd done her best to part—'

'Her best wasn't good enough, was it?' Dominic put in huskily. 'I just didn't want to upset you.' His lips touched her temple teasingly. 'I thought you'd had enough upsets for a pregnant lady.'

'Oh, Dominic!' Ruth's eyes were filled with tears. 'But how did you find out?'

Dominic smiled. 'Tim Connor told me. You remember Tim Connor, don't you? I told you, it was he who found out all about your family history.'

Ruth frowned. 'So you knew all along?'

'No.' Dominic shook his head. 'I thought his investigations were complete, but he rang me the night I got back from the north of England. You remember, the night I went to see Davina.' He grimaced. 'He said that as I was apparently interested in your welfare, I ought to know all the facts.'

'Oh, Dominic!'

'It's all over now. Forget about it.'

Ruth shook her head. 'I can't. I don't want Aunt Davina's money!'

Dominic shrugged. 'Then don't keep it. If—when—you eventually do inherit, you can always hand it over to some charitable trust as a gift, or keep that good-for-nothing son of hers in comfort for the rest of his life.'

Ruth sighed. 'Martin means well.'

'Martin is a troublemaker,' retorted Dominic dryly. 'Did you never have cause to wonder how your aunt found out about me?'

'She—she spoke to your mother—'

'Correction, Martin spoke to my mother's secretary, Ginny Harris. It may have been at his mother's instigation, but I believe it was the morning you got back from Switzerland. It was he and not your aunt who wormed the information out of her. Poor Ginny, as you know, is very gullible.'

'Poor Ginny dotes on you,' retorted Ruth, with some heat, and Dominic grinned.

'Yes, she does, doesn't she?' he averred comfortably. 'I'll have to remember that.'

'Don't you dare!' Ruth looked up at him fiercely,

then melted beneath the look in his eyes. 'Oh, Dominic, I do love you.'

Dominic drew her towards him. 'Not here,' he murmured, 'not now. Tomorrow, when we're several thousand miles from here.'

'A belated honeymoon,' sighed Ruth with some satisfaction. 'Do you think your son will be all right?'

'What? With at least three women drooling over him?' remarked Dominic briefly. 'He'll be completely ruined by the time we get back.'

'That always happens with only children,' Ruth countered saucily, giving him a mischievous smile, then darted away before he could retaliate.

Dominic was right, she thought, slanting a loving glance in his direction, as she tried to pay attention to what her father-in-law was saying. There would be time enough to sort out Aunt Davina's problems. Her own life was much more important, and someone with so much could afford to be generous.

ANNE MATHER

Anne Mather is one of the highest selling novelists in the world, her sales to date exceeding 90 million copies. Her first novel, *Caroline*, was published in 1966 and met with immediate success. *Stormspell* is her ninetieth. Her novels have been translated into Afrikaans, Danish, Dutch, Finnish, French, German, Greek, Hebrew, Italian, Japanese, Norwegian, Portuguese, Serbo-Croat, Spanish, Swedish and Turkish. Her work, *Leopard in the Snow*, was made into a successful film, which is now much sought after on video. *Leopard in the Snow* also has been chosen to appear in the Alpha series of the Oxford University Press.

Anne Mather was born in the North-East of England and still lives there. She is married with two teenage children.